Godforsaken

Tarryl Janik

ISBN: 069219763X
ISBN-13: 978-0692197639 (Hellbound Books)

For Sam.

1

Jack Warren is an enigmatic drunk. There is a black Ruger P95 9mm pistol pressed firmly against his right temple and he has yet to brush his decaying teeth this morning.

Halitosis.

Fetor oris.

Twelve cavities. Two silver fillings. Sensitive to both hot and cold.

There are faded black letters tattooed into his fingers spelling out the four-letter word **HATE**. He is left handed. Always remember where you came from is what he tells people who ask him about it.

Somewhere within the confines of a quaint yet visibly run-down trailer park called Royal Acres a cell phone rings.

The ring is drowned out by the noise of a nearby locomotive, the traffic on a two-lane rural highway, an obese woman outside screaming obscenities at her three children who are throwing rocks at each other, and some stray barking dogs.

The dogs have mange; their hair falling out, bald in spots, flaking red skin.

Jack peers out the adjacent window and sees a crooked, flickering lime green fluorescent bar sign that reads *Happy Tap* hanging across the street, someone must have left it on all night. There is a pile of dead bugs at the foot of the window — a large moth lies motionless like those pretty butterflies in glass cases at universities pinned to boards; glued to cardboard, lying in cotton swab sarcophaguses.

This particular decrepit trailer is the home of Jennifer Thomas, the town cum dumpster. She prefers to call herself an *entrepreneur*. Or sometimes an *entertainer*. Or *dancer*. Her title depends on the audience.

Rotted pine sheeting creaks under the heavily trodden grey carpeting. The carpet maintains a constant ambiguous and ubiquitous odor, likely from spots saturated with cat urine and spilt booze over the years. In the corner of the living room there is a cat litter box that hasn't been cleaned in weeks — hardened granules, clumped, and moldy — spilling out onto the floor. Even Shelby the calico cat walks by in disgust, coughing up wet hairballs. Brown, hard water streams out of the faucet, but only after the air is flushed from the lines. Banging pipes clang and clunk before spewing out a curious mixture of watery sludge.

Not a poltergeist, just poverty.

Jack ignores his ringing cell phone as he pours another glass of Jameson and continues to contemplate blowing his brains all over the trite, antiquated, scratched, wood paneling behind him. A splintering bullet hole wouldn't be the first hole in the wall, he thinks. Nor the last. Five photos hang sideways, covering the holes where Jack put his fist in a drunken rage.

"Damn Jack, you know I don't like guns," she says.

"Shut up," he says.

Jennifer has a decent body for a single, forty-three-year-old, mother of two. Some would even say she is a "milf", as long as she never took her shirt off. She can never wear a two-piece bathing suit. She has stretch marks from hell. A terribly wrinkled lower abdomen. Like bubble gum. Big chew. A body ruined by childbirth. They cut her from vagina to anus during her second pregnancy. She had four stitches and wore gauze in her panties for weeks.

The sting of antiseptic after each wipe.

Jack only fucked her with her shirt on or in the dark. It was silently mandated and never talked about.

Her hair was dirty blonde, her complexion pallid. Gaunt. Leathery.

She is wearing brown puppy dog slippers, a dark blue dingy baseball tee, faded pink panties with little yellow stars, and smoking a non-filtered Marlboro.

Stained yellow fingers.

Stained yellow dentures.

He is continually perplexed by his hesitation to pull the trigger.

She lasciviously makes her way over to Jack, takes a long drag off her cig, exhales in his face, smothers it out in an overloaded ashtray, kneels, and pulls Jack's semi-aroused stretchy cock out through the escape hatch in his checkered brown boxers.

Her white dried pussy juices are still visibly encrusted in his pubic hair from last night's charade.

Heavy panting.

Exhaustion.

Flaking off like dandruff now.

A crusty cocktail of discharge and semen.

She pops out her dentures and sets them on the nearby end table, right next to the ashtray. Milky white saliva drips slowly down off of them and pools on the dusty oak veneer mixing with black ash, turning the fluid grey.

Noir.

Jennifer may be a nympho sycophant, but she has a rare gift for deep throating dick. A talent. Most women can't fit an entire penis in their mouth without gagging or vomiting, but not Jennifer. She takes it slow and works it down the shaft after lubing it up with just the right amount of spittle.

Practice made better than most.

The swoosh of spit and lips smacking.

She gums it vigorously, as if there was a tootsie roll in the center or some sort of prize for a job well done.

Enough lube is key.

She takes pride in her work.

She is careful not to pop the blister in the corner of her mouth.

Her oral herpes are agitating.

The phone keeps ringing, but Jack lets it go to voicemail. He rests the Ruger on the couch, it's still loaded. Safety off. His eyes roll back white as he orgasms and shoots a thick load of baby batter on her tonsils. Cottage cheese in texture.

Gritty, salted, snot-esque.

Warm.

Jennifer swallows hard before putting her teeth back in and lighting another cigarette.

She's a chain smoker, amongst other things.

Some people in town call her *Judas*.

"Feel better now?" she asks.

"Ya," he says.

"You better check your phone, it could be important."

Jack stuffs his now flaccid penis back in his boxers, takes a drink, and keys in his password.

9999

Sure enough, it's Roy, his boss.

"Jack pick up your damn phone, I know you're there, I need you to come in. You know Jessica Mills? The daughter of Tom and Darla Mills...who own the Chateau Restaurant down off of Highway 21 toward Red Granite? Ya well, apparently she has been missing for over two days and I..."

Jack hits "end" and calls back the last number.

Roy answers on the third ring.

"About time Jack."

"Two days huh?"

"You could just answer the damn phone you know..."

Jack pours another drink. "It's my day off," he says.

No ice.

"I need ya on this Jack, you know the Mills family right?"

He sort of remembers.

"Ya, I know them, I'll be right in. Just give me twenty minutes."

Jennifer walks past him with a disappointed look on her face and almost gets her hair stuck in one of four fly strips hanging from the ceiling. Jack slaps her on the ass.

Hard and firm with a slight sting.

Tart.

Stimulating.

She giggles and coughs, then perks right up.

Fly strips filled with flies; buzzing, wings caught, trapped, legs kicking relentlessly.

They eventually give up and die. Much like Jack has on the inside.

The fly strips are a mirror, reflecting past calamity — events that continually haunt him.

Some older types of flypaper were toxic to both humans and animals. They contained metallic arsenic, which some murderers would then extract by soaking them in water before poisoning their victims.

She hacks a lung thrice, it's deep and guttural — barking like a bullfrog — then spews a dark brown sputum into the sink. It's the kind you get with pneumonia or bronchitis.

She's smoked since she was thirteen.

The pipes bang loudly as she rinses the aforementioned brown mucus down with even darker questionable sludge water.

Not a poltergeist, just poverty.

The water smells of septic.

Jack's holding the phone in the crook of his neck. Roy is still talking.

"Good, meet me at the rest stop on Highway 22, south of town. That's where we found her vehicle."

Jack grabs the gun off the couch and holsters it. It seems his mistress, *suicide,* will have to wait another day.

She's a patient courtesan.

Unlike *Judas*, who licks her lips and tells him how wet she is.

2

The rest stop on Highway 22 is used minimally, there is never more than four or five cars that visit at a time on even the busiest of traffic holidays. The only building, surrounded by tall black oak trees and gravel, which houses the restrooms, is a light tan dilapidated brick and mortar. A pale cracked concrete wall with a small vent in the center about six inches from the ceiling separates the men's side from the women's.

If you listen carefully on a Saturday afternoon you can hear middle aged truckers spanking their meat to the sound of Chatty Cathys and soft voiced teenage gossip. And, if you pull in late at night on a Friday, one might catch Devin Sanders meeting up with men from Craigslist. His fellatio is arguably better than that of Judas herself. Just ask father Reynolds from St. Peters, he is one of Devin's most satisfied customers. Devin also does anal and gives blumpkins if the price is right.

His seductive blue eyes lined in thick black mascara.

Petal soft lips.

Painted with beige glitter Chapstick.

Long blonde hair, sometimes worn in pigtails for pulling.

Tugging.

Spanking.

Thrusting.

There are two entry doors: the men's facing south, and the women's facing north. Both fail to curtail the urine odor, even when left wide open for ventilation. Both are shielded by a small discolored wooden privacy fence that extends just beyond a pad of worn concrete. Both conveniently block the view of any would-be passerby rubberneckers, which makes giving blowjobs or smoking weed behind them all the easier.

Like most rural Wisconsin rest stops, drivers from both directions can turn in at all hours of the day or night. There are no personnel on duty, outside of Joe Schneider the maintenance guy who works for the county part-time. Joe mows the lawn, changes the garbage, and replaces the urinal cakes — he is supposed to maintain the restrooms twice daily.

He also picks up the fecal covered dildos left in the grass by Devin's late night escapades. Hardened like coprolite. Some of Devin's clients have very specific ass fetishes — requests made for reaming, fucking, felching, sniffing — one john even has a serious hyper butt-licking fixation.

Coprophiliacs aroused by scat.

Then there is omorashi Tuesdays.

The "Kentucky Klondike bar."

The "Panamanian Petting Zoo."

Men in town call Devin *queer* or *faggot boy* in public, they make fun of him in front of their wives, girlfriends, and friends. The *Argus* writes about Devin's continual arrests for soliciting sex and prostitution. The articles say he is a troubled youth with a storied past. They say something about addiction. The same men who demonize him in public are the men who call him *lover, baby,* or *the best they ever had* in private — when Devin's girthy cock is deep inside them, or vice versa.

But if anyone saw what happened to Jessica Mills, or knew why her abandoned car was left at the rest stop, Joe would be the one to ask. Not Devin, since Devin is currently sitting in the county jail doing six stiff months for meeting an undercover cop for sexual favors. Joe on the other hand, oddly enough, no one has heard from him in over a week.

***

"What do you mean Joe has been on vacation?" Jack asks.

"Ya, I guess he hasn't been to work since last Monday." Roy shrugs his shoulders.

"So, you mean to tell me that Joe just happens to be on vacation at the same time Jessica goes missing and leaves her car here? You know I don't believe in coincidences Roy."

Jack makes his way around Jessica's dark blue 2002 Chevy Impala, being careful not to disturb any potential evidence.

"So, when was the last time her parents heard from her?"

"Friday evening, she was headed to Montello to see a movie with her boyfriend and she never came home."

"Did you call the movie theater to see if she had been there?"

"Ya, she was there, she stayed through the whole film too."

Everybody knows everybody in this area.

"Who's her boyfriend?"

"Scott Hickey."

"Isn't he the kid who won first at state in wrestling last year?"

"Yep, that's him, she rode with him to the theater, they watched, get this — *Valentine's Day Massacre*. I already talked to both Scott and his parents. I guess her and Scott had some sort of fight and he dropped her off at home right after the movie around 11 p.m."

"Thinking intent?"

"Nah, he's a good kid."

"I'm sure Jeffrey Dahmer and O.J. Simpson were good kids too."

"His story is good, his parents corroborated..."

"Ya, well..."

"So how did her car end up here?"

"That's the question, no one knows."

Jack notices that both the keys aren't in the vehicle and that it is locked.

"You find the keys?"

"Nope," Roy replied, "No keys...nothing. It's like she just vanished."

"Maybe or maybe not. If I was an eighteen-year-old girl and came here late at night, I would take my keys and lock the doors too...did you find anything in the bathrooms?"

"Not yet."

"What about the woods?"

"Nope, deputies walked them, and not a damn trace."

Jack scans the surface area around the exterior of the building, the interstice of the tattered and torn privacy fence by the women's bathroom reveals *something* upon closer inspection — a small piece of red fabric, cotton, caught on a splinter of wood. Jack quickly puts on a pair of XL McKesson powder-free vinyl exam gloves and carefully wiggles it loose. Suddenly out pops a freshly polished, yet clearly broken off pink fingernail.

"Roy, I've got something over here."

3

Roy Samuel Hutchinson was a

anachronistic grizzly man from a bygone era. He was an Iraq war vet and a father of three overweight, spoiled boys. Brats. He spends his time writing poetry, fly fishing the Mecan River, and tying flies out of bucktail. Roy is a good cop, but a mediocre detective. When it comes to Jack, he knows that Jack is an alcoholic, but he also knows Jack is a great detective when he wants to be. *If* he wants to be.

He knew, that at the end of the day, Jack would come through for him, even if Jack never came through for himself anymore. Being a cop in a small town comes with its pros and cons — you know everyone, but everyone also knows you. The whole community sticks their nose into all your business and gets involved in every dirty little thing you *do* or *don't do* whether you like it or not. That being said, everybody knows Jack is a drunk with a hooker girlfriend, but given his particular circumstances, everyone just puts up with it. *Everyone* meaning *Roy*. Roy turns the other cheek knowing what Jack has been through. If Roy wasn't Sheriff, Jack wouldn't have a job. No one straight out of the academy would put up with him.

Not these days anyway.

***

"What is that, a fingernail?"

Roy holds the evidence bag up to the sunlight to get a better look.

"Yep, I think we can rule *runaway* out here, cause I'm willing to bet that is both a piece of Jessica's clothing and her fingernail."

"Think so?" Jack was being facetious.

"Dick."

"Well c'mon man. Pretty obvious."

"We should show these to her parents to confirm that they're hers."

"That ought to go over well," Jack says sarcastically.

"What? Why not?"

"You show them that and suddenly we have panic on our hands — we'll have the whole town thinking there is a murderer on the loose."

"Ya I suppose, but what if there really is?"

"We don't know that yet."

"You really think telling Tom and Darla that we found something is a bad idea?"

"Do what you want, but unless you want a circus of reporters and media descending upon our beloved little village, this horrid township, this godforsaken place...I'd hold off. Besides, we know it's hers. There was a bottle of the same pink nail polish in the center counsel of the car."

"Seriously?"

"It's called observation, you should try it."

"Dick."

"Where'd you get your degree, online?"
"Fuck you."
They both laugh.
Jack steps lightly toward the women's bathroom, perusing the vicinity, making sure not to disturb any more potential evidence. The smell of piss is overwhelming; it is obvious that this place hadn't been cleaned in quite some time.
Jack pulls out a notebook and writes *find Joe*.

***

The women's bathroom has three stalls, one of which is completely missing a door, and all of which were empty. The interior of the toilets were splattered with brown excrement and the tile floors were rock concert sticky. Jack walked into the first one on the right, put the toilet seat down and popped a squat. His Chaps leather size twelve shoes are now wading in what-can-only-be vomit. A vile pool of stringy, chunky, clustered baked beans and ramen noodles. Someone had a cheap dinner he thinks.

The stall reads, "Sarah Marks is a slut bitch," and "Marty was here," the typical clichéd scratching found on restroom walls. It was nothing out of the ordinary. On the adjacent wall there is a massive cock in dark permanent marker ejaculating the numbers 666, the mark of the beast, toward the drain in the floor. How Christian of them, he thought.

"Now that's interesting," Jack says to himself.

"Surrealism? Impressionism? Abstract? And in the women's bathroom none-the-less," he mutters with childlike amusement.

It was a caricature of President Ba"rack" Obama taking Hillary "Rod"ham Clinton's meaty beaver basher with the words "democracy" and "Merica" scratched into the side of her blue-veined sausage.

***

"Hey Jack you in here? You decent?"

"Ya and yes," he replies.

"Good, I didn't want to stumble in on you wanking it or anything," Roy jokes.

"Right."

"I'd say you never get laid, but well..."

"Shut up."

"What do you see in her," meaning Judas. "anyway?"

"She doesn't ask me stupid questions like you do."

"Funny."

Roy peeks his head around the stall door and says, "Well, whatever, I'm gonna head over to the Mills' place. Want to come with?"

"For what reason?"

"Just to offer them some peace of mind."

"About?"

"It's the right thing to do, you know."

"Uh huh, no thanks."

Jack looks at his watch and then at Roy.

"Nah, I'm gonna head home. Have Nick finish this up...call me if anything significant arises. Oh, and I'll stop by Joe's on the way and see how his *vacation* is going."

"You ok bud? You don't look so good."

Bulbous nose.

Shaking.

Irritation.

"Ya, just tired, long night and all that."

"Ok," Roy says, knowing better.

"See ya later."

"Yep."

Jack's demeanor was noticeably changing. He was starting to get on edge, sobriety was his anathema. By "tired" Jack meant it was time for his "liquid dinner." Roy knew this, hell everyone knows this. Just like everyone knows that Jack is a real asshole when he doesn't drink. Upon Roy's leaving, Jack makes his way back to his car and reaches under the driver's seat, pulling out a small bottle of liquor. It's a fifth of whiskey.

Jack unscrews the cap and takes a hearty swig. The bitter-sweet fluid splashes his taste buds, instantaneously satisfying his craving. Just the thought of drinking makes him feel better, much less the act. The first swill goes down like water and he swooshes it around for a minute like mouthwash. He savors the euphoric feeling it gives him but he needs more. Once down-the-hatch, Jack pounds another shot without hesitation. His nerves begin to calm. The shaking subsides a bit and he relaxes. Like a man possessed he gulps down one last mouthful as he turns the key in the ignition clockwise and slides the car into reverse. As the new hire, Nick, wraps up the crime scene, Jack sets the now half gone bottle in the plastic cup holder hanging from the ashtray and puts the car into drive.

The sun sets over the green field of soybeans in the distance. The sky is pink like rose quartz, grey and white stratus clouds dangle ever so softly, dark blues intermingle and offset their long, curved edges.

***

Somewhere in Royal Acres, Judas is lighting up a non-filtered Marlboro after making fifty dollars for a gum job. Her fellatio is well known in these parts. Rivaled only by Devin Sanders. Her client asks her if she enjoys urine play. Salirophilia. She wipes the cock snot from her eye and tells him how she has a tarp in her closet for such special occasions. She also tells him that she'll even drink pee for an extra Benjamin Franklin. She calls letting someone urinate into her mouth a "fish bowl." During a fish bowl she lets her cheeks fill up wide like a chipmunk before she swallows.

For two hundred she will do an "Alabama hot pocket."

She has a special stool with a hole in the center for her clients with coprophagia.

A "cold lunch" and a "Birmingham booty call" is always on the menu too.

She's an *entrepreneur*, an *entertainer*, or *dancer* depending on the audience.

4

Joe's place was a small, ranch-style home. A typical modular with a dash of red brick on the front, which was no doubt the explicit handiwork of the resident housing and community development board. It has a small two car garage. Across the street there is a large yellow "Watch for Deaf Child" sign, and a nearby flickering street lamp illuminates the suburban cul-de-sac. Just off the overgrown lawn is a plastic, largemouth bass mailbox flopped open and packed tightly—puking white envelopes.

Jack pulls in the blacktop drive at dusk. The house is pitch black, not a single light is on. It looks like Joe hasn't been home for awhile. Jack shuts the car off and reaches over to the glove box opening it. A bottle of aspirin, a black Sig Sauer, and a Mag flashlight spill out onto the floor of the car next to some empty fast food containers, soda cans, and coffee cups.

"Goddamn it."

Jack grabs the bottle of aspirin, lines up the arrows on the cap and slides the childproof lock over. It takes him two tries to achieve success. He pops it open and dry swallows at least four white pills. The fifth he chews up with what teeth he has left—it tastes gritty. At least he didn't snort them this time. With flashlight in hand he vacates the vehicle and makes his way toward the front door. He stumbles. A faint sound of music echoes from the recesses of the basement. He can just barely make out the words.

Thundering machine gun drums, wailing guitars, "Of course," he says, "*Behemoth.*" Even having grown up on metal music, Jack thinks this is an odd choice for Joe, and for a house with no lights on, but who knows maybe Joe sleeps to the soothing sound of death metal and not jazz or American roots. He doesn't know Joe *that* well. Jack decides to walk around to the back of the house—to get a better look.

As Jack turns the corner, a flashing thin white light streaks across the amber, fall leaves in front of him from the basement window, and a sharp chill swipes through and cuts the mild November air. Treading carefully, Jack closes in toward the window only to find abysmal darkness. His gut tells him something isn't right, so he slowly peeks his head around the back corner of the house, noticing that the sliding glass door has been left wide open.

The back porch is discolored and grey, boards bow as Jack steps on them. The wind picks up. Leaves scatter, tossing and twirling across the yard. Out comes the Ruger P95 from its holster. The very same gun that was so firmly pressed against his temple earlier now precedes his every step as he cautiously makes his way inside through the open door and into the dark abode.

Panning the flashlight toward the wall just inside the door, Jack attempts to turn on the lights in the dining area, but flicking the switch yields no results; the breaker must be out. In the process, he gets a talcum-like substance on his fingers, but pays no attention.

"Goddamn it," he says to himself.

The music stops abruptly. A loud bang rips through the pitch black adjacent hallway just off the kitchen, only feet in front of him. The air is cold, Jack can see his breath. The heat is off. He itches his nose and quickly wipes the sweat from his brow, forgetting about his powder covered digits.

Dishes piled up in the sink.

Mold on bread.

A rotten smell coming from the vicinity of the fridge — likely spoiled meat.

Far gone.

"Joe is that you? You home? It's Jack, Jack Warren from the Waushara County Sheriff's Department."

No response.

Then suddenly, another bang from the hallway, followed by a baritone grunt or groan somewhere underfoot—from the basement.

Maybe poltergeist, not poverty.

"Waushara County Sheriff, if anyone is here make yourself known," he calls out.

A crash of broken glass startles Jack, he spins clockwise and shines his light on the living room just off the kitchen. It is piled with magazines. There is a broken picture frame on the floor, as if someone threw it. Jack is too inebriated to be afraid. His Ruger is aimed and ready for action. Without warning a soft woman's voice speaks to him from the dark hallway now on his nine.

"It's good to see you Jack," she says.

The smell of burnt rubber permeates the air. He thinks it must be coming from outside. Maybe someone is burning tires in a bonfire or something. Typical here. Typical of this place.

Jack quickly points his flashlight toward the direction of the voice and sees a silhouette of a woman on the wall. She is standing just out of sight. The silhouette motions to Jack to come closer.

"Put your hands where I can see them and come out slowly."

"Jack Warren, still a white knight in shining armor I see," she whispers.

"Come out with your hands up!" Jack shouts.

He has her dead to rights, or so he thinks, watching for furtive movement.

Nothing but silence.

Jack inches his way across the kitchen toward the hall; the smell of burning rubber intensifies. It burns his nostrils and makes him gag, cough, and spit, distracting him just long enough...

The woman quickly dashes down the hall toward the doorway to the basement and says the name, "*Haven.*"

The name drifts through the silence like a phantom, sending chills down his spine.

"What...did you say?"

A door slams.

Jack catches his breath and follows in pursuit shining the light down the blackened hallway — it starts to flicker.

"Police department come out or I'll shoot!" He postures.

Again no response, the flashlight batteries die. He immediately regrets not having changed them since he bought it. That figures. The light from the waning moon streams in through the nearby window and Jack's ears start to ring. He hears footsteps quickly descending the stairwell, the air is fumigated with the stench of burnt rubber, and now a subtle hint of cherry blossoms. Perfume. A fragrance all too familiar to him.

Surreal.

Suddenly the lights in the house come on. Simultaneously the music starts again, this time it's the soothing sounds of *Frank Sinatra*. Low toms, followed with piano...

Jack rushes down the hallway checking his corners, he swiftly moves past the bathroom and the spare bedroom. He is clearly flustered by what he *thought* he heard her say. Sinatra, much like the odor of burnt rubber is overwhelming, loud and consuming, his hands start shaking. The overload of his senses only exacerbating the situation.

***

Joe Schneider was a pack rat. Some call him a *hoarder*. A *dirt ball*. He had spent years collecting other people's junk from auctions and yard sales. Air hockey tables, bowling trophies, hand tools, beer mirrors, baseball cards, vinyl records. Boxes upon boxes of *things*, memorabilia, stuff labeled with permanent marker. Blue books, repair manuals, old *Playboy* magazines. That musty smell was a good sign that he had found a treasure. Joe was single, never had any kids of his own, always wanted to, but just never knew how to talk to women.

The closest thing to a "relationship" he ever had was with a woman named Rhonda whom he met playing an MMORPG. Rhonda was jealous, over dramatic, and sexually repressed. So when she found out about his love affair with old pornography, she dumped him. Rhonda couldn't handle the thought of Joe masturbating to pictures of other women being pounded by massive amounts of beef whistle, even though, Joe knew she harbored a nine-inch fleshy rubber dildo named *Lean Luke* under her bed in an old shoe box. The fallacy of the phallus he called it.

***

Nostrils flare, the harsh taste of burning tires, flashes of memories, to a midsummer night where a young girl wrapped her car around a monstrous oak tree, her collar bone snapped, unconscious, head against the wheel, the trickle of warm blood down the steering column.

The horn wailed in continuous monotone...the smell of gasoline.

The lights go out in Joe's house again just as Jack treads the final step into the basement.

"Jack, over here," she says.

Flashlight on palm, palm on flashlight, still nothing. Jack searches for a lighter in his pants — more nothing. Something is tossed, scraping the ground, it stops just under his feet.

"Pick it up," a deep guttural voice says.

Bending over, Jack scans the surface of the concrete floor with his fingertips. His nails scratch the ground, it is rough to the touch — cold — he feels a butane lighter and snatches it. Flick, click, flick...flame. He gets some more powder, or residue, or dust, on his fingers but again ignores it. Sinatra repeats, wall to wall boxes labeled with permanent marker — *Playboy, Penthouse, Hustler, Busty, Playgirl.* A cornfield like maze, a narrow pathway between boxes leading somewhere, amidst a serious collection of vintage smut mags.

"Warmer, warmer."

A light flashes and shines over the boxes as Jack turns the corner. He wipes the sweat from his face, again forgetting about *whatever* he got on his fingers. Grey hues, permanent marker, plastic sheets hanging from the wood beams, leading to the pathway's end. A strobe light flashes, there is a silhouette of a figure standing on the other side. Behind the plastic, the smell of burnt rubber is intoxicatingly noxious. Was the tire stench coming from inside the whole time? He stumbles to find solid footing. Something's not right. His body doesn't feel right.

"Come and see, come and see," the woman's voice whispers.

Just as Jack peels back the plastic, careful as to not blow out his flame, the lights come back on.

He doesn't feel very well.

NAUSEA.

A cd player is hanging from Joe's neck. The extension cord is tightly wound around his throat, making it hard for him to breathe. He is seated on a barstool, wide eyed, his pupils rolled back. Joe is coming in and out of consciousness. There is shit and piss all over the floor, the putrid smell of foul urine and feces.

Jack is feeling woozy.

"Joe, it's Jack Warren, I'm going to get you out of here."

"JJ..aack," he stutters.

Careful as to not step in the brown and yellow mess Jack moves forward slowly and approaches with caution. His balance is off and it's not from the alcohol. Then he steps in Joe's mess anyway. The lights go out. His flame is gone. He must of dropped it. He loses control of his motor skills. Jack is immobilized, he cannot move. His body frozen, every muscle tensed — locked up. A strobe light flickers, the silhouette of the woman appears behind Joe in the chair — Jack gets goosebumps; hairs begin to stand up. Prickle. Jack falls to his knees.

"I missed you," she says.

Her dark silhouette grows and seemingly splits apart. There is crunching, cracking, snapping sounds, tentacle like things—audibly wet. They stretch and entangle Joe—constricting, wrapping violently—enveloping his body and then squeezing tight. Jack's vision goes fuzzy. Blurry. He thinks he sees Joe's eyes pop almost completely out of their sockets. Is that blood spewing forth from Joe's nostrils and mouth? Oozing down his lips?

"HAVEN!" Joe screams. A visceral, violent, exsanguination ensues and Joe is devoured. His bodily fluids extracted. Juiced. Drained. Consumed. Words like *hematophagy* and *anthropophagy* come to mind. Is this real?" Jack wonders. He tries to lift his arms but nothing happens.

Paralyzed.

Jack can do nothing but look on as the tentacle-looking things flay Joe's skin apart, barbs piercing and ripping, stabbing bones, tearing flesh like razors. Whatever is eating Joe lets out a loud belch then regurgitates milky white pus covered parts of him onto the floor. Joe is dead. His carcass is left steaming on the concrete.

The fervent smell of burning rubber and a hint of cherry blossoms precede Jack's sudden loss of consciousness.

Enter foreboding darkness.

5

The Guyana highlands.

South America.

"Peter! Come quickly, over here!" the Patamuna guide yells.

The Yawong Valley was a thick jungle; dense, hot, moist. Dark greens, shades of brown, earthy, rich, futile. Looking south toward the Ireng River, toward the border of Brazil is anthropologist Peter Faxneld. He had learned that an urn burial had been discovered just north at the head of the valley in a small cave—Kuyali'yen, Macaw Cave.

"Brilliant! On my way!"

Peter excitedly wiped the sweat from his brow, adjusted his backpack, tapped a cigarette loose from his pack of Camels, blew the tobacco from the filter, cupped his hand, flicked the lighter, and inhaled.

Pale rock formations, thick weather hardened trees, a dark entrance into questionable territory. The Macaw Cave resembled a 14th century hellmouth; a gaping maw, where the damned would go to suffer for eternity in Christian fairy tales.

This was no fairy tale.

"Right then, let's have a look shall we?" Peter climbed up only to find disappointment.

"Well, this is rather very small, right?"

His Lokono companion shrugged his shoulders, not knowing what to think.

"Definitely not big enough to contain a complete human set of remains."

The urn burial was accompanied by a small *tumi* offering bowl, the Patamuna guide was getting nervous.

"Peter, we should leave this be. It's no good."

"What? Not before I get a few photographs. Then we can go."

The Patamuna guide backed away slowly as the Lokono companion picked up the small ceramic urn. Without thinking, he moved it toward the cave mouth so Peter could photograph it.

Click, flash. In the focal plane, the shutter opened and closed, a split second that would come to define the moment and redefine the archaeological expedition. Peter picked up the urn, then gently repositioned it for another photo op. The Patamuna guide had good reason to back away, for the urn contained human skeletal and tissue material, very recent, and not archaeological as Peter had been told.

"Very good, although quite disappointing right?"

The Lokono companion shrugged his shoulders and pointed to the sun. Deep blues, hues overtaken by dark green tree tops, the sun heading west toward setting.

"Indeed, we should head back to the village, I'm starving."

"Why the long face?"

A finger pointed at the Patamuna guide; he is clearly upset, repeating something under his breath.

"Kanaima, kanaima...not good, kanaima."

"What's that you say?"

"Peter, that urn is no good, it's kanaima...we should return to the benab of Posira, he'll know what to do."

"Kanaima? I don't follow man, we're heading back to the village."

Peter, his Lokono companion, and their Patamuna guide climbed back up to Paramakatoi, only to find that news of their discovery had already spread throughout the village. The Patamuna guide was excited, clearly vexed, and he kept repeating the word "kanaima."

The villagers thought this was an excellent development, enabling the Walter Roth Museum, who funded the archaeological expedition, to let the world know the truth about Kanaimas.

"I'm rather sick to death of this whole kanaima thing man, I'm starving."

Peter and his Lokono companion headed to the refectory, where an old Makushi woman came in and offered to cook for them. As she did, she too started to talk about kanaima, Peter nor his companion spoke Makushi and her English was too difficult to understand.

She had wrinkled dark skin on her hands, varicose veins, and long hair. She stirred *casareep* (manioc juice) into a bowl of rice and dried shrimp vigorously.

It tastes horrible, absolutely horrible.

"Gawd, this is awful stuff man."

The Lokono companion just shook his head and smirked. The Patamuna guide was nowhere in sight.

After finishing the meal Peter began to feel very ill...

Stomach cramps.

A bitter taste in the mouth.

A buildup of phlegm.

Dry mouth.

Periodic gastric pain.

The symptoms would only intensify all night into morning. As Peter set back off onto the trail in the Yawong valley the next day, all he could think was "food poisoning." The *droghers* (carriers) were concerned about taking him into the bush in his condition.

"Still not feeling well?" one of the *droghers* asked.

"No I reckon it was the lousy food the Makushi woman cooked for us last night."

"You let that Makushi woman cook for you? Well, that was a stupid thing to do."

"Why's that?"

"Don't you know she lives by Posira?"

Of course Peter didn't know, how could he? But he suddenly grasped what the *drogher* was suggesting—it was not *food poisoning*, but it was the *poisoning* of his food that had made him sick.

The hike continued and Peter's condition only grew worse.

Fever.

Diarrhea.

Sweating, panting. Loss of breath.

Dizziness.

At the summit of Aluatatupu on the other side of the Yawong valley, Peter collapsed on the forest floor with severe retching and stomach cramps. His companions carried him to the summit, laying him down by the waters of Akaikalakparu.

Peter had felt terrible before, having had malaria and pneumonia, as well as "normal" food poisoning, but this was different. This was an attack.

Peter came to a crossing of a small creek, with a submerged stone. Carved on it is the face of *Totopu* (spirit guardian) who—come to find out—died right there, in this very spot from exhaustion. Peter's gaze was caught up by *Totopu's* pale face, and in that moment of reflexivity he cried.

Everyone was scared that he, like *Totopu*, might die.

Never one to give up, and fighting off the persistent cramps, the sweating, the shortness of breath, Peter rose.

The *droghors* distributed his load amongst each other, and helped him to the nearby village.

Then out of nowhere, Posira and two adolescent boys passed by on the trail, addressing no one, disappearing off into the thick of the bush and out of sight. Whistling noises came and went from somewhere behind the aphotic leaves and vines, but the group paid no attention.

Once at the village, the group was greeted politely and offered bowls of *cassiri* (manioc beer). Only one of them accepted. Peter knew this was a real breach of etiquette. Taruka was a Makushi village, and the Makushi were believed to be associated with Kanaimas.

The refusal of *cassiri* would only bring about more trouble.

Unsurprisingly, suddenly no one in the village had any food to sell. This was bad news, since there was no food left, and the only place to buy it was Monkey Mountain, which lingered off in the distance, some twenty miles away near the Brazilian border.

The group was stuck, Peter couldn't go on, for he could hardly even make it to the bathroom, much less a twenty mile hike to Monkey Mountain for food.

His symptoms got far worse—constant diarrhea and nausea.

"Can I do anything for you?" the Lokono companion asked.

"Just help me up, I've got to take a squat."

Peter staggered out the door, made it some twenty-yards away from the house, hunkered down, and looked out over the savanna toward Siparuni mountain.

The moon was bright, waning, it was majestic, the way the light danced on the tree tops. Amidst the night of the jungle and his ever persistent diarrhea — there was a calm.

Then in the distance some movement.

Two distinct figures moved along the ground toward him.

They looked like dogs, but as they turned to flank him they took on the shape of anteaters, with long snouts and tails.

Peter pulled up his pants, in the time it took to look away and adjust his trousers, they were gone.

Everyone else was unsettled by this. The group believed that the two distant figures were Kanaimas.

Kanaimas, whose attention now centered upon them, and especially Peter.

No one slept easy.

In the morning the group was fortunate enough that someone finally sold them some eggs and pieces of *tasso* (dried meat). One of the *droghors*, named Walatu, persuaded someone to fetch a horse so that Peter could be carried down the trail to Monkey Mountain.

They were going to make a go of it.

Tired and weak, progress was slow.

Every so often the group would stumble upon wild cashew trees in fruit, which inhibited Peter's diarrhea in the meantime. Then, finally, after a day's journey, the group arrived at Monkey Mountain and settled in for the evening.

Peter needed to rest. He decided to lie in his hammock while the others went to the local shop. Then, out of nowhere, one of the youths who had been with Posira on the trail appeared in the doorway.

"Hey you, what's your name?" Peter asked.

He didn't say a word, nor did he respond in any way to Peter's question.

The boy, who looked about twelve or thirteen, was gaunt, dark skinned, long haired, and wore only pants. He started to speak rapidly in Patamuna, much too fast for Peter to understand.

Walatu, Yabo, and Hama saw the youth as they returned and they shouted at him. The strange boy ran off into the jungle.

"He came out of nowhere and just started to ramble on in Patamuna, so fast, I couldn't make out a word of it."

"Peter, he was sent to check you out," Walatu replied.

"He was threatening you."

"Great."

"We have to get you out of here. I'm going to radio Zeek, the bush pilot, it's no longer safe for you to be here Peter, especially in your condition."

"I agree, we should leave now before things get out of hand and something worse happens."

The point of the archaeological expedition had been to establish the antiquity of the Amerindian presence in the Guyana highlands. Peter was supposed to do this through both excavation and ethnography, but it was clear that this was no longer reasonable or *reasonably safe*. t was evident that the ritual vessel he disturbed was significant to the practice of kanaima assault sorcery.

"When we come back, we will make kanaima the focus of our investigation," Peter said.

The group was extracted the next morning and flown into Georgetown, where Peter was frightened again when he started urinating blood.

The locals recommended that Peter seek out someone who had knowledge of bush medicine — to fight fire with fire.

Within a few days of treatment, finally Peter saw recovery.

6

Jessica Mills is a drama queen. She is fashionably anorexic, 5'4, bleach blonde, and enjoys e-cigarettes — vaping. Apple, banana, mint, hazelnut coffee, plum, vanilla, cotton candy.

E-juice. Liquid.

Inhaling, a bright blue light, exhale, cherry licorice.

Lipstick marks.

Her boyfriend Scott is a decorated high school wrestler for the Wautoma Stingers, they were the clichéd jock cheerleader romance.

Jessica was spoiled, although, no more or less than the average middle-class teenage girl. iPhone, Juicy Couture, a name brand txt-aholic.

Raspberry Menthol.

Cappuccino.

Coconut lip gloss.

Jessica's father Tom is a religious man, a hardened factory worker who takes the bible at faith value. Sin and damnation every Sunday before brunch, then football, closed doors, internet porn, and dirty tissues.

Mother Darla is a wine-o. One glass a night became two, two became four, four became a bottle. If you ask her if she thinks she has a drinking problem she would say "No, it's been scientifically proven that a glass of red wine every night is good for your health."

The typical defense of a reticent wine-o housewife in small town Wisconsin.

Merlot, Molly Dooker, Chardonnay...

"It helps me sleep," she says.

It helps her pass out, she means.

***

It was supposed to be a typical date night for Jessica and Scott. A late night movie, some foreplay in the parking lot before show time, and after curtain call a late night masquerade in the back seat of the car at the nearby rest stop.

Jessica would ride him, hands pressed firmly against the ceiling, he would use a condom. After climax they would smoke E-juice and cuddle, the windows fogged, her hair a mess.

Then just before midnight they would part ways and Jessica would arrive home, panties soiled, smelling of rubbers and spermicide.

Trojan, ultra ribbed, for her pleasure.

Propaganda.

Tonight would not be left unscathed.

Jessica finishes penciling in her eyeliner, feeling the gritty slide of the black tip in her peripheral. The radio plays her favorite song, it's hard for her to resist singing along, but she's running late this evening. Scott will be here soon.

***

Scott's engine warms up, his Grand Am smells of vanilla air freshener and black pleather seat covers. Purple accent lights illuminate the blue dragons on the floor mats.

He checks the center console for condoms.

He disposes of the leftover McDonalds in the back seat and tosses it in the trash.

Nothing kills the moment like the crunching of day old french fries under bare butts or wet soda spilt — leaking and sticky — between toes while mid coitus.

He checks his phone, 7:05 p.m.

The click of the seat belt.

The smell of exhaust.

Scott puts the car in reverse and backs out the driveway. The neighbor's cat runs across the front yard into the bushes as his headlights scan the suburban Wautoma streets.

***

"How do I look?"

"Like a hooker, go change," Tom replies.

"I do not!"

Jessica adjusts her bra in the mirror — black lace.

"Oh Tom cut her some slack, all the girls are dressing like this these days...don't be so old fashioned," Darla chimes in.

"Ya I saw Molly Cyprus on that award show the other night, I'm well aware of what 'all the girls' are up to. And I don't like it. It sends the wrong message."

"Don't be ridiculous Tom," Darla sips her Lancatay malbec.

Jessica rolls her eyes.

A horn honks from outside — just in time.

"K see ya guys later, love ya," Jessica grabs her coat and makes for the door.

"Try to be home on time tonight, huh?" Tom says.

"She's not a child anymore," Darla says.

"Be home by 12:30 if you want dear."

"What? Why would you..."

The door slams shut. Jessica hurries toward the black Grand Am parked in the driveway.

Jessica looks back to see Tom and Darla clearly still debating their little girl's curfew in the living room window. The muffled sound of a screaming match.

The car door opens.

"Hey babe."

Jessica gets in, shuts the door, leans in, and gives Scott a kiss. His breath tastes like cigarettes, her lips taste like coconut lip gloss.

"What is that, vanilla?"

"Ya, you like it?"

"Not really. It's kind of putrid, makes me nauseous."

"So what's playing tonight? Anything good?"

"*Valentine's Day Massacre*. It looks decent. It has that one guy from that TV show you like in it."

"Which one?"

"The one with the two brothers who hunt demons..."

"*Supranatural*?"

"Ya that's it. One of those guys is in it."

"Sweet! I hope it's Liam...I'm definitely team Liam."

"Whatever."

Scott leans back and settles in for the drive. Steering the wheel with his left hand, he turns up the radio and rests his right arm over the passenger's seat. Jessica leans into him and sticks a fresh piece of gum into her mouth — strawberry lime. Her phone vibrates.

She checks it, swiping her freshly painted pink nails across the touch screen. The text message reads — *be home by midnight.*

7

Jack wakes up in the ditch of some backwoods rural highway. He is face down in knee high, wind bent, fawn brown grass.

Straw rough.

Covered in frost.

Crunchy.

What the hell, he thinks.

He is groggy with a slight headache. He kneads his temples briefly with his callused knuckles, then cracks his neck at a forty-five degree angle like his chiropractor used to do.

A cold breeze.

Clouds cover the moon.

Nothingness.

Onyx colored sky.

Am I going crazy? he asks himself.

Jack's brain is mush. Overloaded like Judas' ashtray. He starts talking to himself while spinning in circles. His mouth moves, but it's almost mumbling, more like muttering, maybe murmuring, but nothing that sounds like language. He is attempting to logic out, put together, make sense of, what now seems like some sort of twisted dream, or pseudo reality, or maybe nightmare.

Where am I? How did I get here? Joe's dead! I've got to call this in, he thinks.

He grabs his phone from his jean pocket and turns it on, but there is no signal. The phone has some sort of powder on it—maybe dust or dirt. He pays it no attention.

It says 11 p.m.

Low battery warning flashes.

"Wait a second, I know this place," he speaks out loud.

Jack makes his way to his feet and looks up at the towering shadow of an oak tree swaying over head. It has cafe noir bark. Its limbs look like a myriad of thin little arms swinging and clawing, reaching out, as if to grasp him. It has so many arms, like Kali, dark mother. Goddess of destruction. They resemble a thousand snakes hanging by their tails on jungle vines. Like a Medusa's head. Maybe this is the tree of life, he thinks.

He turns on the flashlight app on his cell and pans it around in front of him. There is a white wooden crucifix sticking out of the ground just a few feet away. The paint is chipped, you can tell it has been there awhile. A now forgotten memorial.

Not attended.

The mark of unfortunate death.

Of community sadness.

A family's pain.

Suffering.

Anguish.

Recklessness.

A family's longing.

Someone died young. Right here, in this very spot.

Memories seep in.

They rush back.

Past nightmares flooding his mind.

Taking over his thoughts.

Memories he had blocked, hidden, stored away for so very long...

He now remembers.

"Haven," he whispers.

No car, no radio, no phone signal.

Jack rubs his tired eyes, he scratches his itchy face.

"This is impossible," Jack says.

Jack feels something crawling on the side of his neck and quickly snatches it up. He traps it between two fingers, his index and thumb, and shines the light of his phone on them, in order to examine *it*, whatever *it* is.

He recognizes *it* immediately.

"I hate ticks," he says as he flicks it away.

"Damned blood suckers are everywhere."

PARASITES.

Parasitic pests is more like it.

Ticks are attracted to their hosts by body heat, odor from the skin, and carbon dioxide.

A chill of disgust. Now everything feels like a tick crawling on him.

"Goddamnit, I hate ticks."

I HATE TICKS.

Headlights appear off in the distance. Jack makes his way up the ditch toward the road. He thinks about flagging the vehicle down. He takes his eyes off the lights for just a moment, a split second to watch where he is going. He must, in order to avoid stepping in a partially decomposed raccoon.

He looks up and the lights are gone.

"Damn, must of turned off."

The breeze picks up, the temperature drops, he walks the dark road until he smells something familiar that makes him come to a roaring halt.

Cherry blossoms.

Another set of headlights appears in the distance, this time he doesn't let them out of his sight. Not for a second.

They get closer and closer.

Jack waves his arms.

The vehicle's lights start cutting across the center line, then back, then forth, then all the way right into oncoming traffic. Lucky for whoever it is, there is none out tonight, not in this beloved little village, this horrid township, this godforsaken place. Jack continues to wave his arms hoping they see him. Whoever *they* are.

The lights shine brighter, closer, now only a few hundred yards away. Jack hears the roar of the engine and its acceleration.

The lights shift across the center line back into the right lane and partly onto the shoulder. They shoot straight toward Jack, aiming right for him at the last second. He leaps out of the way just in the knick of time. He narrowly avoids being run down by what he now suspects is a drunk driver.

The car flies off the road, spinning its tires, throwing dirt, and slams head-on into the enormous oak tree with a loud crash. It sits just feet from where the white wooden crucifix juts out, just feet from where he sent the tick flying.

The smell of burnt rubber permeates.

Without hesitation Jack runs for the car knowing someone may be injured and in dire need of help. Again, demonstrating his innate white knight nature. The tail lights flicker, one headlight illuminates the woods, the other cuts in and out, on and off, blazing into the night sky, lost unto its forever darkness. Exhaust steams, gathers in a small cloud and billows. Tires still spinning. A foot is obviously stuck on the gas pedal.

Sparking wires.

A steady and persistent horn sounds off culling the silence for miles.

Monotone.

Coyotes hoot and howl.

At the car, Jack runs around to the driver's side where a head rests motionless upon the steering wheel. Limp. Dead weight. A chin sits on the horn. Bright red blood is running down onto the steering column, the door is locked, and the windshield smashed in where a forehead bounced off of it. The glass is spider webbed with a large hole in the center.

A woman is trapped inside.

Her seatbelt locked tight.

There is moaning and then groaning, the woman starts to regain consciousness and sits up.

The horn stops.

"Oh, my head...my head," she says while looking at her hands.

Two broken fingers. Twisted and folded over.

"Miss, don't move. I'm going to get you out of there."

Her white knight to the rescue.

A damsel in distress.

Small pieces of glass, very minute shards, are embedded deep under her skin like slivers. Her skin all torn up. Like a shaved ham.

Jack tries the back door, it's locked as well.

"Miss, just stay calm. I'm going to get you out of there."

As if repeating himself changes anything, but it makes *him* feel better.

Her moans grow louder, then something intelligible...

"Why did you do this to me? WHY?!" She yells. Then more grunting and groaning.

Even hissing.

She struggles against the seat belt.

Jack kicks the passenger window out.

"WHY!" she screams.

Eyes wide, she bares broken teeth on her tongue, then swallows them grinning.

She laughs about it.

A malevolent snicker.

She must be in shock, Jack thinks. It must be brain trauma, or mental illness, or drugs, or alcohol. He thinks she surely must be on *something*, even if it's just adrenaline.

He remembers seeing police training videos of heroin addicts with superhuman strength — beating up legions of officers.

He remembers watching news stories about people cannibalizing each other while naked. They were gnawing on faces, chewing on noses, while high on bath salts.

Jack reaches inside the window to unlock the door and she pounces on him.

She was waiting for just the right moment to attack. Like a big cat on the hunt in the Sahara who just took down a gazelle. Like a Nile crocodile snatching up a thirsty water buffalo at river's edge. A wolf crying wolf. She grabs his arm as fast as a viper strike, sinking her fingernails deep into his flesh.

"WHY! Jack Warren! Why did you do this to me!" She grabs his arm with her other hand too, sinking her long yellow dirt smitten fingernails deep under his pale white skin.

She breaches the dermis layer. Then the subcutaneous. Jack writhes in pain and screams. He shrieks like a banshee.

Infection.

Calmly, she asks in a cute manner, "Did you think I forgot about you, Jack?"

Her eyes roll white, blood streams down her face and into her mouth, augmenting her bright red lipstick. Black goo seeps out of her broken nose, it is dented and crooked from hitting the steering wheel upon impact.

There is pieces of glass in her hair from the shattered windshield. There is pieces of glass jammed into her forehead. There is one long shard sticking out of her ear causing red and yellow pus to trickle down her neck.

"Now you will pay! YOU WILL PAY!"

She sinks her fingernails deeper and deeper until...arterial spray. She thrusts her face into the bloodstream, licking at it, sucking all she can get, tonguing the grume.

She looks up at Jack, her face dripping gore, and in a soft, mildly sexy voice she says, "You make my pish flaps ache Jack." She then looks down at her crotch and Jack's eyes follow suit. Her lap is moist, stained red, wet with menorrhea.

Jack is mortified.

"What's that I smell...gasoline?" she asks. She lets loose a hysterical and maniacal cackling, then sticks out her tongue at him.

"Get off of me you crazy bitch!"

"Oh no no no..." she squawks.

Jack tries to get his arm free, but pulling away only digs her nails in deeper, like fish hooks.

A spark ignites under the hood of the car and flames burst out firing upward, rolling over the metal. The heat is melting, bubbling, boiling, the chartreuse paint.

"Fire! Fire! Purifies, oh yes! YES!" she hollers.

Jack yanks with all his might and rips his arm loose, screaming in agony. Strips of his skin are left dangling from her fingertips. She waves them around and shakes her head — thrashing her neck against the headrest of the seat.

A hot pain rushes in, first there is burning, then there is stinging. Then nothing. He backs away slowly, grasping the shredded arm in shock. It's numb, he can't feel a thing.

This can't be real he says.

The fire engulfs the entire front end of what looks like a Ford Taurus. Thick black smoke rolls. Tires still spinning, mud spitting, the radio starts playing...blasting...

Sinatra.

"Jack! Come back here! They're playing our song baby! My meat wallet yearns for you!"

The fire makes its way toward the gas tank, it's only a matter of time until...

"JACK!"

The car explodes.

Just as Jack falls to the ground a surly large man in a maroon flannel catches him.

"I've got you, was there anyone else in the car?" the man asks.

Jack can barely speak, he tries to, but it's just not happening. He looks up to see a brown, well-trimmed beard. The man takes off his belt and ties it around Jacks wounded arm, constricting blood flow. Compressing.

"What's your name friend?"

"Jaaack..."

He finds his vocal chords.

"Ok Jack, well hold on man, my wife is calling 911 right now. Help is on the way."

The man takes his flannel shirt off and covers Jack gently. The flames of the wreck brighten the night sky. Cars begin to pull over to see what all the fuss is about.

Spectators.

Cameras.

Snapshots of violent death.

Uploading onto social networks.

Car accidents, the ultimate spectator sport. People driving five miles per hour just to get a glimpse of the latest chalk line, rear end, roll over, or decapitation.

Mutilation.

Immolation.

The roar of sirens creeps up from miles away.

"It won't be long now," the surly man says.

Local police move in quickly, fire trucks pull up, paramedics rush over.

"Sir, I'm going to have to ask you to step back so we can do our jobs," a female paramedic says.

Jack looks up. There is a beautiful blonde woman — maybe thirty — taking the belt off his arm, cleaning it, and applying a tourniquet wrap. She smiles and says "It's gonna be ok, it's just a flesh wound. You're lucky to have survived the crash. Your name's Jack right?"

She has beautifully tapered cupid lips with a subtle heart-shaped curvature. They're the kind you only see in TV commercials or those gorgeous vintage tobacco advertisements in gentlemen's magazines.

More delicate in flavor, too...for those with keen, young tastes.

Jack smiles and asks her name.

"I'm Haven," she says.

Jack swallows hard, his blood pressure drops, the burn of antiseptic, the pukey taste of saline flushing his IV.

Smoke surges upward as the fire trucks douse the flames. The car is black lung charbroiled.

Next stop, Berlin Memorial Hospital.

This can't be real, it just can't be real he thinks.

8

"Kanaima."

A term that within the Patamuna region of Guyana South America elicits both fear and respect.

"Dark shamanism."

Corporeal violence.

A criminal act.

Kanaima is a form of dark shamanism. A term anthropologist Peter Faxneld brought attention to through his fieldwork.

The term kanaima signifies both the doers and the act. Kanaimas (dark shamans) do kanaima (assault sorcery).

Kanaima is a unique religious practice that involves the prolonged harassment, torture, mutilation, and then murder of its victims.

"So who wants to know the dodgy details?" Peter asks.

The eager 600 level class of well-to-do anthropology grad students unknowingly, and arguably mistakenly, seek the answer.

There are some things you can't unlearn.

The class is entitled *Anthropology 666*.

Day one of the fall semester.

Peter is tall, handsome, enjoys four o' clock tea time, and relishes in academic discussion. His long hair is reminiscent of a British rock and roller, yet he always enjoys a good intellectual back and forth. He stays true to his arguments, making others see that violence needs to be understood within particular contexts.

Peter is a paradox.

He says that violence was and is no more horrific in Guyana than it is in Iraq or Afghanistan.

"It's all how we look at things ya know. Kanaima, although quite viscerally gruesome is no less violent than dropping a bomb, firing an assault rifle. Violence is language, it's communication, it's theatre."

There are three types of shamanism within the Guyana Highlands—piya, alleluia, and kanaima. Piya shamanism involves both curing and killing. Alleluia shamanism involves chanting, and kanaima is assault sorcery...murder.

Violent death.

"The kanaima ritual involves the mutilation of both the victim's mouth and anus. They are forcefully and horrifically violated."

Desecrated.

Immobilized.

Abused.

Tormented.

"Once dead and buried, the killers will seek out the body of the victim in order to consume the juices of putrefaction."

At this point, student's mouths go wide.

You could hear a pin drop as the class struggles to come to grips with what Peter just said.

"Kanaimas hunt in packs, when a fatal attack takes place, victims are always struck from behind and physically restrained."

A young girl gets up and leaves the class.

Disgusting.

Heinous.

Repulsive.

"Once restrained, the victim has their tongue pierced with the fangs of a snake and is then rolled over onto their stomach and ravaged anally with either an iguana or an armadillo tail. The goal here being to strip the anal muscles out through vigorous rubbing."

Another student, this time a young man, a Christian, gets up and leaves.

Appalled.

Surely the work of the devil he thinks.

"The Kanaima will then press on the victim's stomach and a section of the sphincter muscle is forced out and sliced off."

Two more students exit, ubiquitous "ewws" reverberate around the room. Looks of shock and horror, of interest and fascination, simultaneously undulating.

You could cut the tension with a knife.

"Before releasing the victim, their body is rubbed down with astringent plants and a tiny piece of wood is jammed into the rectum. This opens the anal tract, making it possible for packets of herbs to be deeply inserted. The Patamuna say these herbs begin a process of auto-digestion which gives off the special aroma of magical death — rotting pineapple."

"Fucking gross," a student says.

"Indeed," Peter replies. The class laughs.

"Once let go, the victim cannot speak or eat. They lose all bowel control and the clinical cause of death is acute dehydration due to diarrhea. And as mentioned, the Kanaimas will try and locate the burial place of their victim in order to drink the juices of putrefaction in the corpse. They do this by inserting a stick through the ground and into the cadaver. The stick is retracted and the honey-like juices are sucked off. Once the corpse is sweet enough, the Kanaima tries to retrieve a section of the anal tract of their victim. Not just as a trophy, but in order to use it as ritualistic paraphernalia. They say pieces of the victim's rectum help in seeking out their next victim."

Peter clicks through the PowerPoint slides, showing his class images of his fieldwork, the ceramic ritual vessel, the entrance into Macaw cave.

Hands go up all over the room.

"Ya, Matt..." Peter calls on the young man in the front.

"So what's the point?"

"Well, that's the question, right? Why do Kanaimas do kanaima. Power, fear, religion, native autonomy. The answer is multi-faceted and we'll get into it."

"Still pretty gross," a girl in the back says, filing her fingernails.

"It's the theatricality of violence," another student says.

"Indeed," Peter says, "it captures the imagination! Kanaima captures the imagination and the way they kill people is quite consciously designed to have an imaginative impact. Just like the suicide bomber has that sort of impact on us. It's not simply about how many you kill, what really scares us is the way it's done. So too the kanaima right, people die, but the way people go about it is what really kind of worms into the mind."

9

The bright lights of the city at night, a packed parking lot full of teenagers necking, an elderly couple holds hands on their way out of the theater. The windows of Scott's Grand Am are fogged, the doors locked, Scott caresses Jessica's breasts while simultaneously tonguing the roof of her mouth. He slides his hand down the front of her pants as she leans into him, the wet between her thighs is inviting, she moans as he fingers her under the light of the parking lamp. Jessica looks over and says it's almost eight o'clock and that the movie will start soon.

"We'll only miss the previews," Scott says.

Thrusting, the smacking of wet fingers, he picks up the pace.

"Oh my fucking god," she says.

Clitoral stimulation, excitement, pleasure.

Scott slides his pants and underwear to his ankles, Jessica removes hers too and mounts his lap.

Grinding.

Jessica's soft, moist pussy sliding up and down on his bulging protein spigot — entreating him to come inside.

No condom.

Her breath picks up as he inches his way inside of her, it won't be long now.

Scott grabs her waist trying to count backwards from ten so he doesn't cum.

Focus.

Concentration.

Resistance.

All for not.

Scott tries not to think about how good she feels or her moaning, or how her nails dig into his shoulder, or how she bites his neck.

It won't be long now.

Jessica is about to climax and he knows it. It feels so damn good. Scott's holding back, thinking of his mother, of dead fetuses, abortion doctors with coat hangers, and vacuums sucking up dead babies. Mucus membranes and his mother's sagging aged titties. Suction aspiration, suction curettage, scraping uteri. His friend Dave said it works for him every time—thinking of his mother so he doesn't jizz early that is. Then Jessica clamps down on his penis, muscles tight.

She does her kegel exercises.

"Oh fuck I'm gonna cum," he announces.

"What? No, I'm almost there!"

Scott quickly throws her off and blows his load all over his stomach.

"I was so close," she says in frustration.

"Sorry babe."

He cleans up with a used McDonald's napkin.

Dilation, evacuation, forceps dismemberment, and violation.

Prostaglandin chemical abortion. A baby's brains are sucked out and the skull collapses.

Maybe thinking of his mother wasn't the answer he thinks.

The two get dressed quickly, the awkward silence is unanimous. Scott's humiliation festers, while Jessica's tepid attitude accentuates their mutual unpleasantries on the way into the theater. A half cracked smile, the rolling of eyes and batting of hair, a loose, cold, weak grip while holding hands, it's obvious expectations have become disappointments.

Teenage angst and premature ejaculation is always a recipe for insecurity and bitterness.

The whole ordeal tastes of chocolate but chews like broken glass.

"Two for *Valentine's Day Massacre* please," Scott says politely.

He was always such a good boy.

A momma's boy.

The swiping of plastic, VISA, torn ticket stubs, wall to wall red checkered carpets, illuminated movie posters, popcorn on the floor, and salt spilled over next to the straws.

Gum stuck in carpet fibers, hardened, with dark soda stains.

Coke products.

Over-priced candy and day old popcorn smothered in butter.

The slurping of straws, crunching of kernels, it was another cliché American Friday night.

"Want anything to eat or drink?"

"No," Jessica says while checking her phone.

"Theater six," the acne-faced ginger behind the counter says.

Two kids run passed eating pixie sticks, laughing and snorting.

Scott and Jessica walk down the hall, bypassing the concession stand. Scott, the gentlemen that he is, holds the door open, they make their way down the dimly lit ramp toward the back of the theater just a few seats in.

Their feet stick as they walk the isle, the rusted springs of the worn maroon reclining chairs groan as they take their seats.

Dry mouth.

Scott wishes he had gotten something to drink.

Snail trails.

Jessica's crotch is still dripping wet. Scott must of came inside of her a little bit. His pre-ejaculate oozes out and runs down the side of her leg. Jessica squirms a little and re-adjusts, nonchalantly wiping it into her pants.

Scott's semen dying on denim.

No reason to worry though...

Altavera, Beyaz, Cesia, Ortho-tri-cyclen...there is a birth control pill for every letter of the alphabet.

Previfem once daily.

Plan B or plan a through z, Jessica's friend Sara says that taking eight tablets in twenty-four hours can also end an unwanted pregnancy through miscarriage.

It's only $500 for the abortion pill. A lucrative mixture of RU-486 and *Misoprostol*, causing uterine contractions expelling the embryo. Side effects vary; abdominal pain, nausea, fatigue, uterine hemorrhage, vaginitis, and even rigors. A select few have excessive vaginal bleeding.

Not a word is spoken between them as the movie starts.

10

Cleaning and dressing open wounds are important to avoid infections.

Yellow discharge, pus, the goal is to remove any debris or contaminants without damaging any healthy tissue. Surgical wounds, pressure ulcers, infections requiring IV antibiotics, amputations, necrotizing fasciitis, and chemical debridement.

In not so ancient history, fly maggots were used to treat wounds, specifically to prevent necrotic spread. Some species of maggots only consume dead flesh, leaving the living tissue all but unaffected. Although this practice died out after the inception of antibiotics, it has resurfaced with mild success in contemporary cases of chronic tissue necrosis and gangrene.

If only maggots could treat the earth's wounds, maybe best the human infection.

To clean a linear shaped wound such as a long deep scratch mark, gently wipe from top to bottom in one motion, starting directly over the wound and moving outward. The type of cleaning agent you'll use depends on the wound type and its characteristics. Sterile 0.9% sodium chloride solution is the most commonly used cleaning agent. It provides a moist environment, promotes granulation, tissue formation, and causes minimal fluid shifts in healthy adults. Antiseptic solutions, such as chlorhexidine, povidone iodine, and hydrogen peroxide, are also used to clean infected or newly contaminated wounds.

Once the wound is clean, it will start to granulate, new cells will form, and eventually it will close.

Time will heal all wounds they say.

Jack Warren is living proof of the counter thesis.

Jack's psychological wounds have began to fester, they are necrotizing, black, decayed, cold, and foul smelling.

Twisting into psychosomatic illness.

Drowning in alcohol and Bayer aspirin.

Contemplating suicide as the only antidote. Once daily.

Anti-venom.

"Son of a bitch!"

A burning sensation.

White hot.

"You ok, Jack?" Haven asks.

"Sure," he replies as the ambulance pulls into Berlin Memorial—sirens off.

The hospital was sepia brick and mortar, not to be confused with light tan. Small evergreens line the blacktop parking lot, faded yellow paint, cracks and potholes, rows of disabled parking stickers hanging on rear view mirrors, blue and sun drenched. A legion of elderly folks in wheelchairs await escort at the main entrance, staring off into oblivion. A growing herd of cancer patients sit in the oncology waiting room come morning.

6 a.m.

How is time passing so quickly? Jack wonders.

Haven walks Jack into the E.R.

A young man is crying with his head in his lap at the registration desk.

"So, you're a cop?"

"Ya, sometimes," Jack replies.

"I thought about being a cop once."

"I think about not being a cop everyday."

"That bad, huh?"

"Sometimes."

Jack and Haven round the corner through two large brown doors. A young woman is wheeled by with a sense of urgency, she is on her way to get an emergency C-section. The female doctor follows steadily behind, not wearing any shoes. The husband stands peering off in dismay with utter dread on his face as the doors close, leaving him behind.

It was supposed to be a normal delivery.

Modern medicine.

Structural violence.

Panacea.

"This way, Jack."

A short strut down another hallway, bypassing rooms full of broken bones, heart attacks, and hypochondriacs.

Patients trying to manipulate doctors for pain meds. Playing the system.

There is moaning, the smell of urine and bleach.

Chemicals, cleaning agents, janitors, white name tags, and white coats.

Color coded socks, laundry baskets, cold stethoscopes on warm skin.

Open up and say "Aaah."

"I also wanted to be a prison guard at one time too, well until I heard about inmates throwing AIDS blood and piss at guards as an act of autonomy."

"You'll have that," Jack replies.

Innocence lost.

Jack looks down at his arm and notices ichor starting to soak through his bandages.

"That will require stitches," Haven says.

Haven leads Jack to room 321. Two registered nurses named Nicole and Shanon make their way into the room.

"I'll be back in a little bit," Haven says.

"Oh that bandage is going to need redressing," Nicole proclaims.

Nicole is rotund, two large dimples on her cheeks, her brown hair in a bun, she is wearing cartoon covered scrubs. She says kids like it.

Shanon is her yang, she's thin like a skeleton, with yellow teeth, long worn fingernails, and a barb wire tattoo on her wrist.

Her hair is dirty blonde and in dire need of a root treatment.

She has crow's feet.

"I'll take his blood pressure if you want to start redressing that wound," Shanon states.

Nicole peels back the dressing, uncovering sticky fresh blood, crusted in at the seams. A foul smell is released, both nurses gasp. A wretched stench.

"Oh lord."

"What is that?" Shanon asks Nicole.

Nicole peels the rank bandage back some more, something wiggles underneath the last layer closest to the skin. Nicole does a double take. Jack wasn't paying attention. Shanon places the blood pressure cuff just above the elbow of his free arm and begins to pump.

"Ah, Shanon..." Nicole has a scared look on her face.

The smell intensifies, nostrils flair. Smiles turn to grimaces.

"Ya, I'm going to need your help here. Can you grab me that scissors?"

"Sure."

"Is that smell normal?" Jack asks.

"Just be patient dear," Nicole says.

Shanon hands Nicole the scissors.

Cutting slowly, something wiggles again, the smell is quite overpowering. Black dark blood stains, the tattered dressing hangs — snip snip snip.

Rotten.

"I just about have it..."

Nicole gives the dressing a little tug, it bursts open and slides to the floor. Black ooze explodes all over like a shotgun blasting a watermelon. The putrid juices hit Shanon right in the mouth, drenching her. The inky fluid has a hint of dark greens and maggots are covering Jack's arm like a bee's nest. They are crawling out, wiggling their way up from the deep scratches and lacerated skin.

"Oh my god!" Nicole screams.

Horror on all faces.

"What the...Get them off me!" Jack screams.

He violently shakes and flails his arm sending maggots flying everywhere. Some hit Nicole right in the face, then joggle down her dimples. Jack continues to shake like a wet dog fresh out of the tub, doing everything he can to get the worms off his arm.

"FUCK! FUCK! FUCK!" he shouts.

It's raining maggots, not men.

Now everyone is screaming.

The smell in the room is rotten eggs, like a road kill that has been sunbathing in eighty degree weather for a few days.

Bloated.

Oozing.

Festered.

Foul.

Maggots are all over the floor, the sink, even the multi-parameter patient monitor.

11

Valentine's Day Massacre ended

around 10:15 p.m. Scott and Jessica still weren't talking, not a word spoken since the opening scene of the film. The sky is full of overlapping grey clouds, a light fog rolls in from the east, and in an effort to quell the awkward silence Scott makes small talk.

"So what'd ya think?" Scott asks.

"About what?"

"The movie..."

"It was ok. Liam being the killer was a little bit too predictable, don't ya think?"

"Ya, they don't make horror films like they used to."

"Ugh, remakes are the worst."

"Totally."

Scott unlocks the Grand Am and they both get in, only a few cars remain in the parking lot. The lot is vacant, quiet, the moon peeks out for a few moments from behind the clouds.

"So about earlier, I'm..."

Jessica rolls her eyes and abruptly cuts him off, "It's ok...and speaking of predictable," she says while checking her makeup in the dual mirror/protective cover of her smartphone.

"Ya, right," Scott says while turning the key and starting up the engine.

"I didn't mean it like that," Jessica says.

"Sure, nah I got ya."

Scott backs the car out and guns the gas pedal with his right foot holding the break. He shifts the car into drive and releases the break rapidly, squealing the tires, smoking them, leaving behind ten feet of burnt rubber in his wake. Black stains on pavement. Jessica just rolls her eyes.

"Seriously Scott you need to grow up, I don't like it when you act like this."

"I need to grow up? That's a joke right? All you do is cause drama, you're an attention whore."

"What the fuck did you just say? Really? There are tons of guys who would **LOVE** to put up with my 'drama', not to mention give me attention, mister premature ejaculation."

Scott steps down on the gas pedal, 65 in a 55.

"Fuck you, you're such a bitch."

"Just take me home, I'm sick of you calling me names."

The needle rises on the speedometer, as does Scott's anger — 70mph.

"Fine, I'm so goddamn sick of you anyway," he says.

"Whatever."

Jessica turns away from him and scoots toward the window puffing on her e-cigarette, sweet cherry licorice on the inhale, yet a strong resentment on the exhale.

Tensions remain high.
75mph.

The fog is dense as Scott pulls up at Jessica's house. The lights are off. Everyone must have gone to bed early. Scott starts to feel guilty.

"I'm sorry babe..."

The car rolls to a stop and Jessica immediately unclips her seatbelt and opens the door.

"Fuck you, Scott."

Shot down.

She's feeling vengeful tonight.

Jessica steps out and stands up, then abruptly turns around, bending down in the doorway of the Grand Am, looking him right in the eyes.

Their eyes meet.

"And another thing, I lied...you do have a small dick."

She smirks and slams the car door shut.

Emasculated.

Enraged.

As Jessica walks toward the house Scott guns the gas pedal again and turns up the radio. He shifts into drive, peeling off around the corner, and into the night, leaving a trail of smoke and dust—with music blaring. Jessica decides to get into her Impala and listen to some music. She just wants to chill out and vape rather than go inside and deal with more Tom and Darla drama. Music is her only means of catharsis.

Well ok, maybe not her only means of therapy. Daddy's little princess does have her vices.

"Fuck it, I'll text Casey, see what he's doing," she says to herself. Casey knew how to get her off, unlike Scott. She dated him a few months ago and he was hung like a horse—nine inches. Although, rumor has it that Casey has a minor case of genital warts. It might just be hearsay, besides the thought of Casey's massive throbbing dong made Jessica super soaked and she needed a good romp after dealing with Scott's Freudian neurosis.

Although there is no clear cause for premature ejaculation, some argue that PE is the direct result of masturbating too quickly in order to avoid being caught by one's parents or an adult during adolescence. Others postulate that it has to do with performance anxiety or an oedipal conflict. Freudian theory states that it is a symptom of neurosis and that the man, consciously or unconsciously, doesn't like women. Thus, he orgasms fast on purpose, satisfying himself instead of his lover.

What an asshole, she thought. The fog is so thick. Jessica can barely see the house anymore, even the street light is clouded in a deep murky grey haze. Little water droplets build on the exterior of the car and run down the windshield.

10:30 p.m.

She texts Casey.

Whatcha up to?

She mouths the words to the song on the radio and takes a hit of her e-cig, sucking, then blowing half-assed smoke rings toward the cracked driver's side window.

Casey replies.

Not much, just hanging out u?

Can I come over?

Sure, what's up?

I miss you

You miss me or just miss fucking me? lol

lol maybe both

Ya come on over I'll be up

k :P

Jessica takes a puff of cherry licorice, exhales, then dry swallows a morning after pill — it's her pre-morning after.

She puts the car in reverse and backs out the driveway. Casey lives only a few miles out of town right off of hwy 22. The fog is antagonistic, she has to keep her brights off in order to even see the road.

10mph.

Fuck I have to pee she says to herself, a bright blue sign appears in the mist in passing, it says *rest area 1 mile.*

She squeezes her legs together and drives slowly. It's only a mile to the rest stop and it's open at all hours.

She refuses to stop and squat on the side of the road. She would rather wet herself. She is *that* kind of girl.

A warm drop of fluid seeps out of her urethra and trickles down her thigh. She can't hold it back much longer.

A mile of anguish.

Constant pelvic shifts.

Uncomfortable.

Finally Jessica turns into the dimly lit rest area, within walking distance to the women's bathrooms. Her headlights briefly scan the gravel parking lot as she pulls in and parks her car. Another vehicle is parked on the men's side and it looks as if no one is in it, but through the dense fog it is hard to tell.

Cigarette butts and ash are all over the ground. A crumpled candy bar wrapper and a full diaper sit just short of the overflowing garbage can. It's clear no one has cleaned this place in awhile.

Jessica gets out of the car and locks the doors, gently clicking the button on her key fob. Pain strikes in her uterus, she clenches her vaginal muscles, her clitoris numb, she enters the bathroom. A long dusty fluorescent light flickers over a porcelain white sink and cracked mirror.

Paper towels are piled up in the corner. Two of the toilets are full to the brim with shit and toilet paper, clearly clogged. Caramel stains meander on the concrete, a used tampon sticks ominously to the side of the brown stall, the color of dried crusty black blood. A puddle of something suspicious beckons on the floor. And of course there is no clean ass wipe. It's all out.

"Wipe front to back," Darla always said. "You don't want to give yourself an infection," she would say, "no one wants shit in their vagina."

Well, no one except Judas, but she's an *entertainer*, an *entrepreneur*, or *dancer* depending on audience.

Through the disgust Jessica quickly makes her way into the middle stall and drops her pants, hovering over the grime on the toilet seat, she sighs and releases.

Gushing, not to be confused with squirting. Almost better than sex.

Casey has warts, it says on the stall in black permanent marker.

Whatever, she thinks, rolling her eyes.

Suddenly there is a noise, the bathroom door opens and shuts, then a clicking sound. Jessica sees two muddy brown work boots walk past her stall toward the sink...clunk, clunk, clunk...leaving thick clay tracked behind them. She strives to remain quiet, as to not draw any attention to herself. She doesn't move a muscle.

Her phone goes off, it's a text message.

Where r u?

The muddy work boots start to move, clunk, clunk. The sink faucet turns on. Water running, pulsating. Not to be conflated with vibrating.

Jessica pushes the last of the urine out of her bladder, waiting in anticipation for the muddy work boots to leave. Her pants are still around her ankles and her muscles are tiring from hovering the toilet seat. Straining. Failing. She decides to slowly sit down on the toilet, cringing upon impact.

Poop in her vagina.

The muddy work boots start whistling — *Sinatra*.

The bathroom air dryer turns on.

The muddy work boots walk toward the stalls and stop in front of the middle one, the one with Jessica in it.

The water faucet is still running, thrashing, the valve all the way open.

Jessica squeaks and pulls her feet back toward the toilet and away from the door. Her phone beeps again, another text message.

Are you cumming? :P

The muddy work boots don't move, not an inch.

"Ah, can I help you? This stall is occupied," Jessica says.

"I know," the muddy work boots says.

A man's voice.

Her heart stops.

Panic sets in.

Remember to breath.

Then Jessica hears a zipper pull, the man pulls out his yogurt gun and starts pissing on the door. The pee splashes, pools, and drains toward Jessica's feet. She lifts them up.

"What the fuck man! Leave me alone, sicko!"

He starts whistling again.

Jessica quickly pulls up her pants and digs into her purse for her pepper spray. It's in there somewhere amidst the lip gloss, condoms, and loose change.

The whistling stops.

Pepper spray found. She pulls it out and readies it for battle. War. Just then the air dryer shuts off and the muddy work boots are gone. Disappeared from under the door.

Adrenaline rush.

The faucet is still running, full force.

Jessica opens the stall door and hops out armed with pepper spray, ready to attack.

"Don't fuck with me motherfucker, I've got pepper spray and I'm a black belt in Karate," she says.

No reply. Just the sound of rushing water.

The light flickers above the sink, the water is still gushing. Not to be confused with squirting.

"Fuck this," she says, heading for the exit door. She pushes on the door and it won't budge, it's locked. "What the fuck," she says, slamming her hands into it, trying to break it loose. The creaking of rusty door hinges, the clunk of work boots on the concrete, the last stall opens, and the muddy work boots step out. Clunk, clunk — it's a man in overalls, but something's not right with him. Not in the slightest.

The fluorescent light above the sink flickers faster and faster...

"What the fuck man! You better stay back pervert, I'll fuck you up!" Jessica says.

Heart pounding.

Pulse racing.

More adrenaline pumping.

The animal has been cornered.

Fight or flight.

The man steps forward slowly not saying a word, mud still caked onto his boots. His eyes are rolled back white. Something yellowish, snot green, is oozing and sliding out from his mouth.

Gurgling.

Rope like, it falls out and hits the floor.

It looks like a pig intestine covered in mayonnaise and Vaseline.

Clear, slimy, coiling into a pile.

"Gross," she says, maintaining a Kenpo defensive stance.

The man keeps moving forward, unaffected, unmoved by her threats.

The pile of snot rope on the floor starts to gyrate.

Jessica thrusts down on the trigger of her pepper spray, letting loose a stream of irritant at the man's head hitting him right in the face. Then she turns, Karate-kicking the door as hard as she can, busting through the flimsy brass bolt. She has a sidekick from hell, her Sensei told her.

The lights in the bathroom go out.

Just as Jessica makes it out the door something attaches to her leg, dropping her right on her face. Her two front teeth slice through her bottom lip and break off as they hit the concrete. Her cell phone flops out of her pocket and beeps upon hitting the ground. Still entangled, entrapped, and now terrified, Jessica kicks her feet and starts to scream for her life.

"Help!" she barks, as *something* starts to drag her back into the darkness of the bathroom. Jessica grasps onto the wooden fence in the entryway, digging her pretty pink nails into the fibers. Her red blouse is hung up on a loose nail.

Slivers in cuticles.

Something wet like a tongue grabs and coils around her other leg as well, sinking sharp spikes into her flesh and piercing straight to the bone.

The excruciating pain makes her light headed, the onset of shock.

With one vicious pull her pink polished nail snaps off, leaving it behind in a crevice in the wooden fence. Her finger begins to bleed. She finally notices the pooling blood from her mouth on the ground in front of her, it is caked with dirt and clay. Upon seeing this, she loses it completely.

Screaming turns to crying.

Her blouse tears loose.

In desperation Jessica lets out one final hoarse squall before being yanked back into the bathroom. The door slams behind her and there is nothing but silence.

12

Grey and blue hairs in wheelchairs drooling, struggling to remember their own birthdays. Tiny complex spirals in the worn carpeting. Wrinkled newspapers, patterns of beige, half-full hand sanitizers squirting dirty palms. Roy sits in the waiting room patiently, the elderly woman across from him stares off into space, her body rigid like mummified remains. She doesn't move a muscle. Her eyes are sunken deep into her skull. Her tight lips are dry and cracked, accented only by her pale, crinkled, rawhide skin. Daytime television echoes in the background. Soap operas, sex scandals, and talk shows observed by catatonic, blank, distant, disassociated eyes.

"Attention, we need first responders to the Bean Cafe," a woman says over the loudspeaker. There is an unconscious choker on the first floor.

Roaming children probe the germ infested playground that is the hospital waiting room. Fingers in mouths, then on magazine pages, and wooden jigsaw puzzles. Exploratory little fingers picking yellow boogers. Cute little hands not covering their mouths while coughing.

A college girl sits nervously in jogging pants, unkempt, awaiting her gynecological exam. She hopes the doctor doesn't shove her finger up her ass this time. Plastic fake smiles on the receptionists faces, they regurgitate the word "perfect" after every verbal exchange with incoming patients. They say things like, "Do you have your insurance card? Perfect." Obese RNs wander the hallways calling up patients by name—Clarence, Dorice, Lou, Lajon. They are clearly not upholding the model of health and wellness they proselytize to lifelong smokers.

At least you're not fat with lung cancer.

Thinning hair and warts, banal wildlife art hanging on egg shell vinyl interior, a pamphlet for every occasion—hysterectomy, appendectomy, orchiectomy, teen pregnancy. Middle-aged divorcees thumbing through perfume ads, crying babies, and automatic doors opening and closing.

A hospitality cart makes its rounds offering granola bars, fruit, orange juice, and watered down coffee in Styrofoam cups. Trail mix, almonds, all natural powdered creamer, and little red stir sticks.

Cane syrup, vegetable glycerin.

This is how waiting is done at Berlin Memorial.

"Excuse me sir, Jack is awake if you want to see him now," a nurse says, her name is Betty.

Betty is filling in for Nicole and Shanon on short notice. They went home early, something to do with maggots they said.

Jack was sedated but conscious, his roommate was a 28 year old prurient male named Seth.

Seth was rushed to the emergency room with a broken penis. He had torn his tunica albuginea, the outer sheath of his penis' inner chamber. This happened while pounding his girlfriend Lizzy's gash during rough sex. Hardcore. She was on her back, legs spread, he pinned her legs back toward her head and dropped his body weight onto her with each thrust.

Neighbors could hear the smacking over their T.V., it echoed through the thin walls. It only took a moment for Seth to slip out of Lizzy's wet box—her taco soup—and hit her perineum by accident. He heard a snap, immediately lost his erection, then saw blood spurting out. It was a rush of blood from the tip. Thus, he needed an operation.

Seth didn't break his penis jelqing. Penis enlargement exercises, commonly referred to as "jelqing" are all but mainstream these days. Research has shown that men who jelq five days a week end up **BIGGER**. Seth gained over two inches from jelqing twenty minutes a day for a year.

To start Seth would take a hot shower to increase the blood flow. Then, for five minutes, he would tightly grip his deep V diver at the base with his right thumb and forefinger in order to keep the blood from flowing back out of the spongiosum. From here, he would gently grab his clam hammer in the same manner—with his left hand placed above his right—stroking upward pushing blood into the head. He would do this for five minutes a day, five days a week.

If you get hard you have to stop and wait for the erection to subside.

Then start again.

The other notable part of Seth's routine, his penis workout, was flaccid stretching.

To do this Seth would seize the base of his limp noodle and pull it straight outward, slowly stretching the ligament. He did this three times a day, five days a week.

It worked or at least *he* thought so.

Just moments ago Seth was being prepped for surgery, having his pubic hairs shaved by an elderly woman named Ethel.

She must LOVE her job, he thought.

It was awkward.

He had wished his dick wasn't retracting toward the warmth of his body, but the old lady's wrinkled hands were ice cold.

All the jelqing in the world couldn't have prepared his penis for that.

Ethel had a tattooed wedding band on her fleshy finger. Tattooed eyeliner, eyebrows, and lips.

They say cosmetic tattooing can improve the appearance of nipples after breast reconstruction. They say that complications are rare, but can include infection and allergic reaction to dye.

The surgeon, who was also the urologist, said that complications from Seth's fracture include: erectile dysfunction and/or scar tissue, known as fibrous plaques, can form causing his piss weasle to have a permanent bend. The procedure didn't take very long and now Seth and Jack sit across from each other, juxtaposed, exchanging war stories.

"So what do you think Jack?"

Jack cringes, "I think I'm going to be sick."

"Ya well, I'm just happy it's over with."

"I imagine."

"It could be worse, I could of bled to death or something right?"

"Ya," Jack says laughing a bit.

Seth was in good spirits.

There is a knock on the door.

"You have a visitor Jack," nurse Betty says.

In walks Roy, just as Seth's girlfriend Lizzy shows up blushing.

If Seth only knew that in three months he would be diagnosed with an aggressive carcinoma and that he would have to endure twelve weeks of chemotherapy, he wouldn't be smiling, or laughing, or making jokes.

He will lose all his hair.

Weight loss.

By his fourth cycle a skeleton will be peering back at him in the mirror.

He won't even recognize himself.

The good news is that his cancer won't impede his future jelqing.

Nor will it kill him.

He will survive to live another few years in this beloved little village, this horrid township, this godforsaken place.

The smell of chemotherapy drugs will permeate Seth's sweat and urine, he will hallucinate, he will become weak, and, eventually, bedridden.

Elderly terminal cancer patients will look at him with pity. His five day, five hour chemo regimen will be excruciating; he will have over thirty IVs set into his hands and wrists, he will eat stale crackers, drink flat soda, and watch daytime soaps while large bags of steroids and poison drip ever so slowly into his bloodstream.

The Young and the Restless

Vomiting.

Anal fissures.

A metallic taste in his mouth.

"Roy, it's good to see you," Jack says.

"So what the hell happened? Last thing I knew you were headed home."

Jack shrugs his shoulders and takes a drink of his aspartame laden diet cola.

"Look Jack we still have no leads..."

"Joe's dead."

"What?"

Roy looks puzzled.

"I stopped by Joe's house and long story short...he's dead."

"Why didn't you call it in?"

"I was attacked...knocked out by *something* or *someone*...I don't know."

Jack sets the Styrofoam cup down spilling a little soda on the table, his hand trembling.

"There is something really fucked up going on here Roy. I think Joe has something to do with Jessica's disappearance."

Roy takes out his cell and calls it in.

Seth and Lizzy are holding hands, she is running her fingers through his black, combed over hair, telling him that everything will be alright.

Problem is, nothing's ever alright here, not in this place. Not now. Not ever.

"How's your arm? The nurse said you had some sort of hallucination or something?"

"What do you mean?"

"Ya Betty said you freaked out on a couple nurses, that you were running around screaming about being covered in maggots..."

Jack doesn't understand, he looks down to see the bandages and they are there just like he remembered them.

"Apparently you made them so upset they both went home. Nice one buddy. You have such a way with the ladies." Roy lets out a chuckle.

Jack just looks at Roy dumbfounded.

Speechless.

Questioning his own sanity.

"Anyway, you rest, I'm sure you can use it...I'll see about Joe," Roy says.

Jack's heart rate rises to over 100 beats per minute on the monitor. Tachycardia.

13

Roy's thumbs are covered in scars. They are cracked, torn, and bleeding at times. He picks at them relentlessly, with a fury. Scar tissue. If he didn't trim his nails regularly his thumbs would need stitches from all of the tearing and scratching—it was his nervous tick.

This is why he had to be extra cautious when thumbing through the fetid pile of meat that used to be Joe Schneider. Joe's corpse was rank and it stunk. Latex gloves are a must at times like this. Roy didn't want to catch Hepatitis C or HIV in his ripped apart pollices. Not to say that Joe had either disease, but it's good to be cautious with any kind of bodily fluids when you have open wounds.

Sure enough, Joe was dead, just as Jack said he was. But *how* is the explicit question. The bones that weren't crushed were curiously clean, as if they had been soaking on a stove, boiling in borax. Joe's muscle and skin slid right off of them, tendons loose, hanging freely, elongated and stringy. Joe's eyes were questionably wide, set forward and apart, past the eyelids, his pupils dilated, and his sclera bloodshot—maybe proptosis—obvious subconjunctival hemorrhage.

Roy couldn't help but think about the bruised and battered face of an eccentric geriatric who he ran into on his way out of Berlin Memorial. She had small cuts on her left cheek, two hoses jammed up her nostrils, and an oxygen tank in a stretched green bag on the floor. She donned a fur hat and was dragging two small white Pomeranians with fuchsia gloss toenails behind her. They wouldn't quit yelping. They just wouldn't shut up.

What's left of Joe resembles a fleshy roadkill that had been repeatedly run over for a day or two on a busy highway — a malodorous heap of entrails, bones, skin, and hair, swarmed by flies. Once Roy had a tire on his pickup puncture from running over a similar mess a couple years back.

Sharp jagged bones perforating rubber.

Roy notices a bright yellow pill shining from within the bloody muscular tube of Joe's large intestine. Roy pulls the gooey skin back carefully, hair sticks to his wet latex gloves — probably chest hair — it's short, black, and curly. It might be pubic, it's hard to tell.

Joe's work boots are caked with mud.

Maybe the autopsy will reveal something useful, he thinks.

Neon pink hues striate the blue sky as Roy finishes up his walk through at the crime scene. He looks through each room of Joe's cluttered house and finds himself in front of a well-locked door. It was Joe's home office. Lucky for Roy, his father was a locksmith. Roy picks the lock and finds himself in a room that is, for the lack of better words, an homage to the strange and stranger still. Satanism, the occult, and South American mythology. Hanging on his wall was a diploma, Joe apparently had a Bachelor of Science degree.

Here was a guy who cleaned toilets with a college education. It's nothing he ever talked about. No one had any idea.

As Roy's eyes scan the room he notices an alter with black, scented votive candles, behind him there are two Balinese masks hanging ominously on the cream-colored wall—eyes bulging, with large white fangs. In the corner on a shelf are three red samurai swords reflecting a fading sun, and a brass mold of Shiva dancing— creating and destroying the world.

Joe was into some weird shit by society's standards—the taboo. Not just vintage pornography. Roy couldn't help but notice all the books—a hoard of books—shelves of nothing but books lining the walls. There was one entire section dedicated to *witchcraft*.

"Interesting," Roy says while jotting down notes in a turquoise notepad.

Demonic possession.
Fire walking.
Shamanism.
Books galore.
Roy is writing "key words."
Voudou.
Sex Magick.
Cannibalism.

And there, pinned with a small thumbtack to the wall in the middle of the black candles on the altar, just past the dragon's blood incense, was a photo...in it Joe had his arm around a pretty, black haired teenage girl. The girl looks familiar, but Roy can't quite put his finger on it. He pulls the tack out and turns the photo over — on the back in squiggly black cursive ink it reads, "Haven and I in Guyana."

Roy puts the photo down and takes notice of a strange powder all over his fingers. It has no smell. He ignores it and carries on, brushing it off on his slacks. *It must be dust or dirt,* he thinks.

Curled, hardened chicken feet, tanned animal skins, and small dog bones in finger smeared jars. Joe's office was not just a strange place, it was a *cabinet of curiosities.* On his desk was a diagram, a schematic, it was some kind of structure, an architectural floor plan of a small building. It looks like Joe was up to something, but *what* was anybody's guess. On the top of the blue diagram it read, "Highway 22 Rest Stop."

"Well I'll be damned," Roy said, for now it was clear that Joe had been up to something nefarious. Jack was right after all. On the floor plan in black permanent marker there was a large, black circle drawn in and around the maintenance closet in-between the men's and women's bathrooms. Seeing this, Roy knows what he has to do. He folds up the documents and puts them in his pocket on his way out the door.

Dusk settles in comfortably as Roy starts up his car and makes his way to the rest stop. He doesn't bother to wash his hands before eating the rest of his chicken sandwich. Twenty minutes go by and suddenly Roy isn't feeling so good. He begins to sweat profusely.

Light headed.

His stomach churns ever so slowly.

Roy takes a drink of cold coffee from the mug in his counsel and pulls into the rest stop.

No cream.

No sugar.

Black.

Darkness falls.

Roy gets out of the vehicle and stands up. He forgets his flashlight. He ducks back in the car to grab one out of his tactical equipment bag.

With flashlight in hand he shuts the car door and makes his way toward the bathrooms — the light tan brick and mortar. Not to be confused with sepia.

His stomach churns more ferociously, knotting, twisting, spiraling upward.

A sharp pain strikes his nervous system, he rests his left hand on the cold concrete wall of the building. Teeth clenched, it fades momentarily.

A cold sweat.

Brisk air.

A high of, maybe, thirty degrees outside.

The waning moon looks on advantageously, peeking out from behind the grey cumulonimbus clouds as if to sneak a peek at Roy's torment and laugh about it.

To take note of his suffering.

Roy makes his way around the building and sees a large brown door with a silver handle, it says *maintenance* on it in stenciled black letters.

To his surprise, it's unlocked.

Roy opens the door to a set of concrete steps that lead downward. A string hangs from a light bulb overhead. He pulls it and the light comes on. As he descends the staircase the door catches a gust of wind and abruptly slams behind him, jarring his senses.

The air smells heavily of incense, much like Joe's office, but far more overpowering.

You could taste it, it was almost hypnotic. Hallucinogenic. Euphoric.

It reminded Roy of college and the hot sex with Darla Young, his high school sweetheart. It reminded him of her pulsating, super tight vagina.

She goes by the name Darla Mills now.

The mother of Jessica Mills.

He too knows the Mills family, it wasn't just Jack. But Jack didn't know about this—their sordid history.

Darla had the tightest vagina he had ever experienced. He would finger bang her with the familiar odor of dragon's blood smoldering in the background.

Roy's stomach churns again, another sharp pain sends him keeling over, this time straight down to the concrete floor. Half open paint cans, used turpentine, and mouse traps with peanut butter are strewn about.

The pain washes over him and he stands himself back up. He is confronted with a T-intersection with two narrow corridors, one leading under the men's room and one leading under the women's. He opts for the latter.

Fever sets in. *Maybe it's food poisoning,* he thinks.

Maybe he had some foul chicken.

Maybe it was salmonella.

Another light string hangs from the ceiling, he yanks it. The light repels some of the darkness of the basement.

There are large muddy boot tracks leading further toward the women's side, so he follows them.

It's then that he hears something peculiar, a voice maybe—a whimpering of some kind—further down the blackened corridor.

It gets louder.

And louder.

Then a violent spasm in his abdomen drops Roy to his knees.

This time he retches and throws up, spilling out chunks, emptying everything — even the chicken.

Surely it had to be food poisoning he thought. He reassured himself that it would pass. That this was temporary. And that things would get better.

Roy looks up from his knees to see a flickering of light from a room at the end of the corridor, directly under the women's bathrooms. The light dances off the walls. Shadows boogie, creating imaginary worlds. Seeing them reminded Roy of Plato's allegory of the cave.

He unholsters his weapon — a Glock 9mm.

Another light string dangles, he pulls it, but nothing happens. There is no bulb. Only shards of broken glass left sticking out of the socket. And a burnt filament.

Roy regains his composure. He wipes the bile from his lips off onto his pants.

His body starts to shake from chills, *maybe it was influenza,* he thought.

The distant whimpering now mutates into a low moaning, a deep groan, nothing intelligible, but definitely *human* in nature.

Light continues to glimmer and pirouette, back and forth, here and there, brighter and brighter, all over the aged stone walls.

Roy proceeds with caution, pushing the cracked wooden door open ever so gently, ever so quietly, then stepping inside, pistol at the ready.

Cocked.

Safety off.

He enters the room.

His eyes cannot believe what he sees, his hands shake, his stomach moans and groans.

Gurgles.

The walls are lined with candles, half of which are burning brightly, the others just blackened wicks. There is a large altar in the middle and there, to his disbelief, is Jessica Mills lying on it. She is naked. Tied down. She has duct tape on her mouth.

She looks over at Roy and moans louder. She is trying to say *something*.

The altar is draped in bright red cloth, there are rose petals strewn about, Jessica's nipples are red as a ripe strawberry. Her body tight, her tits perky and perfect.

Roy swallows as his eyes acquire the smallest of details, his gaze fixed upon her tied up body. He looks intently at her impeccably trimmed pubic hair. At her flawless, painted toe nails.

Blood rushes to his loins as he witnesses such a beautiful tragedy.

There are strange symbols painted on the walls, and on the floor, in what looks like blood. Here, in this beloved little village, this horrid township, this godforsaken place, beauty rests eloquently amidst violence.

The intoxicating smell of incense opens a flood gate of Roy's pornographic memories.

"Jessica, don't worry I'm going to get you out of here," Roy says.

He sounds like Jack.

Another white knight.

Another damsel in distress.

Another cliché disempowered woman in need of saving.

Another woman in need of a man.

Just like in a thousand stories told before.

Another female victim.

She returns noise, words muffled by grey tape.

Roy starts to feel dizzy, but fights it and makes his way to the altar. He holsters his weapon in the process. He pulls out his pocket knife and cuts the ropes on her feet. He thinks about unholstering his pleasure python and jamming it vigorously into Jessica's perfect little snatch.

Besides, who would know right?

Sinful thoughts.

Oh, what it would taste like, feel like to have another dance with Darla he thinks.

He sets his lust aside and cuts the ropes, his morality subdues his inner devil.

Another stabbing pain drops him to his knees, his body heaves and haws, it tries to throw up. His muscles contract and his mouth opens, but only hot bile makes its way out onto the floor. And not much of it for that matter.

Jessica's legs are wrapped with gauze and white wound dressing.

Roy uses the altar to get back to his feet. He grabs onto the tape on Jessica's mouth and tells her that this might hurt a little.

It comes off quickly. She cries out, some dead skin tears off and causes her red succulent lips to bleed. Fresh red blood drips and streams down the side of her chin. Roy moves to cut the ropes around her wrists and tells her it will be ok, that he is here to help.

Saying so makes *him* feel better.

Jessica doesn't say anything. Not a word.

Roy tells her how her parents are worried sick about her and how everyone will be so happy to see her.

He cuts the last rope.

"Even Jack?" she asks in a curiously calm voice.

"Yes everyone," Roy says, "even Jack."

"That's good news," she replies.

She sits up on the altar and stretches her arms out wide, "Oh that feels so good," she says. She twists her neck, cracking it, relieving tension.

Roy offers his hand to help her down off the altar and she just looks at him and smiles, it's then that he realizes something isn't right. He backs away slowly.

Beauty is in the darkness, beauty is the darkness.

More gut pain makes Roy cry out and hit the floor. He whimpers. The wheels start to spin in his head — words like *poisoned*, *tricked*, and *escape* flash in between agonizing debilitating abdominal spasms.

"Not feeling so well Roy?" Jessica asks.

How kind of her.

His rectus abdominis contracts tighter and tighter, he dry heaves repeatedly — uncontrollably. Out of the corner of his eye he sees Jessica hop down off the altar and start walking toward him like a runway model. Almost prancing, but not skipping. Like a goddess, a seductress, a temptress. "It will be ok Roy, I'm here to help," she says.

A white knight in distress.

A woman empowered.

In charge of her own destiny.

She needs no man to save her.

She is no victim. Not anymore.

"You know, you really shouldn't touch other people's things Roy," she warns, "they can make you sick."

Her bare flesh still very much excites him, but the sight of it is now so very bittersweet.

Roy is in too much pain to do anything but maintain a solid constant fetal position on the floor.

"Poor devil," she says as she soccer kicks Roy in the head, knocking him out cold.

"Stripping naked is seen in civilizations where the act has full significance if not as a simulacrum of the act of killing, at least as an equivalent shorn of gravity."

–Georges Bataille

14

Stuporous.

His head tender, sore, Roy has a splitting headache. Cephalalgia.

Ironically Roy awakes upon the same altar he thought to have saved Jessica from — his legs and wrists bound by tight, blood stained rope, rubbing his skin raw. He is naked, his mansicle just lying there exposed, flaccid, his testicles cold. *This is what Seth must of felt like.* He tries to speak but his lips won't move, they are ducttaped shut. His facial hair pulling snug, prickly sharp hairs tug at skin with each movement — it is a bad time to be sporting a thick mustache.

"Welcome back," Jessica says.

She is mixing something in a small bowl. She stirs it, then kneads it with her hands.

Roy can do nothing but look on anxiously.

"You probably have lots of questions, don't you Roy? The first being, why you are all tied up right?"

Roy nods his head and grunts, hoping she will remove the tape.

Jessica puts down the bowl and walks over to him. She places her hands on his stomach, they are freezing. Morgue cold.

"I know what you're thinking Roy, but your premise is all wrong."

She reaches down and places her left hand around Roy's cock, stroking it gently with soft hands. The blood begins to flow, hardening it, making it grow. First against his will, then to it.

"That's it, it's hard wired you know...you can't fight it. Carnal instinct. My naked flesh, my wet pussy, you desire it, even now, bound and vulnerable. See? Your cock rises to the occasion."

Jessica's free hand, the one she isn't jerking — not to be confused with jelqing — Roy's dick with, quickly rips off the duct tape.

He screams.

"Pleasure and pain Roy...they are one in the same...you'll see," she says, "They are inseparable."

She puts Roy's hard member in her mouth and deepthroats it.

She is no Judas.

She is no Devin.

Roy closes his eyes and envisions Darla Mills. Her mother. Now it feels so damn good. It had been a long time since he had a blowjob — years. Even now with the duct tape off, he can't find any words, he only yearns to orgasm. To finish on her perfect lips.

Jessica abruptly stops and looks him in the eyes, her lips still wrapped around his penis...she smirks and spits it out.

"Like I was saying Roy, your premise is all wrong. But you don't care anymore, do you? You just want to cum...cum inside me. Am I right, Roy? Do you want to blow your load inside my tight little pussy?"

She grabs him by the face squeezing his cheeks.

"Well?" she asks sternly.

"Y...es," he replies.

"What did you say? I can't hear you...SAY IT AGAIN."

"Yes."

"Again!"

"YES!" he shouts. His inner devil takes over.

"You just want to be inside me spilling your seed don't you Roy?"

She releases her grasp.

He nods yes, not saying a word.

"I don't think Jessica would mind," she says and hops up on top of the altar, straddling him. She rubs her wet vulva back and forth, all over him.

"It's not like she has any say in the matter anymore anyway, she's dead."

Roy looks up, not fully realizing what was just said, his carnal lust is tired of foreplay, he yearns to fuck. He is puzzled by what she is saying, but just doesn't care; lust becomes him.

"You see Roy, your premise is wrong...wrong because I'm not Jessica," she says stuffing his blood filled rod deep inside of her, grinding her clitoris upon his pelvic bone.

Roy's eyes roll to the back of his head while asking who she is. Because if she isn't Jessica, then who is she?

"I am everything you want, everything you desire, I am the wet hole you fill called ecstasy. Now shut up and cum for me baby."

She grinds harder and harder, faster and faster.

Roy moans, releasing everything, his cum shooting inside her, filling her with his darkest secrets. Quenching desire, pleasure magnified, at the very height of orgasm, as he strains to maintain control of self, as the blood rushes to his head, endorphins flowing, she pulls a knife and thrusts it deep into his stomach.

A fatal wound, it punctures him to his very core.

Dichotomies of pleasure and pain she says. As Roy lies there in shock, having just came and now bleeding profusely from the belly. The girl who should be Jessica stands up, grabs the bowl from earlier, and places it between her thighs and under her creampied clam. She winks and pushes out Roy's seminal fluid into the bowl — squeezing out every last drop.

"Was I the best you ever had?" she asks., "Well, I'm the last you'll ever have."

His tummy is warm as fresh, bright red blood pools into his belly button and overflows onto the floor.

She mixes *whatever* is in the bowl with his semen and begins to brush the questionable substance on his forehead.

Ritual.

"Who are you?" he mutters.

"I'm not Jessica. And soon enough...you won't be Roy."

***

Jack turns the key and unlocks the door to Judas' trailer. The deadbolt creaks and slides back, a newspaper lies at the base of the door, the headline reads **Still No Leads in the Case of Missing Local Teen**. Jack kicks it aside and shuts the door behind him, his arm still a little sore from the dissolvable stitches.

The air is musty, his cell phone alerts him that he has messages in his voicemail. Jack sets down his keys and plays the messages on his way to the liquor cabinet—the oak doors are worn and scratched. He pulls a small dirtied glass out of the dishwasher and rinses it in the sink, then pours himself a drink—Jameson Irish whiskey—per usual.

"Jack, it's your mother. Call me."

Two messages to go.

"Hello Jack this is Bernice from..."

Surely it's a debt collector. He presses forward onto the final message and takes a swig.

Bitter yet calming.

"Jack, it's Roy, I'm headed over to Joe's house to see what I can dig up. If you get this give me a call."

End of messages.

Jack throws back what's left in the film-coated tumbler and dials Roy's number — there's no answer.

He calls again.

Still no answer.

Jack pours another double, slings it back like water under a scorching noon sun, as if his throat was parched, and violently throws the glass at the wall shattering it into bits.

"Goddamn it," he says.

Glass shards litter the once plush carpet, it has stain protection, but not enough. There is a thick layer of dust on crooked hanging picture frames.

Judas isn't home.

Cigarette burns spot the Maya teak sectional sofa.

There are stained panties on the floor in the kitchen.

A black and gold roughed up cardboard box of 9mm blazer brass still sits upon the Noguchi coffee table. 115 grain, 9 x 19, the bullets wait patiently for Jack's return, right where he had left them when he first got the call about Jessica having gone missing.

"Not today," he says to himself.

Jack grabs his keys and makes his way out the door, he staggers slightly.

Being back was depressing.

Jack knows what he has to do, he has to head back to Joe's and find Roy. Joe is the only lead he's got.

He thinks he shuts the door on his way out.

He trips and falls into Paul, his pretentious overweight neighbor.

Paul is in need of a quickie, he is headed over to see if Judas is home, which she isn't.

"Watch it," Jack says.

He uses the railing to guide himself down the steps, the hydrocodone he took said "not to take with alcohol."

He drops his keys while fumbling to unlock the car.

"Goddamn it," he says loudly.

Jeanna, a stunning red head who lives across the street looks on in disgust while pushing a stroller, even the infant looks perturbed.

The car was unlocked the whole time.

Jack still inserts the key and unlocks it again being none the wiser.

He slams the car door shut and starts the car up.

Everything is a little cloudy, like peering through mildew on a glass shower door.

He puts the car in reverse and the car goes forward.

It looked like reverse.

Jack backs out and zooms through the parking lot. A silver Toyota comes to a sudden halt and the driver flips Jack off. He mouths the words "stupid motherfucker."

Jack pays no attention.

He is oblivious to his surroundings.

The double lane blacktop becomes a quadruple lane as he heads toward Joe's place. The car sways back and forth in-between the white and yellow lines at 70 mph. This may seem like a unique event, something leading toward another tragedy, maybe a scene with some sort of gravity, but it's just another day for Jack Warren.

And that in itself was the real tragedy. This was his life, the day-to-day of a drunkard, an unrepentant alcoholic. Uneventfully he will make it safely to his destination, for Jack was *that* kind of cop.

Today it was hydrocodone and Irish whiskey. Tomorrow it would be Irish whiskey and aspirin. The per usual concoction.

15

As Jack pulls down the street toward Joe's house, a call comes across the radio. It's about an abandoned car at the rest stop. The description of the vehicle sounds a lot like Roy's. Jack has a photographic memory. Jack picks up the radio and says he is in route, then whips a U-turn and slams on the gas toward Hwy 22, toward the rest stop.

The moonlight illuminates Jack's left arm as he drives with the window open, exposing his imperfections. The wind sifts through his vellus arm hair, flecks of dead skin scuffle and blow away. Jack usually keeps the driver's side window open when he's drinking just in case he has to throw up. He does this out of necessity. He's had to wash vomit out of his jeans on more than one occasion. Speaking of, Jack grabs his bottle off the passenger seat and goes to take a sip—it's empty.

His mouth dry, his hands shaking.

"Goddamn it," he says tossing the bottle in the back seat amongst old crumpled hamburger wrappers and empty Little Debbie boxes. Oatmeal Creme Pies and Star Crunches, the breakfast of champions.

A moldy banana peel stuck to the floor mat.

Dead bugs in the back window, dried pink gum in the ashtray.

Sometimes Jack would chew watermelon twist Trident and drink whiskey at the same time, he said it tasted like the south.

A Brett Favre bobblehead jiggles on his dash, an old sun drenched bridal garter hangs from the rearview mirror—it was from Roy's wedding—when Jack was the best man.

Jack's never been married, *what a bullshit ritual,* he thought. And there was Roy, all jazzed up, tossing the garter to a bunch of drooling single men. Thirsty. And of course Jack had to be the one to catch it.

The wedding garter tradition started sometime in 14th century Europe. Catching the garter was supposed to bring about good luck. *What a crock of shit,* Jack thought. He hasn't had good luck in years.

The thought of marriage appalled him, it was a repugnant suggestion. Jack has had some serious girlfriends throughout the years, but none of them were anything to write home about. There was Shelley the dance club skank, Sara the loose bartender, Kimmy the pothead, and Laura the high school sweetheart. None of Jack's flings lasted over a year and a half and there were plenty of reasons for that. No one worth reminiscing about now, at least not since Jack became an alcoholic. Not since Judas. Not since Haven...

***

Haven Schneider had dark black hair, she was in her early twenties, and every guy in Wautoma wanted to fuck her. I mean REALLY fuck her. She was *that* girl, the girl everyone wanted to bang but no one could. She would date guys for months and still not put out. She was a prude pragmatist. She believed in love but just didn't have the time for it. Eventually, men would just give up and move on but not for lack of trying. That's how she weeded out the bad ones and they were all bad ones. Haven didn't drink, she didn't do drugs, and she didn't stay out late. All she did was study. She was a bookworm. A nerd, but the most gorgeous kind. She wanted to be an anthropologist, she wanted to work in faraway, remote regions of the world and write ethnographies.

Sometimes during the summer, she would go with Uncle Peter to South America. She would accompany him while he was doing fieldwork in Amazonia. She wanted to be like him, get a PhD, and travel the world. You know, do something important with her life. Something that has meaning. She wanted to make him proud and she inevitably did. Not like her brother Joe who barely finished college and who never did anything with his degree. Peter liked Joe but Haven was his favorite. She was valedictorian of her high school class and held a 3.8 GPA at university.

She was fascinated with other people's worldviews and she loved asking questions. She was a needle in a haystack. While most of her high school class started getting fat after graduation, working at dead end jobs, attaining C-section scars and hideous stretch marks from pregnancy; Haven was cramming for exams, writing research papers, and working out. Haven was *that* girl. She didn't fit the mold, she didn't follow the path of least resistance, she carved her own way.

Jack met Haven a few years ago. Haven had come home from university for Thanksgiving break and was somehow coaxed into going out with some girls she knew from high school. A night on the town with Lindsey and Margo. They had heard Haven was back visiting her family via Facebook, so they invited her out. Surprisingly enough, she agreed.

Upon entering the local pub downtown, Haven turned heads. She was tall, thin, and beautiful. Maybe a whopping 120 pounds. And, of course, there were many more familiar faces out that evening than she had expected to see. Half of the starting lineup from the Stingers basketball team was there. Even now, years later, they were bulky with muscle and sporting tightly-trimmed beards.

The town tramps and bar sluts, on the other hand, were just as fat as the guys were burly. Their clothing was garish and miniscule, their love handles folded and spilling out over elastic. Their butts were stretching nylon, taking it to its limit.

When juxtaposed, it was as if a runway model had just walked into a tavern full of whales in tights. Haven was *that* girl and she never stopped talking.

Her beauty held everyone's attention. Even that of the new detective sitting at the end of the bar named Jack Warren. Jack was the only one not buying Haven drinks. He knew better, he knew Haven wasn't fucking anyone after bar time. At least not by choice. Besides, Jack would rather spend his money on himself. Jack was *that* guy. And he was off duty.

Jack didn't drink much at that point but tonight would change that. Tonight would send him spiraling toward rock bottom.

Guy after guy with hulking shoulders and square jaws would find any reason they could to talk to Haven, to try and break the ice and get her digits. Time and time again she would politely entertain their conversation, not realizing that being polite was the wrong thing to do in this beloved little village, this horrid township, this godforsaken place.

The men here equate conversation with being interested in sex.

The whole Stingers team surrounded her, like husky wolves encircling a winded doe just before the kill. Their liquor breath permeating, they spit and slobber when speaking, the juke box plays Sinatra. It was Haven's choice. She had an eclectic taste in music.

One drink became two, two became four, and it wasn't long before Haven was a little more than tipsy. The has-been Stingers, with their colossal frames, did what they did best—they got Haven drunk. She was smashed. Trashed. This way she would be easier to fuck, to manipulate, because passed out girls can't say no. Naive to their intentions, Haven not only chatted them all up, but started dancing.

Jack sat at the end of the bar sulking but not staring. He was entranced by her perfect hips, her tight ass, and her long legs. Every dick in the bar was already fucking Haven in their minds but she didn't care. She was grooving, she was letting go, and Sinatra would take her there. The would-be-scholar was just plain having fun. The fat girls were seething, giving Haven the evil eye. Tonight, every long dong silver was standing at attention for Haven and every patron knew it.

Then Bill Kimball, the Stinger's pack leader, the old point guard in his tight, worn, faded blue jeans, in his orange trucker hat, hatched a diabolical plan. It was a plan that would have dire consequences for all parties involved.
***

Bill worked in a meat processing plant. His face was beat red from a consistent thirty-degree temperature, like freezer burn. He grew the beard to hide the worst of it and the rest of the pack had followed suite. The factory was full of miserable wrecks with cold-nipped fingers and noses dripping; pulling product and labeling.

The hum of cooling fans drove everyone crazy. Smoked turkey thighs, pork hocks, habanero beef snack sticks. Leaky packages oozing animal juices, throats parched, raw, a case of mild hypothermia. Long underwear, smoke breaks and cancer, the woes of working in a refrigerator. Meats sorted, packed, shipped, sold, cooked, reheated, ingested, bifurcated, defecated, becoming drainage — septic stew.

Recycled.

Ten-hour shifts.

While Bill spent fifty hours a week at work, the dishes stacked in his sink. There was dried gravy and solidified fat crusted onto dinner plates. Spoiled milk curdling, reeking like a bloated carcass on the side of some bypass on the out skirts of some overpopulated metropolitan wasteland.

***

Bill tongued the pizza burn on the roof of his mouth.

Haven told him about her big plans after college. She told him, "I'm only home visiting."

It was then that Bill seized his opportunity, he offered to give her a ride to the "after party." He told her that everyone was going and that she had to come. He told Haven that he would give her a ride back to her car later and that he would take good care of her. He convinced her that the "after party" was the place she wanted to go and that she would have the time of her life.

***

Sure enough, the vehicle is Roy's. The rest stop was empty except for a vintage, white and tan RV parked just off the bathrooms. It is a Ford Econoline camper with long, dark brown stripes trickling down its sides. Meanwhile, two young children are playing tag and circumambulating it, stirring up bits of gravel and dust under the dark sky. Their hipster parents look on smiling, as they walked their large black Rottweiler named Obie. Obie sports a red collar and is sniffing a puddle of antifreeze. They jerk the chain leash, pulling him back just before he can get his licks in.

Jack walks up, asking them if they were the ones who called in the abandoned vehicle.

"So there was no one in the car or in the bathrooms then I take it?" Jack asks.

"Nope, it seemed odd too."

"Why's that?"

"'Cause when we were pulling in, I swear I saw someone go in the bathrooms on the women's side, but Arlean here said there wasn't no one in there either."

Arlean's two front teeth are missing, but it was only noticeable when she spoke. Jack tries not to stare at them — or her blackened meth gums.

"Yep, there was nobody in the lady's room so I told Dwayne here to call it in. I heard about all those rest area rape cases in California and you know it's only a matter of time until it comes here."

"That's right honey bun, and I ain't 'bout to let no rapist stick his pecker in some poor girl on my watch," Dwayne says.

His handlebar mustache is almost as absurd as his high water cut off shorts. His pockets hang just below the fringes. He is sporting a red and black flannel shirt, he has yellow untrimmed toenails protruding from open-toed sandals, his ears are gauged and stretched, and there is hardened, yellow pus smothering the thick black plugs in his earlobes.

Even though they smelt funky, Arlean would still nibble on his crusty lobes during sex. She would lick at them — tongue at the infection.

Dwayne's earlobes remind Jack of the time he caught the clap.

Gonorrhea.

It reminds him of the moment the thin, clear membrane over his urethra busted and its non-stop itching. It reminds him of being politely asked to hold his testicles out of the way so the doctor could examine the tip with his cold cracked hands — covered in blue vinyl.

They said "powder-free," they were supposed to have a smooth finish, be non-sterile, single use only, latex-free, and ambidextrous. "Ceftriaxone should clear this right up," he said.

It could have been worse, it could've been MRSA. Jack had seen that once, on his now deceased grandmother's ass. A deep ulcerated wound, leaking, burrowing progressively into hip bone. Nurses irrigating it daily, splashing bacteria infested fluids into their eyes, mouth, and open cuts.

It starts with a boil.

The doctor fingered his urethra open and jammed a cue tip inside, swabbing for Syphilis.

This is Jack's photographic memory at work.

16

Jack watched as Haven left the bar with Bill. She was saying things like, "This will be so fun!" and "You promise you will drive me back to my car right?". Which Bill avidly and aggressively reassured her was the case.

Jack ordered another beer and turned his attention to the basketball game. It was around 11 p.m.

The drive was short, Bill lived on the edge of town. He rented a three-bedroom home from his parents, paying only the taxes and electricity.

"Right this way, darling," Bill said.

Haven staggered, stumbled, and then upchucked all over the sidewalk leading to the front porch. Chunks of pot roast and little pieces of Jell-O splattered onto the cement and wedged into the cracks. The motion light turned on. Haven was now centerstage, performing, white light distributing shadows all over the damp grass. Her shadow mimicking every dry heave. Every gag.

"I'm ok," Haven said, wiping her mouth with her free hand. Her other was perched, grasping her tummy.

Bill held her hair back, she smiled and then heaved up some bile.

"I've got ya," he said.

"Thanks. Just give me one more second," she said, "I'll be right in."

Bill let her hair go and walked inside where the other hulking Stingers were waiting.

Haven fell over, passed out drunk in the lawn on her way toward the door. Black out drunk.

Minutes later, Bill noticed and carried her inside, upstairs...to the master bedroom.

Four guys followed suit behind him.

There were five men in the house and what they did next would have dire consequences. More than they could ever imagine.

The wind picked up, lightning just off in the distance. Then a rumble. The sky growled with discontent, alerting everyone to a coming storm.

A Portent.

From here there is no going back.

***

Haven came to slowly, still heavily intoxicated, she felt a sharp pain in her abdomen. There was ubiquitous grunting, a barking of low tones and cackles. The air thick with Escada Magnetism, tequila smells, and thick must, sweat and old socks — body odor. Another sharp pain, her body rocking back and forth violently, swaying to an ensemble of groans and barks. Bedsprings flexed and creaked. The air damp, moist with perspiration. Evaporation. Harsh sounds reverberated throughout her skull, piercing her temples — giving her a splitting headache.

She tried to move but her hands and feet were stiff and immotile. Her sight blurred. Head pounding. She was dehydrated and wet. Naked. Haven was face down on an old queen mattress — used from the Pfitzer hotel — draped in Lino teal linen, dark and drenched in spots, soaking up bodily fluids. She turned her head and feels something warm start to trickle and slide down the side of her cheek. A loud guffaw rupturing the din of reverberating barks, she finally came to.

"Hey guys, she's waking up," a voice said.

The alcohol's analgesic properties wear off and stabbing pains shot up from her vagina toward her stomach. Rupturing, thrashing pain. She tried to move again, but there were multiple arms holding her down, hairy legs in her peripheral, boxer briefs, and guys stroking their erections. Then she felt an icy hot sting on the side of her face and her right ear began to buzz.

Someone pulled her hair and calls her, "Bitch."

"Slap her again." Someone.

"Fuck her ass." Another voice.

Haven looked up to see Bill. She trusted him. She asked him, "Why?" Why were they doing this to her? He responded with a fiendish grin and then hocked a large, slimy gob of spit on her cheek.

"Shut up," he said.

Another stinging sensation on the side of her face, both of her ears humming, like a refrigerator just clicked on.

Running black mascara.

Smeared rouge lipstick.

Another slap and then another. The pain rendered her speechless, unmaking her world. A symphony of slaps echoing and stinging all over her body. There are red hand prints on top of red hand prints. Her skin raised and purple, the art of violence. The Stingers basketball has-beens continuously slapped Haven bright red as they spit on and raped her.

"Flip the bitch over," Bill says, "I want her to see this."

Haven is turned over onto her back and can now see everything.

The yellow walls were warm, rich, zingy. Her cooter red and swollen, puffy, irritated and sore. Five men surrounded her, laughing, smiling, calling her bitch and slapping her tits pink, then white.

A welling of tears.

Welts permeated her legs. There was a thick lather of sweat and spit building up onto, what can only be described as, a canvas of bruises.

If rape was art, Haven would be a Francis Bacon.

Her mouth parched. Dry. Her lips chapped. Semen trickled out and down her vulva, vaginal fissures seeping blood.

Tears.

Two men still aggressively stroked themselves as Bill stood naked in front of her. Someone slapped her face so hard it culled all noise in the room, but for only a moment.

"Hold her down good and tight," Bill said.

"Stop!" Haven cried out, "Why are you doing this to me she asks? Please just let me go."

Another damsel in distress.

Another cliché disempowered woman in need of saving.

Another woman in need of a man.

Just like in a thousand stories told before.

Another female victim.

"Shut up whore."

"Bitch."

"I came so hard in you slut."

"Dude we should piss on her."

"My turn," Bill said.

He jumped up onto the bed and the springs popped and creaked loudly, bouncing and shaking, buckling under his obesity. Bill dropped to his knees and lifted her legs up, Haven tried to kick her feet, but took a fist to the face.

Bill punched her twice, the collision of knuckle and cheek bone.

Blood running out of her nose, her face fattening.

Her eyes swelling with tears.

The sting of salt.

"Fight back and I'll hit you again, you fucking cunt."

Haven lost circulation in her arms, they go numb from being pinned so tightly. Even so, she bucked and attempted to kick Bill off again.

Instinct. Fight or flight.

"Fuck you," she said.

Bill punched her right in the mouth.

Blood streamed out, squirting down her chin, her lip punctured by her front teeth.

"Fucking bitch," he said as he spit on his hand and then grabbed his cock.

"Hold her fucking tight, you dumb shits!" he shouted.

Bill hocked a loogie on Haven's anus, then rubbed the tip of his dick up and down on her brown star before thrusting it in.

"Oh ya, your ass is so tight bitch. Is this how your daddy gave it to you?"

"Tear that ass up Billy!" someone yelled.

Bill porno fucked her back door, thighs violently colliding with buttocks.

Haven cried out, a vile burning sensation.

Then a shitting sensation.

A woman empowered.

In charge of her own destiny.

She needs no man to save her.

She is no victim. Not anymore.

"Goddamn man look at her squeal!"

"Squeal bitch! Squeal!"

"Can I piss on her yet?"

Haven went quiet.

"What's the matter bitch, cat got your tongue?" Bill asked.

Haven doesn't hold *it* back, she let *it* go. Suddenly, just as Bill went to thrust inside her, a dark brown substance exploded out, covering his entire frontal region.

"Motherfuck!" he cried.

"Oh shit!" someone yelped.

No pun intended.

Haven defecated all over him, chucks of digested proteins painting his beer gut. All the drinks they bought her had given her the runs.

Diarrhea.

Poetic justice.

There was utter silence. Shock.

"What's wrong baby, cat got your tongue?" Haven asked.

Someone started throwing up, blowing chunks all over the blue plush carpet.

She started laughing.

"Fucking bitch!" Bill rushed her and two guys stop him. None realizing they just let her go in the heat of the moment.

"Billy don't!" one yelled. There were shit stains on the sheets and fecal matter in chest hair.

Another has-been Stinger upchucked.

The air reeked of a men's restroom and regurgitated alcohol, of rotten hops and a full diaper.

Haven made a break for it and rushed the door. One of the guys tried to grab her, but his hands slide right off. She slipped his grip and bolted passed him, out the door.

"Gross," he said looking at his soiled palms.

"Guys she's getting away!"

"Get her!" someone hollered.

A herd of naked and half-naked bodies stormed out of the bedroom door after her down the hallway.

"I'll kill her!" Bill cried out.

Haven quickly made her way down the steps and for the front door grabbing Bill's car keys from the table. A stampede of swinging dicks and scrotums behind her, yelling and screaming.

She slipped and fell on the hardwood floor, hitting her funny bone, but paid no attention. She got right up and made it to the door. She turned the deadbolt and swung it open, making a clean getaway.

"Fuck! Get her!" Bill howled, trailing behind all the commotion.

The night air was damp, after a swim wet.

Haven hopped down the sidewalk and sprinted toward Bill's car in the driveway.

"Fuck!" Bill screamed.

"Everyone back in the house!" he exclaimed.

The city streets were empty, a young boy looked out his bedroom window to see Haven in Bill's car, naked. The interior light exposed her violated bare flesh to the blackness around her.

Haven was unable to speak, her lips are purple, her teeth are chattering.

17

The storm had begun, a vicious downpour ensuing. Searing cracks of lightning flay the darkness, raindrops stinging skin through the open window. Haven turned on the wipers, but they could hardly keep up. She was shaking ecstatically, her naked flesh sticking to cold vinyl and hard plastic. Her body sore and red, she was in shock, trying to keep the car on the road amidst the violent thunderstorm. Amidst the full realization of the violence that was done upon her.

There were little stones caught between her toes, going unnoticed as she stepped down harder on the gas pedal. She was not consciously aware of where she was going, but she knew she must get there—wherever *there* was. She had to get away, and anywhere but here was her destination. Anywhere not in that beloved little village, that horrid township, that godforsaken place.

She was just driving and driving fast. Sixty miles per hour became seventy. The rain pounding harder and faster, tears streaming down her cheeks, her eyeliner still smeared. She was shivering cold. She turned the heat on full blast. Nothing but cold air. She didn't notice that the air conditioning is on.

Then she is freezing.

Her hands could barely grasp the wheel. Her petite fingers with chipped rose polish cracked at the joints.

She smelled of sex and feces, a stygian reminder of what has been done to her. Of what men are capable of.

Stomach pain. The burning between her thighs analogous to the burning behind her eyes.

Enraged.

Screaming.

Feeling vengeful.

Hurt.

Scared.

Alone.

She was sure that somehow, someone will blame *her* for all of this. Maybe they will say *she* had it coming, or that how *she* dressed gave *them* the wrong idea. Surely someone will say it was *her* fault. That being raped was God's justice, that being violated was her karma. Somewhere some man will tell *her* that what happened to *her* was justified.

They won't even see jail time she thought.

The newspapers would make her out to be some kind of whore, or worse, make Bill and the has-been Stingers out to be the victims.

These thoughts made her see red.

These thoughts made her want to kill.

These thoughts made her want to hunt them all down and force feed them all their own below average size dicks.

She would smile as they choked to death on them, if she could.

These were her thoughts, they belonged to her, and in them she made them fucking pay.

The road was carved with flashes of lightning, blurred only by the steam accumulating on the windows. The rain beating down harder and harder on the glass until she could barely see the road at all.

A tight curve in the road ahead.

She cranked on the steering wheel, fishtailing the rear end, over the deepening puddles in the blacktop. She thrusted the wheel in the opposite direction, narrowly keeping the car on the road, spitting mud and gravel up over the shoulder.

Her heart sinking into her chest.

Just as the car straightened out it starts to hydroplane and swerve.

She was losing control.

***

Jack turned up the volume on the radio on his way home from the bar, the rain drowning out his visibility, so he slowed down and turned the wipers to high. *Another night alone, with no one to go home to.* This was his life. Well, this was his life before he became an alcoholic. He turned on the heat to circumvent the fog building up on the windows. Warm air circulating inside the vehicle, lightning pops and crackles just yards away hitting a tree, splitting it in half. Sparks scattered, a flame burning hot white then orange. A car's headlights emerged on the roadway and swayed back and forth in front of him.

Eyes wide.

Body stiff, his foot hovered over the brake.

***

Haven tried to keep the car straight but her speed made it impossible. The car veered left, then right, then left again. The sides of the car started raising. The back end swayed. Her shaking hands, her chattering teeth, her battered and bruised body could not react quick enough to gain any traction. The rain was relentless, a bolt of lightning hit a tree just as the car headed for the ditch. Mud and gravel spitting, tires spinning, all she could do was brace for impact. There wasn't even enough time to scream.

She forgot to put her seat belt on.

***

Jack's hairy knuckles cracked as he braced the steering wheel, the car in sight veered off the road and into the ditch smashing head-on into a massive oak tree. Jack slammed on the brake and pulled the car over. The vehicle's red tail lights acting as a beacon in the night. Jack opened his door and darted for the smashed car. The rain soaked through his clothes, drenching him in mere seconds. Thunder sounding off overhead, Jack raised his arm as if to deflect it.

A loud monotonous horn blaring.

Jack slipped and fell on the grass, mud caking his already wet jeans, nevertheless he jumped right up and rushed toward the car.

He was slipping and sliding.

Heart pumping.

Adrenaline.

Somehow the driver wasn't ejected.

It was a naked girl, her head resting on the steering column. Warm blood streaming down her face, she was unconscious.

Jack tried the door handle, it was unlocked but jammed, crushed from impact.

"Goddamn it," he said.

"Hold on, I'm coming," he touted.

She couldn't hear him.

The smell of gasoline.

The urgency that is intrinsic to a car accident pummeled Jack in the pit of his stomach. Jack circled the vehicle, nearly slipping again, thunder crackled and echoed across the night sky. The rain died down. There was mud caked onto his boots. He had that itchy feeling you get when you're wearing wet clothes long enough. None of the doors would open, so Jack decided to break the passenger window. He told her to hold on again and that everything would be ok and that he was here to help.

She didn't hear him, but started to come to. Broken glass was stuck in her forehead, she was sliced open, draining blood. The steering column was pinning her chest tight, her collar bone was snapped in two. Her left leg was broken and her petite toes crushed under folded metal. She couldn't feel anything, even pain. Her vision was blurred from the thick hot blood in her eyes. Her head was a mess from the concussion. She had no concept of where she was or what she had been through. Her mind was as jarred as her body.

Whiplash.

Half of her front teeth were missing, half of those missing, she swallowed.

Jack immediately realized it is Haven, the girl everyone wanted to fuck but couldn't.

She heard an intelligible voice ramble at her from the passenger window and clarity started to come — it fading in and out.

"Haven I'm gonna get you out of here, hold tight ok," he said.

Jack realized she was in a bad spot and that moving her could be detrimental to her health — maybe even kill her. He pulled out his cell phone and dialed 911, describing the place and requesting an ambulance. He took off his wet sweatshirt and covered her naked torso, he said it would help keep her warm.

She reached over and gently grabbed his forearm with her free hand. Jack turned and their eyes met, she said, "Bill."

"Jack," he said, telling her his name is Jack and that he is with the sheriff's department and that help is on the way.

"No...it was...Bill," she said.

"Bill?" he asked.

"He and his friends raped me...they hurt me."

She tried to say more but couldn't. Her lungs were filling up with fluid, she had internal bleeding.

She was feeling tired.

Cold.

Shivering.

Then suddenly warm.

Still, there was no pain.

18

She is crushing up *gueio* leaves with fresh cut nails and bangs of hair — pulverizing them between two stones. Hands taut. The juice of the *gueio* is mixed in thoroughly as she pours the concoction into his nose.

She speaks to him as if he is alive, but he is not, he is legally dead.

No heartbeat.

No brain functions.

They say she cannot be killed, however violently she is attacked.

This is how she raises the dead. She knows because she too was brought back to life. She was brought back from the abyss in this same way, brought back by her brother Joe Schneider. *But now Joe's dead for good* she thinks. *Good riddance* she thinks. His death was a power play. She would answer to no man. Never again.

Zombies are never free.

They are forever slaves of their masters and so too can be said of their ancestors in Haiti. This is where zombie making comes from. It is indigenous to the Haitian people, not an import from Africa like everyone has been told all these years.

She whispers to him softly ten times.

They say once made a male zombie cannot be killed unless his testicles are torn off. She tore everything off of Joe. Just to be sure.

The *buhuitihu* doctor is also invincible once the cohoba powder is inhaled.

Intoxicating.

Purging.

In Haiti it is snorted as an affirmation that they talk to spirits — the *cimini*.

She clasps her hands around his cheeks and blows air into his mouth.

His fingers begin twitching.

Rigor mortis came and went. Come and gone.

His eyelids flutter ever so softly, begging to see the world for the first time since his human death.

Zombies crave life but too much of a good thing is never a good thing. Not in this place. Not in this beloved little village, this horrid township, this godforsaken place.

His erection under the cloth subsides, they say that dead men still get it up in morgues. A death erection, also known as "angel lust" or a "terminal erection" happens post-mortem and is typically observed in the corpses of men who have died by hanging. Execution. In hung women, their labia and clitoris will become engorged, which is sometimes followed by a discharge of blood from their vagina.

Pop-culture also believes that zombies crave brains, but in reality, the zombie only sees chains.

Zombies are forever slaves. Slaves to their masters.

Roy Hutchinson opens his eyes and sees the world again for the first time. He is no longer dead but he is no longer Roy either.

She grabs his wrists and pulls him up onto his side.

He scans the perimeter, his vision is blurred, but his sense of smell is heightened. She smells of cherry blossoms, a light but not too potent perfume cascading down her neck.

What is this place? he wonders. The paint is dry and cracked, the walls rough from years of water damage. The smell of mold lingers subtly in the background. He doesn't recognize her or this place. He makes his way over to a cracked mirror on an old vanity, what he sees ignites no memories whatsoever, he doesn't even recognize himself.

"Who am I?" he asks.

He turns and glances over at her with feelings of insecurity.

Of fear.

"Come, sit," she speaks gently, patting the vinyl of an old bar stool next to her.

Roy is hesitant, but makes his way over and sits down. Her presence is warm and safe. It is both inviting and reassuring.

She caresses the hair over his eye and rests her hand on his shoulder.

"You are my child and I would never let anything happen to you. You understand this, don't you?"

"I think so," he says.

"Good."

"Now, son...your given name is Roy, but we call you Hutch for short."

"Hutch?"

"Yes."

He smiles and says, "I like it."

"You always have, son. Now, come and let me show you to your room. You need your rest, you have a big day tomorrow."

"Tomorrow?"

"Oh, don't worry, everything is fine dear."

She could sense his self-doubt, his diffidence, his uncertainty. Newborns are always anxious at first. They are rightly confused by their new surroundings, the adaptation to a new world.

"Here, this way, I'll show you to your room."

"I have my own room?"

"Yes, dear. You always have."

"I'm hungry."

"I know dear."

She takes his hand and ushers him down a corroded corridor with water stains all over the ceiling. Buckets line the floor catching constant water droplets. Their silhouettes fade into the candlelight. Voices turn to whispers, then turn to echoes — then fade away into the night.

***

Jack is standing just outside the women's bathrooms, the door is cracked, with no lights on. He pulls out his weapon and nudges the door ever so slightly, as to remain unnoticed by anyone that might be inside. Thunder echoes off in the distance. There is a rattle of metal reverberating off the hanging door latch. It's broken. Like someone kicked the door open from the inside and busted it off the hinge. He didn't notice that before. The smell of urine invades his nostrils as he pushes the door open further and makes his way into the brick and mortar building.

"Police! Anyone in here? Say so now."

The lights flicker and spark, then come on. No response.

Jack walks slowly toward the stalls and kicks them open one by one.

Nothing.

No one.

All the stalls are empty. Jack stands still assessing the situation. Maybe they crawled up into the ceiling he thinks. He looks up and there is no way anyone is hiding up there, it's wide open and the beams are exposed. Then he looks down. His eyes follow a questionable stain on the floor...it leads to a large drain.

That's it, right there. The basement.

Jack rushes out the door and around back to the other side of the building to the maintenance door. It's locked. A padlock dangles and reads *Master Lock.*

We'll see about that, he thinks.

Jack runs to his car, pops open the trunk, and grabs a small, black unfinished prybar. He jams it behind the lock and pushes with everything he's got. It pops and snaps, the metal bends and caves to the pressure. The door opens.

The steps leading down are dark, he reaches up to pull the light switch and it works. The bulb burns bright illuminating his descent.

Descent into the unknown is always cause for trepidation.

It stinks like patchouli incense, at the bottom of the staircase. He follows the scent, left and down the corridor. He moves with speed, checking his corners, like he was taught in the academy. He approaches the same room Roy discovered and kicks the door open.

"Police!" he yells.

Nothing, no one.

An altar stands before him, candles with black wicks, burnt, there are no signs of recent activity. There is blood all over the altar, stained into the cloth and all over the floor. Jack pulls out his cell phone and calls it in. This must be where Jessica was taken...*Roy too,* he thinks. The words *occult* and *cult* come to mind. He cannot describe it any other way to dispatch.

He thinks about Heaven's Gate.

About Jim Jones.

About Charles Manson.

Scientology.

Tom Cruise.

Waco.

About Catholic priests molesting children.

Jack lets his guard down, lowers his weapon, then holsters it. *Surely whoever did this won't be back anytime soon,* he thinks. He walks the room, surveying it, looking for evidence, for anything that could lead him to Jessica...to Roy.

He finds nothing. *Whoever* did this was thorough, well except for of all the blood. Which is also cause for concern. *Who does it belong to?* and *are they still alive?* he wonders. *The state crime lab ought to have a field day with that,* he thinks. Then, out of the corner of his eye, he sees something, something at the base of the altar, so he moves in for a closer look. He bends down to examine it— turns out it's nothing, just a piece of loose concrete.

Jack stands up and turns around. To his surprise, there is a woman standing right in front of him.

She smiles.

"Jack, I presume," she says.

"Jessica?"

Before he is able to do anything, she takes the butt end of a shotgun and hits him square in the face. Everything goes black as Jack hits the ground. Like turning off one of those old black and white TV sets with the dial knobs and numbers.

With Jack unconscious, a large man enters the room and picks Jack up off the floor with no effort at all. He is huge, maybe seven feet tall. He is built like a linebacker. Like William "The Refrigerator" Perry. No, even more like a refrigerator. He carries Jack like a sack of potatoes over his right shoulder and stuffs his limp body into the trunk of Jack's own car before driving away.

Red, thick blood seeps down the side of the Econoline camper door. Like something hit it and exploded upon impact. Great force. Obie lies dead in the gravel not far from it. Blunt force trauma to the head. His skull is so caved in you can't even tell it was Obie anymore.

Arlean and Dwayne are nowhere in sight, neither are the children.

Flies start to buzz and linger.

A raven in a nearby tree feeds on one of Dwayne's gauged ears.

There are sirens in the distance.

19

SWEAT.

The taste of burlap is fibrous, bland; the smell potent to the nostrils. Everything is dark. Jack can't see a thing through the dry, scratchy bag taped over his head. He is sitting in a metal desk chair, his hands and ankles tied tight to it with hiker's cord. People are talking in a nearby room, but he can't make out the words. His shoes are gone, he is barefoot. Ventilating fungus. His wrists are sore, fingers a little numb. His ulnar nerve twitches. The floor is cold to the touch, it is an old hardwood. He knows this by the wide spaces and uneven junctures — its collapsed crevices. He feels them slowly with his toes. Then gets a sliver. Needle sharp.

In the distance he hears traffic, but nothing familiar enough to distinguish his surroundings — this is not a place he knows. The walnut butt stock of the shotgun is coming back to him. He struggles against the rope for a bit hoping to loosen it, but no such luck.

A door opens and feet walk into the room, maybe two, no three sets of shoes.

He feels a sharp pain as someone kicks him in the chest sending the chair violently to the ground, knocking the wind out of him. His head bounces off the floor, a neck muscle pulls.

Someone starts pouring water on his face, he tries to hold his breath, but has none. He gasps for air.

He is drowning.

This is how the CIA tortures terrorists.

Waterboarding.

The water keeps coming, Jack gags and chokes, the water is getting into his lungs.

He tries to turn his head but two hands are holding it firmly in place.

Someone sits on his chest.

"That's enough," a voice says. It's feminine, which should not be mistaken for comfort.

The water stops.

"Pick him back up," she says.

Hands grab him and thrust him back onto his feet in the chair. He is once again sitting upright, but now cold and distraught—coughing repeatedly. His neck hurts.

Waterlogged.

"Get rid of the bag," she says.

Hands cut the duct tape on the back of his neck and rip it off. His hair is soaked. He still struggles to breathe.

Someone punches him in the left cheek. He feels a ring cut his flesh and blood seep out down his chin. The punch is hard enough to hurt, but not hard enough to knock him out.

She hits him again, the right side this time—evening things out. Like an accordion playing a fine tune.

A tooth feels loose. He tongues it.

"It's good to see you, Jack. About time you caught up with me. To tell you the truth, I kind of expected this sooner. What took you so long? All that drinking finally taken its toll?"

Jack looks up, still a bit out of it, but cannot believe what he sees. Or what he *thinks* he sees.

Blurry.

"It can't be you, you can't be here, I watched you die," he says.

"True, you watched the weak part of me die, but sometimes we get second chances, Jack. Death is just another door, one that swings both ways if you have the right skill set."

This can't be real, he thinks.

"Go ahead Jack, say my name."

He is frozen in disbelief.

Shellshocked.

She screams, "Say my name!" and strikes him again, this time much harder.

Jack spits out blood on the faded hardwood under his feet.

"Say my goddamn name, Jack!"

He resists ever so slightly, only because he fears for his own sanity.

She winds up...knuckles clenched white and tight ready to deliver another blow.

"Haven," he mutters.

Defeated.

Confused.

Indignant.

Mentally unstable?

"There we go.Now you're coming to terms with the here and now," she says.

One man's muse is another man's misery.

He grits his teeth. His mouth full of sour, the kind before you vomit.

"Being that you're finally here, Jack, I suppose I should tell you what's going on...better yet, I'll show you."

His lower lip is rubbery in texture, like string cheese. His skin is cold like sliced turkey. His mind still coming to grips with the impossible. Then, a familiar face.

"Bring him in," she says.

Roy steps through the door like he has experience doing so. Like he has been here before. Done *this* before. At first Jack is happy to see him, but his eyes are off. His eyes look milky white, like a shark's before the bite...something's wrong.

The milky substance turns black, thick black, and pops, then runs down his face. Jack can only look on in horror.

"Roy, you ok?" Jack asks.

"Never better, friend."

So polite.

The black ooze is streaming down his face and chin and onto the floor. Bubbling. Vexed, Jack notices that Roy seems to be completely unaware of *it* — the black ooze.

Suddenly, a naked man wearing a dog collar is led into the room by a chain. Reminiscent of the days of gladiators and man-eating tigers, when Christians were executed in hot iron chairs. Haven orders the man to be chained to a small steel ring that is bolted to the floor.

Heretic.

Apostate.

"Go ahead son, I know you're hungry...eat," she says.

The naked man is screaming, begging, pleading for his life and pulling on the chain, but no one answers him.

"Help!" he screams, his plea met with awkward smiles.

Roy's body dislocates at the shoulders, his arms flap aimless, his palms and inner forearms open and split apart through large slits, exposing juicy suction cups and spikes. There is no blood. Just white mucous membrane, squishing and smacking. Thick black ooze streams out of small minute pours. It is poison—like anesthetic. The man shrieks as Roy steps closer to him. Within moments, the man is entangled and Jack hears bones snap and crunch. Roy is eating him alive. Jack has seen this before, *with Joe*, he thinks. *This can't be real,* he thinks. Blood pools out of the remains and runs down the hardwood, seeping into various cracks.

Jack hears an unsettling sound coming from the basement. A symphony of roaring and whining. A cackle of growls and moans. *Something* stirs ferociously underneath the floorboards. The hairs on the back of Jack's neck raise to a level he had never felt before.

Roy hisses and thrusts his shoulders back upright—back into joint. The slits in his arms close and reform, his tendons swirl back into place. Roy's eyes once again roll milky white—then hazel—then normal. He must have been parched. He seems livelier and oddly enough, more...human.

There is a familiar pile of meat on the floor—just like Joe. Things start to come into frame, Jack starts to understand what is going on. Or at least that he isn't crazy. The whole foundation seemed to wiggle when the fresh blood fell through the interstices of the floor. *Surely there are more of those things* Jack thinks.

"Better dear?" Haven asks.

"Yes mother," Roy replies.

"Good, now say goodbye to our guest and off to bed with you."

"Bye."

Roy waves at Jack in a childlike manner. Wrist flaccid. So polite.

Haven walks over and grabs another metal chair from the wall and drags it slowly across the floorboards, scratching the surface, she places it right in front of Jack and sits down, sighing deeply.

"Now, what are we to do with our Jack? Such a problem child. Don't you think boys?" Two bodies stir in his peripheral. One of them is huge. Monstrous.

The humor evades them.

"So, if you are alive...you're one of those things?" Jack asks.

"Yes Jack, I too am one of those *things*. As you put it."

Jack sighs, "How should I put it then?"

"Oh, my little Jack, you are swimming in a world of sharks now...and I don't answer to chum buckets."

She laughs and stands up.

"It was good to see you Jack. It really was."

"Re-bag him," she says sternly.

"Wait, no..."

Before Jack can speak the words, a wet burlap bag is thrust over his head and duct taped tightly, leaving him to once again gasp for air.

Starchy particles in his mouth.

His neck itches.

Footsteps echo as the door slams.

There is nothing but silence.

The nearby carcass bubbles and pops, it fizzes from what can only be digestive enzymes — stomach acid — dissolving it.

The stench of death seeps into his nose, it is overpowering. *Is this karma?* Jack wonders. Is he being castigated for past wrongdoings? And, *what the hell are those things?* he asks himself. Jack pauses for a moment to take it all in.

It has been Haven who was playing me the whole time, he thinks. She led him to believe he was losing his mind, but he wasn't. She was behind everything — Jessica's disappearance, Joe's death, even the hallucinations. Deep down Jack was happy to see her, but he had to remind himself that she wasn't really *her* anymore...she is *something* else entirely. She is *something* both horrific and oddly desirable.

Haven was wearing a tight, red v-neck with blue jeans. Her breasts still perfect and perky. Her hair was medium brown with caramel highlights — no longer black. Her roots were not showing. Her eyes were lined with black mascara, her lips a soft shade of red, maybe vermillion. She is as beautiful as Jack remembered. Her fingernails were painted light pink with white accents and her aroma was a delicious hint of cherry blossoms.

20

Down the hall, in a heavily insulated
room, Bill Kimball, the Stinger's pack leader,
comes to. He is face down on an old queen
mattress — used from the Pfitzer hotel — draped in
Lino teal linen, dark and drenched in spots, likely
from bodily fluids. He immediately recognizes it
as his own, from his own house, but this is not his
house.

The walls are exposed drywall, taped-in at
the seams. Unfinished. There is an old brick
chimney running upward into the ceiling. Unused.
There is the rustle of a red squirrel's nest coming
from inside it, there are chattering sounds.
Chirping noises.

Bill feels a hot sting in his wrist, he looks
over to see that it is wrapped in rusty barbed wire
and tied to a bed post. His tetanus shot is not up-
to-date. He suddenly realizes that he cannot move
any of his limbs without feeling that same hot
burning sensation — of metal barb tearing into
flesh. Both his ankles and wrists are strung to
posts with barbed wire and he is stark naked.

He is Leonardo da Vinci's "Vitruvian Man."

At this moment, he hears a door open and
feet walk into the room behind him. Bill turns his
head and notices a woman in his peripheral and
what might be four or five, maybe even six men.

She orders them to stand around Bill in a circle, on the sides of the bed, like husky wolves encircling a winded doe just before the kill. Her voice is familiar. She hands each of the men *something* about a foot long, *something* grainy, *something* with rough edges. They are whimpering, shaking in fear, but obedient. They are acting like they know that they must do what they are told or there will be dire consequences.

They too are all naked.

There is a colossal man standing in the corner, looking on patiently.

The woman shuts the door and walks over to a small dresser, there are objects on top of it. Objects designed to cause pain. To hurt. For torture. She picks one of them up and walks up to Bill.

"What the hell is this?" Bill asks adamantly, "What the fuck is going on? Let me go right now."

"Bill Kimball, still bossing everyone around I see," she says.

"Who the fuck are you?"

"What? You don't recognize an old friend?"

She walks over and leans down, putting her face right next to his.

Bill comes to terms with what he sees.

It is Haven. The same girl he beat. The same girl he raped. The same girl who died in a car accident.

"What the fuck! This is impossible...you're dead."

"Am I now? Do I look dead to you?"

The gravity of the situation smacks Bill in the chest. He now realizes that what goes around, is surely about to come around. Before he can say another word, Haven slaps him in the face and hocks a large gob of slimy spit into his eye.

"You see Bill, what you did to me, only made me stronger. What I'm going to do to you, is far worse."

She takes the object from the dresser, a small hooked blade, made for skinning, and slices off some meat from his cheek.

Bill screams in agony.

She discards his flesh onto the dirty hardwood floor.

"And look Bill, I brought your buddies to play with us."

The men standing around the bed are the other Stingers, the ones who wanted to piss on her, slap her, and rape her.

"You fucking bitch! I'll fucking kill you!" he screams.

"You won't be doing anything this time, dear."

Haven looks at the has-been Stingers and tells them to take their objects—wooden sticks—and line up behind the bed, right between Bill's legs.

"This is going to hurt you more than it hurts me," she says laughing.

The Stinger has-beens look over at the large man in the corner, knowing that if they do not follow directions, they will have to deal with him. And no one wants to deal with him.

There are no erections this time.

No one is stroking their cocks.

No one is laughing.

Or making jokes.

Bill pleads.

He begs.

He'll do anything to make up for his actions, he says.

He fights against the barbed wire, only to watch as his wrists become saturated red with blood.

Haven nods at the first Stinger in line, motioning him to do as he had been instructed.

"I'm sorry man," he says.

"Shut up and do it," she says.

The Stinger takes the rough wooden object and jams it into Bill's anus — rubbing it repeatedly.

Thrusting in and out.

Back and forth.

Ripping him, tearing him.

There is bleeding.

Screaming.

And more screaming.

Jagged edges twisting.

Turning.

Shredding.

This goes on for five minutes.

"Next," Haven says.

There is blood and shit all over the bed. All over the stick.

All the Stinger has-beens take turns raping Bill with their wooden phalluses.

Each for five minutes.

Bill is in so much pain that he cannot speak.

The room smells of sweat. Of feces. Of Must de Cartier. It is earthy.

Palpable.

There are splinters in his rectum.

Haven orders the men to stop and to stand against the wall. Their dicks shriveled, their hands shaking, their teeth chattering.

"My dearest Bill, I have big plans for you. Some would call them...just deserts."

"Pp..lease," he stutters.

If rape was art, Bill Kimball would be a Hieronymus Bosch.

"You will become the food of the gods, I will erase you not just physically, but ontologically from the face of this godforsaken place."

He can do nothing but stutter and sob. Bill Kimball isn't ordering anyone around anymore. He is the boss of no one.

His throne usurped.

Haven grabs the small hook knife and reaches it under and between Bill's legs. She makes a thrusting and swiping motion, then pulls out his severed penis and testicles. She tugs at them — yanks them free.

"Hungry Bill?"

Haven then proceeds to stuff all of it, the bloody meat mess, into his crying mouth and holds his nose and mouth shut.

"Chew it up!" she screams.

Bill gags, but bites down, feeling the gooey texture of his own genitals between his teeth. It reminds him of cutting up raw chicken. How it would slide around on the cutting board. How it would soak through his cutting gloves. He is simultaneously vomiting and swallowing, then vomiting and swallowing again and again. And again, until Haven forces it all down.

"Now it ends," she says.

Haven grabs a machete off the dresser and proceeds to hack at him.

She flails it back and forth, side to side, slicing and cutting, carving and striking. The has-been Stingers look on in horror as Bill is ripped apart. Pieces of him dangling, but not free.

Blood is everywhere.

Flying and staining up everything.

And everyone.

Bill gurgles and finally dies.

Haven saws at his neck, then strikes it with all her might, cutting his head loose.

Haven stops, she is out of breath.

She turns and looks at the has-been Stingers who are standing against the wall, cold and naked. Blood spattered. She asks them if they are hungry.

It is a rhetorical question.

She drops the machete on the floor and orders them to eat every last bit of Bill. She tells them that if they don't, they are next.

The Ravening

Tarryl Janik

"If the life blood pulse of evening finds you gone, into my dreams once more until the dawn."
-Megan Doering

1

Devin Sanders is seated comfortably near the edge of a Jacuzzi. Feet wet. Dangling over the edge. His toenails painted Brandeis blue. He is patiently waiting for his guests to arrive at The Pfitzer luxury hotel — an iconic and historic building. He is having a soiree, a "get out of jail" furry party — he will host as a silver wolf. It is his power animal. Devin's sexual proclivities include: bondage, dominance, and kink.

Being tied up.

A furry sex slave.

Role playing in fur suits.

Zoophilia.

Plushophilia.

Yiffing.

Furry fandom is a subculture built around the anthropomorphic fixation of animal creatures and is inspired by allegorical fiction novels having to do with science fiction and fantasy. The concept of furry derives from a science fiction convention that took place sometime in 1980. Sexual attraction is key.

It is supposed to be both a celebration and an orgy. Devin not so subtly advertised it on Craigslist. Doing so adds a dash of anonymity, who knows who will show up. It's anybody's guess.

Devin just finished six stiff months in the Waushara County Jail for soliciting sex from an undercover police officer. This is why tonight's party is free. The exchange of money complicates things. Tonight is about reciprocity.

In this godforsaken place...we say, "that by gifts one makes slaves and by whips one makes dogs."

The Jacuzzi bubbles fizz and pop as the jets push and swoosh the water. Thrusting outward. A small pool of heated water used for hydrotherapy — saturated with dead skin, dirt, and tiny particles of fecal matter — yet still, the warm water is relaxing. So much so that Devin decides to tea bag it prior to full submersion. His testicles expand as his buttocks finds the coarse, submerged concrete.

Soothing.

Devin pees a little.

He remembers hearing a story about a man who got his ramburglar stuck inside a swimming pool suction fitting. His dick was so swollen that he couldn't get it free even with the pump shut off. The paramedics had to spread a thick layer of lubricant around the suction fitting to get it loose. It took forty minutes. Knowing this, Devin leans forward and lets the rumbling water from the jet pound at his anus.

Stimulation.

Vibration.

Pleasure.

It helps to kill the time.

He is wearing an azure Speedo, showing off his male prowess. It matches his carefully painted toenails. He has a thick cock and his fellatio is rivaled only by Judas, the town cum dumpster.

Devin keeps his head and neck just above the water, he doesn't want to get his blonde pigtails wet.

He wears them sometimes for pulling.

Sometimes for tugging.

While thrusting.

While having bareback sex.

Without a condom.

Devin's gaze meanders toward the swimming pool. The Pfitzer natatorium is a stagnant oasis. A cesspool. Floating in it is like wading in a bog of urine. It is overcrowded and over chlorinated. And no one can hold their bladder. You can taste it.

There are smiling children in wet, low-hanging diapers. Soggy bottoms.

Hotel guests enjoy the sting of chlorine in their eyes, the harsh smell of it in their nostrils. They call this a "vacation."

The scraping of pruned wrinkly skin on the rough concrete.

Open cuts and sores bathing in community fluids.

Overweight mothers in two piece bikinis that eventually become one piece swimsuits.

Bellies engorged, bloated, threatening to burst neoprene. Like a ripe carcass on the side of some forgotten highway; imploding with maggots, exploding with gastric juices.

Some swimmers are new moms sporting pounds of baby fat. Others are just portly from years of practice.

There are dads with once-toned bodies, now holding up sympathy weight.

Beer guts, flaccid arms, loose skin, arched backs, thick arm hair, curled backhair, balding scalps, and Rogaine. Tawny brown specks pattern the floor amidst carefully positioned fake plants and bored teenage lifeguards sexting on cell phones. There is a slight breeze from an open door. Sunlight pours in through large bay windows. There are kids in life preservers stepping on water spouts, accidentally splashing someone's grandmother and her walker—hitting her right in the face. There are small bare feet dancing by urinals in the nearby restroom, stepping in piss puddles. They say urine kills foot fungi and that if you pee on your feet in the shower this will help circumvent a bad case of athlete's foot.

Devin checks his phone, it says 6 p.m.

His guests will start to arrive soon.

Devin stands up in the Jacuzzi and makes his way to room 321, he doesn't bother to grab a towel. Heads turn and eyes diverge, pretending not to notice his large genitalia. Well everyone but grandmother that is. She stares right at his bulging banana hammock while licking her chops and smiling. Her top lip is thin and dry, topped with a light postmenopausal peach fuzz mustache. Her chest is spattered with questionable brown freckles and large abnormal moles. Dysplastic nevi and melanoma. Moderate dementia. An acute confusional state. Under her white compression stockings are thick webbed varicose veins. She hasn't tasted flesh flute since before her husband passed away from ass cancer. The radiation treatment melted his urethra, he had to have a catheter in it for years.

Although sex with grandmother is slow and sloppy, for sixty-nine years old she knew she could still fuck like she was forty. She can really take a thrill drill, if only someone would be interested in finding out. She is hideous to look at, her tits hang past her waist and her skin stretches when you pull it. She bruises easy. She carts around an oxygen tank in a green stretched bag. A lifelong smoker.

Yellow stained nails.

Yellow stained dentures.

This is what Judas will look like in another twenty-five years, including the emphysema. Assuming she lives that long.

Grandmother's white Pomeranians are at the kennel, the hotel doesn't allow dogs. She paints their toenails with fuchsia gloss.

They just never stop yelping.

They just won't shut up.

She used to have cats, but her daughter Lizzy had them put down. Lizzy's boyfriend Seth aided in rounding all twelve of them up. Her cats were filthy — they would piss on, behind, and under everything — Lizzy caught one of them even shitting in the toaster once. She had to tell grandmother that it was diarrhea, not peanut butter.

Then there were the maggots from the moldy cat mess in the back of the coffee pot, where the water goes. The dead ones looked like floating rice in water. It was the last straw; after that, the cats had to go.

And away they went.

Euthanasia.

They blew chunks before their hearts stopped.

It's hell to get old.

Devin takes out his key card, slides it, and opens the door to his room. Inside, there are full unopened liquor bottles, lines of cocaine, bowls of marijuana, and Seagram's wine coolers. The curtains are a dull shade of tan. There are two queen mattresses, both with comforters plastered with maroon patterned orchids and juniper green vines. The scarlet red plush carpet is moderately worn, the pillows have little specialty chocolates on them. Dark chocolate truffle.

Putting chocolates on pillows started sometime in the 1950's thanks to actor Cary Grant. Cary, although married, would frequently meet a woman at the luxurious Mayfair Hotel in St. Louis Missouri (now the Magnolia). Each time the couple met he would have a staff member place a trail of chocolates in the room leading to the bed and up onto the pillow. The hotel manager, having heard about this, liked the idea so much that he decided to make it one of the hotel's standard amenities.

Not long after Devin finishes preparing the room, the guests begin to arrive and the party gets underway.

Tonight would not be left unscathed.

Brown Fox, the first to show up, is snorting lines and pounding shots of tequila.

Patron.

Silver Wolf, the host, is sipping a wine cooler and engaged in some heavy petting.

Sniffing.

Licking.

Sucking.

"You smell tasty," Devin grunts as he takes off his head piece.

The Beastie Boys spin in the background.

Grey Mouse, who showed up shortly after Brown Fox, pulls out his meat and jams it into Devin's wet mouth. He slides it passed Devin's chapped, beige lips. Grey Mouse yanks on Devin's pigtails while making squeaking noises.

Brown Fox subtly lifts, then pulls open the slit in Devin's back door, under his fluffy tail, while simultaneously spitting on his hand and lubes up Devin's rectum with just the right amount of spittle.

Devin is both giving and taking, he is in a generous mood.

Brown Fox inches inside Devin as Devin sucks Grey Mouse all the harder and moans. Grazing teeth on soft flesh.

Grey Mouse is uncircumcised. The extra foreskin slides back and forth over the tip of his action Jackson as Devin tongues it.

Just as Grey Mouse starts to climax...

Just as Brown Fox fires a hot load into Devin's brown star...

There is a thunderous bang at the door.

Penguin abruptly enters the room, it is unlocked.

Brown Fox pulls out and cordially walks over to Penguin, welcoming him to the party with a vigorous blowjob. He gets down on one knee—genuflection—takes off his head wear, and carefully pulls out Penguin's ramming rod. He stuffs it in his mouth while aggressively rubbing it. Penguin reaches over and shuts off the light. Devin and Grey Mouse hear groaning, then gurgling and crunching—questionable snapping sounds.

"Hey man turn the fucking light back on," Devin barks.

No response.

A low moaning. Then more crunching. The room is pitch black. Tempers flair.

"Yeah, what the fuck Penguin? Don't be a dick," Grey Mouse squeaks.

Grey Mouse leans over and hits the lamp switch near the bed. The lamp turns on and illuminates some of the room.

Penguin is still standing by the door but now he's covered in deep red blood.

Aghast.

"What the fuck man!" Grey Mouse squeals.

Brown Fox is lying on the floor, his costume visibly ripped apart. There is loose, fluffy stuffing all over the carpet and the bed. It too is wet with fresh, sticky blood.

There is blood spatter on the amber walls.

The wood door.

The large golden mirror.

Penguin's arms are dislocated, tentacle like things hang freely, snapping and whipping the ground violently. There are suction cups and spikes oozing a thick mysterious black liquid. Penguin steps forward out of the doorway and toward the bed.

"Oh shit!" Devin howls.

Before Grey Mouse can do anything, Penguin snatches him up.

Penguin's arms entangle him, squeezing tight.

Grey Mouse is screaming. Gasping for breath. Eyes bulging. Like a feeder mouse succumbing to a ball python in some kid's bedroom, in a mite infested, soiled, and smeared glass aquarium.

Sharp barbs pierce his flesh.

Tear his stuffing.

Sink deep into his muscles and suction bodily fluids.

Devin franticly throws the lamp at Penguin and makes a break for it out the door, leaving his expensive, one of a kind, custom, commissioned, silver wolf head behind. It has an articulating jaw, a silicone tongue, and is made of ultra soft, plush, faux fur. The lamp crashes against Penguin's shoulder, glass and sparks scatter.

Penguin is unmoved and pays Devin no attention as he devours Grey Mouse like a juice box. Compressing and slurping, extracting his juices.

Down the hallway, Devin hears ubiquitous screaming. Blood curdling shrieks of terror echo throughout the corridors as he dashes toward the elevator.

At the elevator, he repeatedly fingers the down button and waits anxiously.

There are loud crashing sounds followed by desperate pleas for help.

They are coming from everywhere.

And from everyone.

The elevator slowly makes its way down to the third floor. It has hardened doublepane glass doors.

It seems like it takes forever.

Just then, Penguin steps out the door and into the hall. They make eye contact.

"Oh, fuck," Devin yelps, "Come on, come on!"

Penguin's arms are whipping and spinning. Tendons like rubber bands.

Stretching.

Audibly wet.

"Fuck!"

The elevator dings and the door opens, there is a hot, steaming, stomach-churning carcass inside.

It is the bell boy or at least what's left of him.

Devin jumps in and the door shuts just in time.

Penguin's tentacles slam on the glass as the elevator makes its descent. The glasspane cracks slightly from the force of Penguin's blow, then spider-webs outward. Radial lines.

The stench of death in the elevator is overwhelming.

Pungent.

The smell of shit and piss permeates.

Looking down, Devin can see more of those things like Penguin in the foyer and realizes that he has to act quickly if he wants to survive.

He knows the things in the vestibule will surely see him if he doesn't do something.

He gets an idea, he saw it in a film once, but it will take some moxie.

Devin has a strong stomach, years of fulfilling anal fantasies with truckers at the local rest stop have surely prepared him for this.

He lies down next to the mucus covered, blood soaked, gooey remains of the bell boy and starts to cover himself up with the gore like a blanket. He is sure to tuck his fluffy tail out of sight. It smells horrible. The skin slips out of his hands as he paints himself with what is left of Craig.

At least, that's what the name tag says — Craig — the bellhop.

The door opens and Devin tries to remain still. He even holds his breath.

The things in the lobby look over but don't see him.

The elevator doors start to close. Devin attempts to move to stop it, but the bellhop is too slippery. Too heavy. The doors shut and the elevator starts to ascend, back toward the third floor, back toward Penguin. Devin's heart races. His adrenaline pumps. As the elevator stops on the third floor and makes a dinging sound, he sees the silhouette of Penguin through the doublepane glass doors.

Devin slowly scoots next to the wall as the doors open and Penguin turns around. Devin holds absolutely still. Shallow breaths. Penguin looks over the mess on the floor, for what seems like an eternity, then steps in and turns his back to it — to Devin.

The elevator doors close and they begin the descent back down to the lobby.

Petrified.

Terrified.

Shaking.

The smell of Craig begins to bother Devin's nose.

Devin does everything he can to stay as still as possible — to be absolutely quiet.

Sweating.

The elevator stops on the second floor.

Devin's right eye twitches. The dried blood is itchy. His skin tingles all over. Like an opiate itch.

Another thing gets on the elevator. Now there are two of them.

The doors close.

Another dinging sound.

As the elevator continues its descent to the foyer, Craig's corpse makes popping noises.

Digestive enzymes.

Stomach juices spitting.

Dissolving.

Penguin and the other thing in the elevator take notice and turn around to have a look.

The elevator stops at the lobby and the doors open. Another ding.

Penguin and the other thing quickly lose interest in the mess that used to be Craig upon hearing grandmother scooting down the hall with her walker. She is unaware of what is going on and cussing loudly about linens. She says something about needing fresh towels.

She is hard of hearing.

Penguin and the other thing step out and head toward her, in the direction of the commotion she is making—down the corridor.

Devin takes notice and quickly throws what is left of Craig off of himself. He gags. He is still covered in skin, hair, and blood—like he rolled around in rotten animal remains—like he bathed in it. Still scratching, he peeks around the corner and sees grandmother saying something about how no man scares her. He hears her say something about her husband, something about abuse, and that the thing in front of her should give her his best shot.

Devin rushes for the revolving entry door of the Pfitzer. *It's too late to save the old bag*, he thinks.

He looks back to see one of those things rip grandmother's head off and chuck it down the hall. Blood spurts out of her neck, painting the wall as her lifeless body hits the floor. Astounding power.

Grandmother's head rolls and lands face up—rictus grin—just shy of Penguin's feet. Penguin sees Devin in his peripheral but doesn't bother to give chase.

The revolving door turns open, Devin steps out, and he doesn't look back again.

2

When Jack Warren was eight years old his father was blown up in an explosion at work. Robert Warren was the lead purchasing agent for an industrial cleaning company called Advostock.

Outside of the main office there was an underground fuel storage tank, recently filled with gasoline. Someone accidentally left the pump switch on, it was running, pumping, and leaking—pooling above ground near the main entrance to the building.

Robert was a chain smoker. Three packs a day. He took his coffee with a dash of cream. He was also a lieutenant in the U.S. Army. He was drafted during Vietnam. Now honorably discharged. A civilian.

Americans used to spit on Vietnam vets, they used to call them "baby killers."

Having noticed the leak outside his office window, Robert immediately called emergency services. Seconds after hanging up the phone he looked outside and noticed Mindy from accounting smoking a cigarette in the parking lot—she was walking toward the pooling gasoline.

This is where Jack's innate white knight nature comes from. It is hereditary.

Robert quickly hung up the phone and rushed out of his office, he made quick strides, taking only seconds to get outside.

He didn't notice the deep puddle of gasoline under his feet, his freshly brun polished loafers soaked it in. Saturating leather. His nostrils bathed in the fumes.

He had a thick brown mustache and dark, combed-over hair. Parted neatly. He wore a silver wrist watch and a buttoned white and blue cotton striped shirt.

"Mindy get back!" Robert yelled, waving his arms wildly.

Just as she was about to flick the spent cigarette, she saw Robert and heard him shouting, although she couldn't make out the words. Mindy looked to the left of Robert and noticed the expanding liquid in and around the underground fuel storage tank. She also noticed that Robert was standing in it.

She backed away and carefully snuffed out her smoke.

Robert breathed a sigh of relief and turned around to head back inside the building.

At that moment the nearby cooling fan kicked on.

Air conditioning.

The air conditioner, like Robert, was wading in the gasoline.

In the second it took to click on Robert felt the blast wave and saw a bright flash of light.

Blown off his feet.

Sent flying.

Ignited by a spark.

Mindy screamed.

Robert was blind, his ears ringing, his back was resting on the blacktop. There were little flames shooting out of his legs.

The front of the building was gone. It was blown clean off. Black smoke billows.

Robert was looking up at the sky, but didn't know it yet.

The wind got knocked out of him.

The explosion took mere seconds to sweep him off his feet, to incinerate all of the hair from his head, face, arms, and legs.

His polyester undershirt and cotton socks melted into his skin. The rest of his clothes, his cotton dress shirt, his dress pants, and his boxers were all gone. His skin literally on fire.

His eyes began to focus as he sat up, unaware that over seventy percent of his body was now covered in third and fourth degree burns.

His skin was blistered and slipped off of his hands.

He looked like he was dipped into a deep fryer.

Boiling, bubbling, the yellow fat cells in his skin exposed bone.

Fingernails black.

Charred.

Yet, he could feel no pain. His nerves were too deeply affected.

People around him began to panic; screaming, scrambling, not sure what to do.

Mindy rushed over sobbing, patting out the flames on Robert's legs.

Robert tried to stand up, but he was in shock. He didn't realize how bad of shape he was in. His head was a mess.

Having heard the commotion outside, Steve from marketing acted fast. He was a first responder. Berlin Memorial Hospital was just down the street, maybe two, no three minutes away by automobile. Steve ran to his car, turned the key over, slammed his door and quickly drove it up to the building. He grabbed Robert and helped him into the backseat.

Robert could barely speak, he could barely breathe, he had yet to come to terms with the here and now, which was likely a good thing.

Mindy was in the backseat trying to comfort him — keeping him conscious and calm.

"Robert, you're going to be ok, but we need to get you to the hospital."

Robert's skin stuck to the leather upholstery. It was peeling.

Mindy held his head against her chest. There was blood and pus, a yellowish mixture of fluids that lathered into, what felt like, Vaseline on her designer blouse.

"What...happ...ened," Robert mumbled.

70 mph in a 55.

"You were in an accident."

"Wh..aaat?"

"We are almost there."

She had the voice of an angel.

"...where?"

"To the hospital."

Steve pulled the car into the parking lot and toward the Emergency Room entrance. His tires squealing as the car rushed to a stop and he got out.

He wasted no time, picking up Robert and thrusting him upright onto his smoldering feet. He carried him through the doors all by himself. Mindy following behind.

"Help! Now!" Steve shouted.

Nurses looked on and gasped in horror. Thunderstruck.

Doctors were called, pagers went off, paramedics rushed over. The E.R. staff placed Robert on an emergency stretcher. They cut a hole in his throat to help him breathe. A tracheotomy.

Months went by.

Robert endured endless skin graphs. Multiple operations. Salt baths and iodine. Hours of scrubbing and screaming.

He let out cries of anguish from the "tub room" where nurses scraped and yanked off his dead flesh.

Daily ritual agony.

Hard bristles on sensitive skin.

He was "tubbed and bronched" –suspended on a stretcher over a tank of water where nurses would irrigate his wounds and use a variety of brushes and sponges to clean them before bandaging. The doctors used a dermatome to slice off good skin from his thighs, belly, and buttocks. This "good" skin was then draped onto the damaged skin without stitches or adhesive. He had to wear a tight fitting nylon garment over the burned portions of his body for twenty-three hours a day. This was supposed to help keep his scar tissue from growing leathery. He was given intravenous saline solution to replenish the bodily fluids lost through all the oozing and evaporation via open wounds. He was given cocktails of heavy drugs that induced hallucinations.

Many thought Robert might not survive.

The doctors told him that he would never be able to work again.

His two children didn't even recognize him.

To Jack, his father looked like an alien, like a monster, especially without his signature mustache.

Robert spent almost a year in the hospital before finally returning home.

He would eventually settle a lawsuit with Advostock, something to do with negligence and liability.

This experience profoundly affected Jack. As did his father's eventual exit.

Robert Warren would survive, only to divorce and leave a few years later.

Jack wouldn't see him again until he was twenty-one years old.

The marriage was irreconcilable.

Elegiac.

3

Judas Thomas is mid-ménage a trois. She is scissoring a thirty year old named Debra while sucking the cock of Debra's husband, Larry. Debra's wet vulva is locked, entangled with Judas' meat wallet—the same vagina Judas would stuff illegal drugs into to smuggle to well paying cons in prison. A prison wallet.

Rubbing.

Grinding.

Spewing discharge.

Tribbing.

Their clitoris' firmly erect, their legs are wrapped, straining to hold tight, while climaxing. Thighs shaking.

Judas is deep throating Larry, her fellatio is rivaled only by Devin Sanders. Larry is grunting and groaning. The bed is soaked in sweat and pungent feminine juices. Debra cums and Judas lets go, Debra pulls Larry by the dick, motioning for him to fuck her in the missionary position. Meanwhile, Judas stands up and makes her way over to a pink and black tiger-striped suitcase in the corner. She opens it and grabs a black leather harness and dildo. She steps through and adjusts the strap-on — time for some pegging. Larry looks back and pulls out. He transitions to cunnilingus on Debra while sticking his buttocks firmly in the air. That was Judas' cue.

She grabs the lube off the dresser and thoroughly coats her six inch phallus.

Rubbing it.

There are wet sounds and squishing noises.

Like mud between toes.

She slaps Larry on his rear and gently wipes the tip of her man-hole digger clockwise around his rectum.

He practically dies with anticipation while nibbling on Debra's soaked pussy curtains.

Judas flips the dildo upside down so that she can massage his prostrate.

She slides it in and fucks him with moderate pressure. Penetrating him just right. He closes his eyes as he laps up Debra's wet box. Debra grabs Larry by the hair and squirts all over his face as she orgasms.

Female ejaculation.

Is it pee? A French study in the Journal of Sexual Medicine argues that urine is indeed involved. The study found that during sex women's bladders fill up, then afterwards — after they squirt — their bladders are empty. There is a caveat however; the researchers also found prostratic secretions in their samples, meaning that the fluid secreted by women while squirting is a combination of both urine and prostrate juices.

Skene glands.

"Mmm...you taste so good," Larry says. His face drenched and dripping.

It only takes him minutes to cum as the tip of Judas' dildo kneads his walnut shaped prostrate.

Judas pulls out and Larry sits up. Judas stands up and they both put their phalluses in Debra's face. Debra jerks Larry's dick as he spurts hot jizz into her mouth and onto her tongue. Debra licks both the fecal covered dildo and Larry's hard member. She looks up at them with a duck face.

Bright candy red lipstick.

Thick black mascara.

Cover up and pockmarks.

The air is hot, moist, and smells like a dance club. Like ten shades of perfume.

"I want you both to DP me next time," Debra says.

Double penetration is an extra twenty-five bucks.

Today would cost Debra and Larry only three hundred dollars.

***

Months have passed since the disappearance of Jessica Mills, Joe Schneider, and Jack Warren. Judas missed Jack, but at the same time she is happy he is gone. She figures he finally quit his shitty job and moved away from this godforsaken place. Or at least that's what the story is around town.

Some people even say that Jack and Jessica ran away together and that her whole disappearance was just an orchestrated cover up so that he wouldn't lose his job for having sex with a teenager.

Joe's house has new tenants, but no one knows who they are. The windows are always covered. One of them is huge, a man maybe seven feet tall, all muscle, and who always wears a dark blue, hooded sweatshirt.

Stan, who lives next door, says they are drug dealers.

Wendy at the coffee shop thinks they are on the run from the mob in New York City — in witness protection. Rats. Whistle blowers.

Tom and Darla Mills are getting divorced, or in the midst of. Definitely separated. She signed the papers yesterday — the stress of Jessica's disappearance was too much for them both to handle — they blame each other.

Oddly enough, Roy has been visiting her more often and since then, Darla seems just fine. Tom thinks she was cheating on him all along and when he brings up their missing baby girl, she tells him "don't be stupid" and to "shut up." Something isn't right with her he thinks, not in the slightest. He blames Roy, he thinks Roy is brainwashing her. Turning her against him. Rumor has it that Roy and her were banging all along, and that they (meaning Roy and Darla) just needed a good reason for her to finally walk away so they could be together.

What Tom doesn't know is that Roy isn't Roy anymore, just like Darla is no longer Darla. Zombies are forever slaves to their master.

Haven has taken control of the entire town, the entire city council, the police department, the Berlin Memorial staff, the mayor — anyone and everyone who has any sort of influence, power, or control within city limits. She has turned them all into zombies. This is only the beginning. The first act. She is calculated, cool, and methodical. She has just taken over The Pfitzer hotel — it will be her base of operations for the pogrom to come.

***

Judas cleans up in the shower. Her loofa is soaped up and she is scrubbing her snatch. She hears her phone going off in the next room, the music on her ringer says something about being worth it. Larry and Debra got dressed and left the money on the table — they wasted no time in heading home. Home for them is a duplex, forty hour per week jobs, cold dinners, and routine. Judas is the only reason they stay together. She is the glue that keeps them bound, keeps them interested, and not completely indifferent to each other's existence.

Relationship rehab.

Judas picks up her phone and it says she has a missed call from a number she has never seen before. She calls it back. After two rings someone picks up, but there is no talking on the other end.

"Hello, I missed your call...who is this?"

No response, just some light breathing.

"HELLO...look bitch, I don't have time to play games..."

A baritone male voice cuts her off and asks, "This Judas?"

"Who's asking?"

"A potential client, I was referred to you by someone you know real well."

She adjusts her bra while holding the phone tightly in the crook of her neck.

"Oh ya, and who might that be?"

"Jack Warren."

She hesitates to speak. She hasn't heard that name in months.

"I got your attention now?"

"How do you know Jack?"

"Come by The Pfitzer hotel at 8 p.m. tonight, room 321...and come alone."

He hangs up.

"Hello? Goddamn it," she says.

Judas looks in the mirror and struggles to maintain her composure. She doesn't want to ruin her dusk eyeliner. That deep seeded part of her that loves Jack, the part of her that misses him dearly, that yearns for his touch, won't stay down.

She tried to forget about him, she tried to move on...but now, she realizes that it is impossible.

Just the thought of him being alive and in town is enough to get her to show up. Besides, what's the worst that can happen, right? She always carries a small pink handled pistol in her purse, just in case — a 9mm.

Jack taught her to always take precautions.

Tonight would not be left unscathed.

4

Anthropology 321. Health and Disease. It's the third week of the spring semester. Peter Faxneld is talking about curing and killing. Ethnobotany. Hunting and poison making.

"Curare is a poison used by Amerindians in South America. Curare weakens the skeletal muscles and causes death due to asphyxiation when administered in high doses — the paralyzing of the diaphragm. The poison is usually delivered after being applied to the tip of either an arrow or blow dart. Indigenous peoples typically utilize curare for hunting small to medium sized game, although it has been used on humans as well. It inhibits motor function and causes paralysis in its victims. It is a dark viscous fluid, bitter to the taste. It is made by boiling down very specific species of jungle leaves and can be used on anything from small rodents to humans. While paralyzed, it is near to impossible to confirm consciousness through medical means. Every muscle except the heart, but including the eyes will become immotile. It can take up to eight hours for the full effects to wear off."

Peter pulls out a small leather vessel and hands it to one of the students in the front row. "Pass this around," he tells her.

"What you see here is a pouch that contains curare tipped darts. I acquired these while doing fieldwork with the Waiwai. Now don't go sticking each other with them ok. However tempting that may be."

The class laughs.

"Also notable is the material that the pouch was crafted from...it is made out of pig testicles."

Looks of both disgust and intrigue percolate throughout the room as the students continue to pass the container around.

"Moving on," Peter says as he turns to the next PowerPoint slide.

"Much like in Amazonia, the Haitian bokor prepares poisons with the utmost caution—using precise calculations. Tetrodotoxication can induce a state of apparent death. Like curare, its effects depend on the dosage and method of administration. There are four degrees of tetrodotoxication, the first two include numbing sensations and the loss of motor control. The third includes paralysis of the whole body, difficulty with breathing, low blood pressure, and cyanosis. The fourth and final degree is death due to respiratory failure. Blood pressure drops and the heart pulsates for a bit even after breathing has ceased."

"The bokor must be careful when handling tetrodotoxins, since first degree symptoms have shown up in those who merely come into contact with them. If ingested, third degree is imminent. Therefore, the Haitian bokor takes great precaution in preparation, application, and dosage."

A poison made from the sea toad *Sphoeroides testudineus* can cause the skin to peel off before death.

"So, how do they administer it?" a student asks.

"The poison is never placed in food, rather directly on the skin or in open wounds," Peter says, "Consuming it might kill the victim immediately."

"What about if you inject it?" another student asks.

"Tetrodotoxin is forty to fifty times more potent when administered parenterally."

Victims are conscious when paralyzed, thus they are passive observers at their own funerals.

"Usage of tetrodotoxin goes back over five thousand years to Egypt."

"So tetrodotoxin comes from the puffer fish?" Jessie in the back asks.

"Indeed, various species are used...toads are also used in poison making," Peter states, "The Bufo Marinus has large parotoid glands on its back that secrete two dozen potent chemicals, especially when irritated. The final product is buried in the lap of a dead child for forty-eight hours."

The most toxic poison is made with human remains.

Disinterring coffins.

Grating human bones.

Grinding, then mixing them into a fine brown powder.

The powder supports the magic and the magic supports the powder.

Ethnobiology.

In large doses, saponins induce vomiting and extreme nausea.

Leaking secretions from respiratory passages — the victim can drown in their own bodily fluids. Pulmonary edema.

Magic Noire.

There is a knock on the classroom door, it opens, and Linda, the student aid from the anthropology department, walks in. Peter is the chair.

"Excuse me Peter...you have a phone call," she says.

"Can it wait? Class is over in twenty minutes."

"The girl on the phone says it is an emergency. She says that once you know who it is that you will understand."

"Well, go on, who is it?"

"She says her name is Haven."

Peter's eyes go wide, he turns and abruptly addresses the class, "Alright then, we're going to end early today. Do your assigned readings and be prepared to talk about it on Thursday." Peter grabs his bag, quickly shuffles some papers into it, and tells Linda to send the call to his office. He tells her that he is on his way there now.

5

Last Fall, shortly after Jessica Mills went missing, was the scheduled birth of Kabe's son Zion. Kabe, a tall handsome man, cleanly shaven, with a muscular frame, was surprisingly relaxed — he thought he was prepared.

The nurses at Berlin Memorial started the Pitocin drip at 7 a.m. and for three hours Kabe and Scarlet Abraham sat in a cramped hospital room waiting anxiously for the doctor to arrive.

Scarlet was exhausted, she had been enduring intense contractions for what seemed like forever. There were little beads of sweat building up under her long, red hair. Kabe was laying on a small blue couch in the corner, facing a hanging television. Scarlet struggled with her overwhelming need for pain medication. Opiates. Possibly an epidural. She initially turned it down, but she was reconsidering it.

Agonizing sharp pains.

There were stiff, plain, rectangular cushions on the couch—hard like plastic.

Bored.

Tired.

Obdurate.

There would be no epidural.

The Abrahams were ready to get this over with.

They met in high school.

At junior prom.

This was everything but fun for the Abrahams.

Scarlet hated being pregnant. She dreaded the thought of stretch marks, of gaining weight. She was otherwise 5'2 and 120, but with baby she weighed in at 145.

Kabe also hated her being pregnant. He dreaded her possible stretch marks and the possible weight gain. He was otherwise 6'2 and 220, with worn blue jeans and bright arm tattoos. Angels and flames.

Then finally, as if she was reading Kabe and Scarlet's minds, Dr. Brohm, the Abraham family OBGYN arrived. Brohm was a tall, slender woman in her forties. She had short dark brown shoulder length hair and was very well versed in facilitating child birth — she delivered over five hundred babies a year.

The Abrahams had been reassured by Dr. Brohm weeks earlier that Zion's birth was going to be a "normal one."

"Let's have a look," Dr. Brohm said, as she carefully checked Scarlet's cervical dilation. "Well I think we're ready to break your water."

Amniotomy.

Labor would have to be induced, Scarlet went full-term.

She was passed the due date.

Near expiration.

Now with gloves on, Dr. Brohm slowly pulled out a large steel hook — an amniotic hook — and carefully inserted it inside Scarlet's swollen vagina, as to not hit the placenta. Brohm had one hand firmly set outside of Scarlet's snatch while the two fingers on her opposite hand were jammed inside to help guide the tip. Scarlet cringed with discomfort while words like barbaric and titillating came to Kabe's mind.

Suddenly the hard cushions on the blue couch didn't seem so uncomfortable.

Kabe mouthed the words, "Oh my gawd."

Brohm rubbed the tip of the hook against the amniotic sac and pierced its membranes. She then removed her hand from Scarlet's vagina and paused to monitor the draining fluid.

The Abraham's eagerness quickly turned to shock. Repulsion. Fear. There was thick, red blood streaming out and pooling between Scarlet's legs. It soaked through the white sheets, staining them — something is wrong.

"What's going on? Why is she bleeding?" Kabe asked.

"I don't know, let me try again," Brohm said.

Once again, Dr. Brohm inserted the large steel hook — this time the words masochist and penetrate came to mind as Kabe looked on in both horror and disbelief.

"This isn't right, let's check the baby's heartbeat," Brohm said to one of the on looking nurses.

Dr. Brohm grabbed a stethoscope and placed the cold steel end onto Scarlet's engorged abdomen.

She looked like a bleeding grapefruit from the chest down even though she only gained twenty-five pounds during pregnancy.

Some women use being pregnant as an excuse to overeat. Gluttony. They tell everyone that they are eating for two, when it's really just an excuse to get fucking huge — to let themselves go. Take a break from taking care of oneself. And why not? After a lifetime of staring into mirrors, stepping on scales, and smearing lipstick...don't women deserve a little time off?

Kabe's best friend Lenord got his girlfriend Tanya pregnant a week after they had their first baby. Lenord couldn't wait a month for her vagina to heal, his needs had to be met, otherwise he would sleep around on her. Slap her up.

Scarlet's friend Tammy once told her that breastfeeding made her orgasm. Tammy would constantly feed her baby just to get off. She breastfed little Joseph until he was two years old.

During a heated argument, Lenord's friend Erik found out that Lenord banged his wife Angela while he was away for work, so later that evening Erik "accidentally" rolled over onto their (Angela and Erik's) newborn baby while sleeping next to it on the couch. Erik didn't think the baby was his, so he quietly snuffed it out like a cigarette. The paramedics called it "tragic" and said that "accidents" like this happen all the time.

The baby was Erik's.

It turns out, Lenord had gotten a vasectomy not long after his girlfriend Tanya gave birth. After finding out that Lenord couldn't have children, Erik "accidentally" fell onto his twelve gauge and blew his head off. The coroner ruled "accident" out.

Only in this godforsaken place.

Scarlet was distraught, her face was pale white.

She just didn't want her baby to be born sleeping.

This was every woman's nightmare.

"I'm not getting a heartbeat. We have to do an emergency C-Section right now!" Brohm yelled.

The nurses started running around frantically, grabbing everything but the kitchen sink.

Kabe's eyes met Scarlet's — panic set in.

"Did you hit the placenta?" Kabe asked nervously.

Dr. Brohm was also in a frenzy. It didn't take long before the blood stained hospital bed with Scarlet in it was ready to move out the door toward the operating room.

"I don't know. We won't know anything until we have the baby out," Brohm said. Dr. Brohm was missing her shoes.

After doing over five hundred births a year, she still wasn't prepared for this.

Scarlet wanted to cry upon hearing the news. She was terrified of having a C-section; it was something the Abrahams discussed at length only days before.

Brohm and the nurses pushed the bed out the door and Kabe followed.

A nurse gave Scarlet some liability forms to sign and turned around toward Kabe, "You can't come with us, you'll have to wait here. I'm sorry."

"What? Why can't I be with my wife?"

Brohm chimed in, "Because it's an emergency and there isn't enough room in the operating room. Just stay here, we'll have the baby out quickly and a nurse will be back in ten minutes or so."

And just like that they were all gone.

On their way out the door, they passed a man holding his lacerated arm and a paramedic he called by the name Haven as they rushed down the hall and around the corner toward the large brown doors — the paramedic, whose real name was Holly, not Haven, called the drugged man Jack.

All parties were too busy, too frantic, too immersed in their own crisis to notice each other. And they do know each other. They are blood relatives. Consanguinity. Kin.

Kabe's stomach twisted into knots — he started pacing — burning circles in the already heavily worn square patterned beige carpet. Ten minutes passed and still no sign of anything. Kabe's walking sped up, as did his heart rate. Then finally, after fifteen minutes — a nurse appeared in the corridor.

"What the hell is going on?" Kabe asked, "Are my wife and son ok?"

"I'll check," The nurse said, quickly exiting back out the double doors.

Why didn't she know? Why does she have to check? What the hell is going on?

Twenty minutes and still no nurse — still no answers. Kabe was more than flustered at this point, deep in his gut he knew that something was terribly wrong. Twenty-five minutes went by before the nurse walked back through the double doors, back into the corridor. The off-white look on her face said everything.

"Are they ok?" Kabe asked.

Her polite smile disappeared, as did Kabe's breath. He knew something bad was coming.

"I don't know how to say this, but your son died. Dr. Brohm is performing aggressive resuscitation on him right now, other than that, we don't know anything for certain."

It was supposed to be just another day, it was supposed to be just another delivery — normal.

Kabe fell to his knees in the doorway, he could do nothing but cover his face. He tried to hold back the tears.

The nurse came closer. "Do you want me to call a priest?" she asked.

Kabe didn't speak to her, her suggestion disgusted him. Repulsive. He refused to accept that his son was dead, therefore silence was his only reply. *Where is God now? Where is God now!* Kabe wonders. Then, in a moment of clarity, he looked up from the floor to read the nurse's name tag—her name was Sheryl.

"Sheryl, is my wife ok?"

The nurse, who now has a name, answered, "Yes, she's in recovery and doing fine."

"Can I see her?"

"Not yet, she's still out from the general anesthesia."

Kabe reached into his pocket. "Can I ask you to check on my son again, and maybe take my camera in to take a picture?"

Kabe must see him. All of those months that he couldn't wait to see what his son Zion would look like. Even if he truly was dead. Kabe needed something tangible. He needed some kind of verification that this was real—that this was really happening.

"Sure, I can do that."

Sheryl grabbed the digital camera and made her way back through the double doors, back into the operating room.

To Kabe's surprise, it wasn't but two minutes before Sheryl returned with camera in hand. And, oddly enough, her bright pink face, smile, and wide eyes radiated something rather peculiar—it was hope.

"I don't want to get your hopes up Kabe, but your son is alive! Dr. Brohm brought him back!" Sheryl exclaimed.

Kabe could feel the life returning to his body as well.

"How long was he dead for?"

Kabe had to ask, he just had to know.

"At least twenty minutes."

6

Winter is waning. The snow outside is hard, muddy brown, and melting. Slush during the day. Ice at night. Snow banks look like dirt mounds. One wouldn't want to play king of the mountain on them, they are littered in trash, speckled with debris, and covered in bird shit. Squirrel droppings and urine.

There are massive piles of snow left by plows in empty parking lots still hanging tough.

When snow melts it refreezes as a solid, becoming more dense. Thus, it takes longer to melt. The dirt actually aids in its thawing. It absorbs the sunlight, warming it up. The dirtier it gets, the more sand that is exposed, the more sand, the more sun absorbed — the more it melts. Like everything, it involves some give and take.

Judas is wearing tan knockoff Ugg boots, tight black yoga pants, and a blue down jacket. The hood is lined with synthetic white fur. She walks in the street to avoid the ice on the sidewalk. Someone driving by yells at her, telling her to get off the road. She pays them no attention. The only thing on her mind is Jack Warren. Is he alive? And if so, why hasn't he contacted her? Or why bother to now? Especially if the rumors are true and he ran off with Jessica Mills. None of it makes sense. Maybe this is an elaborate trick someone is playing on her. Maybe someone is being mean. Cruel. Toying with her emotions. Her mind is set ablaze, which only makes her feet move faster. She is only blocks away from the Pfitzer hotel, blocks away from an answer.

The streets are oddly quiet for 7:45 p.m. The wind is blowing her hair around, she continually has to swipe her hair from her eyes. *I should of wore a hat,* she thinks. It takes time to look this good — men have no idea.

The hotel is within sight. All the other shops nearby are closed. Lights off. Even the houses look abandoned. As Judas makes her way up the concrete steps toward the entrance she notices two men standing, arms folded, looking out upon the road — as if they are guarding something. Stationed at a post. She thinks this is weird but doesn't really care. It is none of her business and Judas is one to always mind her self. She is that kind of woman. She never calls the cops and she never sticks her nose where it doesn't belong. She knows better.

She had learned the hard way — lessons that only years of poverty can teach. Street smarts are not innate to human nature, they must be acquired through experience. It's not something you can pick up from reading a book. Judas has a PhD in spousal abuse, drug addiction, juvenile delinquency, and childhood neglect. Her mother was a heroine junkie and her father...well Judas was a rape baby.

She doesn't know who her father was.

Nor did her mom.

Judas' mother was raped at gunpoint.

Judas was conceived in the back of a 1971 baby blue Ford Pinto.

Her father forcefully rammed his pleasure stick back and forth while saying things like "move and I'll kill you" and "don't look at my face or you're fucking dead."

This was before DNA testing and rape kits became available.

This was a time when men couldn't rape their wives and women who dressed in a provocative manner supposedly asked for it.

Maybe times haven't changed.

People in town called her mother Harley Harlot. She was a lady of the evening.

A streetwalker.

Judas enters the lobby. It smells of bleach and other potent industrial cleaning supplies — the kind that remove blood stains from carpeting. The man behind the front desk eyeballs her, a large man is standing by the elevator pretending to read a magazine. It all seems quite set up. Judas knows this because she too is an entertainer, depending on audience. Her gut reaction is to leave, to turn around and calmly walk out, but she knows that if her hunch is correct, it's already too late for that — the men by the doors will surely stop her. She is beyond the point of no return. Judas knows that the only thing she can do now is to keep moving forward. Besides, maybe Jack is here, and that in itself is enough to keep her motivated — to court explicit danger like this.

People do some really stupid things for love.

Judas walks up to a gilded gold-framed mirror in the lobby and calmly fixes her wind blown hair. She puckers her lips and lines them with a fresh coat of rouge.

If she was going to die, then she was going to leave an exquisite corpse she thought. She would bleed goddamn Marilyn Monroe.

Judas struts toward the elevator, heel to toe, and pushes in the button with the up arrow on it.

The music in the lobby is Frank Sinatra's "Witchcraft."

The elevator makes its way down, in it are a man and a woman, they are kissing each other passionately. Obsessively.

Judas instantly recognizes the man, only because he has arrested her in the past. It is Roy Hutchinson.

The elevator dings and the couple step out. Roy has his left arm around the woman, she is wearing a fur-lined designer coat and they are chatting, laughing, and smiling.

The woman is all dolled up.

A subtle shade of blue on her eyelids.

Juicy red lipstick.

A hint of blush on her cheeks.

Judas and Roy lock eyes, but only for a second, then he winks at her and smirks. The last time she had seen Roy, she was in handcuffs and not the fun ones with the pink fur either, these ones bruised her wrists from being closed too tight. Naturally, Judas gives him the finger. The woman pays it no attention. She is simultaneously walking and sucking on Roy's neck as they make their way through the lobby and toward the entrance. She says something about how wet he makes her and that she is starving.

"Stupid asshole," Judas says under her breath.

After Jack disappeared, all Roy repeatedly told the media was that Jack was on a leave of absence and not available for comment.

What a fucking liar she thinks.

Judas gets in the elevator, pushes the button for the third floor, and the doors close. As she ascends, three men enter the lobby dragging a young blonde girl by her arms, she is yelling at them to let her go. Judas is starting to regret her decision to come here, to this godforsaken hotel, in this horrid township.

It's too late now, the third floor awaits.

Ding. The elevator stops and the doors open to the third floor.

The brass sign on the wall says rooms 310 through 330 are to the right.

Judas peeks her head out, looks both ways, like she is crossing a busy intersection, and sees that the hallway is empty.

Red checkered carpets with ivory swirls.

A musty smell with a hint of lavender.

Low lights and beige walls.

An old storage closet with white stenciled letters that read INCINERATOR.

Judas steps out and takes a moment to compose herself. She takes a deep breath and opens her purse — double checking that her 9mm pink pistol — a SAR B6 Pavona with a pink polymer frame is still loaded and ready, just in case.

Nervousness sets in.

She walks the hall slowly but not too slow as to incite suspicion from any possible onlookers. She does have to maintain appearances after all, she is an entertainer, entrepreneur, or dancer depending on audience. She bypasses rooms 315, 317, 319, and then sees it, her destination — room 321.

The brown door has a small silver peephole and a silver handle.

Head up, tits out, ass tight, Judas knocks three times and then steps back, again scanning the hall from side to side.

There is a clicking sound, like a chain latch being removed, and then a thud.

Someone was peering out the peephole, checking to see who it was, someone was about to open the door. Was it going to be Jack? Judas sure hoped so.

Anticipation.

Enthusiasm.

Suspense.

All for not.

"Come in," a woman's voice says loudly.

Judas is caught off guard, she assumed that whoever it is would at least open the door for her.

Maybe chivalry really is dead, she thinks.

Judas grabs the silver handle and pushes open the door. She gets some sort of powder or dirt or dust on her hand. It feels like makeup— loose powder foundation or press powder. She looks up, brushing whatever it is off onto her yoga pants, and sees a woman sitting comfortably in a gold chair in the back of the room by the windows.

The shades are drawn and the lamps are all on.

"Judas I presume, come...sit. Welcome to my hotel."

Judas is confused, but no longer afraid. Women don't scare her.

What's the worst that can happen? she thinks.

The beds are made and there is no luggage, there are no clothes strewn about.

"Who are you? And why am I here," Judas asks.

Judas sits down on the edge of the queen size bed, facing the dark haired woman. She has caramel highlights and her aroma is a delicious hint of cherry blossoms.

"My name is Haven."

"Can I smoke in here Haven? Being it's your hotel and all."

"Of course."

Judas pulls out a pack of unfiltered Marlboros and massages the tip slightly before sticking one in her mouth and lighting it up. She forgets about whatever it is that she got on her fingers. The flavor is somewhat bitter but she pays it no mind.

Judas exhales and continues her line of questioning. "So why exactly am I here? You know my time isn't free right?"

"Whose time is free these days? You are here because I too know Jack Warren."

"Then you probably know Jack is missing...and that I haven't seen him in months."

Haven laughs and offers Judas a drink — Jameson whiskey. Judas is quick to pick up on what her gesture really means.

Jameson was Jack's drink of choice — it was part of his per usual concoction.

"I don't have time for this, or your games, tell me what it is that you want."

Judas takes another drag of her cancer stick and suddenly doesn't feel so well.

Nausea sets in.

"Well to be quite honest Judas, you are here, because you still love him."

Judas tries to finish her smoke, but her stomach is churning. A sharp pain sends both her and the cigarette to the floor. It smolders on the carpet, burning its fibers, turning them curly black.

Melting.

Upset stomach.

Writhing in pain.

"What the hell did you do to me, you bitch?" Judas looks up at Haven from the floor as she begins to dry heave. Then she throws up.

Haven leans over and picks up the burning cigarette and takes a drag. She sits back in the chair and exhales. Her legs are folded real proper, like a real lady.

Genteel.

She has elegant posture. The kind you only see in those gorgeous vintage tobacco advertisements or on TV.

She is wearing black peep-toed heels with thin straps.

Black nylon stockings.

Haven takes another drag and exhales in Judas' direction.

"You know in Amazonia, tobacco is very auspicious. Infact, tobacco is central to shamanism and witchcraft," Haven says.

Spell blowing.

Curses.

Haven takes another puff and blows a thick cloud at Judas, who is kneeling on the floor.

Haven says something under her breath. You can barely hear it.

Haven sits up and tells Judas that she is only going to give her what she has coming and that it is her love for Jack that will be her undoing. She tells her that she doesn't like ex-girlfriends, that she isn't fond of their desperate nature. She says that she also isn't fond of her life choices — her being an entertainer, an entrepreneur, or dancer depending on audience. She says something about how women like Judas have no real purpose and that she is going to give her one — that she is going to "save her from herself."

Judas can't feel her arms or her lips, she tries to move them, but nothing happens. As Judas falls to the floor she sees Haven stand up, toss the smoke to the ground and step on it, abruptly snuffing it out.

Like Lenord's friend Erik did the baby.

She hears Haven say that she needn't worry, that she should rest now, and that it will all be over soon.

7

Judas wakes up to the sound of a door slamming shut behind her. Her head hurts and she has an acidic, chalky, sour taste in her mouth. She's looking up at the ceiling of some room, it has grey popcorn texture, there is a single white indoor flush mount ceiling fixture with a dangling string and bulb. She attempts to move her arms but they are firmly strapped down in cracked leather cuffs. So too is her head, there is a shabby tortilla brown strap around her neck. She is naked lying on a Prussian blue vinyl padded board. The oval board is jutting through the wall in front of her and so are her pelvis and legs.

The hole is big enough to fit her entire body. It is draped with a black linen fabric to prevent anyone from seeing in or out on either side. Privacy. It looks like an enormous glory hole. It is an enormous glory hole. Like a Prague fucking house.

Judas tries to move her legs but they too are taut and immotile. On the other side of the wall she is spread eagle with her bare buttocks and vagina exposed. Her legs are fastened in the air to relieve muscle tension. She can hear voices on the other side of the wall — whispers — on the side with her anus and vagina unprotected. The whispers are discussing who will go first.

The door behind Judas opens and footsteps approach. They stop behind her head. Haven leans over and looks down at her — face to face.

"Awake I see...good," Haven says.

"What the fuck! Let me go bitch!" Judas shouts.

"Temper, temper, my dear. It's far too late for that."

"For what?"

"Posturing."

"Why am I naked? What the fuck!" Judas struggles against the straps and grits her teeth.

"Shhh, come now Judas...I am giving you a purpose. You really should be thanking me."

"For what? What purpose? What in the fuck are you talking about?"

"Unlike what your name implies, you will bring about the new Aeon...a new age...you Judas...will help give birth to my legions."

"You're fucking crazy!"

"I know it's hard to understand without seeing, without feeling...but you will, eventually. Soon enough it will all make sense, but for now...just do what you do best."

Haven smirks and softly places both of her hands on Judas' cold cheeks.

"And what's that exactly?" Judas asks.

"Don't be Judas, be the Whore of Babylon."

Haven bends forward and kisses Judas on the lips.

Sensual.

Soft.

The kiss of Judas.

Ushering in the dawn of a new age.

Before Judas can respond, she feels something wet wrap around her left leg. It feels weird. Rubbery. Oily. Sticky. Her other leg is quickly entangled as well. She feels pressure circulating on her thighs, as if little glass jars were placed on her skin. Like cupping therapy.

Haven abruptly exits and closes the door behind her.

Nervous.

Terrified.

Vulnerable.

Then Judas feels it, whatever it is, touch her vulva. It is gooey, but warm to the touch. Like dipping your toes in a lukewarm bath. It starts to vibrate. It finds her clitoris and then picks up speed. It feels amazing. Judas' eyes roll back and she starts to moan. It feels so damn good. It feels better than any vibrator she has used before; and she of all people is an authority on them. Her nipples harden, her breath picks up, and she now finds herself dripping wet. The suction on her legs tightens and it pulsates into what can only be high speed. Judas is licking her chops, she wants to fuck really bad. She hasn't wanted intercourse this bad since high school. Not since Jack.

Then it splits open — the gooey tendril — uncovering a long phallus while still fixed, shaking, and shuddering. Judas can feel it thrust inside her inch by inch and it feels like nothing she has ever experienced before. It is covered in small ridges, as if it were designed specifically for a woman's pleasure. It pushes deep inside her, deeper than any man has ever ventured. Any human. It slams right into her cervix and forcefully thrusts back and forth, it too is vibrating.

Judas can do nothing but orgasm. She cums hard. She can hear moaning on the other side of the wall too, whoever it is, whatever it is, enjoys banging her immensely. Judas is taken to new levels of pleasure, far beyond the capabilities of mortal men.

This sex is otherworldly.

Underworldly.

Stygian.

Undead.

Whoever is on the other side of the wall groans hard, raucously — even she knows what is coming. At the height of pleasure, as both her and whoever, or whatever, is on the other side get off simultaneously. Whatever is inside her rams into her cervix again, but this time she feels a horrible pain within her cervical cavity. Needle sharp. A stinging sensation. As if something was injected into it through a needle. Then suddenly, a rush of fluid fills her entire pussy before gushing out onto the floor. Like her water just broke.

Draining heavily.

Whatever it is pulls out.

Whatever is wrapping her legs lets loose.

Whatever it was blew its load and then left without saying a word.

Judas' abdomen is sore and bloated.

Distended.

She has no words. Although distraught, although repulsed, and now feeling dirty, she also feels strangely delighted.

Oddly ok.

The whole experience was somehow erotic.

Before she can catch her breath, regain her composure, she feels more wet tendril like things envelop her legs — wrap her thighs — and another vibrating phallus start to explore her now sloppy nether regions.

Her legs tense up as she braces for more.

***

Devin is home now. He locks the door and quickly slams the dead bolt. He is out of breath. Terrified. Shaking. He cannot believe what he just saw, *it cannot be real,* he thinks. This kind of stuff only happens in horror movies, or nightmares, not in the real world he tells himself.

Devin lives in a low income housing complex — apartment 21A — a single bedroom and bath on the second floor of an affordable housing unit overlooking a parking lot and the Mecan river. His blinds are white and dusty, grimy, like he never bothers to clean them. The walls are eggshell white, his furniture is worn, and bought used from the local thrift shop. His couch has questionable stains on the underside of its cushions.

He flipped them over and threw a blanket on them, it was cheaper than buying a new one.

Devin is into comic books and Manga pornography. It clutters his walls.

Hentai Manga.

Animephile.

Amaetai Fucks.

Mama wa Boku ni Koi o Soru.
Yaoi Hentai Manga.
Lady boys and big toys.
Art imitating life, life imitating art.

Devin throws the gore covered furry costume into a black trash bag and ties it up. He hops into the shower and cleans up. The water under his feet turns red, little pieces of Craig, the bell boy, fall out of his hair. He gags. He has a strong stomach, but this is more than his gut can handle. Devin soaps up and rinses off. He grabs a towel and begrudgingly calls the sheriffs department from his landline. Calling 911 doesn't seem logical at this point, so he doesn't waste his time. He presses the number two for non-emergency.

His cell phone was still back at the hotel. He always hated the fact that Uniontel Phone forced him to have a landline in order to get DSL but now, in this moment, it seems sort of useful.

Devin tells the operator something about being attacked.

Waushara county dispatch informs him that they will send an officer out to speak with him shortly. Devin suddenly realizes that there is a large bag of weed on his coffee table — half an ounce — he snatches it up and stuffs it in a sock in his dresser drawer.

He has dealt with the police well enough to know that they wouldn't be searching anything, but leaving it in sight would cause problems.

Twenty minutes goes by and he hears a knock at the door.

"Who is it?" Devin asks.

"Roy Hutchinson, Waushara County Sheriff's Department."

Just great, Devin thinks. He knows Roy and they weren't on the best of terms. Devin's "sexcapades" at the local rest stop made sure of that.

"Come on Devin, open up. You called us, remember?"

"Yeah, yeah, one second."

Devin turns the bolt and flips the lock on the handle opening the door. In the doorway stands Roy and another officer he doesn't recognize. This new officer is huge, maybe seven feet tall. He is built like a linebacker, like a refrigerator, he is a behemoth of a man. The behemoth has to duck his head under the doorway upon entry.

"So what's up Devin? Why'd you call us? Who attacked you?"

The large man stands silent, he cracks his enormous knuckles.

Devin shuts the door and makes his way to the couch.

"Look, this is going to sound crazy...I mean completely nuts...but whatever attacked me wasn't human."

"Are you still on your meds or did you stop taking them?" Roy asks.

"No! Listen Roy, I'm serious. I was at the Pfitzer hotel and something attacked me, I don't know what the fuck it was, but it sure as fuck wasn't human."

"Ok, ok, settle down. What then, some sort of animal? What do you mean it wasn't human?"

"I don't know, it had tentacles and it fucking killed people man! You gotta believe me!

"Settle down, tentacles you say?"

Roy nods his head at the giant man, who then steps in front of the door ever so slightly, blocking the exit.

"And at the Pfitzer hotel you say?"

"Yeah man, you gotta go check it out.These things didn't just attack me, they were killing everyone."

"Things? As in more than one?"

"Yeah man. I barely made it out alive."

"Lucky you, then," Roy says as he sits down on the edge of the couch and scratches his head. "That's funny, wouldn't you think someone from the Pfitzer would of called 911? I was just down there and everything seemed fine to me...so what is this...some sort of joke?"

"What? No I swear it's no joke man! I know what I saw!" Devin shouts.

"Ok, well...I tell you what, why don't you come down to the hotel with me and show me what you are talking about? If you aren't making up stories, that shouldn't be a problem, right?"

"No way man! I'm not going back there! Fuck that."

Roy leans back on the couch and rests his chin on his hand, sighing.

"I'm not fucking with you, I swear!"

Roy tires of playing coy.

"Oh I know you're not, you moron! I'm just deciding whether or not I'm going to kill you or eat you or both."

Devin looks up at Roy, dumbfounded. His gaze then moves toward the behemoth in front of the door.

"Oh shit! You're one of those things too?"

Roy stands up. "Silly boy, I think I'll do both. I am starving."

Devin dives over the couch and dashes into his bedroom, slamming the door behind him. He locks it and pushes his twin bed in front of it. Roy looks over at the behemoth and gestures at him to do something.

The behemoth wastes no time, he swiftly moves in to open the door. He tries the handle, to no avail, then begins slamming it with his fist.

Devin forces open his bedroom window and kicks out the screen. He catches his hand on a large sliver in the windowsill, but ignores it. He is only two stories up, so he jumps.

As soon as Devin jumps the bedroom door bursts open and the behemoth tosses the bed out of the way. He rushes the window and sees Devin getting up off the ground below. He looks back at Roy, awaiting his command.

"Don't worry about him, Devin is no threat to us...besides no one will believe him. He has no friends. We have more important things to do."

Roy's cell phone rings, he answers it and listens to whoever is on the other end of the line carefully.

It is Haven, she tells Roy something important before abruptly hanging up.

Roy looks over at the behemoth and says, "It has begun."

"Abashed the Devil stood and felt how awful goodness is and saw Virtue in her shape how lovely: and pined his loss."

--John Milton

8

This godforsaken place is

burning — it is all on fire. As Kabe peers out of the front window of the Abraham house he can see the heat from the blast wave across the street melting the skin right off of the wretched beasts, or things, or monsters, but they are still getting up. The ubiquitous screaming is overwhelming, the neighbors — the Pattens — are outside doing anything they can to escape the madness, but it is a hopeless endeavor. The wretched things, whatever they are, are merciless, they are killing men and capturing women and children. Anything deemed male is on the menu.

Women and children are being hauled away.

Tied up and gagged.

Forced into the back of semi trailers like cattle.

Like holocaust Jews.

They are left bawling as they watch their boyfriends, husbands, fathers, grandfathers, and uncles be devoured voraciously — eaten alive.

Ensnared in tentacle-like things and ripped apart.

Omophagia.

The ravening.

"Scarlet! We have to leave now!" Kabe yells up the staircase.

Staying is no longer a viable option, it is a war zone outside.

"Come on! We have to fucking move! We don't have much time!" Kabe shouts up the stairs again, but this time with a greater sense of urgency. Kabe's patience is dwindling fast because he knows that it won't be long before the fight is right on his doorstep.

"I'm coming!" Scarlet barks as she rushes down the stairs. "I had to grab Zion and the last duffle bag."

The Abrahams bolt down a dark, narrow hallway into the dining room toward the back door to the house.

"We're going to have to move fast to the car. I'll go first and clear a path," Kabe says.

Kabe chambers a round in his shotgun and gives Scarlet a kiss on the cheek. "Give me ten seconds and then follow behind with Zion."

Nervous.

Afraid.

Heart pumping.

Adrenaline rushing.

"Kabe wait, what about Sammy?" Scarlet asks.

"He's coming with me. Come on Sammy, let's go boy!"

Sammy is short for Samurai. He is the Abraham's family dog. He is a pit bull terrier mix. He is an amalgam of other pure breeds, the kinds in fancy dog shows, circling bright green turf and winning trophies. He is a mutt.

Kabe opens the door and steps out.

The pogrom has begun.

***

"Step on it!" Kabe howls.

The Abrahams made it out the back door of the house and to their silver Ford Expedition unharmed. The suburban Wautoma streets are now soaked in blood. Painted in death. Tainted in violence. Scarlet is behind the wheel so that Kabe can shoot anything that tries to prevent their escape with his trusty Mossberg 500 shotgun. As the vehicle turns the corner onto Main Street, Kabe sees Scott Hickey, the decorated Stinger wrestler, wrestled to the ground and ravaged in his front yard. He is shrieking in pain, bellowing and crying out. His intestines are being strewn about. Tugged on. Torn. Disemboweled. His feet are kicking wildly as he is eaten alive. There is blood all over the side of his Grand Am.

"Just keep going!" Kabe shouts.

Another man is shooting the wretched beasts, or things, or monsters rapidly from his porch. As mangled and full of holes as they are it doesn't stop them, not in the least. They keep coming. They have divine hunger. One of them is wearing a penguin suit.

Ravenous.

Blood thirsty.

Ferocious.

Feasting.

A couple miles down the road, it is quiet again.

It takes a few minutes to calm Zion down.

"Where are we going Kabe?" Scarlet asks, sniffling a bit.

"To see Grandpa."

"Does my dad know we're coming?" Scarlet asks.

"No, my cell phone lost signal before I had a chance to call him. But it's no big deal, he'll be there."

Scarlet's father, Robert Warren, lives just south of the rest stop on Hwy 22 in the woods. He owns two hundred and fifty acres.

Highway 22 is wide open. It is clear of vehicles since the wretched beasts, or things, or monsters are now ravaging the city.

Oddly enough the police have just blocked the roads both in and out of town.

The Abrahams narrowly escaped, they were almost trapped in the city. For now, they are safe—startled—but safe. They are still coming to grips with the situation. They are digesting it and letting it settle in their minds—taking it all in. Soon enough they would be at Grandpa's house planning out their next move.

Dark grey clouds hang overhead. It starts to snow.

***

Jack Warren is eating his second meal for the day. Eggs on rye with a side of orange juice. It is dry. Grainy. He is being kept in a locked room in some decrepit abandoned house, the same one that used to have a horde of zombies in the basement. The four letter word HATE on his left hand, tattooed on his knuckles, shines in the light from the nearby barred window. His brown hair is unwashed, but combed, and he is sporting a scraggly beard.

Now, it is just Haven, her bodyguards, and Jack. Haven visits him periodically throughout the day and has been for some time now. She tells him that she loves him and that one day he will love her too.

Jack does love her. More than anything in this world. More than anything in this godforsaken place, but he also knows that she isn't really Haven anymore. She is something else. He tells her this when she reads to him at night under candle light. She reads Nietzsche, Shakespeare, Palahniuk, King, and Rice. She reads J.K. Rowling, Dew, Barker, and Bruce Lee to him.

She reads him Lovecraft.

Poe.

Aleister Crowley.

She has an eclectic taste in books, as she also does in music.

It is hard to distinguish the Haven now, from the Haven before. Even though Jack knows she is not human, he struggles to maintain that observation. Besides, what really makes someone human? How do we define something like "life" and "personhood?" Science defines life as having self-sustaining biological processes. This definition is supposed to distinguish the living from the dead — the inanimate and the animate. These processes include: homeostasis, organization, metabolism, growth, development, adaptation, response to stimuli, and reproduction.

Homo sapiens.

Human nature.

Aristotle defines being human via genus and species, arguing that humans are "rational animals."

Haven is obviously a sentient being; she uses language, has the ability to use complex tools, and she can make rational decisions. What then about biological processes? What of reproduction? The line between human and inhuman is becoming increasingly difficult for Jack to define.

Then, a knock at the door. The turn of a key, the slide of a bolt. Two men enter the room and tell Jack that he is to come with them and to not ask any questions. They don't bother to put a bag over his head nor do they use any sort of restraints. Jack tells them ok and follows suit. He follows them down a dimly lit corridor, there are water stains on the ceiling and the smell of moth balls — like that of a thrift store. All three of them turn the corner and stop at a rickety flight of wooden stairs leading upward, toward the attic. The two men motion to Jack to go the rest of the way alone.

Jack isn't nervous.

He is strangely enthusiastic.

Excited.

Happy.

As he ascends the staircase, he looks back and the two men are diligently guarding the hall below. There is a flickering glow of light protruding from beneath the white oak door at the top of the stairwell. Jack can hear the faint sound of music echoing from behind it. Low toms and piano — it is Sinatra. Jack knocks and slowly turns the door handle opening it. The door creaks and Jack walks in, closing the door behind him. There are lit candles all over the room and the air smells like dragon's blood incense. The walls are covered by an old Victorian floral pattern, they have an elegant Tuscan bronze finish. Wallpaper. There is a king size bed set against the back wall with a large, beige, padded headboard. The comforter is white with black swirling patterns. Like vines. On the bed, in silk black lingerie, is Haven. She is lying proper, like a lady, smoking a filtered cigarette, legs crossed just past the knees. Genteel.

Jack steps forward toward the front of the bed. Haven scoots toward him and stands up, they are now only feet apart. Face to face. Jack's eyes peruse her perfect hips, her tight, perky breasts, her dark eyeliner, and red rouge lipstick. Haven snuffs out the smoke in an overloaded ash tray on the dresser and walks around him while swaying her hips to the sound of Sinatra. She gently swipes her hand around Jack's shoulder, just brushing his neck, and spins in front of him, her back is facing his now bulging front. She slowly rubs her buttocks on him from side to side and throws her arms up and back around his neck while leaning into him. Her nails scratch his ears.

Her long dark hair with caramel highlights splashes past his face.

Her scent is a delicious hint of cherry blossoms.

Her skin is soft and glowing.
Erotic.
"What's all this?" Jack asks.
"A celebration," she says.
"What are we celebrating?"
"To new beginnings babe. To a new world."

Jack gives in and puts both his hands on her waist. He wants her more than he had ever fathomed; he wants to be with her, whoever she is, even if she is no longer Haven. His hands slide up and down her thighs and around onto her bare abdomen. He feels every crevice, every imperfection, though to him she is perfection. To him she is like a dream. Jack embraces her and starts to kiss her neck. He licks her ears and nibbles at them. She feels the wet of his tongue graze her neck, she moans and spins into his arms. They lock lips as she undoes his belt and massages the lump in his pants.

Jack unsnaps her bra, unveiling the most gorgeous set of breasts he has ever laid eyes, and now hands, upon. He slides her panties over and stuffs his thick fingers inside her dripping wet pussy. She opens Jack's pants and tugs on his hard cock. Milking it. She thrusts Jack onto the bed and jumps up on his chest; she is on her knees with her feet facing his chin. She puts her hair back and leans forward, now straddling his face. Jack slides her black silk panties over and licks her soaking slit. Sixty-nine. He tongues her rapidly as she sucks and strokes. Reciprocity. She tastes bitter and his whole face goes a little numb. Haven sits up and spins around. She tosses her panties onto the cold hardwood floor. She slides up and down on Jack's groin and pushes his pants down to his ankles with her pristinely painted little toes. She feels amazing. Powerful. Her wet lips cause his dick to tingle as he thrusts inside of her. As Haven grinds on top of him, moaning, Jack suddenly feels something moving inside her vagina, wiggling, vibrating. It slides out of her, passed his penis and toward his taint. It is wet and soft, but long and phallus like. It starts to nudge his rectum. Reaming it. Lubricating it. Jack is nervous, but caught in the heat of the moment. Before he can think, whatever it is thrusts inside his rectum and pokes at his prostate. Gyrating and shaking.

Now they are both inside the other, simultaneously giving and taking. They both gasp and grunt as they ravage each other's bodies. It is euphoric. Hallucinogenic. Phantasmagoric. Haven says she is going to cum, which only makes Jack want to orgasm as well. His dick hardens as does whatever is inside him, they both blow inside the other. A gush of fluid flushes Jack's anus like an enema and spurts out onto the mattress as Jack blows a hot thick load of semen deep within her.

They are both out of breath and creampied. Whatever it was that penetrated Jack retracts back inside of Haven. Still leaking. Dripping milky liquid. She rests silently on top of him; they are both sweaty and exhausted.

Jack holds her tight.

For the first time in a very long time, he doesn't even think about alcohol.

For the first time in a very long time, he feels content.

Like his old self.

He feels a range of emotions—love—but he doesn't dare say it.

Haven slides over and rests her soft head of hair in the crutch of his arm. She runs her fingertips down the space between his pectoral muscles and tells him how beautiful he is. Jack pulls her in close and closes his eyes.

He tells her that he loves her.

She tells him that they can be together forever.

He kisses her forehead and says that forever is not long enough.

9

Sunset. Darkness falls as the Abrahams pull into grandpa Warren's snow covered, gravel driveway. The Warren family has lived in this godforsaken place since the 1960's; since great grandpa Leo first discovered Wautoma while on vacation from his factory job in Milwaukee.

Scarlet has a lot of good memories fishing Silver Lake as a young girl with her brother Jack.

Robert settled here shortly after the divorce and he's been making a decent living as a maintenance man for the local snowmobile outfitters in town ever since.

The large, white birch trees hold a warm place in Scarlet's heart. She remembers tearing off their bark and coloring on it with her Crayola crayons. The natural beauty of these woods is something most people take for granted, but not Scarlet. She loves the feeling of walking an old logging road and just taking in the scenery.

Nature.

It is her escape.

Catharsis.

Upon pulling up to the house, both Scarlet and Kabe notice that the garage door is open but no vehicles are inside. Nor are there any visible lights on. Thus, leaving them to wonder, *is the old man even home?*

"Do you think he's home?" Scarlet asks.

"I don't know. Let me go in and check things out first before you and Zion come in. Ok? Lock the doors and if I'm not back in ten minutes…well, never mind, I'll be back. Just lock the doors."

Sammy is sleeping in the back.

Kabe shuts the car door and turns the safety off on his shotgun, then heads for the front steps. *It's strange that no dogs are barking,* Kabe thinks. Robert has three Irish setters with long red hair that bark their brains out whenever anyone comes near the house and, for the first time, Kabe hears nothing. Kabe cautiously and slowly nudges the front door open. It is unlocked. As he walks in, his trusty shotgun takes the lead.

"Robert, you home?" he calls out.

Nothing.

No one.

Not a sound.

Kabe makes his way through the living room. There are old, smoke-stained Audubon pictures on the walls — loons and geese in black dusty frames. The fireplace is still simmering and there is a light on over the electric stove.

"Huh, I guess nobody is home," Kabe mutters.

He relaxes and lowers his shotgun.

"Hello Kabe," a voice says from behind him.

Kabe quickly raises his gun and turns around to see the back of a man looking out the bay window in the dining area. He is wearing dirty jeans and a torn red and black flannel shirt.

"Robert, that you? Everything ok?"

"Oh, I'm fine son...just dandy."

"Jesus Robert, why didn't you answer me? Where are the dogs? Are you sure you're alright?"

"Like I said, I'm just swell, but please, don't talk about Jesus. Just the thought of that no good charlatan makes my blood boil."

"What?"

"Did you ever notice how beautiful they are, Kabe?" Robert is staring out the bay window, but something isn't right.

"How beautiful what are?" Kabe asks while steadily moving in closer to see what Robert is gazing at.

"The crows son, the crows...you know they say that a crow can cross between the realm of the living and the dead? That they are intermediaries...such a gorgeous creature isn't it?"

Robert is still facing out the window.

He has shoulder length grey hair with a large bald spot on top.

A "skullet."

Earned from years of wearing an old snapback baseball cap.

"Yeah they are amazing, aren't they?" Kabe says humoring him.

"I've been seeing things a lot clearer lately, thanks to you. Infact, I've been waiting for you to arrive Kabe. I have a message for you that you really need to hear."

"A message? What are you talking about?" Kabe asks.

Robert turns around at a snail's pace. His chin is dripping gore and his eyes are missing. Only two bloody dark sockets remain. Half of his face is mutilated from something eating it. Something gnawing it down to the bone. Kabe can see Robert's tongue through the side of his cheek when he speaks.

Exposed fat cells.

Black and yellow.

The smell of infection permeates Kabe's nostrils.

Robert is scratching at the holes in his face and neck, at a jaw that is no longer there. His fingernails are sliding through flaps of moist, rotten skin. He has a gaping neck hole that is oozing a questionable substance.

Repulsion.

A hideous stench.

Putrid.

Mortified.

Oozing.

Festered.

Foul.

Maggots are wiggling out of his pus filled eye sockets, dropping onto the tile floor. Squirming. They must be what is eating his face. Seeing this reminds Kabe of squamous cell cancer. His mother passed away from it when he was a young man. It looks and smells similar when let go without treatment.

Kabe wonders how he sees the crow outside the window with no eyes.

The large bird is pecking at some raw meat. Has Robert been feeding it? And if so, what has he been feeding it?

There are large piles of long red dog hair scattered all over the porch.

Kabe quickly realizes what happened to Robert's three Irish setters.

Kabe notices the flies buzzing, he hadn't before. He tries not to look at it, Robert's face, but finds it impossible.

"Oh my..." Kabe says.

Robert abruptly cuts him off, "God...I believe god is the word you're looking for," he says.

"What the fuck happened to..."

Robert again speaks over top of him, "You're not listening boy, I told you I have a message you need to hear...NOW SHUT THE FUCK UP!" he yells.

"Ok, ok…what message?" Kabe asks, stepping backwards a bit.

Kabe breathes through his mouth to circumvent the rotten stench.

It doesn't really work.

"The mark your son Zion bears…the one on his arm…he has been chosen."

"His birth mark? What do you mean chosen? And how do you know about…"

"That mark! You have to get rid of it! If you know what's good for you you'll cut it right off of his arm and burn the flesh!"

"What does it matter, it's just a birthmark?"

"You fool! I don't have much time left, you have to listen to me…it's only a matter of time before…AARGH!"

Robert screams in pain and drops to his knees.

"Robert!" Kabe shouts as he moves in closer to help.

"Stay away from me!" Robert throws his arm up, gesturing at Kabe to stay back. "Now LISTEN! You have to get rid of that mark. It will bring about terrible things as long as he has it. Until you get rid of it, you and your whole family are in grave danger."

Robert clinches his head in agony, his nails dig deeper into the blackened flesh hanging from his cheek. He claws at it. Rips at it. Tearing pieces off and tossing them. Kabe can tell he is fighting off something horrible, but what it is, is anybody's guess.

"They know about your son, they know everything, and you don't have much time..."

"They who?"

"Never mind that! Do you remember how to get to the section of the woods we hunted last fall...the thick pines over by Snipe Lake?"

Behind Robert's property is four hundred more acres of public hunting land and Snipe Lake sits square in the middle of it.

"Sure I do, why?"

Robert strains to talk. He is wrestling with something dreadful inside, something gut-wrenching. He is now face first on the floor and squeezing his temples with his thumbs. It is debilitating. Excruciating. Horrendous. The pain is unmaking his world.

"Go there, those woods are thick and they go on for miles. It will at least buy you some time....Now GET OUT OF HERE!"

Robert thrashes around violently on the floor, convulsing, foaming at the mouth. The juices from his face splatter and stick to the Brazilian cherry wood floor. Whatever he is fighting, is something dark. And it is taking him over.

Suddenly Kabe hears a loud, high pitched wailing outside the bay window. It is the large black crow. It is perched on the deck railing, peering inside — glaring at Kabe. Staring right at him with its devilish yellow eyes. It looks hungry.

"But Robert…"

The body that should be Robert looks up from the floor and says, "Robert's not here anymore, Robert is gone. Leave a message after the beep motherfucker."

The body that should be Robert Warren starts laughing maniacally.

"What the fuck is going on?" Kabe asks.

The body that should be Robert Warren stands up and cracks its neck loudly. It has no eyes, but yet somehow it is still looking directly at Kabe. Worms dripping. Falling. Squishing under foot.

"Robert, are you ok?"

"Oh don't worry about dear old grandpa, what I'm going to do to you and your family is what you should be worrying about. We've got big plans for you and your kin…fantastic fun plans."

The body that should be Robert Warren lunges at Kabe, grabs him by the shirt, and violently tosses him to the floor — right through the coffee table. It splinters and crumbles, Kabe drops his shotgun upon impact. The shotgun slides across the floor toward the couch. Still loaded, safety off.

"Sheesh I'm starving, honestly I've been waiting here for you for weeks. You are going to taste marvelous."

The body that should be Robert Warren licks its lips and grins from ear to hole.

The body that should be Robert Warren spasms, its shoulders dislocate, and split open at the seams, unveiling large wet tentacles with gooey pus covered spikes. Like what Kabe witnessed from the car on the way out of town. Like what he witnessed from his house.

Kabe struggles to move, he might have a concussion, but somehow he manages to crawl toward the gun — toward the couch.

"Go ahead, get your gun, those things are useless against us...come on, I dare you...pick it up tough guy."

Kabe grabs the gun and staggers to find footing. He musters all of his strength, breathes heavy, and stands up.

"Go on, take your best shot kiddo. Bing, bang, boom." The body that should be Robert Warren mimics Kabe in jest.

Kabe raises the shotgun, unleashing hell, spreading the monster that used to be Robert Warren all over the living room.

If death by shotgun was performance art, the body that should be Robert Warren would be a Ron Athey.

Kabe is extremely good with a shotgun and the intensity of the moment coupled with the velocity of the rounds rips whatever it is to shreds. Fills it with holes. Kabe empties the entire contents of the gun and now feeling satisfied tosses it on the couch. Surely nothing can survive that he thinks. And he is out of ammo.

The wretched thing hits the ground steaming. Juices spill out and splatter onto a little bit of everything, even Kabe.

The smell of gunpowder.

Kabe sniffs his fingers.

For some reason he loves it. It reminds him of John Wayne. Of Clint Eastwood. He feels like Dirty Harry.

The good, the bad, and the zombies.

Scarlet hears the gunshots echo and ring from the car.

Then, just as Kabe turns to walk out the front door, the huge black crow flies in. Its wings graze his face. It lands on the steaming mess that used to be Robert Warren and pecks at its neck, pulling off a strip of thin, long, bubbly skin and then swallows it. Kabe ignores the bird, he takes a step forward, but stops when he hears something start to stir behind him on the floor—where the bullet ridden corpse should be. Kabe spins around post-haste and cannot believe what he sees—the mangled body of Robert Warren is getting up. Just like he had seen in town. The wretched thing spits out some dark black fluid, a ball of maggots, and clears its throat.

"Oh...that's not very nice...you know...hurting Grandpa like that," it says.

The wretched thing spits up some bloody mucus, it dribbles down what is left of its chin, making room for a hearty chuckle. It is at this moment that Kabe realizes that he is in for a long night and that things are about to get real messy.

"Oh shit," Kabe says.

The body that should be Robert Warren replies by hacking up another mouthful of dark black ooze and worms before spitting the fetid mixture onto the floor.

Kabe cracks his knuckles and eyes the iron poker by the fireplace.

10

Night. Scarlet Warren hurries to exit the car. She fumbles with her keys, tells Zion that mommy will be right back, and locks the doors. Sammy is barking. Zion is playing with a little red toy fire truck on the edge of the window, under the moon light. He yawns. His eyelids grow heavy.

It begins to snow. Flurries. It is cooling down outside, it's maybe fifteen degrees. Scarlet can see her breath. There is a loud commotion coming from inside Grandpa's house and just as she steps to the front door, she slips on a small patch of ice, slamming her elbow into its hard, unforgiving surface. Scarlet hears roars, shrieks, and something that sounds like metal chipping away at concrete coming from within the now dimly lit abode. Her elbow is bruised, but not broken. She gets up and pushes the door open, yelling Kabe's name. What she sees leaves her speechless.

Kabe is standing over the body that used to be Robert Warren holding a rusty iron fireplace poker. It has a curved handle and a slanted fish hook front end. There are bits of bloody skin and guts hanging from it. Stuck to it. Clinging. Kabe stops dead in his tracks, arms raised, ready to lunge the rod deep into the meaty mess on the floor that used to be Robert Warren. The odious thing is still wiggling, there are thrashing foot long severed tentacles with sharp spikes oozing black fluid dancing and sliding about.

"What the fuck are you doing?" Scarlet demands to know.

"This godforsaken thing won't fucking die!" Kabe shouts as he gasps for breath.

He is worn out.

Bone-tired.

Zonked.

All his energy is spent.

Frustrated.

Covered in gore, dripping ichor.

"Where is Dad?" Scarlet asks.

"Yeah, about that..."

Scarlet looks down at the higgledy-piggledy pile on the floor that used to be Robert Warren and recognizes her father's favorite tattered flannel shirt.

"Oh my gawd! Kabe, you killed Dad! What the fuck is wrong with you?"

Kabe lowers the poker.

Tentacles still flapping aimlessly, legs still twitching. In spasm. Knees bending. Flexing. Feet kicking.

"He's not your father anymore honey, just look at him."

"No shit! Look what you..."

Scarlet is hyperventilating. Her asthma is acting up. She isn't able to finish her sentence. She's had asthma since she was a teenager. It is a constant aggravation whenever she becomes upset or engages in physical activity. Scarlet strives to catch her breath—she grasps her chest. Kabe drops the rod and quickly comes to her aid.

"Sit, breath, it'll be ok, love...everything's ok."

Problem is, nothing's ever ok here, not in this beloved little village, this horrid township, this godforsaken place.

Kabe gently rubs her back, forgetting about his gore drenched hands. He unwittingly smears them onto her white sweater. It is a v-neck with two brown buttons augmenting her engorged size C cleavage. Scarlet is still breast feeding Zion.

The advertisement in the women's magazine she bought the sweater from said that it was stain resistant, patented, and tested.

Now Scarlet too, like Kabe, is wearing some of her father.

Speaking of, there is a rustle on the floor. Kabe and Scarlet both look over from the couch and witness the body that used to be Robert Warren sit up. It's skull is punctured and pitted, caved in from thrusts of iron. Its neck is discharging questionable black sludge and its arms have been completely torn off. All that is left is a bullet ridden torso, its groin and legs.

"You have got to be kidding me," Kabe says in frustration.

Scarlet shrieks and sits back. Feet up.

"Ok, that's it. I've had enough of this," Kabe says.

The wretched thing can no longer speak. It doesn't have a mouth. Kabe smashed it in a fit of rage.

Kabe runs to the kitchen and grabs the biggest knife he can find. A butcher knife. The kind used for heavy duty chopping. Dismemberment surely must be the answer he thinks.

"Alright time to end this motherfucker," he says.

Just as Kabe raises the knife, the wretched thing's head makes a snorting noise and bursts. It spews out a vile explosion of maggots and black ooze. It covers everything, startling everyone. It douses both Scarlet and Kabe thoroughly. Her once white, name-brand sweater is now three shades of brown and green. Maggots crawl in-between the stitches, Scarlet screams and yanks it off—undressing down to her bra. White little worms smack the TV and wiggle down the LCD screen. Kabe is unmoved.

He wipes the pulpy mushy rancid substance from his eyelids and spits before going to work on what's left of Robert Warren. Kabe straddles the torso and hacks away at it like a madman. Pieces start tearing loose. Fluids pool. Maggots squirm and joggle.

"Now the goddamn legs," he says.

Kabe starts at the ankles and makes his way upward on both legs. He tosses a boot, with Grandpa's severed foot still in it, to the side.

"Scarlet, you don't have to watch this," Kabe says, pausing just a moment to catch his breath.

"No, I think I do," Scarlet says.

"All that's left is...well...his dick and balls," Kabe says.

What's left of Robert Warren on the floor is still moving. The gooey tentacles are still flinching.

"Fuck it, the dick and balls it is..." Kabe says.

Kabe unbuckles the body that should be Robert Warren's belt and grabs onto the penis. He stretches it out and slices it off in one quick motion. The blade gets stuck in what's left of the lower abdomen. Kabe tugs on it, forgetting about Grandpa's sliced weiner in his other hand. Then he feels it move. Somehow it, Grandpa's pecker, was still animate. Disgusted, Kabe chucks it against the Puritan Pine wood-paneled wall. It slides down and shimmies around on the floor like a caterpillar, like a giant maggot.

"Fucking gross," Kabe says.

Then finally Kabe jerks on the only pieces of Grandpa left—his testicles. They are morgue cold and swollen. He jams the bloody blade into them and musters enough energy to cut them off.

A rush of fluid streams out, at least a gallon or more, a white creamy concoction. It splashes Kabe in the face, it gets in his mouth.

Semen.

Kabe throws up.

Then Scarlet throws up.

Then Kabe pukes again after seeing Scarlet's vomit.

Finally the body that should be Robert Warren stops moving. So too the maggots.

"Go figure, it was the balls the whole time," Kabe says jokingly.

He grins at Scarlet who is not at all amused.

They both look like they had taken a bath in Robert Warren. There are bits of him stuck in Scarlet's hair, her sweater, and even in her ear. Robert's eviscerated corpse bursts and spews forth a noxious gas. Putrid. Then another loud sound comes from what is left of his rear end—Robert's anus lets loose.

The whole room now reeks of piss, stinks of feces, and smells of decayed meat.

It would be a long evening.

11

Sweltering heat. The air is moist—damp—small water droplets build upon the plank Shiplap, distressed wooden walls. Judas is psychosomatically exhausted. She is breathing heavily, panting, her muscles spasm, quivering uncontrollably. Her toes are numb. Her wrists are sore. Her vagina feels like a swimming pool, she can feel liquid still slopping around inside her uterus. Zombie semen. It splashes back and forth whenever she shifts her weight. She tries to push it out, like she used to do after letting a john cum inside her, but to no avail. This is different. Abnormal.

Thus far she has been fucked by ten of them, the wretched things—all of which blew their loads in her pussy. They flushed her nether regions with gallons of undead spunk. The last creature left about five minutes ago. These five minutes are the first respite from rape that she has seen all day.

"Someone! Anyone! I can't take anymore of this!" Judas yells, "Please!"

She begins to weep.

The door behind her opens, a man wearing a Wautoma Stingers basketball tee walks in and says that it is lunch time. He tells her that he is going to release her, but that if she tries anything he has orders to kill her on the spot. He lifts up his shirt unveiling a black pistol. Judas catches a glimpse of it in her peripheral, which is neither here nor there, since she is far too tired to try anything anyway. She sighs in relief. At least this meant that she was getting a break.

The man unbuckles her.

As good as it felt to be fucked by the wretched things, she couldn't handle anymore. She has tasted ultimate pleasure and realizes that anything beyond that is pain. Like how eating too much candy will make you sick.

Upon standing up she tastes sour grapes and gags.

Dizzy.

Weak.

Starving.

She grasps her belly, it doesn't feel right. It feels like her insides are loose. Then suddenly, thanks to gravity, a rush of fluid spews forth from her vaginal canal, emptying onto the grimy tile floor. Like her water just broke. The watery substance splashes her feet.

She had taken life's delights and given birth to its vile excesses.

The man, an out of shape character wearing open toed sandals, escorts Judas out of what he calls "the fuck room" and down the hall. She passes multiple doors, each of which play a unique tune. Some, soprano with high pitched moaning, women reaching orgasms, others baritone with raucous groans and howls. Yowling. It is clear that she is not the only woman being raped in the building—there are more. *How many more are there?* she wonders. *And why? What is going on?*

"This way, you slattern cunt," the man says.

"Fuck you, dick jockey. I'd rather be a slut than somebody's bitch like you," she says.

The man stops, as if he wants to do something violent like put his hands on her, but continues moving forward without saying a word.

A bitch indeed.

The hallway reeks like a sweat shop. The lighting is sparse. This is not a place that Judas recognizes or has ever been before and she has seen every crevice this godforsaken place has to offer. She has bathed in all of its delights and has explored every seedy back door. Every nauseous nook and cranny. She is a purveyor of hedonism, a goddess of obscenity, of indecency, in the underworld. In her line of work, nothing is new, everything is either passé or passion for a price— well, until now.

Until today, she was merely an entrepreneur, an entertainer, or dancer depending on audience.

A demimonde.

A cam girl who would sleep naked and let men pay to watch.

Voyeurs tugging on their testicles, pinching and pressing on their taints, milking themselves like cash cows, paying her bills.

Sometimes she would sleep with anatomical decor shoved in her anus. A steel ball shaped butt plug with a baby blue crystal end. Rear end decoration.

She wore a black and red corset so no one would see her bubble gum abdomen, the one with hideous stretch marks, the one wrecked by child birth.

The same disfigured abdomen that Jack refused to look at while fucking her.

It was silently mandated and never talked about because it reminded Jack of his father's skin graphs. His burn scars, from the explosion.

Thinking about that makes Jack cry.

"In here," the man says.

He opens a locked door and turns to the side, cutting Judas off, funneling her into a room like a cow led into the squeeze shoot in a slaughter house stall.

Judas hesitates, she attempts to peek inside before entering, but feels a hand abruptly push on her back and shove her forward against her will.

"Have fun, ladies," the man says before slamming the door and locking it.

Judas' eyes peruse the room cautiously. She can smell food — pork and beans — and maybe chicken. Her mouth begins to water. Her taste buds writhe in agony. Salivating. She is still stark naked, her nether regions still sloppy and slick.

Oily.

Greasy.

Oleaginous.

There are two green military cots on the floor. Each with a white pillow. The room stinks like urine. The only light is coming from an old gilded lamp sitting on the floor in the corner.

"What's your name, girl?" a soft voice from the corner by the lamp says.

It is feminine.

Judas looks over, straining her eyes, waiting for them to adjust, and finally sees a young girl sitting on her haunches, she too is naked. She has long, ass-length, red hair and blue eyes. There are little freckles on her cheeks and a tattoo in black cursive on her forearm that reads *Your Life Is In Your Hands*. She has purple, chipped fingernails.

"People call me Judas."

"Like the one who betrayed Jesus?"

"Yep."

"I'm Reagen."

"How long have you been in here?" Judas asks.

Without warning, Judas and Reagen are interrupted.

"Lunch," a man's voice says.

The door to the room opens and a tray of food is set on the floor. It is a can of pork and beans, some chicken, and a cup of water. Its odor is delicious. Judas hasn't eaten in what feels like days.

"Judas, come get it. You will need your energy," he says.

Judas wastes no time and dives for it, she snatches and slurps up every morsel, every last bit. She is famished. Or at least feels like it. Her stomach gurgles and groans. She pays it no attention.

"I just got here, I was taken along with my mom and sister."

"What do you mean, taken?"

"You're kiddin' right?"

"About what?"

"The whole town is being rounded up. All the women and children. Hundreds of us shuttled onto semi trucks and hauled here. It's like Nazi fucking Germany out there...except weirder."

"What do you mean, weirder?"

Reagen's voice lowers down to a whisper, she doesn't want them to hear. "They aren't human, whatever is taking us are aliens or something. They have tentacles and are eating people. One of them ripped my neighbor Greg's head off with his spine still attached. It's pretty sick shit..." Reagen looks around suspiciously before finishing her sentence. "...and even the cops are in on it. I saw them. They are working with the aliens. No lie."

Judas is speechless.

"I know it's hard to believe, but I'm telling you the truth."

Judas now comes to grips with what has been done to her. She puts two and two together. It all starts to make sense.

The rape, the otherworldly sex that she endured isn't about pleasure, it isn't about being a glory hole, it is about breeding.

Before Judas could speak, the room door opens again and the man in the Stinger basketball tee walks in. He tells Reagen to get up and that she is coming with him. He again lifts up his shirt, brandishing his black pistol. He tells everyone that if anyone tries anything that he has strict orders to kill them. He grabs Reagen—who is crouched in the corner by the lamp—by her beautiful red hair and drags her across the floor toward the door. She is screaming and kicking her feet wildly. She looks at Judas with her scared blue eyes bulging as she is yanked out the door.

Judas doesn't have the heart to tell Reagen that her life is not in her hands anymore.

12

Peter Faxneld is driving down highway 22 at sixty miles per hour. The sun has begun to set on the horizon. Its warm rays splay the tree tops, their glare lighting up the filled-in cracks in the uneven blacktop. The scene is warm, bright—comforting. The snowdrifts on the sides of the road are stuck, frozen in waves, there is a soft breeze carving them upwards then spilling them over onto now empty corn fields. Soy bean fields and straw-rough fawn brown grass. A blue sign appears in the distance—it reads Rest Stop One Mile. *Oh what the hell, might as well,* Peter thinks.

He has been holding his bladder for a good hour now.

He puts on his blinker and turns into the gravel drive of the rest stop, parking his green Jeep just yards from the brick and mortar building. His phone vibrates, distracting him just long enough so that he doesn't notice the putrescent mutilated corpse of a hipster on the edge of the lot in the bushes, half buried in snow. The cadaver is somewhat preserved by the cold weather, but missing a gauged ear. Desiccated. Four yards further back in the woods, the hipster's wife, Arlean, is strung up from a pine tree, decomposed yet visibly frozen, her skin torn and stripped, icey and stuck to thistles. Her head is caved in, her mouth bashed, her teeth black from years of drug addiction. Every so often ravens fly in to peck at what is left of her — their rough beaks pounding and scraping hard bits of iced flesh.

It doesn't take long for Peter to realize that he doesn't want to enter the bathroom to see a man about a horse, it reeks like a bloated carcass stuffed with spoiled diapers. The fetor of the public lavatory.

"Oh good gawd man, that's just plain unsanitary," he says to himself.

He pinches his nose, shields his mouth, and turns toward the bushes at the edge of the drive; the same bushes where the hipster named Dwayne is stuck rotting at a snail's pace, thanks to the tundra-like Wisconsin climate. Peter's phone vibrates, another text message, another distraction. He pulls out his todger and lets loose a hot stream of urine into the snow, abruptly melting a hole in it. He is looking up into the trees, nodding off into space, worn out from the long drive, body stiff, ass sore, not realizing that only feet in front of him his pee has begun to further uncover Dwayne's carcass. The yellow stream exposes Dwayne's entire head and chest, splashing over broken bones and draining into torn, faded, dirt covered, blood stained, flannel. Peter is oblivious to it, his eyes are closed, he is enjoying the silence that is intrinsic to being in the woods as opposed to the hustle and bustle of the city that he is so used to.

Peter zips up his fly and, still without managing to look down, turns and heads back to his Jeep. Peter, is none the wiser that he just gave Dwayne a post-mortem "fish bowl." As the piss spills out of what is left of Dwayne's cheeks, Peter checks his phone, swiping it, revealing a text message from Haven.

It says, "Tell sheriff Roy Hutchinson that you are my uncle and that I'll explain everything when I see you."

"Well that's not concerning in the least," Peter says to himself.

Peter stops and takes another moment to breathe in the fresh country air. To observe the night time sky, dusk having just fallen. Peter loves the darkness. So peaceful. So wonderful. Serene. Some would say he has nyctophilia. Others say scopophilia, others meaning the ones who don't understand his fascination with ethnopornography. The sexual encounters and collisions in colonial Mesoamerica.

Alternative sexualities.

Sodomitical subcultures.

Gas mask fetishes.

Queer Nahuatl.

Bodily transgression.

Pleasures of the flesh.

Sanguinarians.

Sex and Conquest.

Sacred pain.

***

"Are you ready yet?" Jack asks.

"Almost," Haven replies.

Haven sprays some Tsubaki blossom perfume on her wrists and rubs them together before touching her neck. A Japanese secret.

"Ok, ready."

Haven opens the powder room door and Jack's mouth drops. She is wearing a skin tight red dress that stops just below mid thigh. Tantalizing. Exotic. Petal-soft. Her luscious breasts barely being held in by the fabric, a silver gemstone necklace with four black onyx is gracefully draped mid v-neck. Sultry. Tempting. Her legs are bare and shaven, her feet encased in sleek black combat boots with grey and white puffy fur tops. Her black hair is slightly combed over her left eye and hanging shoulder length, exposing a small tattoo on the right side of her neck—a symbol in black ink—the Japanese kanji for strength. Lavish. Seductive. Her sexy red dress is lined with a thin black belt resting subtly on her waistline. Silky perfection.

Her eyes lined black—the art of mascara. A brush for every look. Lacquer liner. Infallible. Plumper. Fuller. Voluminous.

"Wow, you are breathtaking."

Bold, matte, smoky, shaped and styled. The architecture of face.

"I'm not wearing any panties," she says.

Jack's nether regions start to fill with blood. Harden.

"Don't tempt me, we can stay in too."

Submission is everything.

"There is plenty of time for that...tonight we celebrate our union...and my conquest. Besides, uncle Peter will be here soon. You're gonna love him. Then, after dinner, if you're lucky, I'll let you have desert."

"If I'm lucky huh?" Jack laughs and grabs his black leather jacket. It has the eye of Horus embroidered on the back of it.

His hair is clean and styled, his face shaven.

Jack throws his arm around Haven, kisses her on the top of her head and says that he can't wait to meet her uncle and that he doesn't need luck because he makes his own.

13

"O death, where is thy sting? O grave, where is thy victory?"

-1 Corinthians 15:55-57 (KJV)

Devin kicks in the basement window of Lakeness Funeral Home & Crematory, an old two story with an eggshell white facade. There are three large granite pillars decorating the edifice, the kind you only see on old mansions resting atop thousand acre southern plantations — the kinds that had black slaves prior to emancipation. The basement sits just under a rustic yet modern brick addition, beneath the funeral parlor where services are held and loved ones are grieved for. Wails heard in unison, wrinkled hands emptying Kleenex boxes. Drying eyes and dabbing sniffling noses.

The "American" way of death.

The glass shatters upon impact and Devin quickly kicks at the loose shards, hoping that no one sees him breaking in under the bright, yard spot lights. There are over ten of them, illuminating the outside of the building under the otherwise cloudy night sky. The glare from the fresh, powdery snow augments their luminance. Devin crawls through the basement window on his belly and falls into the darkness below. Some snow also makes its way in, scattering lightly, floating, creating tiny glistening specks before melting away on the pickle green tile floor. White grout lines. Freshly polished.

Devin is careful not to make much noise, even though he knows no one else is in the building. *What better place to hide than with the dead?* he thinks. *No one will find me here* he tells himself. The glow from the broken window is just strong enough to allow Devin to find the light switch. He flicks it upwards. It is clear that this is no ordinary basement — this is a place where bodies are embalmed.

Preserved.

Decorated.

Cared for.

The beautification of the dead.

Some argue that the therapeutic value of funeralization starts with a properly prepared and presentable body. But what is aesthetically pleasing? What makes for a stylish sendoff? A proper bon voyage? Whomever works here, in this godforsaken place, is a passionate mortician. The room is immaculately clean, organized, and everything is shelved and labeled. Nothing is out of place.

Curmudgeonly obsessive.

In the nineteenth century, coffin designers experimented with all types of materials — glass, cement, celluloid, papier-mâché, and India rubber. Rube Goldberg contraptions called "life signals" were also created, made from wires and bells, to alarm if the occupant in the coffin should accidentally be buried alive.

Mourning symbols have also ran the gamut — the skull and crossbones once being a widespread favorite.

Funerary extravagance in medieval England and colonial America saw elegant and elaborate mourning clothes — ornate vestments — as well as paid mourners and extravagant feasting for days. Funeral flowers did not become popular in America until sometime after the middle of the nineteenth century, which of course first took off in direct opposition to church leaders.

Until this time period family and close friends would attend to a body themselves, washing it and draping it in a winding sheet. They would order a coffin from the local carpenter and dig the grave with their own hands. Between death and burial, the body would be placed in the family parlor so that mourners could mourn and so that it — the corpse — could be monitored for signs of life. Embalming still hadn't come into style. It was primarily used during the summer, to preserve bodies during the sweltering heat, to forestall putrefaction, but profiteers would change that. As would the body count of the American Civil War and the growing need to preserve the dead during travel over long distances.

Today, embalming is primarily done for viewing purposes, so that strangers and loved ones can sate their morbid curiosity.

Prior to the discovery of formaldehyde, arsenic was one of the early chemicals commonly used for embalming, even though eventually it was found to be both hazardous and toxic.

Contaminating ground water.

In this room, in this godforsaken place, there is a large, steel mortuary table where corpses are laid in the supine anatomical position, their heads elevated by a head block. Their bodies are naked, their genitals are sometimes covered with a modesty cloth. The remains are disinfected and then massaged to relieve rigor mortis. The eyes are posed, the mouth sutured shut with a needle or adhesive. This is called "setting the features."

Modern embalming takes hours to complete, it involves special injections of embalming chemicals to displace blood and interstitial fluids. Drainage. Arterial embalming. Injected with a centrifugal pump. The embalmer continues to massage the body to break up circulatory clots and ensure proper distribution. After embalming, the dead body is rewashed and dried. This is followed by the application of moisturizing cream. Once dressed, cosmetics are applied, and baby powder is used to eliminate odor.

Corpses are displayed under pink colored lighting for a warmer looking complexion.

As Devin walks through the room, he knows that whoever works here is meticulous, earnest, and borderline obsessive compulsive. There are neatly packed glass cabinets filled with different colored chemicals, a prep arm for localized exhaust ventilation, boxes of blue sterile gloves, a coiled hose hanging from the ceiling, and glass jars filled with mysterious substances. There are rows upon rows of plastic containers filled with Introfiant arterial, Metasyn, SynCav, Juandofiant Basic, Metaflow, and Plasdopake. Frigid Cavity 55, water clot guard, perfect tone, tissue guard 32, Frigid Contact embalming spray, and a white bucket of Fulfill Autopsy Compound.

A Porti-Boy Mark IV Embalming Machine.

A Brute Magnum Hydraulic Embalming Table. Only $1897 plus shipping and handling.

Aron Alpha high strength bonding adhesive.

Velva post mortem massage cream.

A tissue dryer set and an incision spreader.

Devin advances, he heads for a large grey steel door, and opens it. It makes a swooshing sound, like when air is released and decompresses. The temperature in this room is considerably lower, like that of an ice box. As he steps in an automatic fluorescent light kicks on, unveiling a large, steel wall with what looks like little refrigerator doors lining it. Devin can see his breath, he knows exactly what this is—a holding room for the dead. This is where they store the bodies.

There are two dead bodies lying on steel tables, covered up to their chests in light, white linen. One is an elderly woman with purple lips and the other is a young man, maybe in his mid twenties. His skin is taut, his shoulders are broad and muscular. Devin moves in for a closer look.

"A damn shame this one," Devin says, "I bet you were all the rage."

Devin looks back at the door, as if to avoid spying eyes, and then lifts up the sheet to see just what the dead man is packing. His testicles are large and swollen, his pork sword is filled to the brim with blood—it is hard and long.

"Oh my...just gorgeous," Devin whispers.

Watchful, Devin puts his warm hands on the dead man's cold, buff upper body.

He runs his painted fingernails through his coarse black chest hair.

Devin slides his hands downward, trailing ever so gently across the dead man's abdomen, combing through his well groomed pubic hair and then firmly grasping his engorged member. Suddenly the corpse doesn't seem all that dead anymore, but he is. Stiff as a board. Devin kisses the tip of his cum gun and licks it.

He looks up at the dead man, stares into his emotionless face, and then deep throats his prick, jamming all eight inches down his throat hole — far enough that his wet lips just touch nuts. After a few minutes pass, Devin releases and spits all over the lifeless cock, massaging it enthusiastically, working up a thick lather, smearing it in saliva.

Devin then drops his pants, kicks off his underwear, and hops up on the table, straddling the lifeless body — just enough to squat down and thrust the now lubed up phallus in his rectum.

It feels incredible.

Breathtaking.

Spectacular.

Devin moans and sways, his legs spasm, as he grinds his pelvis on it — simultaneously jerking off.

It won't be long now.

One of the dead man's arms fall over the edge of the table as Devin bounces up and down on his dead dong. Devin tugs harder and faster on his piss weasel, banging the meat of his hand on his ball sack. He starts to sweat. Then, the rush comes, the endorphins release, and he grits his teeth as he busts all over the remains. Semen shoots forth, splattering the dead man right in the face. It fires across his left eye, down the side of his head, and drips off the table onto the floor.

Devin is no necrophiliac, just an opportunist.

He is a romantic, desiring a non-rejective partner.

He yearns for something real.

And in this desperate yet beautiful moment, he found what he is looking for.

Sex with the dead although rare, does happen. A morgue attendant from Ohio recently admitted to having intercourse with over one hundred dead women.

In Pennsylvania, a man was recently found guilty of videotaping himself sleeping with the corpse of his step daughter after shooting her in the back of the head.

In Los Angeles, a nurse was arrested for fornicating with a corpse at a hospital.

If you stimulate the sacral root nerve of a beating heart cadaver, oxygenating it, it is conceivably possible to bring a corpse to orgasm.

In Wisconsin, necrophilia is a class G felony.

14

The sign reads "Wautoma, population, 2,218."

In the distance Peter sees vehicles in the road — two police cars — blocking both lanes of traffic. There are two officers standing in front of the police cars, one of which is putting his hand up motioning for Peter to stop. Peter brings the car to a stand still and puts it in park. He rolls down his window as the officer, dressed in tan with brown stripes, approaches the driver's side.

"Sorry sir, but the road's closed. No through traffic," the officer says.

"Is Roy available?"

"Who wants to know?"

"Haven's uncle, Peter."

"One sec, I'll be right back."

The officer, sporting a crew cut — high and tight — with a neatly trimmed mustache walks over to deliberate with his partner who is holding a black twelve gauge. They speak for a moment and look back at Peter thrice before coming to a decision.

The officer walks back to the car and tells Peter, "Just wait a few minutes, I'll fetch Roy to come speak with you. Shut the vehicle off please and step out."

"I'm quite fine waiting in here," Peter says.

"I wasn't asking."

"Is there a problem officer?"

"Not yet, so I suggest not creating one."

Peter rolls his eyes and turns the key to off before stepping out. Meanwhile the other officer, also in tan with brown stripes, is talking in the radio attached to his shoulder. He says something about Roy, something about uncle Peter, and the voice in the radio says something about not harming him and that he will be there shortly — whoever he is.

"Would you mind coming up here and sitting on the bumper?" the officer asks.

"I don't suppose I have a choice now, do I?" Peter says.

"Nope."

About ten minutes pass before a black sedan pulls up with a bearded, grizzly fellow driving. He steps out and wastes no time with introductions.

"You're Peter Faxneld...you got some ID?"

"Yeah," Peter pulls out his wallet, fingers forth his driver's license and puts it into Roy's hands, "Roy I presume?"

"You got it bub and don't you forget it."

Roy takes a look at it and hands it back.

Peter notices Roy's ripped apart pollice with a dried black substance inlayed between the cracks.

"Uncle Peter it's a pleasure, Haven awaits. If you don't mind, I'll have one of the boys drive your car over, in the meantime you can ride with me."

"Well...I don't feel comfortable letting..."

Roy talks over him, "Don't worry about it, besides, this way we can get to know each other."

Roy pats Peter gently on the shoulder and motions toward the black sedan.

"Fantastic," Peter says under his breath. "Sure, why not...if you insist," Peter says faking a smile.

Roy grins and assures Peter that his car is in safe hands, that Haven is only a few minutes away at the Pfitzer hotel, and that everyone is thrilled to see him.

The interior of Roy's car smells like a teenager's bedroom.

Incense.

Vape.

Perfume.

"If you don't mind me asking, what's the deal with all the security?"

Roy takes a sip of whatever is in his travel mug and says, "The town is on lockdown due to an escaped felon...you know...got to look out for the people...keep everyone safe."

Roy winks and puts both hands on the wheel.

Ten and two.

"I see. And what exactly does Haven have to do with it? She's no police officer."

"Look Mr. Faxneld, you'll just have to talk to her. She'll tell you...you'll see."

The wind picks up outside, tree branches sway and swoon, it starts to snow.

"You warm enough?" Roy asks.

"Yes, thank you."

"Yeah, it's suppose to snow tonight. Reports on the news say up to a foot."

Peter's eyes scan the vacant streets, the empty parking lots, the closed stores. It doesn't take long for him to realize that something isn't right here, in this beloved little village, this horrid township, this godforsaken place, but given the circumstances, the best thing to do is play along.

The car pulls into the front of the hotel. There are two large men standing in front under the deep red awning, both trying not to look armed and dangerous, but failing miserably at it.

The snow really starts to come down, the wind gusts wildly. Peter opens the door and thanks Roy for the ride. Roy tells him what a pleasure it has been meeting him and that he looks forward to seeing him again soon.

Peter pulls up the collar on his jacket to cover his ears and dashes toward the revolving entrance door. The gleaming foyer. The man on the right motions toward the vestibule and says, "Right this way Mr. Faxneld."

The lobby is quiet and before Peter can say anything he sees her—Haven—rushing toward him from the hall.

"Uncle Peter!" she shouts as she jumps into his arms and offers the tightest of hugs.

Speechless.

Shocked.

Terrified.

Suspicious.

Peter whispers in her ear, "Haven my dear, how can this be?"

Without leaving his arms she whispers back, "Does it matter? I'm alive, isn't that all that counts?"

Peter grabs her by the waist, creating some space, then looks her in the eyes and says, "You are alive, but...how matters."

Haven bites her lip softly and quickly diverts the conversation. She smiles and turns toward Jack behind her. "Uncle Peter, meet Jack Warren."

Haven steps to the side and Peter and Jack shake hands. A firm handshake, not limp wristed, nor awkward.

"Jack Warren? That name sounds familiar," Peter says.

"I get that a lot," Jack says.

"You're not the same Jack who went missing a few months back...you know the bloke who was all over the news?"

"Nah, must have me confused with someone else...like I said...I just have one of those faces."

Haven grabs Peter's hand and says, "Anyway, let's go...dinner is waiting."

"Indeed, I'm starving. I haven't eaten since this morning," Peter says.

"Great!" Jack says.

Peter's eyes continue to scan the hotel, its deep, rich vibrant colors, its vintage gilded archways, its handcrafted hardwood furniture with soft velvet cushions, and its peculiar security detail.

The trio enters a large dining room with early 19th century Persian rugs strewn about on the floor. Silver gilded candle sticks, decadent art, and low lighting. Silver chalices, lotus folded napkins, Wedgewood Chinoiserie Gilt decorated octagonal dessert plates, Royal Worchester Green dinner plates, exquisite early Victorian plate flatware.

As they sit down, Peter immediately notices the unusual size of the waiter. He stands at, what can only be, seven feet tall. An enormous fellow. A behemoth of a man. He doesn't talk, not a word. He starts pouring drinks into the silver chalices. He pours what looks like red wine into Peter's and Jack's, but then pours something else, something thicker and steaming, into Haven's.

Virgin menstrual blood.

Jack pays it no attention, which draws Peter's attention.

"So Peter, tell me about your work. Haven tells me you are an anthropologist?" Jack says while politely folding his napkin on his lap.

"Yes," Peter clears his throat, "My fieldwork, as I'm sure you already know, has to do with shamanism in South America."

The behemoth brings out a gourmet appetizer—carpaccio.

Raw meat served with lemon, olive oil, and parmesan cheese.

"Shamanism huh? You mean those hippies who take hallucinogenic drugs and go on spirit journeys?"

Haven gives Jack the evil eye.

Peter laughs and says, "No, that sort of thing is reserved for bloody Americans and their fatuous neo-shamanism. When I say shamanism, what I really mean is a holistic religious practice that takes place in a very remote region of Amazonia that involves both curing and killing. And as Haven is well aware of...raising the dead."

Haven smirks but their conversation is interrupted briefly as the main course is served. The behemoth pushes out a cart with three steaming soup plates on it. In the center is a large steel domed plate with a finial mirror polish. The behemoth dishes out the hot soup bowls and sets the large dome in the center of the dark hardwood, antique banquet table, directly under the Baltic crystal chandelier with its brass drip pan. He smiles and steps off to the side, arms crossed, visibly guarding the door.

Just as Haven begins to speak, Peter interrupts. He has had enough of playing along.

"Alright Haven, out with the truth here huh? You didn't bring me here to play games — nor will I — I know something dark was done here to bring you back from the dead...and from the looks of it...you've taken over this entire bloody town too. So what was it, necromancy?"

Tezcatlipoca.

Mictlantecuhtli.

Machetaurie.

Dumbala.

The behemoth by the door uncrosses his arms and steps forward. Haven thrusts her hand out and abruptly tells him no.

"My father was so Amerindian, he never went to school, but he could kill and resurrect you in one day," Haven says.

"Resurrection does not come without its price my dear," Peter says.

"The burden is mine not yours to bear, both its inherent bliss and its agony and pain. Does it not matter more that I'm alive?"

"But at what cost? And what you've done here, to this town...to these people...this is beyond the scope of imagination."

"Is it really?" Haven stands up and walks over to the dome plate, she grabs the handle, "Is this beyond the scope of your precious imagination?"

The dome cover makes a crashing sound as it hits the floor violently. Unveiled beneath it, now centerpiece — center stage — is a cooked human head and arms, fingers charred, eyes boiled white, with a butter glaze.

"Long pig, is a delicacy in these parts!" Haven shouts.

"The gods may have given you life, but they forever hunger...have you forgotten what a predatory cosmos it is that you have invoked?" Peter asks.

"The gods speak through me now. I am immortal. I am their agent. And the world will soon tremble at the sound of my name. Those who get in my way...will be devoured!" Haven slams her fist into the table spilling menstrual blood soup everywhere.

Peter stands up. "Your rage is dangerous, the divine hunger of the gods can never be sated. I won't stand for this! This magic is not yours to use. It does not belong to you! What you have done here must be undone!"

"I thought you, of all people, would understand," Haven says.

"Understand? I love you so very much girl, but this is too far. What you have done here, to these people, it's not right...don't you see this?"

Jack, having well enough of the argument, takes a drink of his wine, sets it down softly onto the table, stands up, pulls out his Ruger 9mm and shoots Peter in the head. Blood and brains splatter out the exit wound in the back of his skull and paint the wall red behind him. Peter's body falls lifeless to the floor.

Haven screams wildly.

"Now he understands," Jack says.

15

Blood Magic. Many have argued that menstrual blood taboos — seclusion, rules for conduct and sex — are universal throughout human culture.

Symbolic pollution.

Dangerous.

Defiling.

The malevolence of menstrual discharge.

Menstrual taboos, rather than protecting society from a universal ubiquitous feminine evil, instead protect the creative spirituality of menstruous, not monstrous, women.

Menstruation is the potent positive spiritual force that all women inherently contain and this is why Haven desires it.

She prefers it.

Collects it.

Stores it.

Hoards it.

Some have suggested, incorrectly, that menstruating women can wither plants, turn wine, and spoil pickles.

The Imperial Romans used menstruation as a panacea, to treat a wide variety of medical conditions such as; gout, goiter, hemorrhages, inflammations of the salivary glands, erysipelas, furuncles, puerperal fever, hydrophobia, worms, and headache.

Menstrual remedies have been used in many cultures for centuries, for ailments such as epilepsy to infant's eye diseases.

Menstrual blood has also been utilized as a wound healer—dressing open sores and wounds.

Subcutaneous injections of menstrual blood was used to treat liver-bile syndrome.

The menstrual blood of virgins was preferred over all others for agricultural and medical applications.

Haven uses it to commune with the divine.

Blood and tobacco.

These ingredients are central to Amazonian shamanism.

Cosmology.

***

Judas wakes up to a loud bang. The noise is followed by Reagen crawling around on the scummy floor in front of her. There is copious amounts of fluid spewing out from between her legs—the semen of the undead. She is whimpering.

"Are you ok girl?" Judas asks.

"I don't know, I don't feel well. I feel sick to my stomach."

Reagen scoots her butt and back against the wall and rests her elbows on her knees to hold her head.

"What the fuck did they do to me?" Reagen asks.

"Besides the rape, you mean?"

Reagen puts her hands on her stomach and presses, pushing out a half gallon of thick, white liquid. It oozes out from between her legs, from her swollen vagina. It smells horrid. Like a septic tank backup.

"You on birth control, darling?"

"No, why?"

"Because, well, how do I put this? All that mess...yeah, that's monster cum."

"I'm going to throw up," Reagen says before blowing chunks onto the floor.

Judas walks over and holds Reagen's soft, beautiful red hair back as she continues to vomit into the pool of jizz beneath her feet. It squishes between Judas' toes, but it takes more than that to gross her out.

"I'm cold," Reagen says.

Judas gently places the back of her hand on Reagen's forehead. "You're burning up. Come on girl, you need to rest."

Judas helps Reagen over to the other side of the room, onto a green cot and away from the throw up and zombie spunk.

"Why do you...call yourself Judas?" Reagen asks.

"I don't, other people do."

"How come?"

"It's a long story, you just rest girl."

"Will you tell me later?"

"If you promise to get some sleep, I will."

"Pinky swear?" Reagen holds up her pinky, awaiting Judas' response.

"Yeah...sure...pinky swear," Judas says while interlocking her finger with Reagen's.

Reagen smiles and closes her eyes.

Judas sits back and bites her lip, she knows she is in for a long night.

***

Blood.

The warm, thick, sticky substance that all humans contain within their bodies.

Some blood is clean and some is infected with disease — hepatitis C and HIV.

Some desire its taste — salty and sweet.

Some desire to see it flow from their enemies — to the victor goes the spoils.

And some faint at the sight of it — a breathtaking reminder that one day we all too will die.

Human mortality.

To some blood is polluting, to others it is sacred.

To the gods of Amazonia, human blood is vital, it sustains the cosmos. It keeps order. Thus, to invoke their power, to bring back the dead using Amerindian methods, requires human sacrifice.

Blood sucking witchcraft.

The way of the Hoarotu.

Through blood, Haven seeks to commune with Hoebo the Ancient One.

It is said that he has existed since the universe began. Then, when the Lord of Death decreed that spiritual ones were to incarnate into mortal bodies, Hoebo manifested as the Red Macaw. It is said that Hoebo and his parrot people drink human blood from a thirty foot canoe in the sky and feast on human flesh from well stocked larders. The blood canoe, like Hoebo's house and furniture, is said to be made of human bones. Hoebo's sacred domain is said to reek like putrefaction, a gagging rot, and the ground is saturated with coagulated blood. It is also said that in his sky palace one will find wind instruments of human tibias and skulls, and partakers in the banquets are attired in their feather coats adorned with necklaces of human costal bone.

Hoebo's presence is said to bring about complete immobility as his great wings pass over you and his razor sharp beak inspects your flesh — as it sniffs your offering.

Haven bends over the corpse of Peter and sticks a thick cane straw into his flesh. She begins to suck repeatedly, with all her might, cheeks indented, until blood makes its way up into the cane straw and passed her lips.

The gods demand sacrifice.

Haven's eyes water as she continues to slurp Peter's blood.

She knows full well what she is doing and that Peter will be gone forever once she has finished the ritual.

After emptying the rest of Peter's blood into a wooden trough, resembling Hoebo's canoe, Haven carefully butchers Peter's corpse and eats it, leaving only the heart and liver for the supreme Macaw.

Peter's words still echo through her head — the divine hunger of the gods can never be sated.

Haven wipes her red stained hands on her dress and peers out the window upon the well lit city streets. She puts one bloody hand on the glass and says, "It is not the hunger of the gods that they will fear, for it is my thirst that is truly unquenchable."

16

"...the Guaja describe a kind of magical contagion that occurs when the jaguar is eaten. It has the ability to provide those who consume it with strength and is the only food believed to have the ability to confer its properties by being eaten."

--Loretta Cormier

Haven is suddenly struck with searing pain. A rush of ferocious energy. She drops to her knees as her bloody hand slides down the glass of the window, leaving behind a long red streak. The burn is boiling in the pit of her stomach, she clenches her fists and thrashes them against the wall, against the air conditioner, denting it.

A throbbing sensation.

Stinging.

Cramps.

Black ooze streams out of her nostrils, her eyes, and down her cheeks into her lap.

Pooling.

Popping.

Haven's eyes roll back to white, as does the skin on her knuckles from being clenched tight. She sees flashes of white, then blurry images, then a myriad of colors. The pain sweeps upward and burrows deep into her temples.

Excruciating.

Intense.

Agonizing.

It unmakes her world.

The colors swirl and spin until she is completely overcome by visions.

Or nightmares.

Or dreams.

Thick black sludge pours out of her open mouth.

Bubbling.

Gurgling.

Spitting.

She is unconscious, but still kneeling.

Like a samurai in feudal Japan before committing seppuku.

In seiza.

In her vision, or dream, or nightmare, she sees Jack running.

She sees a couple with a young boy.

Screaming.

The boy has a distinctive black mark on his arm.

The couple too is running, clutching the boy, out of breath, in a thick forest of towering evergreens.

They are yelling something. Flailing their arms. Words like daggers, piercing Haven's ears.

Haven looks up, the world beyond the forest is on fire.

Rotten.

Something smells pungent. Like burning oil. Like burning rubber.

The ground is soaked in blood.

Haven looks back and now there are three mutilated bodies lying faceless on the ground. Squirting blood. Dismembered. Hacked. Shredded. Ripped apart.

A large murder of crows blackens the daytime sky and swirls like bats around a male figure on his knees beneath an old white oak tree that is bleeding black curare. He too, like Haven, is kneeling like a samurai in feudal Japan. In seiza. Thick black ooze seeps out from the tree's bark.

Heat lightning.

Thunder.

Haven looks closer to see that the kneeling man is Jack. He is holding something...a stone knife.

Haven peers deeper, concentrates harder, in order to see that Jack is also holding the boy bearing the black mark. Jack looks up at Haven as if he can see her spying on them and whispers the word Kaikuci'ima.

Suddenly Haven is thrust from the vision, or dream, or nightmare by a piercing roar that seems to be coming from Jack. His teeth are shaped like a cat. Large canines. A jaguar.

Haven sees a flash of bright red, then white, then her sight goes blurry as her body falls to the ground, now limber and unconscious.

***

Jessica Mills is still fashionably anorexic, still bleach blonde, and still enjoys e-cigarettes—vaping. She no longer answers to Tom and Darla, she only answers to Haven, her maker.

The room is sparsely lit, candles burn, flicker, and sway as Jessica peers into an elongated mirror hanging on an old rusty nail—held up by wire. She is scrying. She tries her best not to blink. In the foreground the reflection is pale and increasingly fuzzy, the background is darkness.

The last time Jessica had spent this much time in front of a mirror was almost a year ago. When she was human. She was taking selfies. Posting them to Snapchat. Instagram. Facebook. She was so focused on how she looked—in the foreground—that she, like most women, forgot to acknowledge the clutter in the background. The grime. The filth. The hanging undergarments, the used feminine products, and the boxes of junk. Even the mirror itself was disgusting—it had toothpaste streaks, white crusty fluid from popped zits, and specks of hardened tartar from dental floss.

Still, guys would like her social media posts and comment on how beautiful she was. Yet, there were some who paid attention to the details, who, no matter how much cleavage she showed, or how tight her ass seemed, saw through the facade. They saw how dirty she was, how lazy she was, and how she cared more about her looks than cleaning up the pigsty she called a bathroom. Those who noticed would quickly realize why none of her relationships lasted more than a month or two. It was the toothpaste streaks in the mirror that revealed her true nature.

This mirror, not unlike her old bathroom mirror, also reflects more than mere images. After ten minutes, she no longer sees herself or the darkness around her. Then a large shadow rises in the oval frame and she hears a low voice call her name.

"Jessica."

Her eyelids flutter gently as she realizes that the voice is one she recognizes—it is the behemoth.

"Jessica, I'm sorry to disturb you but..."

Jessica turns around and her eyes gaze upon his enormous body. They sweep upward from his legs to his face—in both wonder and amazement.

She has been infatuated with him for months.

He is the man everyone fears.

Haven's enforcer.

And no one knows anything about him.

He too, was made by Haven, but she refuses to talk about him or his past to anyone, and not for lack of trying. Jessica has tried desperately to figure him out, to seduce him, to get his attention—to no avail.

She calls him "hun" and "babe."

He calls her "Jessica," or sometimes "Ms. Mills."

"What can I do for you babe?" she asks.

"Haven would like to see you, at your convenience of course," he says.

Jessica stands up, flicks her hair over her shoulder, and pretends to stumble and fall so he'll catch her.

He does.

The behemoth quickly snatches her up with his bulging arms.

His giant hands place her upright and he tells her that whenever she is ready he will be waiting outside her door to escort her downstairs. Jessica tells him thank you and that she'll only be a few moments.

He turns and walks away.

She smells the air, specifically his musk, and admires his tight backside—his glutes, his legs, and broad shoulders—as they disappear into the darkness of the hallway.

"Damn what a fine man," she says under her breath.

***

Reagen is sweating profusely, she is sopping wet. Her fever is out of control. Her stomach engorged. Huge. Ready to pop. Like a blister. Her heartbeat racing. Frightened. She is gasping in pain. Uncomfortable. Her abdomen is growing an inch per half hour. The rest of her body is thinning, her once full cheeks are now sunken, and her limbs are skin and bone.

Her hair is falling out.

Her nails are turning white.

Her lips are purple and cold.

Her eyes are bloodshot.

Judas looks on in horror as something inside Reagen's stomach starts to move, starts to wiggle, and pushes up on the skin from the inside.

There is something growing inside Reagen and it desperately wants out.

Reagen starts to scream maniacally, wail and moan, Judas backs away in fear.

"Help me!" Reagen yells, "There's something fucking in me! Help!"

Suddenly, the door to the room is thrown open and the man with the Stinger basketball tee enters. He shouts, "Shut the fuck up, bitch!"

"Help me...please," Reagen pleads. She begs.

"I'll help you alright," he says, grabbing Reagen by the arms and yanking her off the cot onto the floor—slamming her on her tail bone.

"Get your fucking hands off her!" Judas yells and steps forward as if to attack him.

The Stinger quickly pulls out his black pistol and points it at Judas' face. "Don't think so cunt," he says, "Get the fuck back."

Judas steps back, Reagen lets out a high pitched howl as two small tentacles shoot out of her vagina and pierce the wall in front of her. The discharge is like syrup. Thick and sticky and clear.

"I said back, bitch!" The Stinger motions for Judas to step further back as he snatches Reagen by the wrist and starts to drag her out the door.

The thing inside Reagen starts to chirp and snarl — make hissing noises. Then suddenly, her pussy is torn apart, ripped from anus to belly button as the wretched thing is born. Reagen goes into shock and passes out. The wretched thing wraps its tentacles around Reagen's torso and squeezes tight, pulling itself out and up onto her breasts. It has human legs, a human head, and tentacles for arms. It wraps its tentacles around her throat, sinking its spikes deep into her neck ferociously. Blood is everywhere, spurting on everyone and everything. Like a yard sprinkler just went off.

The wretched thing continues to eat Reagen as the Stinger drags them both out the door, slamming it shut behind him.

He forgets to lock it on the way out.

17

Escape. Judas wastes no time, she grabs the door handle, turns it clockwise, looks both ways for traffic, and makes a break for it into the hall. She runs as fast as she can; she doesn't know where she is going, but she knows she has to find a way out of this godforsaken place. She ignores the terrifying noises from behind all of the many doors in the hallway. Now she knows exactly what they are — the birthing of monsters.

There is a short stairwell at the end of the hall leading upwards, she quickly ducks to the side, to the wall, just as someone, likely a guard, passes the corridor. Another guard is posted at the top of the stairs — to get away she will have to get through him. She scours the surface area of the hall for anything she can utilize as a weapon. There is a jagged piece of wood jutting out from an exposed board, it is near nine inches long. "That will work," she says as she grabs it, tears it loose, and then holds it like a dagger — point down.

Judas creeps, she sneaks up the stairs quietly. The man at the top guarding the stairwell is oblivious to her, he has earphones in, he is jamming rap music.

Judas grabs his shoulder and sticks the jagged wood into the side of his neck. Blood gushes forth as she thrusts him down the stairs backwards. He tumbles and rolls, she doesn't bother to finish him, she keeps going. She sprints down another hall and trips on a crease in the carpet, she fumbles and gets up. Then suddenly, without warning, a door opens and the Stinger steps out. He isn't paying attention at first, but within moments they make eye contact. Judas eyes the door adjacent to her as he pulls his pistol. She lunges for it, yanks the handle, and opens it, just narrowly escaping being shot.

Judas slams the door, turns the lock on the inside, and whips around. The Stinger goes berserk, he starts shouting and firing his weapon. She ducks as bullets fly through the door and the wall just above her head. One of the bullets hits another man in the head, slicing through the side of his face and tearing into his brain as he sits up out of bed, startled by the commotion.

Judas had broken into his bedroom, but lucky for her he caught a stray round.

The Stinger empties his clip, all fifteen rounds.

Aware of this, thanks to Jack, Judas stands up and looks out the bedroom window. There is nothing but large evergreen trees outside. One of which is close enough to the building to jump to. She tries the window, but it is locked. She grabs a nearby wooden chair and throws it, shattering the glass. The Stinger is twisting the door handle and kicking at it now. *It won't be long before he gets inside* she thinks.

She has to move fast.

Judas, still naked, snatches up a pile of clothes from the floor, tosses it out the window, and jumps. She catches thick, sappy pine branches and crawls her way down to the snowy ground below. Barefoot in snow.

She picks up what clothes she can gather and runs away, as swift as she is able.

Freezing.

Nipples hard.

Adrenaline pumping.

Shivering.

Wet.

The Stinger boots the door, busting it open, splintering the wood around the latch. He notices that Judas is gone, that she got away, and sighs. He knows the consequence of failure like this — death.

Haven would serve him up to the behemoth.

Rather than face such a gruesome fate, and now out of bullets, the Stinger grabs a large piece of broken glass from the window and slices his own throat.

Tears stream down his face as he feels the glass glide across his skin and slice through his jugular.

He chokes, blood spills and stains his faded Stinger basketball tee as he crumbles to the floor and bleeds out.

Now there are only three has-been Stinger basketball players left.

***

There are maroon, plush towels draping the seats with gold letters that say "Reserved." There are beige, corduroy chairs with brass screws, a grey empty casket with a fluffy white pillow and shiny silver handles. There is a small brown crucifix made from stained wood. Devin Sanders is sitting quietly in the room where they hold the funeral services.

Being here reminds him of his grandmother's funeral. It was held here many years ago.

He remembers Somewhere Over The Rainbow and Happy Trails being played over the loud speakers. He remembers the sobbing, the community tissues being passed, the hands on faces — on backs, patting gently. He remembers the bitter thoughts about inheritance and the snide comments — how he didn't do enough, and how he was the running joke of the family. He'll never forget the fatuous eulogy that emphasized love in a room so obviously full of hate.

These thoughts bring tears to his eyes.

He loved his grandmother, but she too never understood his homosexuality.

Even the family that claimed they "didn't care" and "supported" him in his life choices, still acted offish when he was around.

Homophobic.

Conservative Christian.

Some would even have the nerve to tell him about special "classes" that he could take to "cure" being gay, like it was a simple choice or disease. Like it was something that he could just undo on a whim, like it was a sexual preference that he could just make go away. They told Devin that he needed to be honest about his sin, that being queer is evil, that it is wicked, and that he needed to imagine himself as "broken."

Their Christianity got in the way of their ability to accept him for who he is.

They called it, "the glory of God."

He called it, "fucking stupid."

They told him that his being femme was in response to being wounded.

They said he could reverse it through therapy.

He said they were the ones who needed psychological evaluations, not him.

His father refused to accept that he was attracted to men. It was because he thought that his son's being gay directly reflected upon what kind of man he was. In his own mind, it made him question his own masculinity, his own heterosexuality.

So he made Devin suffer. He even started abusing him.

Physically.

Mentally.

Emotionally.

Devin turned to drugs to escape his father's criticism, the ridicule, and the leather belt.

Ecstasy.

Pain killers.

Alcohol.

Devin spent his entire youth in and out of treatment facilities and juvenile detention centers.

He was sent to Rawhide Boys Ranch, it was supposed to reshape his life.

After his grandmother's death, he quit talking to all of them.

After he turned eighteen.

He moved out.

He no longer spoke to his parents, siblings, aunts, uncles, or cousins.

It was if they were all dead.

Estrangement.

There is a part of Devin that hopes that they are all dead.

There is a part of Devin that misses them.

There is also a part of him that wishes they all would have just accepted him for who he was.

And there is a part of him that is too far gone to care anymore.

Indifference.

Antipathy.

Misanthropic.

The dearth of his empathy.

Emotional Flatline.

Devin scours the funeral home for supplies. He checks all its cupboards, closets, and rooms. There is enough food in the pantry to last a few months, even if the power goes out. There are shelves of soup cans, canned vegetables, fruits, and Spaghettios.

If the United States of America lost power, if the electricity never came back on, it would only be weeks before men would force their wives, girlfriends, mothers, grandmothers, daughters, and sisters into prostitution for cans of Spaghettios.

Whoever lived here was also a "prepper." Someone who takes self reliance seriously. Both a mortician and a survivalist.

This leads Devin to wonder, *where is this person?* How could someone so prepared not be here? Or are they here and he just doesn't know it?

Devin continues to walk the funeral home, to explore every nook and cranny. Daylight is fading fast and he needs to be sure that there is no one else in the building with him. He climbs a large curved staircase, its posts are made from rich brown mahogany. Its carpet is sleek, a light shade of emerald green. He dawdles in the hall at the top, but then checks the rooms, the bathrooms, and the storage closets.

He hears a noise. Like feet walking on the ceiling above him. Creaking and squeaking. A grating sound. Rather than try to sneak up on whoever might be up there he calls out, "Hello, is anybody home?"

Then he hears another scraping sound, but no verbal reply.

Devin looks down the corridor and sees a string with a circle grommet hanging from the ceiling. *Of course* he thinks, *the attic!*

Devin hastily struts the hall and pulls the cord, unveiling an old open ceiling wood ladder. He says, "Hello, I'm coming up. I'm unarmed, please don't attack me...please."

He pulls the ladder down and steps onto it. He pauses a moment to listen, but hears nothing. Devin climbs the ladder, it makes loud clanging sounds under his weight, he slowly peeks his head up into the hole — again pleading with whomever might be up there to not hurt him. To his surprise there is no one. Just a bunch of old dusty boxes. Then, without warning, something tugs on his leg and sends him crashing to the ground. Devin's head bounces off the ladder and then the hardwood floor, knocking him out cold.

Minutes later, Devin awakes to the muzzle of a rifle in his face and a heavy set woman with short, stylish brown hair wearing a David Bowie tang top holding it.

"You picked the wrong funeral home, motherfucker," she says as she places her finger on the trigger.

18

Jessica Mills is led by the behemoth into room 321 of the Pfitzer hotel. The behemoth stands guard outside the door. Inside the room are Jack, Haven, Roy, and Darla. Roy and Darla have become inseparable. Attached at the hip.

"Sit down," Haven says, "I have called this meeting because of recent events. First off, Roy, have you found the boy yet?"

"No...not yet, but we are still searching," Roy says.

"What boy?" Jack asks.

"It doesn't matter, I now know who we are looking for," Haven says, "Find Kabe and Scarlet Abraham...they have the boy."

"Whoa, whoa...what boy? And why my sister? I think it's time you tell me what is going on," Jack says.

"God Jack, you're such a control freak," Jessica says.

Roy laughs.

Then Darla laughs.

Jack scowls at Darla then says, "Shut up Jessica, I wasn't talking to you."

"Ooooh, tough guy now...I'm shaking Jack...really. Let's not forget which one of us in the room is still human...still just a doggie treat," Jessica snickers.

"Shut up and sit down!" Haven orders, staring straight at Jessica.

Darla pulls out an emery board and starts to file her pink nails. She could care less.

"Roy, I suggest you check in on Robert Warren...I assume they are hiding out there. Or somewhere on his property," Haven says.

"No problem, I made him last month anyway," Roy says.

"Made my dad? You did what?" Jack asks while placing his hand on his pistol.

"Don't look at me, she told me to," Roy says pointing at Jessica.

Darla smirks.

Jessica rolls her eyes.

Roy swallows hard.

Jack looks at Haven, perplexed and upset.

"Babe, it had to be done...I was looking out for your own best interest. Besides, at that time we weren't together yet. I needed leverage," Haven says.

"You've got to be fucking kidding me," Jack says.

"Let's not forget that Jack killed Peter, shall we," Jessica says, "It's not like he's innocent or anything...tit for tat."

"Shut up!" Both Jack and Haven shout in unison.

Darla looks over at him.

Roy shakes his head.

Jessica smirks at Jack, knowing it will piss him off.

"Alright, enough everyone. Roy, go find them. Take Darla and two of the Stingers with you."

"You got it," Roy says "See you later Jack and good luck with her," he says pointing at Jessica.

Jessica flips Roy off as he and Darla exit the room.

"Why my sister? And what boy?" Jack asks Haven.

"I'll explain everything shortly, but let me finish here first, ok babe," Haven says.

"So...why am I here exactly?" Jessica asks.

"You mean other than being a constant annoyance?" Jack says.

"Suck a dick, Jack," Jessica says.

"Whip yours out and I might," Jack says laughing.

"Fucking hell, enough you two," Haven says, "Jessica I have something for you to do as well, so pay attention. There have been reports of some stragglers on the outskirts of town near the funeral home. Take a Stinger with you and check it out. If there is anyone left, kill them."

"A Stinger? Can't I take him too?" Jessica says pointing to the behemoth by the door.

The behemoth looks at Haven awaiting a command.

"Sure, I don't see why not," Haven says, "But don't think for one second that I don't know why you want him with you."

Jessica blushes.

Jack coughs.

"Ok, let's go hun," she says to the behemoth by the door. She smiles from ear to ear and gives Jack the bird as she exits the room.

"I don't know how you put up with her," Jack says, "Can I please kill her?"

"No sweetness, she's not worth your time. Besides...we have other, more important, things to discuss."

"Like the boy?"

"Indeed."

"I'm listening..." Jack says.

"Many years ago, uncle Peter told me about a vision he had. It was shortly after my first trip to the Amazon. Peter told me that after he went on a hunt with a Makushi shaman, they consumed raw jaguar meat in a ritual. After doing so he was struck with horrific visions, things he said would come to pass — prophecy. Peter said that a child would be born outside of South America, that it would carry a black mark on its arm, and that it would bring about the end of the world. He said the only way this would happen though is if the white man used Amerindian necromancy, it is the only way that Lord Jaguar would incarnate into human form and devour the whole of creation.

Lord Jaguar, Kaikuci'ima, would be sent as a punishment for the white man stealing Amerindian magic. My brother Joe brought me back from the dead, not knowing about this, and now the prophecy has been set into motion."

"That still doesn't explain why you are hunting down my family," Jack says.

"Like Peter, I too had a vision, after conducting a blood ritual with Peter's corpse. I saw the boy, it is your sister's, the one she had months ago. It was born with the mark. If we don't find it and kill it, the boy will destroy us all."

"So that's why you are building an army?"

"Indeed. If we don't kill the boy, if we let him grow to even childhood, we will need an army...and by then it might still be too late. The more the boy eats, the faster he will grow, so we must find him immediately."

"My sister and I have never been close, so of course I'll do anything to protect you. I love you so much."

"I know, our bond is eternal."

"So how do we kill him...the boy?"

"Kaikuci'ima has to be stabbed through the heart with an obsidian knife...like this one," Haven says, showing Jack a ten inch, black, serrated stone blade. "Once you pierce the heart, he should die. There is no other way to kill him."

19

"Wait!" Devin hollers, he begs,

thrusting his hand up as if to shield his face.

"Why should I, Devin?" the woman asks.

"How do you know my name?"

"Oh please, I'd recognize those sissy pigtails anywhere. Everyone knows who you are...and that you're nothin' but trouble."

The stocky woman has short brown spiky hair with blonde highlights. The sides are shaved close to the skin, with steps. She is wearing large black combat boots, black and blue camouflage pants, and a pentagram necklace.

Blue powder eye makeup.

Black fingerless gloves.

"Give me a good reason why I shouldn't kill you right now," she says.

"You need me."

"Ha! You're joking, right?"

"No seriously, I'm no threat to you...besides you're going to need help staying alive with those things out there."

"You broke into my house, why should I trust you?" she says sticking the muzzle of the firearm closer to Devin's face.

"Please...I'll prove myself...I swear. If I don't, then you can kill me."

The woman thinks about it for a second and then lowers the gun.

"Hmm. I tell you what...I'll let you live for now, but if you cross me Devin, I promise I'll shove this gun up your ass and pull the trigger."

She offers her hand to help Devin up and he takes it.

"And another thing...if I catch you fucking anymore of my clients in the basement...I'll feed you to those damned things out there," she says pointing toward the street.

***

"How much further? I'm horny," Darla says, kissing and sucking on Roy's neck as he tries to steer the wheel of his black sedan.

The two Stingers in the back avert their eyes and check the clips in their guns. One of them has a crossbow. The other has a rusty machete, the same one Haven used to hack up Bill.

"Alright already," Roy says pushing Darla off, "Focus, there will be plenty of time for that later."

"There better be, I'm so fucking wet. Must be the thrill of the hunt," she says.

"Two more miles, lock and load. Remember...shoot to kill. No exceptions," Roy says.

"Yes sir," the two Stingers in the back say in unison.

***

Zion is crying.

"Kabe, can you bring Zion in here? I'm sure he needs to eat again," Scarlet says.

"Sure, just give me a second," Kabe says while tossing wood into the fireplace and stoking it.

Kabe walks to the sink, washes his dirty hands, and then picks up Zion, carrying him into the bedroom by Scarlet.

"He just ate a half hour ago, you sure he is still hungry?" Kabe asks.

Scarlet takes her shirt off, unstraps her bra, tosses it to the foot of the bed and raises her arms up saying, "Just give him here."

Her tits are leaking milk.

Kabe puts Zion in her hands and she lays him across her chest. Zion fastens his mouth to her nipple — sucking and biting it aggressively — as if he were starving.

"Jeeze, you weren't kidding huh?" Kabe says.

Then suddenly, Kabe and Scarlet both hear a subtle bang outside. A car door being shut, then another, making simultaneous thuds.

Kabe and Scarlet look at each other, Kabe tells her to stay quiet and that he is going to check it out. He tells her that he'll be right back.

***

"Shhh! You idiots," Roy says closing his door quietly, "You two go around back. Darla and I will go to the front door. Kill anything that moves. And most of all...don't fuck up."

The two Stingers creep through the snow toward the back of the house while Roy and Darla make for the front door.

"Let me do the talking," Roy says.

"Ok," Darla says, placing her freshly filed fingernail on the doorbell. She presses it in.

***

Kabe looks out the kitchen window and sees four bodies get out of a black sedan, two of which head toward the back of the house. The other two make their way to the front door. "Roy Hutchinson," he says to himself as he grabs his shotgun and ducks down behind the wall to the side of the door.

DING DONG. The doorbell rings. DING DONG. It sounds again.

Roy tries the handle, but the door is locked.

"Robert, are you home?" Roy asks loudly.

Kabe stands and walks up to the door, he points the barrel of his shotgun at the head in the glass window next to it, and fires.

The shotgun blast blows Darla's face off, exploding her head like a watermelon being hit by a sledgehammer. Black goo splatters everywhere as do bits of glass.

"No!" Roy screams.

Kabe chambers his gun and fires again, this time right through the door and into Roy's gut, sending him flying backwards to the ground.

"That should buy me some time," Kabe says.

Darla's body is still standing, although now headless, her shoulders start to dislocate and her arms split apart revealing large tentacles with sharp spikes. She thrusts them through the shattered window toward Kabe. The tentacles flail violently, smashing and striking anything within range, ripping into the wall and floor.

Kabe chambers his shotgun and rushes to the back of the house. He hears a commotion in the spare bedroom across the hall from Scarlet and Zion, like glass being broken. He can only assume that it's the two men breaking in through the window.

Kabe steps to the side of the bedroom door and waits for whoever it is to open it so he can ambush them.

The first Stinger steps in through the broken window and then helps the second who follows behind. The first Stinger grabs the bedroom door knob and opens it, stepping through the threshold, unaware that Kabe is fixed and ready — lying in wait.

BLAM! Kabe fires the shotgun at point blank range, the Stinger's head explodes, sending blood and brains everywhere, splattering Kabe's face. He gets some pieces of the Stinger's skin in his mouth. The Stinger's lifeless body folds, his knees drop, and his rusty machete hits the ground. The second Stinger starts shooting through the wall, sending bits of wood and drywall into the air. Dust and debris. Kabe dives to the ground, dropping his shotgun as the Stinger empties his clip over top of him.

The gun makes a clicking sound. It is out of bullets. Kabe eyes the machete, picks it up, and rushes the Stinger before he can reload. With one quick chop, the machete gets stuck in the Stinger's skull — right between the eyes. The Stinger tries to lift the crossbow, but he has limited motor function.

His vision is blurry, his limbs go numb. He falls to his knees, then to his stomach and onto his face, which sends the machete further into his brain, abruptly killing him.

Blood pools.

There is a loud bang in the front of the house, the front door gets kicked in, Roy and Darla enter the living room. Roy has an oozing hole in his gut and Darla is still missing her head.

"Kabe you're going to suffer for what you did to Darla, I promise you that!" Roy yells, "Your death will be long and painful!"

Kabe snatches up the crossbow and shoots a bolt at Roy, just missing his head. It sticks into the wall behind him.

"You think your guns or a puny crossbow are going to kill us? You really are stupid, aren't you Kabe?" Roy says.

Kabe makes a break for the bedroom but slips on the blood in the hallway, the blood from the Stinger whose head he popped with the shotgun. Kabe hits his face upon impact, a tooth in his mouth busts off and he swallows it.

Kabe feels something wrap around his ankle and start dragging him toward the living room.

"Got you now Kabe," Roy says as Darla's tentacle reels Kabe in.

Kabe is disorientated, but comes to when he hears Scarlet start to scream from the bedroom.

The bedroom door opens and Zion walks out. Suddenly, he is a toddler, capable of standing on two feet.

Zion walks forward slowly, his body shaking violently, excess secretions dripping, dead baby skin falling off. Shed. His eyes turn blood red as he lifts his arm up and points in the direction of Darla and Roy.

Suddenly Darla cannot move, her body is locked, immotile.

Zion opens his right hand and makes a pulling motion.

Darla's body lifts off the ground, just inches off the floor, and starts to move toward Zion as if he is pulling her with an invisible rope.

"Darla!" Roy shouts.

Kabe can do nothing but watch as his son, now the size of a 12 month old toddler, pulls Darla toward him, toward Kabe in the hall. Kabe scoots out of the way as Darla passes him by, her toes are just barely skidding across the floorboards.

Roy also just stands in awe and watches, noticing the now thick, black mark on Zion's right arm. Triangular in shape.

Darla stops just shy of Zion's little hand and hangs suspended in the air, inches off the ground.

"Tum tum," Zion says while tapping his tummy.

Zion closes his hand into a fist and, within seconds, Darla's body starts to gyrate and ooze from every pore—from every orifice. The sludge drains out and pools under her feet as she is exsanguinated in front of everyone. Then, Zion opens his mouth, his eyes burn bright orange, and there is a swooshing sound as all of Darla's juices somehow defy gravity and start to stream upward into Zion's jaws. Like a vacuum. A vortex. He sucks her dry. Her tentacles deflate, nothing is left but skin and bone.

At this point, Roy doesn't stick around to see what happens next. He has seen enough. Roy takes off for the sedan, starts it, and guns the gas pedal.

Zion hungrily wolfs down Darla, then the two Stinger bodies as well. He drains all of their inner fluids, guzzles them voraciously, then turns to Kabe who is still lying in the hallway perplexed on the floor and says, "Tum tum."

20

"Roxy, call me Roxy," the woman says.

"Roxy with a y or an ie?" Devin asks.
"A 'y'."
"Ok."
"Hold on, did you see that?"

"See what?"

"There was a light, over there, from that window," Roxy says.

"So?"

"So it could be a car, better check it out."

Roxy and Devin creep over to the nearby window overlooking the street and see a car pull up and three bodies get out. One of them is huge—maybe seven feet tall.

"Oh shit," Devin says.

"What?"

"That big guy, I know him...he's one of those things."

All three bodies cross the street and head to the neighbor's house, the behemoth kicks in the front door. The house is pitch black. Then, gun shots light up the upstairs rooms. Pop. Pop. Pop. Then screams. Then silence.

Jessica and the Stinger are the first to exit the house, the behemoth follows behind dragging a man by his ankles. He is lifeless. The behemoth tosses him into the road and the three of them make their way back across the street and toward the funeral home.

"Oh fuck, they are coming...we have to hide," Roxy says.

"Hide where? Wouldn't it just be easier to run?" Devin asks.

"No, not in the snow...they'll just track us."

"Shit."

"Quick, you head back down to the basement, I'll go up to the attic," Roxy says.

Roxy climbs the attic ladder as Devin makes a break for the basement. Roxy pulls the ladder back into the ceiling just as the front door gets smashed in.

"Knock, knock, anybody home?" Jessica asks in a booming voice. "Split up and make sure no one is here," she says.

The behemoth and Jessica head upstairs as the Stinger starts searching all the downstairs rooms, closets, and doors.

"These places always used to creep me out," Jessica says.

The Stinger opens what he thinks is another closet door and finds the stairs to the basement. He flips the light switch and descends the staircase, pistol at the ready.

Devin is hiding under the table with the dead man who has the nice stiff erection. The one he climaxed on earlier. The white sheet covering the corpse is draped down and floor length, covering the sides. He hears feet descend the stairs and the Stinger say something about how there is nothing down here and that he's just wasting his goddamn time.

Meanwhile, upstairs Jessica skips around from room to room behind the behemoth as he clears them.

"No one here, huh?"

"Would seem that way," the behemoth says.

Roxy is careful not to make any noise. She sits patiently waiting in the corner for anyone to attempt coming up the ladder, her rifle is aimed and ready.

The Stinger opens the door to the holding room, it makes a swishing sound as he steps through it.

"Dead bodies, go figure," he says.

Devin is terrified.

The Stinger walks the room, his feet just inches from Devin hiding under the table, behind the white hanging sheet.

"Huh, what a waste of time," the Stinger says. He loses interest and opens the door to leave.

Then the arm of the dead man that Devin fucked falls over the side of the table making a subtle yet audible whoosh.

The Stinger's feet stop and turn around. He raises his pistol and says, "Come out, come out wherever you are."

Devin knows he's been made.

Betrayed by a dead man, by another lover.

Story of his life.

The Stinger's feet walk forward and stop right in front of the table with Devin under it.

"It's ok, I won't hurt you...whoever you are. Come on out. I'm here to help," the Stinger says as he quickly lifts up the white sheet and finds Devin crouched down underneath.

"Pigtails? Really?" the Stinger points the pistol at Devin and motions for him to come out from under the table.

"Ok, just...please don't hurt me," Devin pleads.

Devin crawls out and stands up.

"You picked the wrong place to hide pigtails, is there anyone else here with you?"

"Nah, just me."

"You wouldn't lie to me now, would you?"

"No, please...it's just me. I swear."

"Alright then, let's go...upstairs. And I suggest not trying anything...I won't hesitate to use this," the Stinger says holding up the gun.

Devin leads as the Stinger follows behind with his pistol aimed at the back of Devin's head. They exit the holding room and ascend the staircase toward the first floor.

"So what's with the pigtails anyway?"

"Oh honey, you wouldn't understand," Devin says.

The Stinger leads Devin into the foyer and yells loudly, "Got one!"

Roxy, upon hearing this, mouths the words "stupid motherfucker," and sighs.

Jessica and the behemoth make their way down to the vestibule to see who the Stinger caught.

"You," the behemoth says.

"What, you know him?" Jessica asks.

"Yeah, this one got away before."

"Looks like your luck just ran out pigtails," the Stinger says.

Jessica laughs and skips around Devin, inspecting him.

"You're different aren't you? I like your pigtails, don't listen to this moron...he has no fashion sense at all. Just look at him, still wearing his stupid high school basketball tee. What a has-been."

The Stinger just looks down, he doesn't dare utter a word. He knows better.

"That's right bitch, you don't say shit," Jessica says.

Upstairs, Roxy opens the attic ladder and quietly steps down onto the second floor. She tip toes and lies down, pointing her rifle at Jessica.

Roxy doesn't know any better.

"Look, you don't have to kill me you guys," Devin says.

"You're right we don't have to, but...it's kinda fun," Jessica says.

Roxy has five rounds in her clip and one in the chamber. 30/06.

"Devin, get down!" Roxy yells, firing her weapon.

She hits Jessica in the shoulder, knocking her to the ground.

She pulls the bolt back and reloads.

Devin leaps to the ground as the behemoth and the Stinger turn their attention to Roxy on the second floor.

Before the Stinger can shoot his pistol, Roxy blasts him in the throat — almost severing his head completely from his shoulders. Blood jets out, erupts, as he falls to the ground, dead. Roxy again pulls the bolt back and loads another round into the chamber.

The behemoth begins to ascend the staircase. His bones twist and turn, his shoulders dislocate, enormous slits in his wrists open and unveil thick, scaly tentacles with four inch spikes. Like armor. He roars and whips them, busting the railing in half.

Jessica gets up, cracks her neck and says, "Oh bitch I'm going to enjoy eating you." She pays Devin no attention as she too transforms and makes her way up the stairs toward Roxy.

Roxy fires her gun again and again, but to no avail.

The behemoth's left tentacle slams right through her chest and into the wall behind her, pinning her to it. The tentacle just misses her heart. Thick, red blood cascades out and streams down her legs as she tries to load her last bullet into the chamber.

"Devin! Get the fuck out of here!" she howls as Jessica ensnares her, squeezing tight, crushing her bones, flaying her fat, and shredding her muscles.

Roxy drops the gun and mutters, "Curse...you."

Devin gets up, grabs the pistol off the floor by the Stinger's corpse, runs out the door, and into the nearby forest.

Jessica, now stuffed, with her stomach full of Roxy, looks at the behemoth and says, "Goddamn, my hero."

SACRIFICE

Tarryl Janik

"Ultimate horror often paralyses memory in a
merciful way."
— H.P. Lovecraft, *The Rats in the Walls*

1

St. Peters is a towering gothic cathedral in the center of town. Catholic. A historic, magnificent building. Granite. Brick. Large oak stained doors. The exterior is second only to its majestic interior. Enormous stained glass windows. Myriad colors. Saints. Angels. Apostles. The pews are dark cherry, the carpet is patterned vermillion, apart from the center aisle. The smell is lemon pine. Fresh.

Father Reynolds has been holed up in the basement for months.

Sweaty. Stinking. Soiled. His hair is greasy, his nails are untrimmed. Long.

Unshaven. Sleeping on a cot.

He eats canned food.

Pickles.

Sardines. Scraps.

He drinks cheap boxed red wine.

He munches on Broadman Church Communion White Wafers.

They have a cross design.

The Lord's Supper.

A box of one thousand.

If used, best by next August.

Unleavened.

Plain.

Sacrilegious survival.

He stopped blessing the wafers months ago.

Father Reynolds only comes upstairs to use the latrine and pray for both guidance and mercy. He made no attempt to help save any of his flock from *The Ravening*. Instead, Father Reynolds locked the church and prayed that he would survive judgment day.

To him, *The Ravening* was the eschaton of his theology. It was revelation made flesh. He thought the Devil had taken over the earth and that it wouldn't be long before all of the followers of Jesus Christ (his Lord and savior) would be saved and transported to heaven. Thus, he hid behind the church's closed thick, oak doors and waited, patiently, for his savior to punish the wicked, to reward the righteous, and to strike Satan back into the abyss.

While Father Reynolds ate caviar, drank wine, and prayed, his flock was being rounded up, raped, and devoured.

Father Reynolds waited for days, expecting good to triumph over evil.

Then days became weeks.

Weeks became months.

And months became today.

Today, Father Reynolds would finally receive his divine answer.

Divine retribution.

Someone knocks on the thick, oak doors of the church thrice.

"Help me. Please," *someone* calls.

Father Reynolds quickly cowers behind the pew closest to the altar. He isn't quite sure if he heard a voice at the door or if it came from inside his own head.

Is he losing his mind?

Dementia?

Another knock.

"Please. I have nowhere else to go," *someone* says, "In the name of Jesus, help me please." *Someone* continues to beg.

Father Reynolds, recognizing that the voice he hears isn't part of his imagination, walks slowly down the chartreuse aisle rug. He steps quietly, tip-toeing toward the doors.

"Are you a servant of Christ?" Father Reynolds asks.

"Yes. Please help me," *someone* says.

The voice is feminine, which should not be conflated with comfort.

Father Reynolds unlocks the door on the left and slides back the large, black bolt. The door opens just a crack, wide enough for Father Reynolds to get a look outside.

"Come close my dear and let me have a look at you," Father Reynolds says.

"Alright. Thank Jesus you opened up," a woman says.

"Why is that?" Father Reynolds asks.

"Because I'm starving!" the woman shouts.

Father Reynolds is sent flying when the church door is suddenly kicked open with great force, sending him hurtling backwards onto his butt and skidding into the aisle. Rug burn. Sun bursts into the chamber, blinding him. Two figures, two tall shadows, stand in the doorway — one of which is at least seven feet tall.

"Who are you? How dare you defile the Lord's house!" Father Reynolds yells.

One of the two figures in the entranceway laughs while the other stands silent, arms folded. The quiet one is a gigantic fellow — a behemoth of a man. He is all muscle, and wearing a dark blue hooded sweatshirt. He doesn't speak at all.

"Defile the Lord's house? Well, then surely your God is really pissed off and I should beg for his forgiveness before he smites me," the woman says as she gets down on her knees and folds her hands in prayer. "Please Mr. Jesus, please don't smite me, pretty please...with sugar on top." The blonde haired woman smirks and spits on the aisle carpet, in the direction of Father Reynolds and hollers, "Fuck your God, it was Nietzsche who said it best...your God is dead! Grab him!"

The large man in the foyer quickly sets upon Father Reynolds, picks him up by his throat, and holds him high in the air while choking the life out of him. Father Reynolds kicks his feet and gags. He gasps for breath as The Behemoth's hands clamp down tighter on his neck, suffocating him. Squeezing hard. Knuckles white. Bruising skin. The sun beams from outside illuminate the altar and the large, granite crucifix hanging behind it. Father Reynolds' shadow lines up perfectly with the cross behind him. The woman and The Behemoth take notice.

Poetic.

"That gives me an idea," the woman says. She pulls out an electronic cigarette and takes a long deep puff — hazelnut coffee — and exhales. "But first we're going to have a little fun. Priest, you're going to tell me everything I want to know about Devin Sanders."

***

In the 1800's, anti-Catholicism in America was virulent. In 1834 a Charleston Massachusetts convent was burned. In 1839 there were riots in Baltimore. Protestants wrote "convent novels" or anti-Catholic literature that functioned as Protestant erotica. The premise being that Catholic priests were sexually depraved, that the celibacy of priesthood bred insatiable sex crazy mad men who were hell bent on ravaging the purity of innocent women in the confessional and especially devout nuns.

Nuns were hyper-sexualized while the priests were depicted as barbaric and abortion happy. The demonic offspring produced through the priest's rape of the convent women were said to be strangled and then tossed into lime abortion pits deep under the cathedral that would dissolve the infant's bones.

Nuns were supposedly confined in dungeons and starved to death. Gagged. Whipped. Hung upside down on crucifixes and the flesh was burnt off of their bodies. Only after being thoroughly physically mutilated, the nuns were then murdered and burnt in secret ovens.

Convent novels during this time period were more like Protestant pornography than reality. Catholic sexual deviance ran wild through the Protestant imagination, yet simultaneously these terrible tales reinforced society's norms and values. Thus, through the demonization of Catholic clergy, the Protestant worldview was maintained. This was the anti-Catholic sentiment in Antebellum America.

This is Father Reynolds' secret passion, his darkest sin. He loves reading these horrific tales from behind his locked office door with tissues and Vaseline in hand.

The violence done upon women excites him. The blood and the gore really work him up into a frenzy. The killing of infants arouses him—it gets him hard.

It's not their death in particular that gets him off, but how it's done that really gets his blood pumping. Which is followed by lots of sweating and grunting, then moaning and vigorous tugging.

Sinners behind closed doors, aren't we all.

2

Jack Warren is no longer an enigmatic drunk. He now chain smokes cigarettes—American Spirit—the teal box. Lights. No tar. Nor chemicals. Additive free. Organic. US-grown. Mild. The Surgeon General warns that smoking cigarettes causes lung cancer, heart disease, emphysema, and may complicate pregnancy. Jack is leaning against the brick exterior of the Pfitzer hotel—his back facing the wind—his chin length brown hair is a mess.

In the distance, Jack hears the roar of an engine and the squeal of tires—it is Roy's black sedan—before it appears, fish-tailing all over the slippery, snow covered road. The car comes to a screeching halt in front of the hotel. Roy kicks open the vehicle door and starts yelling *something* intelligible, he screams *something* about *someone* being dead.

"She's fucking dead!" Roy cries out as he stumbles and strides up the concrete steps toward Jack.

"What? Who?" Jack asks.

"Darla! They killed my baby!"

Roy is oozing dark viscous fluid from his guts.

"What the fuck happened?"

"Kabe blew her head off, shot me too…but then…I don't know…the kid ate her! Sucked her dry!"

Jack tosses his cigarette into the snow, it fizzes and goes out. Jack grabs Roy and orders the two men by the door to stand guard as they rush inside the hotel.

"My baby's gone! Oh Darla!" Roy yelps.

The two make their way into the vestibule.

"Get Haven! Now!" Jack yells at the concierge.

The man behind the desk frantically picks up a phone and dials.

Roy sits down on a plush velvet chair, black goo streams down between his legs and stains the fabric under his groin, like tar entwined in carpet fibers.

"Take a deep breath and tell me what happened," Jack says.

"We went over to your dad's place just like Haven said, but Kabe was ready for us. Waiting. He killed both the Stinger has-beens and shot-gunned Darla in the face through the window by the door. He blew her fucking head off!"

Roy struggles to breath.

Hyperventilation.

"Ok, take another deep breath, what happened next?"

There is the ding of an elevator in the background.

"Kabe shot me through the door, but we had him! Until…"

"Until what?" Jack asks.

There is the click of high heels on tile. "Yes, until what Roy?" Haven asks.

Roy turns his head to see Haven walking toward him from the elevator. She is wearing a skin tight black dress that stops just above mid-thigh. It is accented by long, black, knee high, suede boots. Her hair is brown and curly. Her lips are ruby red. Lush.

"The boy, the one you said should only be a baby…ate her."

"And you ran before he could eat you too, I suppose?" Haven asks.

"I had no choice! He did it without touching her…I don't…"

Roy starts to shake uncontrollably.

"Shhh, calm down dear," Haven says as she sits down next to Roy on the nearby couch. She starts to pat his head gently. "Look, I know how upset you must be from losing your *beloved* Darla, but I need you to focus, I need you to tell me everything, every detail, as best you can. Otherwise, Mommy can't help. Now…what do you mean the boy ate her?"

3

The wind is relentless. Persistent. Incessant. Unabating. Whipping and howling. Snow blows across the frozen ground and scatters. Evergreens bow and bend. Amidst the frigid air, Jennifer Thomas, aka *Judas,* is trudging forward toward an old shack in the distance. The woods are vast, desolate, and dreary. There are hundreds of large white oak, paper birch, northern white cedar, and balsam fir. Black spruce.

Judas is wearing a faded *Wautoma Stingers* basketball tee, some torn jogging pants, and stained socks on her hands like mittens. Her feet are wrapped up in scraps from cotton boxers — two pair — which are layered with pine needles and small flexible twigs for support and insulation. She has been plodding through these woods for what seems like weeks. Over her tee, she is sporting a hooded, down jacket. She found it in an unlocked and abandoned car. A saffron Pinto.

Scavenging.

Dog-tired.

Her muscles are atrophied.

Starving.

Judas has lost fifteen pounds.

Even her stomach looks tighter — the one ruined by childbirth.

Not much farther, she tells herself. The shadow of an abandoned shack looms in the foreground. She presses forward, her eyes are watering. Her tears are freezing on her cheeks. Snot is dripping down into her mouth. She wipes it away with her sock mittens. She makes her way up some creaky, rotten steps and onto a dilapidated porch. She grabs the handle of the door, turns it, pushes hard, and steps inside.

It's an old trapper's cabin. The walls are made from thick logs. Dust covered lumber. The roof is sagging and growing moss. Inside there is an old stone fireplace, decrepit wood cabinets littered with mouse feces, and some rusty old traps hanging from the wall. "It's not perfect, but it will do," Judas says. Judas begins to scour a cupboard and finds some old canned food, a rusty knife, and some dishes. She grabs an old deer skin on the wall and shakes it out. She beats the dust out of it and coughs before bundling herself up in it. She piles a bunch of dried wood and rubbish from the floor into the fireplace and ignites it with a lighter from her pocket. "And then there was fire," she says. "Oh my god that feels so good."

The smoke settles a moment before billowing upward and out of the chimney. Just as Judas settles in, the wind pushes the door open and sends a gush of cold air into the cabin. Judas looks over at the wall by the open door and notices a bottle of liquor on the shelf — half full. She quickly snatches it up, shuts the door, braces it, and hooks the latch.

She twists off the top of the bottle, smells it, and takes a hearty swig.

Whiskey.

"This will warm me up," she says.

Hours pass by. The wind continues to howl outside, pushing snow into swooning drifts. Judas, now lying on her side by the fire, snuggled up tight in an old, hardened deer hide, and intoxicated from the alcohol begins to feel sick — nauseous.

She has had reoccurring nightmares of monsters ripping through abdomens, gooey spiked tentacles tearing flesh, and vigorous, violent rape.

Post-traumatic stress.

When she isn't crying, she is nervous — always watching her back — always on edge.

This is the first time in a while that Judas has let her guard down, that she has felt comfortable enough to close her eyes, to fall asleep…to just let go.

The queasiness is subtle at first but becomes more and more irritating. All she wants to do is sleep but her stomach is churning. It comes in waves. The room spins. *Is it alcohol on an empty stomach or something worse?* she wonders. She can't stop thinking about Reagan and the *thing* that burst forth from her vagina—shredding it. The *thing* that was gnawing on Reagan's remains as the Stinger dragged her corpse out the door still haunts her mind. Judas wonders why she didn't give birth to one of those wretched *things*. She tells herself that it's because she went through menopause early, that her womb is barren, but in truth, she doesn't really know. She wonders if there is still *something* inside her, *something* waiting to eat its way out, *something* wicked. The nausea doesn't help. It only makes her more paranoid. Then, the sour taste in her mouth signals what's to come—vomit.

Judas quickly opens the rickety cabin door, rushes outside into the blowing snow, falls to her knees, and throws up with vigor. First the contents of her stomach burst forth into the snow, they are brownish green, likely the liquor, but then after a few more painful upchucks, the snow turns bright red. Judas is vomiting blood.

Hematemesis.

The blood paints her lips and chin red as the nausea subsides. Judas wipes her face with her hand and notices two black boots on the ground in front of her. They are snow covered, possibly a men's size 8. The boots are still—unmoving. Judas is too sick to be scared. Instead her gaze moves upward from the boots to the figure of a man standing in front of her. She is too tired to react. Too drunk. Too weak. Suddenly, the nausea returns and strikes her viciously in the pit of her stomach. Then another retch, another gag, and Judas throws up, sending a smattering of thick hot blood toward the black boots in front of her before passing out.

"Well don't just stand there. Help her," a soft voice says.

4

Kabe Abraham is stunned. His body fixed. Frozen. Unmoving. Like crisp Jell-O.

Zion wipes his gore-soaked face and again utters the words, "Tum tum." His eyes are blazing red and orange, his gut is bloated and distended from filling up on Darla and the two Stingers. Yet, he hungers for more. His desire to eat is yet to be assuaged. He raises his right arm in the air and with a subtle flick of his wrist picks Kabe up in the air like he did Darla.

Kabe is suspended, floating, and terrified. He tries to speak but his mouth won't budge. Paralyzed, he starts to feel a weird stinging sensation in his abdomen. Like a hornet sting. Zion opens his mouth and motions Kabe toward him, just as he did with Darla before sucking out and snacking on her insides. Kabe's body begins to shake and gyrate, a wave of intense pressure passes through him. His blood begins to boil, his body temperature rises drastically, sweat beads on his crinkled brow, and bright red blood begins to seep slowly from his eye sockets and ear lobes. It also starts to trickle out of his nose. The pressure pops his ear drums and he loses his hearing. It feels like getting swimmer's ear.

Then suddenly, Samurai, the Abraham family mutt, rushes through the front door, leaps, barks, snarls rapaciously, and knocks Zion over onto the hardwood floor. Kabe too falls to the ground. Kabe looks up to see Samurai go flying into the wall and whimper loudly in defeat. Zion gets up, but before he can do anything Scarlet limps into the hallway and yells at him sternly.

"Zion no!" she demands. "Leave them be!" she orders.

Zion looks at Scarlet, then at Kabe and Samurai, giggles, and raises his arms in the air as if he wants to be picked up and held. Scarlet walks forward and picks him up in her arms and tells him that he is never to hurt Daddy or Sammy again. She tells him that he must protect them like he does Mommy.

"Ok," Zion says.

"Are you ok?" Scarlet asks Kabe.

"I think so."

"Are you sure?"

"Not really but I'm better off than those three," Kabe says looking at the dried-up carcasses of the two has-been Wautoma Stingers and Darla.

"What happened to them? One minute I was feeding Zion and the next I was out cold. I don't remember anything," Scarlet says.

"Your son ate them."

"What do you mean 'ate them' and don't you mean our son?"

"Well, those two I killed, but Darla over here, he drank her dry like a red slushy—blood, guts, and all. And he's YOUR son when he's bad, not mine. Need we forget that the damn kid just tried eating me too! Hell, he would have if it wasn't for Sammy…come here boy, good boy," Kabe says as he gently pats Samurai's head and looks him over for any major injuries.

"Do I need to be the one to point out the pink elephant in the room?"

"What's that?" Kabe asks.

"Oh, you know, maybe the fact that OUR son just grew into a toddler in the span of minutes."

"Yeah, beyond his now seemingly cannibal superpower…we definitely have a problem," Kabe says.

Scarlet looks down at Zion, who is now sleeping soundly in her arms. He burps and sighs then snores loudly. She asks Kabe what he thinks they should do, to which Kabe replies, "I need a drink."

"Me too," Scarlet says.

Samurai limps over to the couch, jumps up on it slowly, kicks his feet in the red and black flannel blanket, and lays down.

5

Seth Dillinger was supposed to survive to live another few years in this beloved little village, this horrid township…but *The Ravening* changed everything. His fate is up in the air now, just like everyone else in this *Godforsaken* place.

Seth spent the last twelve weeks doing chemotherapy, he was fighting an aggressive carcinoma.

He and Lizzy, his girlfriend, returned to Wautoma shortly after the *things* took over. They hadn't heard from Lizzy's grandmother for a while and, after numerous unanswered phone calls to the Waushara County Sheriff's Department, they decided to stop and check up on grandma themselves, only to find that the roads in and out of town were blocked and that there were terrible *things* with large tentacles devouring the denizens.

Seth, now seated against a dusty, old log cabin wall, opens his journal and reads the last entry:

"I woke up this morning and more of my hair is gone. I run my fingers through what's left and six half inch bristles are stuck to my fingertips. The acne on my face is getting worse and my skin feels like leather. I haven't had acne since high school. The pores are empty and dry. A sharp pain makes my eyes water when I squeeze them. They sit on my face, ominously looking back at me in the mirror, red and irritated, right under my nose. Sore. My feet are numb when I lie down, swollen when I stand up. The skin on my hands sometimes feels like it's on fire. There was blood in my stool yesterday, I think it is an anal fissure and not something more serious, hence the bright red color on the toilet paper. The doctor says my red blood count is at a nine, that's only half a point off from needing a blood transfusion. I wonder if that hurts too.

Wait just a second, let's take a step back. I'm getting ahead of myself.

My name is Seth Darcy Dillinger and I have cancer.

Embryonal carcinoma to be exact, which in unscientific terms means 'testicular cancer.'

Yes, the kind Lance Armstrong had or has – he's in remission, right?

I hate the sound of that. 'Testicular' implies a lot. I feel stupid when I say it, like a twelve-year-old who can't say the word 'vagina' without laughing. Although, I don't laugh. I tend to scream or cry. Testicular cancer is more serious than you would think. I would argue it's more serious than anyone thinks but truth is that only ten percent of men get it. Lucky me then, right? I drew the short straw. Sometime in between being born and having my sex determined as an embryo in my mother's womb, cancer snuck in and went dormant for twenty years.

This is not a cancer derived from poor lifestyle choices like smoking too much or being exposed to carcinogens or asbestos, this cancer was in my body since my inception. Think about that for a second – philosophically, religiously – where does one even begin to explain or justify that? Was I born to suffer? Anyway, moving on...

I am currently in my second cycle of high dose chemotherapy.

In high dose chemotherapy, you have to be hospitalized during treatment.

Lance Armstrong makes me want to throw up.

I asked Lizzy to kill me two weeks ago.

I hate the smell of chemo in my urine.

My oncologist told me not to have sex with Lizzy because chemotherapy drugs will be in my semen. He recommended condoms if I do.

I have lost 35lbs since January.

When you have cancer, everyone tells you "you look good," but truth is...I look "holocaust good."

My eyebrows will be the last to fall out.

This is what having cancer is really like. There are no bake sales, no colored ribbons, nor fundraisers here. No little coffee cans or jars with my photo on it. It's just me and Lizzy in a hospital room in Marshfield Wisconsin.

Oh, and my various roommates on the other side of the sliding curtain...

Doctors told my first roommate he was going to die.

The room was silent.

My second roommate was wearing a diaper.

He was near seventy years old.

His shit smell made my nausea worse.

I'll be twenty-two in December.

I was first diagnosed with cancer after finding a round, smooth lump on the underside of my right testicle. It hurt to touch it. Although only the size of a marble, it was tender and hard. I told myself that it was probably something like a testicle torsion but I did have enough sense to go get it checked out by my family doctor immediately. That in itself is hard to do as a 'man.' Guys are so self-conscious about the size of their penises. I've heard stories of guys who will let the lump on their testicle grow to the size of an orange before seeking medical attention. All because they are afraid to have someone (male or female) see their dick.

These are the same guys who fight our wars, play physical sports, and beat their wives. But give them a little bump on their balls and tell them they should see a doctor and they will procrastinate until it's so bad they (the surgeons) have no choice but to make an incision through the scrotum when removing it.

You can't pull an orange-sized tumor out via orchiectomy.

Cancer separates the men from the tough guys.

I am not strong.

Everybody loves a hero.

Give a young man cancer, then you see how strong he is or isn't.

And with enough time and 'procedures'...cancer breaks all men.

My oncologist said that one guy not only let it grow that large (to the size of an orange) but he also had noticeable growths jutting out the side of his rib cage. My oncologist said the chemo melted it right off.

I now realize that was part of his sales pitch to me for the chemotherapy.

He told me that without treatment I would die in a year or so.

After dropping my pants and having my female doctor put her hands all over my nether regions, I was sent for an ultrasound.

The doctor was on her knees, feeling me up in front of Lizzy. Yet arousal at this point was impossible.

"Hold your penis to the side," she said.

It was more awkward than sexual by far.

At this point, I realized that I had better get used to having strangers touch my balls. For the next six months, the common phrase used was "I had better check." What that means is that they wanted to continually check my good testicle for cancer.

How? Well, it starts by holding the nut in your hands with your thumbs on both sides – like you're holding an egg. Next, feel around it for lumps. All over, spare no expense. And if you find anything that hurts to touch, don't lie to yourself, go see a doctor – yesterday.

The longer you let it go, the more it will spread into your lymph nodes and toward your lungs.

This means more treatment, more surgery, and a lower survival rate.

Remission rate in testicular cancer is near ninety percent.

Right now, I have a seventy percent chance that I will get remission after chemotherapy.

It's times like these that I remember a dark night years ago.

I was driving slowly on a twisted back road with a long horizontal crack in my windshield.

As the light from my headlights peeked over the hill, splaying the moonlight, there was something in the road.

Blood everywhere.

There was a glare from bright night eyes reflected in my headlamps.

A large doe – a female deer.

It was lying there with its legs tucked under itself in the middle of the road.

As my car crawled forward, its lights beaming bright,
its engine sputtering, I came to a stop.
I knew then what had happened.
A drunk driver had hit it and left it to die for fear of
reprimand.
I knew then what I had to do.
I shut the car off and got out to get a closer look.
Now there were two of us — myself and the doe — in the
middle of the road.
My girlfriend Lizzy was in the passenger seat and my
dog Tuffy, a black and brown spotted cocker spaniel,
was in the back looking on with wonder.
I was wearing ragged, tan shorts with a Slayer patch on
them.
My shoes were tattered and torn with duct tape holding
them together.
I was hipster poor.
This is before hipsters existed.
I hate vinyl records, they seem so useless.
Phil Anselmo, the vocalist for Pantera, once said, "the
trend is dead," but I'm not so sure about those types of
things anymore.
YouTube.
Twitter.
Selfies.
I made my way up to the magnificent animal, its front
leg was almost seared off completely, red liquid was
pooling out — it was thick and creamy, like tomato soup.
I pulled out my cell phone and dialed 911.
The deer couldn't hold its head up, it was limp and
snapped.
I thought about suffocating it.

It breathed hard when I covered its face with my hands but I couldn't find the fortitude to go through with smothering it.

Yet, physically broken, the doe still tried to get up and run.

I hopped on it and held it down. Now I was painted red too.

It was warm and sticky, it felt like maple syrup all over me.

It itched.

I made the call.

It took fifteen minutes for the officer to come out and it was the longest fifteen minutes of my life.

There I was in the middle of the night, in the center of the road, in what felt like the epicenter of the universe, my axis-mundi, under the stars...holding down a one hundred pound plus animal just so an officer could shoot it in the head.

Just so he could stop the misery, end the suffering.

Then I ask myself again how cancer is fair.

Seth quickly shuts his journal and looks up at the unconscious woman on the floor. She is bundled up in an old deer hide and wearing socks on her hands. He thinks about the doe he held down in the middle of the road years ago.

Seth then asks Lizzy if the woman on the floor is still breathing. Lizzy checks her and tells him that she is, that she hasn't thrown up blood for at least an hour, and that they need to keep the fire going.

6

Scarlet Abraham always has to be right. She always has to be right, even if she is dead wrong. And she always has to have the last word. Her particular psychosis, or disorder, or resting bitch face, has always put her at odds with the world and especially with her brother Jack. Truth be told, Jack despises her.

Everybody in town hates Scarlet.

She is just such a bitch.

She's the kind of girl that everyone wants to see die in a horror movie. She's the type of woman who sleeps with married men, who fat shames, and picks on folks with debilitating acne — she makes jokes at the expense of those with psoriasis to make herself feel better.

When Scarlet was sixteen, her ex-boyfriend, Terry Ceeling, spray painted the word **BITCH** in large, white letters on the road in front of the Warren's house. In high school Scarlett claimed she was raped by the town basketball star, but she wasn't. She told everyone that she was sodomized for attention. She ruined Mark Malbrough's life, his reputation, all for attention.

Scarlet still needs constant attention.

If her boyfriend wouldn't worship her, she would quickly move on to the next one who would. Or *whoever* was willing to spend the most money on her. Who, in the end, was Kabe Abraham.

In his eyes, she could do no wrong.

Scarlet caused so much drama between her parents Robert and Karen Warren. Scarlet's underage drinking tickets, her constant coming home past curfew, and her hyper-promiscuity led to many fights in the Warren household. Fights that Jack would have to listen to for years, or at least until Scarlet graduated high school and left home for college.

Jack would hide away in his He-Man tent during the lengthy shouting sessions.

The screaming matches seemed endless.

The silence seemed even worse.

"End of Discussion," Robert would say.

"Asshole!" Karen would holler.

Then doors would slam shut.

Robert would get so angry at Karen that he would throw pots and pans at the walls, he would smash ashtrays on the floor. Then he would chain smoke cigarettes in the kitchen while Karen sobbed in the locked bathroom.

You could cut the tension with a knife after each fight. It lingered for days in awkward silence. Robert and Karen wouldn't speak to each other for weeks if the argument was bad enough. They would just sit at the dinner table staring off into space, chewing cold meat, and swallowing hard potatoes.

"Jack will you ask your mother to pass the butter?" Robert would ask.

"Scarlet can you tell your father to get the butter his damn self," Karen would reply.

Lima beans and carrots. Sour tasting multi-vitamins—chewables.

Jack would pretend to consume them but instead he quickly pocketed his vitamins and buried them in the soil of Karen's household plants.

No wonder Karen's indoor plants seemed to do so well in poor sunlight.

Karen was tall, thin, and gaunt with reddish blonde, straight hair. She had rheumatic fever as a child. She was just **ALWAYS** sick. There was just **ALWAYS** something wrong. A headache. A backache. A cold. She had a different illness for everyday of the week—for years. Eventually, after the divorce, she moved to Minnesota and married some well-to-do guy with an airplane. He was a realtor, he was someone else to take care of her.

This was long after Robert's "accident."

The explosion.

The skin grafts.

The burn center baths.

Scarlet is the type of woman who types a twenty-page letter letting you know "how right" she is. She is relentless, suffocating, and thrives on emotional abuse. The worse you feel, the better she feels. How Kabe puts up with her is anybody's guess.

"She gets it from her mother," Robert would say.

"She's just like her father," Karen would say.

Most people in town think Kabe sticks around because he's too afraid of what Scarlet would do to him—financially—in a divorce. And rightly so. She would wipe him out. Taking half of everything would be a blessing, but Scarlet would make sure he had nothing left. She's *that* type of woman.

Jack and Scarlet have never seen eye-to-eye. They have fought since childhood.

And now, as adults, there is still bad blood between them. This is why Jack has no problem hunting down his own sister, he's always wished she was dead anyway. Scarlet Abraham has been nothing but a burden to the Warren family, a royal pain in the ass, a lying cold-hearted, trouble-making bitch. Or at least that's what Jack calls her.

***

Father Reynolds shouts, he cries out in agony as The Behemoth slices open the skin on his back and rips it apart, exposing bloody, fibrous muscle tissue.

"Please—God—help me!"

"Just tell us where Devin Sanders is and the suffering ends," Jessica says. "But if you don't—your death will be slow—real fucking slow. I promise you that, holy man."

"I—I—don't know where he is," Father Reynolds says. "I haven't seen him, I swear to God!"

"Why do Christians always say that? It's just so cliché. I swear to God! Blah, blah, blah. It's the same old song and dance. When will you Christians learn? I don't give a fuck about your fake God or your scapegoat Devil." Jessica looks over at The Behemoth again and nods.

The Behemoth makes another deep cut and tears off another chunk of Father Reynolds' flesh.

Father Reynolds' screams echo throughout the chamber hall.

Jessica nods again.

Another incision and another piece of ripped skin.

"Ok! God — damn — it! I saw him yesterday but he didn't tell me where he was going I swear!"

"Oh really? So now I'm supposed to believe you?"

"Yes! I swear to God I'm telling you the truth!"

Jessica walks over to Father Reynolds, who is laying naked, face down, on the church altar with his arms stretched out tight and tied down. She places both of her hands on Father Reynolds' shoulders and digs her nails into them — as far as possible.

"Don't swear to your God — SWEAR TO ME!" Jessica shouts as she rips all ten of her nails downward toward Father Reynolds' hips. Blood spews out of all ten tears as she again digs her nails deeply into the meat just above Father Reynolds' buttocks.

"Lie to me again and I'll rip you open down to your ankles, you twat."

"Ok—ok—he said something about heading back into the woods. He told me he was going home."

"Home?"

"Yeah," Father Reynolds' gasps. "He meant his parent's house out in the country off Highway 22."

"See, confession is good for the soul, isn't it Father?" Jessica says, grinning wide.

Father Reynolds breathes a sigh of relief as Jessica pulls her fingernails out of his backside and walks down the aisle toward the door.

"Now, can you do me a favor?" Jessica asks.

"A favor?"

"Tell your God that there's a new queen in town and that unlike him...I'm not so forgiving."

Jessica turns and nods at The Behemoth again and casually walks out of the church smiling.

"Home sweet home," she says.

Inside the church there are horrifying screams, unsettling crunching noises, and the faint sound of Father Reynolds gurgling on his own blood. Then, there is nothing but silence.

7

Haven is pacing the foyer of the Pfitzer, wearing down the handwoven and dyed Turkish carpets. They are from the 1920's. She is thinking deeply about what to do next. She is unsettled and shaking in anger.

Rage.

Writhing in suppressed fury.

Boiling energy.

"I'll go out there and deal with them. It's no big deal, I can handle it," Jack says.

"I'm coming with," Roy says.

"Oh no you're not. You'll compromise everything," Jack says.

"Bullshit! They killed my Darla and I'm gonna make them pay for it."

"Would you two just shut up!" Haven shouts. "For fuck's sake, I'm trying to think."

"Sorry," Roy says looking down at the floor.

"Just listen to me—for one second," Jack says as he puts both of his hands on Haven's biceps and stops her from pacing. "Look, Scarlet is my sister, let me deal with her. I know her better than anyone—Kabe too. And I don't need any help." Jack says while glaring at Roy.

Haven looks into Jack's eyes and says, "I'm sorry love but I can't risk losing you too. And her being your sister is a problem, I'd rather Roy deal with it for now." Haven draws Jack in close and whispers in his ear, "Besides, Roy — unlike you — is expendable."

Haven kisses Jack softly on his cheek before turning and smiling at Roy, "Roy dear, get it done and take as many of my children as you need with you."

By *children* Haven means *zombies*.

Zombies are forever slaves, slaves to their masters.

"I won't let you down again Mom," Roy says with a grin.

"You had better not, for there is a terrible price to pay for such failure," Haven says.

***

Judas comes to slowly, she is swaddled in a plaid fleece blanket with her head propped up slightly by a small, worn backpack. She sees two figures moving around in front of her. They look like dark streaks, shadows dancing in the firelight.

"Where am I?" Judas asks.

One of the figures steps closer and says to the other, "She's awake."

"You're in an old trapper's cabin out in the woods off Highway 22. We found you throwing up blood outside. You passed out and we brought you in. You've been sleeping ever since."

"Who are you?"

"I'm Seth and this is my girlfriend Lizzy," Seth says.

"Hi," Lizzy says.

"What's your name?" Seth asks.

"Folks in town call me Judas but you can call me Judas," Judas says with a smirk.

"Judas, huh, like the one from the Bible?"

"I get that a lot," Judas says.

"Wait a second," Lizzy says. "I've heard of you, aren't you the—?"

"Yeah, I expect you have—and yeah you probably heard right," Judas interjects.

"I'm not judging, I just remember you from the newspaper when I was a kid," Lizzy says.

"Wait, you're THAT Judas? The one who ratted out half the town to get out of a prostitution charge? Oh wow," Seth says. "Is that all true?"

"Unfortunately, yes honey, we all have our regrets and our vices, especially at my age," Judas says, now sitting up. "These days if you aren't sucking cock you're married to one. No offense— Seth, right?"

"None taken and yeah it's Seth. So, what are you doing all the way out here anyway?"

"Same thing I suspect you're doing—hiding from the goddamn monsters."

***

"Follow me," Haven says to Jack.

Haven grabs Jack's hand and steps with purpose toward the elevator. She presses the up button and waits, silent, tapping her foot. Jack doesn't say anything. The elevator dings and the doors open. Haven and Jack step on, she inserts a key into a key slot, turns it, and the doors close. The elevator ascends past the fifth floor, the last floor listed on the panel. It continues to climb up to another floor, a floor Jack is not familiar with. A floor that technically, by all indication, should not exist.

"What's going on?" Jack asks.

"You'll see," Haven says.

"Grrreat," Jack says sarcastically.

"Just wait, you'll see."

The elevator stops, the doors open and Haven and Jack step out onto the top floor. It says 6 on the wall in front of them. There are no lights. The hallway on both sides is pitch black. Haven steps forward and Jack hesitates.

"It's ok. Just trust me," Haven says.

Jack shrugs his shoulders and follows Haven down the right corridor, passing room after room, door handle after door handle. He can barely see but it is clear Haven knows exactly where she is going. Then, suddenly, Haven stops in front of door 666.

Jack looks at the numbers on the door and says, "You've got to be kidding me."

"You can stop talking now," Haven says as she fumbles through her hand bag, searching for a room key.

"Here it is," she says as she pulls out and then inserts a large, bronze skeleton key into the old, dusty, brass lock. "This floor hasn't been touched since the early nineteen hundreds. Not since the fire."

"What fire?" Jack asks.

"In 1960, the entire sixth floor was engulfed by a terrible fire. It killed twenty people. They died of smoke inhalation. Or at least, that's what the papers said. You never heard about it?"

"Why would I have? I wasn't born until twenty-five years later," Jack says.

"Well, anyway, what the papers didn't say is that those folks who supposedly died in the blaze were already dead long before the fire."

"Arson?"

"Nope, it was murder. And this room, 666, is where all the bodies were found."

"All in this room? And why have I never heard of this before?"

"Because Jack, the whole town was in on it. This beloved township, this horrid village, this godforsaken place was run by the Chicago mob in the early to mid-20th century. They built this hotel…they used it to clean their money and make their enemies disappear. This whole place is built on blood."

"Why room 666?" Jack asks.

"They had a knack for the theatrical and an obsession with Frank Sinatra. He used to stay here you know—in this very room."

"Sinatra? What's he have to do with it?"

"Old Blue Eyes had a passion for the occult. Haven't you heard his songs? You know, 'That Old Black Magic' or 'Witchcraft'? How about 'Bewitched, Bothered, and Bewildered' or 'Old Devil Moon' or 'Devil May Care'?"

"So that explains all the Sinatra you listen to," Jack says.

"Indeed, he grows on you. And not to mention those gorgeous eyes of his. Besides, he's the reason all those bodies were found in this room. He would fly in on the weekends, perform ritual sacrifice in this very room, and fly back to Hollywood. This hotel was his secret ritual chamber, for both him and his associates. 'The Rat Pack' is what the press called them but they called themselves 'The Clan.' The Clan wasn't just a supergroup of A-list actors, they were practicing occultists, they were a warlock coven. Frank Sinatra, Sammy Davis Jr., Dean Martin, Joey Bishop, and Peter Lawford were all serial killers. They only found twenty bodies in the fire but I'm sure these walls are stuffed with bones."

"Holy shit," Jack says as Haven opens the door to room 666.

"I know, right? Pretty damn cool when you think about it," Haven says.

Haven pushes open the squeaky door while pulling out a lighter. She then proceeds to walk the entire room, lighting candle after candle. And, as the room begins to become illuminated, Jack is astounded by what he sees. Every candle holder is brass or gold. The floor is draped in one-hundred-year-old rugs. The kind with intricate hand-woven patterns, the kind you only see hanging in expensive specialty shops for five thousand dollars or more—the kind of carpet you want to fuck on just to say that you fucked on it.

The room smells of lavender and cherry blossom. There is a large oil painting of Aleister Crowley, the one with him wearing that big triangular hat and folding his hands toward the sky. On the ceiling is a large painted seal of Solomon. On the wall, there is a large black mirror, large enough that you could walk through it. After lighting the candles, Haven begins to walk the room again. She starts to slowly take off her clothes. Jack is entranced and enticed by what he sees. Everything is so beautiful, so magnificent, *she is a goddess* he thinks.

Haven stops in the center of the room, looks at Jack with her voluptuous breasts hanging perfect before him and says, "What are you waiting for? Take off your fucking clothes."

8

Devin Sanders stops abruptly in

front of a gravel driveway with a tan, polymer mailbox jutting out of the snow just to the left of it. The mailbox has **SANDERS** stenciled on it in wide, black letters. There is a large piece of plywood screwed to the side of the mailbox to protect it from snowplows and teenagers with baseball bats who drive around smashing mailboxes late at night for fun.

Bashing mailboxes is something to do, as opposed to nothing to do.

Art. Masculinity. Ritual. Violence.

There isn't much to do for fun in small town Wisconsin.

Idle hands are the Devil's workshop.

Robert Warren would put bricks in his mailbox so that when a trouble-making kid would swing at it with all his might, the shockwave from the impact would sting so bad that the perpetrator would have no choice but to drop the bat in pain and make a quick getaway.

"Home sweet home," Devin says. "Not quite but it will have to do."

Devin continues to walk down the driveway through a row of perfectly planted pines and knee-high, fawn brown grass that is covered in snow. He is wearing a Brandeis blue cardigan and knitted, black fingerless gloves with matching earmuffs.

His hair is in pigtails.

Sometimes used for pulling and tugging while having bareback sex.

Devin wonders if his parents are still alive. *And, if they are, what can I say to them?* he thinks — especially his father.

Devin's father refused to accept that he was homosexual. He was in denial and, in doing so, he made Devin suffer immensely. Abuse. Drugs. The leather belt. Devin spent most of his childhood being tossed back and forth in-between treatment centers — juvenile delinquent facilities.

Nervous.

Anxious.

Scared.

Devin presses on. He makes his way to the front door of his childhood home and hesitates before knocking. The siding is lemon chiffon. The shutters, chocolate brown. The snow in the driveway hasn't been cleared for a while but there is a shoveled path to the pole shed — his father Stanley's workshop.

Devin finally builds up the courage to knock — thrice — then steps back, awaiting a response. The wind picks up and starts to howl, whipping and scattering snow and debris across the front yard.

No response.

Nothing.

No one answers the door.

He knocks again and sighs. He can barely stomach thinking about the last time he saw his father. The argument was heated, the words hurt, they cut deep. They still do. "You're not my son," Stanley told him. "No son of mine would put another man's cock in his mouth," Stanley would say again and again while shaking his head and looking down at the floor.

"Alright! I'm coming! Just hold your horses," a voice yells from inside the house.

Devin recognizes the voice immediately.

He swallows hard, hearing his father's voice after all this time makes him feel like crying. He takes a deep breath and holds back the tears as the front door unlocks and the handle turns.

The door opens and in the threshold stands Stanley Sanders, Devin's father.

"Can I help you?" Stanley says.

Devin tries to speak, but can't find the words. He just stands there in awkward silence.

"Well, I don't have all day ma'am, what do ya want?"

Stanley mistakes Devin for a woman. It must be his pigtails and bright colored cardigan or Stanley's bad eyesight brought on by old age and cataracts.

"Hi D—ad," Devin says.

Stanley steps forward, takes a long look at Devin and asks, "Devin, is that you?"

"Yeah it's me."

Devin's knees are trembling.

Stanley steps back, takes another long look at Devin, tells Devin that "queers aren't welcome here," and slams the door.

"Please Dad! I need your help! I don't have anywhere else to go—please!" Devin shouts while pounding on the door.

"Go away!" Stanley hollers.

"I'll pound on this door until you let me in!"

"The hell you will!"

"Please, just give me ten minutes to explain..."

Devin pounds relentlessly on the door, every hit echoes in Stanley's head.

"Alright! Enough already! Goddamn it, I'll open up," Stanley says.

The door opens and Stanley again stands in the doorway.

"You have five," Stanley says as he steps aside and allows Devin inside.

Devin sits down on the couch in the living room. It is musty smelling and hard. The cushions are stiff, the fabric is coarse and tight. It is tan with brown swirls.

"You better have a damn good reason for being here," Stanley says.

"I have nowhere else to go," Devin says.

"How's that my problem?"

"It isn't but you're all I have left—the things out there—they've taken over the whole town. Nowhere is safe, not even here."

"Things? What things?"

"Surely you know what's happened?"

"What the damn commies finally attacked? Or ISIS? Goddamnit, I knew it would only be a matter of time."

"No, it's much worse than that—," Devin pauses, realizing that the truth sounds even more ridiculous than a communist invasion.

"What then?"

"Yeah, that's it, it was some sort of terrorist attack, but no one knows who it is yet," Devin says.

"Fuck me sideways," Stanley says. "I knew them damn liberals would get us into a war and how are we supposed to win with all the faggots they let in the military? This is your fault you know, you and your kind."

"My fault? That's bullshit Dad and you know it. You still haven't come to terms with it, have you? How typical."

"Watch yourself boy, you're lucky I even let you in this house."

"You know what—fuck you Dad—you're just an ignorant homophobe."

"What did you just say?" Stanley says, standing up.

"You heard me. You're the problem with this country, not me, or 'my kind,' as you so eloquently put it, you uneducated backwoods prick," Devin says standing up as well.

"How dare you! Do you really think I'm supposed to be proud of my son, who goes around sucking and fucking men for dollar bills? It's not my fault you decided to throw away your life on drugs...you were nothing but a problem for me and your poor mom — God rest her soul — nothing but a goddamn burden!"

"You know Dad, maybe, just maybe, if you and mom would have been supportive of me instead of ridiculing me and treating me like some sort of freak or failure — maybe I wouldn't have turned out like this!"

Devin's tears make his eyeliner run.

"Oh, that's just like you to put it all on us — same ol' Devin — just blames everybody else for his constant fuckups. How old are you now? When does Devin finally become responsible for the dumb shit he does, huh? Or is it just always me and your mom's fault until you die? Sure, maybe we were — I was — hard on you, but you were no angel either."

"I fucking hate you. You're twisted if you think for one second that beating me with a belt didn't fuck me up!"

"A belt? You're lucky I didn't just kill you for being such a goddamn disappointment! And that's the problem with liberals these days, they think everything is abuse. Maybe if more of you queers took a good healthy beating growing up, you wouldn't be so quick to ruin this country."

"Wow Dad, you're a fucking embarrassment. You're right, I should never have come here, you're just a worthless relic, you cling dearly to a dying age of homophobic Christian conservatism to justify your wrongs. Fuck Jesus and fuck you!" Devin shouts as he turns to leave out the front door.

"Oh no you don't, I tell you when you can leave you disrespectful little shit," Stanley says, grabbing Devin's arm.

Devin pulls his arm back out of Stanley's grasp and says, "Don't you fucking touch me, old man!"

Stanley's eyes go wide, his fists clench tight — white — as he says, "Why you little — " before abruptly punching Devin in the jaw and knocking him to the floor.

Stunned, Devin looks up at Stanley from the floor and says, "That's right, if you can't beat me into submission with your words, you have to beat me into submission with your fists. You're the same old weak piece of shit that I remember."

Stanley undoes his belt and starts pulling it out through the loops of his worn blue jeans and says, "It might be the end of the world out there but it's going to be the end of your world in here boy. We'll see if I can't set that smart mouth of yours straight for good."

9

"We have to leave — now," Kabe

says.

"Leave? And go where exactly?" Scarlet asks.

"Your dad said that we should hide out in the woods by Snipe Lake. There's an old trapper's cabin out there, it's hidden by thick pines."

"And my dad told you this? When?"

"Just before he — turned into whatever those damned things are."

"What do you mean turned?"

"I don't know, he was sort of himself, but then wasn't. It was as if he was possessed or something."

"And you think we can trust what he said? What if it's a trap?"

"Well, staying here doesn't seem like it's any safer. Roy got away and it won't be long until he comes back — with more of those things."

"So how far is the cabin from here?" Scarlet asks.

"A little over an hour's walk, so we better get moving. If we hustle we can get there before dark," Kabe says as he opens Robert Warren's bedroom closet and pulls out a couple jackets, flannels, gloves, and stocking hats. "Here put this on and Zion will need these too." Kabe tosses Scarlet a couple of thin brown wool blankets and puts on a pair of Robert's Sorel snow boots.

"I'll pack whatever supplies I can find too, we're gonna need food — especially for Zion. And don't forget about Sammy, check and see if dad had any dog food left over in that cupboard to the left of the sink," Scarlet says.

Kabe and Scarlet grab everything they can find, then take Zion, who is bundled up in wool blankets, and Samurai, and head out the door and into the woods to find the old trapper's cabin.

***

Roy Samuel Hutchinson collects his thoughts as he assembles an army of Haven's deadliest children — there are at least ten of them. And they are all gathered inside the old dilapidated house that Haven and Jack used to live in — the one where Haven first introduced Jack to the new and improved Roy, the one where Bill Kimball, the Stinger's pack leader, met his horrific end many moons ago.

One of Haven's zombies is wearing a heavily worn and blood-stained penguin furry costume, the kind one would use during a furry sex party, the kind with role playing in fur suits. He goes by the pseudonym Penguin. It's his power animal.

Plushophilia.

Yiffing.

"Alright, has anybody seen Malach?"

"Nope," someone says.

"Nah, me either," someone else says.

"Damn, it would be nice to have him with us," Roy says.

Malach Bernstein is a huge muscular man.

His parents named him after the angel in the Torah, the one who did all of Yahweh's dirty work. He didn't grow up in Wautoma, he was just passing through on his way to Madison for a national strongman competition. The kind where there are enormous men who lift enormous amounts of weight. Unfortunately, Malach Bernstein never made it to the competition as planned. He stopped at the wrong rest stop, at the wrong time, just outside of the wrong small town in Wisconsin.

It was there that Malach would meet Haven for the first time, where she would snatch him up, and turn him into a zombie through Caribbean necromancy.

Malach seemed destined to become Haven's enforcer. It just made sense since he was such a behemoth of a man.

"Alright let's go. You four come with me, the rest of you follow behind in Nick's pickup," Roy says.

"You got it boss," Nick says.

Penguin nods.

Nick was new to the force, he was hired two weeks before Jack and Roy investigated the disappearance of Jessica Mills — the daughter of Tom and Darla Mills, who own the Chateau restaurant down off of Highway 21 toward Red Granite. It wasn't long after Roy went missing that Nick also went missing, but by that time, no one had been the wiser. Nick too was turned into a zombie.

Penguin jumps into the back of Nick's brown Chevy and slaps the side, indicating that it is time to go.

Both Roy's black sedan and Nick's pickup speed off toward Robert Warren's place, to hunt down and kill Zion and the Abraham family.

10

Dusk.

Jack Warren takes off his black tee, kicks off his boots, and unbuckles his cracked brown leather belt.

Haven continues to circle the room counter clockwise in the nude and says, "That's it, take it all off."

Jack continues to undress and Haven starts to chant in a language he doesn't know. Haven's body glows bright in the candle light. All her soft curves are augmented by the flickering shadows and the antique silver Lyre candlesticks.

Haven sits down on the floor, on her knees, under the seal of Solomon, and motions for Jack to come over.

"Give me your hands," she says.

Jack doesn't bother to ask why, he is hard as a rock, his cock is stiff in adoration. He sits down in front of Haven, crosses his legs, and reaches out to touch her hands.

They are both seated, facing one another, naked, in the center of the large seal of Solomon painted on the ceiling.

"Do you trust me?" Haven asks.

"Of course," Jack says.

"Completely?"

"Yeah, why?"

"Because it's time we stack the odds in our favor. And we are going to tap into the occult power of this hotel to do it."

"What do you mean?"

"Just like Sinatra did, you'll see, just close your eyes and think about me. Put every single thought you have on me and how much you love me."

Haven lets Jack's hands go and stands up, she tells him to stay where he is, and to keep his eyes closed — to keep focused.

Jack hears a door open, some whimpering, and bare feet walk into the room. He continues to keep his eyes shut and his mind fixed per Haven's request.

The bare feet walk around in a counter clockwise circle and then stop in front of him. Jack can tell that someone is standing directly over him. He can feel the energy change in the room, it's subtle, but unmistakable, like a drop in cabin pressure on a large Boeing aircraft.

"Kayik wechipu molo Ali Akwalu wechipu yau," Haven says emphatically.

Then *whoever* is standing in front of Jack gasps and gurgles.

"Masapula Chisek uya."

Jack's eyes are still closed, but he struggles to keep focused. He starts to feel *something* wet drip onto his forehead, *something* warm, but before he can think a rush of viscous fluid pours onto his head, down his shoulders, and into his lap. It feels like engine oil, the dirty stuff that pours out into a drain pan during an oil change. He struggles to keep his eyes shut and squints to avoid opening them. He clenches his eyelids as tight as possible as the luke warm liquid slowly flows down his nose, cheeks, and mouth.

"Tuse mala Puta piyau." Haven continues to speak in a language Jack is not familiar with. She says, "Puluku yamak kulotak ina yeu noka." And then tells Jack to open his eyes, to bear witness to something beautiful.

Jack slowly wipes his eyes and then opens them to a sight that was worse than what he had feared. Before him was a young woman, maybe in her mid-twenties, her throat was slit, her eyes wide, mouth open, and her blood covering Jack's naked body. Jack is speechless. She looks like a human PEZ dispenser. Haven is holding her upright by her dyed-blonde hair.

Haven tosses the woman to the ground, tells Jack that everything will be ok, and then walks over to kiss him on his bloody forehead. She takes Jack by the hand, softly opens his palm, and hands him a boleen.

Wiccans traditionally use the boleen for cutting herbs but the curve of the blade allows for other, more sinister, applications for practitioners of the dark arts like Haven—dark shamans.

"This is just the beginning," Haven says smiling.

"What do you mean?" Jack asks cringing.

"Tonight is a blood moon and we aren't finished yet. I need your help dear, I need you to cut her—and don't worry, she's quite dead. She won't feel a thing."

"Cut her how?"

"In her chest, but anyway you'd like."

"Why?"

"Do you want to stop *Kaikuci'ima* from devouring the world?"

"Yeah, but this seems wrong."

"Does it only seem wrong because I'm finally asking you to get your hands dirty?" Haven asks. "Let's face it Jack, you've gotten off pretty easy thus far, I haven't asked you to do anything but trust me. And I'm asking you now to trust me again—I need you to trust me. Now cut her."

"What if I refuse?"

"You can only remain impartial for so long Jack. I love you more than anything in this whole world. You know that. I need you, I need us to work together on this. And I really need you to cut her—now!" Haven screams.

Startled but convinced Jack brings the tip of the boleen to the dead woman's breast and hesitates slightly to stick it in.

"Not in her breast—her chest—right over her heart," Haven says while grabbing Jack's hand that's holding the boleen and redirecting it to the exact spot.

"I don't think I can—"

"Now!" Haven shouts slamming down on Jack's hand and thrusting the knife into the dead woman's flesh.

"Cut her open!"

"Ok, ok!"

Jack slices with vigor at a downward angle, he cuts deep and hits bone.

"Tuse anuk la uya mala," Haven utters.

Haven thrusts her hands into the deep cut Jack made and rips open a hole. She gets skin under her perfectly painted black fingernails. There are snapping, scratching, and squishing noises.

"Give me the knife," Haven demands.

Haven takes the boleen and rips it back and forth quickly, with precision, then drops it to the side. She jams her right hand deep into the woman's chest cavity and tugs violently. Haven yanks out her heart. It is still pumping blood as Haven opens her mouth, says some words, blows on it, and sinks her teeth into it. Blood oozes out from the sides and out of the valves onto her bright red lips. It trickles down her fingers and down toward her wrists. Bloodlust. Enamored. A blood-fetishist. With her face now painted red she shoves the woman's heart into Jack's face and tells him to take a bite.

Jack hesitates again but this time follows through without argument. The heart is moist. It tastes squishy. Chewy. Rubbery. Like raw meat.

Haven looks Jack straight in the eyes, kisses him on his blood-soaked lips — with tongue — and says, "You did great, but there are eighteen more to go. So, I hope you're hungry."

"Eighteen more what?"

"People to sacrifice."

"Why did you blow on her heart before taking a bite?"

"It's Patamuna *Taleng*."

"What's that?"

"Black Magick."

"Where'd you learn that?"

"Amazonia."

Haven stands up, drags the woman's corpse to the wall, and sets her upright facing Jack. Her eyes are still wide open, her neck sunken, and her chest gaping. Haven then proceeds to take what's left of the woman's heart and toss it into a large silver bowl on the floor. While doing this, she says more words that Jack does not understand, blows over the bowl, and places it on the floor, directly under the center of the sigil on the ceiling.

Jack looks on in awe of Haven's raw power, she is a woman of sheer will. Jack's eyes continue to marvel at the room itself and notices a phrase, written in red, on the ceiling.

"Do what thou wilt shall be the whole of the law..."

In the meantime, Haven opens the door to the next room, and returns with a naked man. He is bound and gagged. His spam dagger is noticeably pierced. Jack recognizes him immediately, it was Lenord, Kabe Abraham's best friend. Lenord is mumbling, but Jack cannot make out the words. Haven drags him by his long brown hair to the center of the room, utters something in Patamuna, and then hands Jack the boleen. She tells Jack to cut his throat.

Jack has never killed anyone before. His hands start to shake. The shaking reminds him of how his body used to react when he needed a drink—when he was a raging alcoholic. Jack looks over at Haven, she says, "Just breath Jack. Take a deep breath and then slice his throat. Don't think about him, just think about me. Do it for me, love."

Lenord's eyes go wide and he desperately shakes his head back and forth. Jack grabs Lenord by the hair, raises the boleen to his throat, takes a deep breath just like Haven recommended, thinks about Haven's beautiful curves, and draws the blade across Lenord's skin with little to no force. Bright red blood spurts out of Lenord's neck, spraying Jack red. Jack closes his eyes and takes another deep breath as Lenord drops to the floor, dead. Without hesitation, Jack flips Lenord over, thrusts the knife into his chest, and tears out his still beating heart.

Both Haven and Jack indulge themselves on Lenord's heart and then toss it into the silver bowl on the floor. Haven says some words, blows on it, and then drags Lenord's corpse over to the wall and sets him upright beside the dead woman.

"Oh, I know her…I thought she looked familiar! That's Angela Arneson, isn't it? Didn't her husband shoot himself after he killed their kid on accident?"

"Yep and Lenord here used to bang her behind his back," Haven says. "A fitting end don't you think? Now they can be together forever — how sweet."

Adorable.

Lenord's head slumps over and rests on Angela's shoulder.

"If I remember correctly, the husband's name was Erik right? And he rolled over onto the baby while sleeping on the couch or something — pretty sure he suffocated it." Jack says. "Who else do you have behind that door?" Jack asks.

"Be an opener of doors," Haven says laughing, making reference to *something* Jack doesn't comprehend.

Jack sits back down in the middle of the floor, still naked, encrusted with dried blood, and waits for Haven to bring out the next victim.

Lenord's anus lets loose, just as Angela's did moments earlier.

Everyone shits themselves when they die.

The room is starting to smell like feces.

There are seventeen more sacrifices left before the main ritual can begin.

11

Dawn.

Lizzy Laing was born and raised in Wautoma Wisconsin. She grew up on a small farm just outside of town. Her parents owned over one hundred head of cattle. She wasn't much of a looker at an early age, she had curly black hair and sported large square glasses.

She loves animals. She likes to draw and paint landscapes — nature scenes.

Lizzy had a pet dog named Buster, he was a black Labrador mix. Buster would chase chickens and bark at the cows. Buster died from cancer. He had a huge growth on his side that spread to his heart. Lizzy held his head as the veterinarian euthanized him. She spoke softly into his ear and told him that everything was going to be alright, but it wasn't, and she knew that. Saying so made *her* feel better.

It was on this day that she met Seth Dillinger. Seth too was in the vet's office, he was having his dog Tuffy treated for worms — a tape worm to be exact.

Tape worms are passed with bowel movements or by consuming undercooked meat.

If an infected person doesn't wipe very well and then cooks your food, you can get a tape worm.

Tuffy, Seth's cocker spaniel, had a huge tapeworm. When she would sit butt down on the floor, little flat pieces of the worm would fall out of her ass, wiggle, and then dry up. They looked like uncooked linguine.

After de-worming, Tuffy's next three bowel movements looked like huge balls of watery spaghetti. Yet still, the city ordinance demanded that Seth pick it up. He would turn the plastic poop bag inside out and scoop up the shitty worm piles with his thin fingers. He would curse the mayor while doing it. "Fuck Charlie Swenson," he'd say while bending over and combing through bundles of tape worm and watery stool.

Seth was waiting patiently with Tuffy to see the vet when he first laid eyes on Lizzy. She came out into the hallway toward the waiting room, simultaneously carrying Buster's lifeless body and weeping. She was struggling to hold him up. Her muscles were shaking.

Seth, seeing this, quickly offered to carry Buster for her and thus began their complicated long-term relationship.

***

"I'm going to go look for more wood to burn," Seth says as he opens the cabin door and steps outside into the frigid air.

"Good idea," Judas says.

"What are we going to do about food?" Lizzy asks.

"We're going to have to go out and look for that too," Judas replies.

"So, Judas, have you been in town? Have you seen what—"

"Yep and you don't want to know the half of it," Judas says.

"What do you mean? What can be worse than aliens attacking?"

"Aliens? Is that what you're calling them?"

"Yeah, I mean what else could it be?"

"Hmm…"

"What?"

"Nothing, you're just the second person that's called them that."

"Who was the first?"

"Never mind, I don't care to talk about it—let's concentrate on the food dilemma."

"Yeah, I'm starving."

"Me too," Seth says as he opens the door. "I could really go for a nice juicy steak, with sautéed onions and mushrooms—medium rare."

"Or broiled fish. Like a Friday fish fry," Lizzy says smiling.

"Steak? Fish fry? How about this can of SPAM?" Judas asks.

"SPAM? Oh my God, where did you get that?" Lizzy asks enthusiastically.

"Oh, you know, I've just been saving it for a rainy day. Here take it."

Lizzy quickly snatches it up and pops the lid open pulling back the aluminum. Seth jumps in on it too.

Salivating.

Stomachs growling.

The old trapper's cabin smells smoky, like a campfire. The logs are chipped and dusty, covered in hardened sap. It reminded Seth of his uncle's hunting shack up north in Eagle River. Seth would go there every November. And while hunting was the priority, the Dillinger boys would spend at least one or two nights at the local strip club—the Frontier.

The Frontier is the last bastion of old school Wisconsin degradation. Seedy. Filthy. A secluded watering hole filled with strung out strippers, cigarette smoke, and cheap tacos.

"Who the hell wants to buy tacos at a strip club," Seth would ask.

The road to the Frontier is the epitome of a "backroad." The blacktop curves through dense forest and hidden ranch style homes.

The first time Seth arrived at the Frontier, he saw a large white van with a bloody buck carcass spread eagle on its roof. Ichor was dripping down the sides of the van and pooling underneath the vehicle's rusted frame. Next to the van on the ground were piles of crushed, empty, beer cans.

Unlike other strip clubs in Wisconsin, you can see inside the windows from the outside. The cover charge is five dollars, but free to ex or active military. Inside the dim lit building, the dancers allow touching.

On Seth's first night there, one young man wearing an old orange baseball cap was fingering Trixie's butthole.

Meanwhile, the bartender flashes customers and tells them about the perks of the "boom boom room."

Seth was always getting himself into situations that are equally ludicrous and lucrative...

He used to pay his credit card bills by signing up for pharmaceutical medical trials, the kind where you stay for weeks on end and test new drugs that Big Pharma seeks to put to market. He would make upwards of three thousand dollars if chosen for participation.

Seth would answer online advertisements that would say things like: *Seeking individuals for a clinical study for patients with myelodysplastic syndromes or acute myeloid leukemia.*

Or: *Patients are needed to participate in a clinical research study of NEOD001 and placebo to evaluate primary systemic amyloidosis.*

Bladder cancer.

Blood cancer.

Brain tumors and cardiomyopathy.

Cataracts and clostridium difficile-associated diarrhea.

If it was a sickness, it made Seth's wish list. The only catch was that he couldn't have any real illnesses, like STDs, and he had to endure a sometimes bothersome waiting period. The inclusion and exclusion criteria for each study was immense, so Seth chose carefully. He would only vet the research trials that he felt most likely to be chosen for, while Lizzy would be home, playing Xbox, or working afternoons at the local pizza joint.

This was Seth and Lizzy's life before testicular cancer, before chemotherapy, and before zombies took over Wautoma.

"Do you think this is judgment day?" Seth asks Judas.

"Judgment day? As in — biblical?" Judas asks. "I doubt it. I don't foresee Jesus showing up anytime soon with his hipster beard and man bun."

"You think Jesus was a hipster?" Lizzy asks giggling.

"Think about it, the guy was Jewish but not mainstream nor orthodox. He had a beard and long hair and hung out with prostitutes, thieves, and homeless people yet his father was a carpenter? Or better yet, his real father was God? Seems pretty fucking hipster to me." Judas says.

"Ok, but what about the Devil?" Seth asks.

"He was an OG," Lizzy says. "Dude was all like, look at Job, look how cocky he is, he has everything, but I bet if you took it all away he'd turn his back on you...and what did God do? He was like alright, I bet you otherwise, so go fuck Job up. And what did the Devil do? He gave Job boils...the Devil was cool, way cooler than Jesus."

"Yeah he was," Judas says laughing as she high fives Lizzy.

"Seriously?" Seth asks rolling his eyes.

"I tell you what, If I had to pick between the two right now—it's the Devil all the way. Jesus was a little bitch," Lizzy says. "Just think about it, he talked a big game, about having special powers, but he never fought back. So what if he destroyed some gambling tables and turned water into wine, when it came down to dying like a man...dude cried out for his daddy. If I was the son of God I would have jumped off that cross and started nuking people with my mind. So like I said babe, the Devil is way fucking cooler than Jesus."

"You have a point," Seth says. "So, if this isn't the end of the world, then what the fuck is going on?"

"I don't know, but whatever is happening isn't good. And hiding out here in this cabin will only work for so long. Eventually, we're going to have to fight back," Judas says.

"Fight them?" Lizzy asks.

"Yeah, it's that or they kill us too. Those things out there won't stop until we're all dead. I promise you that," Judas says. "And if they don't kill you...well let's just say you don't want to know what happens when they don't kill you—I know firsthand."

"What do you mean?" Seth asks.

"Just trust me, you'd rather die than get caught by those things, that's all I'm saying," Judas says.

"So, what are we going to do?" Lizzy asks.

"I don't know yet, but I'm working on it." Judas says.

12

Kabe Abraham used to work at a campground called Wautoma Camper Land. He was the maintenance guy. He mowed the lawn, cleaned the swimming pool, changed the burnt out light bulbs, and siphoned the shit out of the RVs and campground dump station holding tanks. He would drive an old John Deere tractor, towing a pump wagon and holding tank around the resort. He would hook up a big hose to the shit containers and suck them empty. Then Kabe would spread all the human waste in the nearby field—toilet paper, tampons, condoms, and all. The smell was horrid, but he eventually got used to it.

The mosquitoes were the worst. Kabe never got used to them. They swarmed the poop tanks. It was the amount of heat they gave off that attracted them, and the smell, there was just no avoiding it. Kabe's last day on the job was the day he finally took feces to the face.

Usually, Kabe would kick the holding tanks to see if there was anything in them, but on what would be his last day, he accidently kept his face over the hole while he kicked it — thus splashing fecal matter up in his mug.

"Fuck this job, getting shit in the face for eight bucks an hour isn't worth it," he said before walking out, disgruntled and underpaid.

After that, Kabe refused to work at a campground ever again. He moved on to bigger and better things — like factory work — where the pay was better, the hours longer, the insurance costly, and the days monotonous.

His ennui continued to build.

The American Dream.

Oh, how the dream became a nightmare.

If there was a college class on the subject they should call it: *Life training 101: How the American Dream is Fatuous Propaganda to Keep the Poor Working and the Rich Comfortable.*

Human capital.

Forever labor.

If such a class existed, the university would probably hire an adjunct to teach it in order to avoid paying full-time faculty tenure.

At least I have Scarlet Kabe would tell himself —
as if she was worth suffering for.

That's what his parents never told him, that
without a college education your choices in life are
limited to factories, restaurants, or anything else
that destroys your body long-term.

Nowadays, the media tries to convince folks
that college educations aren't worth the cost. They
say liberal arts majors still end up washing dishes
but now with insurmountable debt. And while
this does happen, what they don't tell people is
that a degree is just a piece of paper, it's how you
prepare to apply for jobs your senior year in
college that really matters.

If you don't work on your resume, your
curriculum vitae, or interview for jobs long before
you graduate, then yes, you'll end up working at
McDonalds with a degree in biology. But, if a
student gets serious and utilizes all of the many
resources on campus, such as resume workshops,
mock interview panels, and job boards their entire
senior year, then college is definitely worth it no
matter the major.

You make your own luck.

Jobs won't just fall into your lap because you graduated with a diploma, you have to get out there and actively prepare yourself for the job market you seek to become part of. This means doing research, this means getting off your ass, this means stop partying. Just because you finish college doesn't mean you are suddenly entitled to a job. It's like anything else in life, success comes to those who put the work in, not those who expect things handed to them because they have a degree and a pulse. If you don't start preparing for the job market a year before you graduate college, don't expect anything less than fast food or factory work. Don't expect to be anybody but Kabe Abraham.

Even Kabe Abraham hates being Kabe Abraham.

And success is definitely about who you know, so get to know everyone. Alumni hire alumni, friends get their friends jobs, so make friends even if only for that purpose.

"How much farther?" Scarlet asks Kabe.

"A few more kilometers and just past that row of pines, then we'll be near the lake and the cabin is just around the bend."

"Zion is hungry again, we have to stop and feed him."

Kabe sighs. "Alright, but this is the last time. After this he can wait until we get to the cabin," Kabe says as he drops his bag and pulls out some graham crackers and hands them to Scarlet.

Scarlet gives Zion the whole packet and he stuffs them all in his mouth immediately, filling up his cheeks like a chipmunk.

"Really? The whole pack at once? Jesus," Kabe says.

Zion eyeballs Kabe as he chews.

Scarlet smirks and puts the blanket back over Zion's head, whom she is still carrying.

"Alright let's get moving, I'd like to get settled in before dark," Kabe says.

***

Roy and Nick pull up to Robert Warren's home and all ten men storm the residence. Penguin kicks open doors and punches out wall hangings. They turn the house inside out looking for Kabe, Scarlet, and Zion, but find nothing.

"There's no sign of them," Nick says.

"Goddamn it!" Roy shouts, kicking over a kitchen chair. "Motherfuckering cock sucking piece of trash!" Roy screams as he picks up all the rest of the dining room chairs and smashes them against the floor, walls, and kitchen stove.

"Where do you think they went?" Nick asks.

"I don't know, but…since there's snow on the ground…go see if you can find any…fresh tracks," Roy says as he leans against the counter and catches his breath.

Moments later, Penguin waves at Nick from outside and Nick quickly checks it out.

"Here we go," Nick says. "Good job man."

Penguin nods.

"Over here!" Nick yells.

Roy and everyone else rush over.

There is a trail of human foot prints in the snow that lead into the dense forest.

"Well looky here," Roy says. "Looks like we got a fresh trail, boys...now let's find them and rip them to pieces...everyone but Kabe...I want him alive. Kabe's gonna suffer for what he did to my Darla."

Roy, Nick, Penguin, and the seven other men quickly head into the woods after the Abrahams.

Tonight, no one would be left unscathed.

13

The Behemoth and Jessica Mills

are driving south on highway 22 toward the Sander's place. Jessica is puffing on an e-cigarette. Vaping. E-Juice. Raspberry Menthol. Daddy's little princess still has her vices.

"You know, I've heard stories about these things blowing up in peoples' pockets. I even saw some post online about a guy who had one of these things explode in his face — he suffered second degree burns and lost seven teeth," Jessica says laughing. "What a dumbass."

The Behemoth looks over at Jessica and sighs.

"What? It's not like it's going to happen to me, the guy probably did something stupid with it. Besides, it's not like it would hurt me anyway."

The Behemoth shrugs his shoulders and puts his hands back on the wheel at ten and two.

The e-cigarette was first introduced into the market in 2007. It is now a billion-dollar industry. There are three primary parts that make the e-cig functional — the cartridge, the battery, and the atomizer.

So, why are they blowing up? FEMA says that over eighty percent of e-cig explosions take place during charging. The primary cause seems to be the use of an alternate charger as opposed to the one that came with the device, which seems to over-charge the e-cig and can have explosive results. The other cases where e-cigs have detonated seem to be linked to the use of a lithium battery. Lithium batteries pack a lot of power into a small space; the kind of power which builds up when the internal temperature rises and can knock out some pretty girl's teeth or melt the skin off of her soft glowing, accentuated, cheek bones.

And let's not forget the adverse side effects from inhaling vape — popcorn lung.

"How much farther?" The Behemoth asks in his baritone voice.

"Only a few more minutes — I can't wait to turn Devin — I'm going to make him my bitch."

***

"I'm gonna teach you respect!" Stanley shouts as he whips Devin repeatedly with his leather belt.

"Stop it!" Devin screams as he kicks his legs and blocks his face with his arms.

"I can't believe you're my son...you're nothing like me! You ungrateful...disrespectful...little faggot!"

"Dad no! Please!"

Stanley takes the belt and loops it around Devin's thin neck. The worn, dry leather tightens and stretches. Devin gasps as it cuts off the blood flow to his carotid arteries.

"Get up, lady boy! That's what they called homos like you, when I was in the Navy—lady boys! And you know what happens to lady boys? They get fucked!" Stanley says, pinning Devin against the couch face first—ass up.

Devin can't speak, he struggles to remain conscious, he manages to get his fingers in-between the belt and his neck, which allows for a little space—just enough to breath.

"But you wouldn't know anything about that would you boy? Well, it's time to teach you a hard lesson—one you'll never forget!" Stanley shouts as he smacks Devin continually and rips his pants down to his ankles.

"Dad...please—no," Devin begs.

Stanley unzips his pants.

"Daaaad...stop...please."

Stanley drops his jeans.

"Daaaad..."

Stanley yanks down his boxers.

"No son of mine is a goddamn lady boy — lady boys get f —," Stanley utters, just before thrusting his erection into Devin's anus.

Devin, barely conscious, feels the tip of Stanley's stiff pecker nudge his rectum and then hears a loud crashing sound.

Then a roaring sound.

Then *something* warm splatters all over Devin's naked backside.

Then the belt loosens from around his neck and he hears another loud crashing sound.

Devin finally catches his breath, turns around, and sees Jessica and The Behemoth, standing in the doorway behind him. Devin then looks down and sees Stanley's lifeless body lying on the floor, the coffee table is smashed to bits underneath him. Stanley's decapitated head is sitting over by the T.V. set — eyes wide, mouth open, and tongue hanging.

The television is dripping blood.

Devin's entire backside is covered in fresh warm gore.

Devin gags and says, "Oh god."

"What's the matter Devin — caught with your pants down?" Jessica says laughing. "Nice dick though…yummy."

The Behemoth cracks his knuckles, his wrists, and then his neck. He is not amused.

Tonight no one would be left unscathed.

14

The public hunting land by Snipe

Lake goes on for miles. It is endless forest.
Deciduous. Birch and white oak. Near the lake
itself, which is just over a football field wide and
twenty feet deep, the ground becomes muck and
swamp. Just beyond the swamp, nestled into the
smaller pines, is the old trapper's cabin—the one
where Seth, Lizzy, and Judas are currently hiding
out.

The origin of the cabin is unknown. It was
likely built in the 1960's, around the time the
Warren family first moved to this godforsaken
place. The only folks who know about the cabin
are the local hunters and Robert Warren. The land
around the lake is part of local folklore, namely
that it is a native American burial ground, but
that's just what the old timers say—no one really
knows for sure.

The old folks say *something* about curses…
They say *something* about Wendigos…

"There it is, just beyond those pines," Kabe
says.

"Finally," Scarlet says, dragging her feet. "I
can't carry this kid another step."

Zion is sound asleep in Scarlet's arms.

Samurai barks and then takes off running.

"Sammy wait!" Kabe shouts. "Damn dog."

"Is that smoke?" Scarlet asks, looking up and pointing toward the cabin.

"Sure is. I better go have a look. Stay put."

"Not this again," Scarlet says rolling her eyes.

Kabe creeps around and walks slowly toward the old trapper's cabin with machete in hand—the same machete that was used to chop up Bill Kimball—the Wautoma Stingers has-been pack leader—now deceased. Kabe hears talking coming from inside the cabin. He moves in for a closer look. He peeks into the cabin window and sees two people, then feels *something* cold placed against the back of his head. It makes a clicking sound.

"Drop it," a woman's voice says. "Now."

"Ok, just relax," Kabe says as he slowly places the machete on the ground next to his feet in the snow.

"I'll do what I want, asshole. Who are you and what are you doing out here?"

"My name is Kabe Abraham and I came out here with my family to hide from, well, those things that have taken over the town."

"Kabe Abraham," the woman says. "How do I know you're not one of those things, Kabe? Or work for them? Turn around."

Kabe gradually turns around to face the woman who is holding a small, black 9mm handgun.

"Jennifer Thomas?" Kabe asks. "You gotta be kidding me."

"Call me Judas, Kabe."

"Sure thing, Judas. Wow, so…have you seen Jack?" Kabe asks.

Judas lowers the gun.

"No." A long pause. "Why, have you?"

"Not in a long time," Kabe says.

"So, I assume Scarlet is out there in the woods somewhere?"

"Yep, and our son."

"Son? Well, you better go get them. It's cold. I'll tell the others you're here."

"Who else is out here with you?" Kabe asks.

"Seth Dillinger and his girlfriend…it's a long story."

"I see. Alright, I'll be right back and Judas…"

"What?"

"Try to get along with Scarlet…please…for me."

"Ok, but only for you," Judas says. "And only because I still think you're cool."

"Thanks. I appreciate it," Kabe says as he heads back into the woods.

"Yeah. Right," Judas says under her breath.

Judas opens the cabin door and informs Seth and Lizzy that they are going to have visitors. She tells them that they are old friends, that she knows them well, and that she needs a drink — like yesterday.

Tonight no one would be left unscathed.

15

The dead bodies in room 666 are

piling up.

There is Paul, Jack's overweight, pretentious neighbor.

Tom Mills, Jessica Mill's father.

Casey Rogers, Jessica's ex-boyfriend with the nine-inch cock.

Judas' clients, Debra and Larry.

Nosey Stan who lived next door to Joe Schneider.

Dr. Brohm, Sheryl, Nicole, and Shanon from Berlin Memorial.

Wendy from the coffee shop.

Tammy and little Joseph, whom she was still breast feeding because it got her off.

Mindy and Steve, who used to work for Advostock, but who are now *permanently* retired.

There are only two sacrifices left to go to complete Haven's ritual.

The entire room is blood spattered. There are fifteen dead bodies seated upright against the east wall of the room. All with their throats cut, their hearts missing, heads drooping, and skin sagging.

The room smells like a decaying rat in a shit clogged toilet.

Lenord and Angela have rigor mortis. The silver bowl in the center of the room, in the middle of the seal of Solomon on the ceiling, is loaded with half-eaten human hearts.

One half must be devoured, the other must be left as an offering to *whomever* Haven is calling down the spirit ladder.

Jack is seated, belly engorged, naked and soaked in blood, waiting for Haven to bring in the next victim.

"Fucking move, you bitch!" Haven shouts as she tosses Emmy, Lenord's dead girlfriend Tanya's mother, into the room.

Tanya died from a brain aneurysm months ago.

"I'm so…hungry," Emmy says. "Please, I'm starving."

None of the victims haven eaten for weeks.

"Shut up," Haven says, kicking her in the ass. "Just move, you sow."

Emmy is the by-product of American welfare and consumerism.

Obesity is an illness, is what she tells everyone as she slurps down one gallon buckets of taxpayer funded ice-cream.

Thousands of dollars in food-stamps.

"God you're heavy. How the fuck can you be hungry? Even your ass is growing asses," Haven says. "But don't worry darling, I'm going to do both you and the state of Wisconsin a favor. I have the cure for your particular kind of disorder."

Death, the only panacea.

Haven drags Emmy over to Jack who immediately picks up the boleen and, without hesitation, slices her from ear to ear — he attempts to give Emmy a Columbian necktie — which isn't possible since the human tongue isn't long enough to be pulled out through the throat.

The Columbian necktie (slashing someone's throat horizontally and then pulling their tongue out through the hole) was a urban myth perpetuated by Columbian drug dealers for intimidation purposes, but in truth, it is not anatomically possible.

"What the fuck are you doing?" Haven asks Jack.

"What? She said she was hungry," Jack says, laughing.

"Quit fucking off and finish it."

"Ok," Jack says as he rips a hole into Emmy's huge chest with the boleen and tears out her massive heart.

Haven quickly snatches it up after saying a few words in Patamuna and blowing on it. She takes a large bite out of it before handing the heart back to Jack and telling him to eat.

As Jack sinks his teeth into Emmy's heart, Haven leans forward and grabs Jack's limp cock and jams it into her mouth. She sucks on it ferociously. She strokes it vigorously. Jack's eyes roll back into his head as he chews. His limp prick gets rock hard. It feels amazing.

Jack finishes with the heart and tosses what's left into the silver offering bowl.

Haven pushes Jack onto his back and jumps on top of him. She grabs his stiff member and guides it into her wet snatch as she quickly sits down on top of it. She starts to grind Jack hard, she massages his testicles with her fingers as she rocks back and forth.

"I love you so much baby," Jack says.

"I love your cock," Haven says. "But it's time Jack, time to finish the ritual."

"One more sacrifice to go, right?" Jack asks.

"Indeed, my love—just one more."

"Fuck. I'm going to cum," Jack says.

"Cum for me baby. Give me everything," Haven says as she grabs the boleen.

"Oh fuck!" Jack exclaims.

Jack cries out in pleasure as he blows his load deep inside Haven's super tight pussy.

At the pinnacle of orgasm, Haven makes her move—she drives the boleen straight down into Jack's heart.

Their eyes meet.

Jack can't speak. He is shocked and speechless. Blood spews out of his mouth.

Haven kisses Jack's bloody lips softly and whispers in his ear, "Don't worry my love, this is just the beginning."

16

"Get in the fucking car," Jessica says.

Devin doesn't say anything. He just hops in the backseat of Jessica's car without saying a word. He knows there is no point in fighting back—not with The Behemoth holding his arms behind his back.

"You're smarter than I thought. You're much more than just pigtails—Pigtails."

"Thanks, I guess," Devin replies.

"You really should be thanking us for saving your life. Ok, well more like your butthole," Jessica says, laughing. "Your dad was really one sick bastard, huh?"

"I don't want to talk about it," Devin says.

"What—ever," Jessica says as she shuts the door. She looks over at The Behemoth and says, "Drive."

The Behemoth puts the car in gear and pulls out onto the highway back toward town—back toward the Pfitzer hotel.

"Can I ask you something?" Devin asks.

"Sure, Pigtails," Jessica says.

"Why not just kill me too?"

"Can you keep a secret?"

"I guess, yeah."

Jessica leans into the back seat and whispers, "Because I like you. And, you'll make a great pet."

"Pet? What, like be your slave or something?"

"Nah, I'm going to make you one of us," Jessica says smiling. "How cool would that be, right?"

The Behemoth rolls his eyes.

"Oh, don't be jealous, you know I only have eyes for you," Jessica says, blowing a kiss at The Behemoth.

"Ms. Mills, I don't think Haven will like this. Or Jack," The Behemoth says.

"I don't give a fuck what they like or don't like, I do what I want."

Then, without warning, a large whitetail deer juts out into the road, right in front of the car. A huge buck. The Behemoth swerves the car to avoid it and loses control.

"Fuck!" Jessica shouts.

The car flies into the ditch and slams into a large white oak tree. Jessica is ejected through the windshield upon impact. Glass shatters. Metal bends and snaps. Sparks fly. Smoke billows from the front end of the car.

The Behemoth is wearing his seatbelt, but his face bounces off the steering wheel, knocking out his two front teeth. He is out cold.

Devin ducked down just before the crash, toward the open seat beside him. He is jarred, but uninjured. He unbuckles his seatbelt and tries to open the door, but it is jammed. He tries the other one, but it too is stuck. He doesn't realize the doors are locked.

Devin leans over and reaches into the front passenger seat where Jessica was sitting and tries the door — it too won't budge. The only door left is the driver's side, and The Behemoth is still unconscious in front of it.

Devin reaches over The Behemoth's lap and pulls the door handle — success — the door opens. He slowly, and quietly, makes his way into the front seat — on the passenger side. The Behemoth groans and stirs, but still doesn't come to. Blood trickles down from his forehead.

Nervous.
Careful.
Scared.

Devin decides to reach across The Behemoth's lap and push the door open further, before attempting to crawl over him - which is the only way out of the car at this point. Devin gets the door open and The Behemoth makes another whimpering sound as his head falls back against the seat rest. Devin swallows hard as he goes for it. *Now or never*, he thinks. He races across The Behemoth's lap and falls out onto the ground.

The Behemoth is still unconscious.

Devin wastes no time and sprints into the woods. About ten feet in, he slips and falls into a pool of fluid—dark black gooey sludge. He is now covered in it. He is flat on his back. He coughs and looks up above him to see Jessica's body skewered like a pig roast on a large tree branch—from groin to gullet.

The large abrasive tree branch is jutting out of her ass and Devin just fell into the contents of her stomach.

Jessica isn't moving, her vagina is torn in half—all the way up to the top of her pelvis. She is literally ripped apart. Her face is unrecognizable, it is completely disintegrated. Under the stress of the accident her arms split open and her tentacles popped out. They are hanging loose and touching the ground. Large spikes are oozing puke brown fluid with green highlights. Jessica is dead and Devin is swimming in her guts, just as darkness falls.

17

Judas and Scarlet see each other for the first time in years. They lock eyes as Kabe takes Zion over to make an introduction. Seth and Lizzy move in close to get a better look at the child, as Samurai walks over and kicks his feet around on Judas' blanket on the floor and lies down.

"Jennifer Thomas, it's been awhile," Scarlet says.

"Sure has," Judas says.

"Jennifer Thomas? I thought you go by Judas?" Lizzy asks.

"I do," Judas says unamused.

"So...have you seen my brother?" Scarlet asks.

"Nope, have you?" Judas asks.

"Wait, I thought you two were friends?" Lizzy asks.

"Not for years," Scarlet says to Judas. Then, to Lizzy, "We don't exactly get along. And no, we're not."

"Can't imagine why," Judas says in a snarky tone.

"What's that supposed to mean?"

"Nothing, Jack just mentioned you a few times, that's all. I don't mean nothin' by it."

Scarlet steps forward and says, "No you do mean something by it. Now, why don't you just say it, bitch—say it to my goddamn face."

Judas too steps forward, toward Scarlet and says, "If I had something to say, you better believe I'd say it to your ugly face."

Kabe quickly steps in-between them and says, "Ok, ladies...look things are a bit tense right now, but we have to set aside our differences for the moment. Those things out there — ," Kabe says pointing toward the door, " — they could show up at any time...and we have to be ready."

"He's right," Seth says. "We don't know if they followed you guys out here or not."

"Followed us?" Scarlet asks. "Maybe they are looking for you two and this dumb whore over here," Scarlet says, pointing at Judas.

"Who the fuck are you calling a dumb whore, you stupid skank! And get your finger out of my face!" Judas says pushing herself forward into Kabe's arm, to close the distance between them.

"Whoa, whoa, whoa...let's just cool down. And for fuck's sake, stop with the name calling!"

"Shut up!" both Scarlet and Judas exclaim simultaneously.

***

"The tracks lead just beyond those pines, to a small cabin," Nick says.

Night has fallen.

Roy grins and licks his chops. He looks over at Penguin and nods. Penguin heads into the forest, Roy loses sight of him beyond the trees.

The snow reflects the moonlight.

"Alright, here's what we're going to do," Roy says clearing his throat, "I want to hit the cabin on all sides. Penguin will storm the back, after I go in the front. Nick, I want you to take three guys and smash out all of the cabin windows. And remember gents, I want Kabe alive. If you see the child, swarm him fast, otherwise we're all dead meat. We have to strike hard. No exceptions." Roy pumps his twelve-gauge shotgun and turns the safety off. "And most of all—don't fuck up."

***

"Don't tell my husband to shut up, you dumb slut!" Scarlet yells.

"I should have kicked your ass years ago, but now would be a good time too," Judas says.

"I'm surprised you can even talk with those dentures, bitch!"

"I'll fuck you up! When I'm done with you, you'll be needing dentures too, bitch!"

"Bring it!"

Arms swing, fists fly, and hair gets pulled.

Kabe struggles to keep Judas and Scarlet separated. "Enough already!" he shouts.

Zion wakes up and starts crying from all of the commotion.

Samurai's head raises up, his ears perk straight, and he starts to low growl, but not at Scarlet and Judas—at *something* else.

No one notices.

Shadows move passed the open windows, illuminated by the firelight.

"I'll kill you, hoe!" Scarlet shouts as she reaches for Judas' long, dirty blonde hair.

"Not if I kill you first!" Judas replies as she yanks on Scarlet's red hair.

Kabe is still stuck between them. He continues to try to separate Judas and Scarlet as they tug and pull on each other's hair. Judas continues to tell Scarlet how she's going to knock out all of her teeth while Scarlet says she'd love to see her try.

Fingernails rip and tear.

Hair comes out in clumps.

Seth steps over in front of one of the open windows to get out of the way. Samurai stands up and starts barking loudly.

Zion cries louder, but more aggressively, and in a deeper tone.

Lizzy tries to help Kabe break up the fight when, suddenly, a loud crash stops everyone dead in their tracks. Two large tentacles with spikes smash through the window behind Seth, wrap around his waist, and yank him off his feet backwards, halfway through the shattered window.

"Fuck! Help!" Seth cries as he holds onto the window frame for dear life. His fingernails tear off as long serrated spikes sink deep into his flesh and pull on him with more force. Seth screams out in pain. He writhes in agony.

Lizzy rushes over and grabs onto his arms. She puts her feet on the window sill and holds on tight. She tries with all her might to pull him back into the cabin, but to no avail.

Her feet start to skid.

She is losing him.

And she can't lose him. Seth is the love of her life. They are supposed to be together forever.

Kabe grabs onto Lizzy's waist and holds her down, he stops her from being dragged out the window as well.

Tears run down Seth's face as he locks eyes with Lizzy.

Shock.

Terror.

Remorse.

A myriad of feelings are conveyed without words, all in one single moment. Everything Seth had wished he had ever said to Lizzy was now bottled up in regret.

In our dying moments, we remember all the things we wished we would have said.

In our dying moments, we remember all the things we wished we would have done.

In our dying moments, we remember how to truly love.

The tentacles pull tighter and cut deep into Seth's torso. They splay open his guts. Blood seeps, then spurts out and sprays everywhere.

Then another tentacle shoots in and entangles Seth by his neck. There is no escape now. Thick spikes sink into his esophagus, they cut off his breathing, yet Seth manages to still find the strength to speak those meaningful last words…

"Lizzy…I love you," Seth utters as blood pours from his mouth.

Before Lizzy can reply, the large tentacles rip Seth in half and drag his head and torso out of the window. His pelvis and legs fall onto the floor.

Lizzy and Kabe fall over. Lizzy is covered in Seth's wet intestines.

"SETH!" Lizzy screams maniacally. Blood splatters in her face as the *things* outside hack and slash Seth to pieces.

18

"Open your eyes, Jack," Haven says in a soft and caring tone of voice.

Jack is lying on his back, on an old Turkish rug. He feels queasy. Dizzy. Dehydrated. His lips are chapped, his throat is dry.

"Can you hear me, Jack?" Haven asks as she snaps her fingers in front of his face.

Jack blinks thrice and asks, "Where am I?"

"You're home babe, at the Pfitzer."

"What happened?"

"We finished the ritual," Haven says as she snorts a green questionable liquid. "And soon he will come."

Jack's ears begin to hum slightly.

"Who will come? I'm so thirsty...what are you doing?"

Haven gets up and grabs a silver chalice from atop an old armoire in the corner of the room. "Here...drink," she says, handing it to Jack. "I'm snorting tobacco juice, it's all that's left to do now."

Jack doesn't bother to see what is in the chalice, he quickly grabs it and guzzles down the fluid within. He is parched.

"Oh my god, that is so good. What is it?" Jack asks.

"Blood," Haven says as she pulls out a bottle of High Wine and places it next to the silver bowl of half-eaten human hearts in the center of the room.

Jack looks puzzled. He looks at Haven and squints in confusion.

"What do you mean, blood? And why does it taste so damn good?" Jack asks, sitting upright. He winces in pain. The pain is situated deep in his chest. He looks down and sees a large wound over his heart with fresh stitches in it.

"Look Jack, my love, the ritual we completed — together — was to summon a *totopu*, like *Kaikuci'ima*, but we needed a powerful empty vessel for him to inhabit...which, my love, is you."

"What the fuck are you talking about? What the hell did you do to me?" Jack asks as he tries to stand up, but fails. He cries out in anguish.

"In order for Lord *Ulupelu* to incarnate into human form, we needed a strong vessel. Someone worthy…"

"*Ulu* who? Tell me what you did!"

"Just take a deep breath, love, and calm yourself," Haven says as she helps Jack lie back down. "In order to make room for Lord *Ulupelu*, the great dragon, we had to rid your body of your *esak*, or lifeforce. And the *esak* can only be scared out of the body through corporeal violence — hence your missing heart."

"How could you do this to me without my permission?"

"Only you, Jack, are strong enough. Only you can defeat *Kaikuci'ima*. You're the only hope this world has."

"Why am I not dead like the others? How am I still alive without a heart?"

Haven stands, walks back over to the armoire, and pulls open a drawer. She then pulls out a silver box and says, "Jack, inside this silver box, is your still beating heart." Once you defeat *Kaikuci'ima*, we'll exorcise Lord *Ulupelu* and I'll put your heart back. It is the source of your *esak*. As long as it's in this box, untouched, you're safe. The only way to kill you now is to destroy your heart. You are otherwise immortal."

"That's fucked up Haven. And it's even more fucked up that you didn't ask me if I was ok with any of this."

"You would have said no Jack, I had no choice."

"You're damn right, I would have said no!"

Jack's ears start to hum louder; he squints his eyes and clenches his teeth. He puts his fingers in his ears to try and make it stop, but to no avail.

"Don't fight it, love, he is coming, and soon he will become part of you. He will give you the power you need to kill *Kaikuci'ima* and stop all of this madness before the world is devoured. Lord *Ulupelu* is a mighty *totopu*. You should feel honored...Once he takes over, we will put together a *wenaiman* and hunt down *Kaikuci'ima*."

The humming gets louder.

Jack sees flashes of red.

He smells tobacco.

"A what-a-man and *totopu*?" Jack asks.

"A revenge team and spirit guardian," Haven says as she begins to paint Jack's body red with a suspicious substance. "Just relax, this will all be over soon."

"What are you doing?" Jack whispers.

He feels woozy.

"The painting of the body with red annatto dye is a signal for the acceptance of a new allegiance."

19

"Get back!" Kabe screams at Lizzy.

Lizzy cannot move, she is shell-shocked. Her teeth are chattering. Her body is quivering. She just lost the love of her life. Before she knows it, Judas tackles her and takes her down to the ground, out of the way of the open window.

Kabe pulls out his shotgun, just as the cabin is assaulted from all sides. Penguin is beating on the back door, while Roy and Nick kick open the front door.

"Here's Johnny!" Roy yells as he sprays shotgun lead into the cabin living room.

Everyone ducks for cover.

Kabe returns fire and hits Nick in the chest, sending him flying into the cabin wall.

Black goo splatters.

Roy quickly runs back out the door. He dives onto the porch and hollers, "Fucking kill them! Kill them all!"

Then more windows burst and more tentacles enter the cabin.

"Judas! Catch!" Kabe shouts as he tosses her his machete. The same machete that sliced up Bill Kimball.

"Stay here," Judas tells Lizzy.

Kabe and Judas attack the roaming tentacles. There is loud gunfire and vicious slashing. Judas hacks and cuts at them. She runs out of ammo firing her small black 9mm pistol. Black ooze spurts and sprays. Kabe fires round after round out the windows. Penguin is still trying to bust down the back door. It has a large iron deadbolt and hasn't been opened for years. It's rusted shut.

Then finally, while Kabe reloads, the men with tentacles for arms climb through the cabin windows.

Kabe struggles to reload the gun. He shakes, but eventually succeeds.

Kabe stands up and yells to Judas, "The testicles! Cut their fucking balls off! It's the only way to kill them!"

Kabe blasts Nick again as he tries to stand back up. He blows his nuts clean off. A large swoosh of gooey black fluid dumps out of Nick's body. Like a bathtub just overfilled and let loose. Nick drops dead on the spot. The fluid splashes Kabe's worn boots as he turns around and shoots another man in the junk. He too empties a gush of fluid onto the floor and dies instantly.

Lizzy is motionless, she is sitting on the floor with her head resting on her knees and sobbing.

Judas continues to swing the machete with vim and vigor. She slices one man right in the arm. The tentacle falls to the floor and flops around like a fish out of water. She then turns the blade on edge and jams it upward and into his groin. He drops to the floor in agony. She pulls out the blade and saws at his nuts repeatedly, until he too dumps a giant gooey black mess onto the floor and dies. She continues to swing the blade, she gets black sludge all over her body—in her mouth and even up her nose.

Samurai is biting at anything and anyone that moves toward Kabe—he is barking and snarling.

Then, suddenly Roy rushes Kabe and tackles him to the ground, he smacks the shotgun from Kabe's hands.

Finally, with a loud smashing sound, Penguin breaks through the back door. He stands in the doorway, observing the carnage. Judas lunges at him, but he quickly bats her to the ground. Penguin continues to walk slowly toward the fight, toward the living room. He stops in front of Lizzy and looks at her curiously.

Lizzy pays him no attention. She just sits there, rocking back and forth. Crying.

Judas again attacks Penguin, but again gets tossed aside into the wall. One of her ribs cracks upon impact.

"Lizzy! No!" Judas screams as Penguin raises both of his hands and swiftly slams them through Lizzy's skull, completely obliterating it.

Lizzy and Seth were supposed to be together forever.

Roy and Kabe wrestle on the ground, they pummel each other.

"I can't wait to taste your flesh," Roy says as he bites into Kabe's arm.

"You mother-fucker!" Kabe cries as he punches Roy in the face, repeatedly.

Roy gets the better of Kabe and pins him to the floor. He tells him that he's going to make him watch as he devours his wife and kid. He tells Kabe that when he's done with him, he'll wish he was never born.

Scarlet and Zion scoot into the corner and away from Penguin as he walks toward Kabe and Roy.

"No! He's mine, get them," Roy says as he points toward Scarlet and Zion.

Samurai rushes across the room and leaps onto Roy. He bites him in the face and knocks him to the ground. Samurai chews on Roy's nose and jaw. Roy screams and hollers. Roy's arms detach and large tentacles slide out of gaping slits in his forearms. They are covered in hundreds of spikes that are oozing a brown mucous-like substance. Roy's tentacles ensnare Samurai and squeeze tight. Samurai's eyes pop out of his skull and he yelps before taking his last breath.

"Stupid fucking dog," Roy snickers as he sits up, right into the barrel of Kabe's shotgun.

Kabe grins and says, "Stupid fucking Roy," then pulls the trigger, blowing Roy's head clean off his shoulders. Black sludge covers everything as Roy's shaking body falls backwards to the ground.

Scarlet sets Zion down in the corner of the room and stands in front of him—in-between Zion and Penguin. "You'll have to go through me first," she tells Penguin.

"Tum tum," Zion squeals as Penguin steps closer.

Scarlet continues to use her body as a shield, protecting Zion at all costs.

Kabe points the barrel of his twelve gauge at Roy's nuts and says, "Fuck you Roy," before pulling the trigger. An explosion of black fluid flushes from Roy's corpse and pools all over the floor.

Out of the corner of his eye Kabe sees Penguin quickly grab Scarlet by the arm and kick Zion to the ground, just as two more men burst through the front door. Kabe kills them both, splattering their ball sacks with his shotgun. Kabe turns around to see Penguin carrying Scarlet on his shoulders, out through the back door.

"Scarlet!" Kabe screams.

Judas is lying on the floor, moaning in pain, holding her side.

Two more men enter the cabin, one through a window and another through the back door.

Zion stands up and roars in rage. His eyes are burning red. Flaming in anger.

Kabe runs out of bullets and gets wrestled to the ground. One of the men punches him over and over again in the face, crushing his nose. The other man strikes his ribs. Then, suddenly both men are picked up into the air and pinned to the ceiling, struggling to move.

Zion walks underneath them both and makes a fist. As he closes his hand all of the fluids from their bodies rains down upon Kabe and Zion. Their groins burst and shower the entire room in thick black goo.

Kabe sits up, his nose smashed, crooked and bloody, and looks at Zion who says, "Mommy gone bye bye," and then roars so loud that Kabe and Judas both have to cover their ears.

"We'll get Mommy back, I swear," Kabe says.

20

Penguin wasn't always into furry

sex. Chris Larson used to be a used car salesman. He used to work at Setian Motors and live off of commission. He would sit at his desk, staring out his office window for hours on end. Every vehicle that would pull into the parking lot, he would attempt to intercept. He would hassle folks until they either left or were hustled into buying a car they really didn't want. Penguin was Chris' escape, his avatar; when donning the penguin costume, he didn't have to be his otherwise boring and miserable self.

Chris was Roy Hutchinson's neighbor. They hung out at each other's houses after work. They would shoot pool in Chris' basement and sip whiskey, neat. Roy and Chris would talk about their jobs, how much they wished they could move out of this godforsaken place and start over — start fresh. They both grew tired of their otherwise dull lives. Roy would sit and watch cars rust when on duty or investigate petty crime. Chris would stare off into the sky or at the clock on the wall and think about how his life was ending one minute at a time and how he had nothing of value to show for it.

That all changed once Roy became Haven's right-hand man. Not long after, Roy stopped by Chris' house and told him that he could finally help him change his life, give him a new start and a new purpose. Chris seemed excited at first, but became more uncomfortable as Roy began to describe the horrific procedure. Roy ended up doing it without Chris' compliance—Roy made him a zombie.

Afterwards Chris, who pretty much lived in his furry suit when at home by himself, decided to just never take the suit off. He wore it constantly, so much so that Roy eventually found out about it. To Chris' surprise, Roy didn't care. He told Chris that it would come in handy since there was an advertisement on Craig's List about a "furry party" at the Pfitzer Hotel and that it coincided with Haven's attack plan. Chris wore the penguin suit so much that he eventually forgot about being Chris anymore.

Now he is just Penguin—Chris is just the guy who used to work at that shitty car dealership for commission on lemons.

Penguin is strong and doesn't take shit from anyone.

Chris was weak, boring, and hated his life.

Penguin is a killer.

Chris is just a distant memory.

***

At first, Scarlet was kicking and screaming, but she eventually calmed down.

She is now unconscious, after Penguin thumped her head against a birch tree in a fit of rage.

She just wouldn't shut up and Penguin has a short temper.

Penguin is moving quickly through the woods with Scarlet on his shoulders. He is headed to the vehicles which are parked at Robert Warren's house and then back to the Pfitzer hotel to deliver to Haven the spoils of war—Scarlet Abraham.

It doesn't take Penguin long to reach Robert's abode. He wastes no time, he tosses Scarlet in the backseat of Roy's black sedan; the car Chris Larson sold him years ago. As he jumps in the driver's seat, he sets his grimy, plush, Penguin head on the passenger's seat next to him. He stops to look at himself in the rearview mirror, and for a second, he thinks about his long scraggly beard, his dirty cheeks, and his un-brushed teeth. The moment of reflection passes and Chris gets back to business—he gets back to being Penguin.

No keys.

Aggravated, Penguin checks the visor and the keys fall down into his lap.

Relieved, Penguin starts up the car, puts it in drive, and zooms down the driveway and out onto the road—highway 22.

Scarlet is still unconscious as Penguin guns the gas pedal.

Not far down the road, Penguin sees a car crash. There is a vehicle smashed up against a tree and a large man walking down the road. The man is huge, maybe seven feet tall. As Penguin drives past the wreck, he notices that the enormous man is carrying a woman on his shoulders — it is The Behemoth and Jessica Mills.

As the car gets closer, The Behemoth turns and looks his way. He immediately recognizes Penguin and waves him down.

"What happened to you?" Penguin asks.

"Car accident," The Behemoth says. "She didn't make it."

"Damn, what a waste of a fine woman — get in," Penguin says.

The Behemoth opens the back door and sees Scarlet, unconscious in the backseat.

"Who's this?"

"Scarlet Abraham. It's a long story."

"I bet," The Behemoth says as he pushes Scarlet over and places Jessica's body down onto the seat beside Scarlet, ever so gently.

"Looks like it's just us now, huh?" Penguin asks.

"Something like that," The Behemoth says. "Let's get back. Haven will know what to do."

The Behemoth walks around the car and opens the passenger door. He sees the Penguin head and says, "Can I put this in the trunk?"

"No, just put it in the middle," Penguin says. "Haven is going to be so pissed."

"Yep," The Behemoth says as Penguin squeals the tires and drives fast, toward Wautoma city limits.

21

Kabe, Judas, and Zion trudge through the snow back to Robert Warren's house. Kabe is carrying Zion, while Judas is nursing her cracked rib. She feels a sharp stinging sensation with every footstep. Adrenaline keeps her going.

The adrenaline keeps everyone going.

By the time they arrive at Robert Warren's place, it is too late, Penguin has already gone. Kabe notices the fresh tire tracks in the snow and puts Zion down.

"Where's Mommy?" Zion asks.

"Goddamn motherfucker!" Kabe yells as he drops to his knees and pounds his fists into the snow. "Now what are we going to do?"

Judas stops and rests against Nick's truck, looks around, and says, "Well, he probably took her to the Pfitzer."

"The Pfitzer? Why there?"

"That's their base of operations — those things."

"How do you know that?"

"It's a long story, but trust me, he took Scarlet there."

"Where's Mommy?" Zion asks again.

Kabe stands up, brushes the snow off of his pants, and says, "Then it's to the Pfitzer we go."

Kabe opens the door to Nick's truck and sees the keys in the ignition. He motions for everybody to get in.

"Where's Mommy?" Zion asks for a third time.

Kabe looks at Zion and says, "We're going to see Mommy right now — I promise."

***

Devin Sanders is still covered in Jessica's guts, but they are now dried and sticky. He is running out of energy from all of the walking, so he decides to follow a deer trail out of the woods and up onto highway 22.

His feet are wet and cold.

His back and neck are sore.

He doesn't have a clue as to what to do next, so he just keeps walking. He has no destination, but he knows he just has to keep moving — putting distance in-between himself and the car crash — putting distance between himself and The Behemoth.

The highway seems to go on forever, but he isn't thinking about the highway, nor the fact that he is getting hypothermia. Devin is thinking about his father and he is reevaluating his life — he is dreaming about a new one. Devin Sanders is lost on the highway of his own mind and searching for some kind of meaning — some kind of purpose.

Then suddenly, he is brought back to reality by the sound of a roaring engine. A vehicle appears on the road in the distance, it cuts through the horizon. Devin quickly dashes into the snow-covered ditch and runs back into the woods just off the roadway. He hides behind a giant oak tree as a black car zooms by. As the car passes, he sees The Behemoth in the passenger seat and *someone* he doesn't recognize driving.

Devin's heartbeat races.

His breath quickens.

He is having a panic attack.

He sits down on his butt, behind the old oak tree with his knees in his arms. He is shaking in fear.

This would last approximately five minutes.

***

Kabe's fingers clench the steering wheel of Nick's brown Chevy pickup truck. He grinds his teeth in anticipation.

"Do you think Scarlet is ok?" Kabe asks Judas.

"For now, yeah."

"What do you mean, for now?"

"Well, I'm not sure how to put this really…"

"Just spit it out."

"Those things don't kill women right away — they impregnate them first."

"Impregnate them? What the fuck are you talking about?"

"When they captured me, I saw some shit I wish I could un-see."

"What did you see?"

"They take the women to a fuck room of sorts...and after raping them...the women give birth to more of those things."

"Are you fucking with me right now?"

"I wish I was," Judas says as she peers out the passenger side window. Rows of dried corn pass by in the distance.

"Do the women survive?"

"Nope—those little things eat them," Judas says still looking out the car window. "It's the stuff of nightmares."

"Jesus."

***

Devin finally snaps out of his panic attack and stands up. He peeks his head out and looks both ways before creeping out of the woods and walking back up onto the highway. His body starts to shake—he is freezing. His lips are purple. Devin can't feel his toes. So, he starts to jog at a slow pace to warm his body up. The gravel on the shoulder crunches under his weight with each step. Devin jogs for about a half mile and then tires out. He is no runner. At this moment, he thinks about when he took the Presidential physical fitness test in grade school, the one endorsed by Arnold Schwarzenegger, the one he absolutely hated.

The Presidential fitness test came to be thanks to Dr. Hans Kraus, who, in 1953, called attention to the declining health of Americans — specifically that children were losing muscle tone due to "the affluent lifestyle of 20th century America."

Thanks to Dr. Kraus, President Eisenhower created the President's Council on Youth Fitness in 1956. In 1966, the Presidential Physical Fitness Award was created by President Lyndon B. Johnson after conducting the second national fitness survey in 1964. The original test included a softball throw, a broad jump, a fifty-yard dash, and a six hundred-yard walk/run. George Bush Sr. popularized the Council and the Physical Fitness Award by appointing Arnold Schwarzenegger chairman during his presidency. To win the award, the student would have to score in the 85th percentile. To do, so a student would have to: finish thirty-eight crunches in a minute, run an eight-minute mile, do two pull-ups, complete a ten-second shuttle run, and reach eight inches past their feet in a v-sit reach.

Devin never did well.

He threw up all over himself while trying to finish the mile run.

To Devin, the test was torture not fitness.

"No pain, no gain," his coach would say.

Do you even lift bro?

Meatheads and gym-rats.

Devin hated doing anything that took effort, but at this moment, he finally understands why being physically fit is important.

Even working out twenty minutes a day can significantly improve one's life.

Devin stops jogging and walks. He feels the phlegm build up in his mouth from exhaustion. He huffs and puffs and shivers as his sweat freezes in the cold air. He is so busy recovering that he doesn't notice the brown Chevy pickup that is driving slowly behind him.

***

"What the hell is that guy doing?" Kabe asks Judas.

"Looks like he is in bad shape, we should stop." Judas says.

"Ok. I'll ask," Kabe says.

Kabe pulls the brown Chevy up alongside of Devin who is panting and walking with his hands on his hips.

***

"Need help, pal?" Kabe asks.

Devin is startled by the sound of Kabe's voice and jumps. He stops dead in his tracks and steps back, slowly, toward the ditch. "Holy shit, where did you come from?" Devin asks.

"It's ok buddy, we're just passing through…do you need help or what?"

Devin peruses the vehicle and nods his head.

"Devin Sanders, is that you?" Judas asks while peeking her head around Kabe from the passenger seat.

Devin laughs and says, "Oh girl, you have to be kidding me? Hey girl! How you doin', gorgeous?" Devin says with excitement.

"It's ok, we know each other," Judas whispers to Kabe, "he's all good."

"Is there room for me in there, or what?" Devin asks.

Judas picks up Zion and sets him on her lap. "For you darling, of course there is — get in."

Devin smiles from ear to ear.

22

The Behemoth and Penguin get out of the car and make their way up the front steps of the Pfitzer hotel. The two guards at the door immediately get out of their way — no questions asked. The Behemoth is carrying the body of Jessica Mills in his arms. Her head is resting against his massive shoulder. Penguin is dragging Scarlet up the steps by her wrist. As The Behemoth enters the foyer of the hotel through the revolving door, his feelings start to overwhelm him. He thinks about waking up in the crashed vehicle, kicking open the door, and finding Jessica impaled on a tree limb. He thinks about their relationship, or lack thereof, and wishes for the things that could have been, but never will be.

True love is found in forever yearning…

Tears fall down his chiseled face.

His heart hurts.

Pain like this suffocates all logic. All he can think about is getting revenge — crushing Devin Sanders' skull with his bare hands and then swallowing him whole. In this moment, The Behemoth falls to his knees in the foyer and cries out in agony. Everyone is shocked by the sounds he makes. No-one can believe what they are seeing. The most destructive force in Haven's arsenal has a heart — a big fucking heart. Penguin just steps aside and stands at attention. Unmoved. The man at the front desk gets on the phone and calls upstairs. He says *something* about coming quickly, *something* about Jessica being dead, *something* about a crazy red head, and *something* about Malach losing his marbles.

The Behemoth smells Jessica's hair, it smells like raspberry menthol — her favorite. He draws Jessica's body in close and holds it tight, he squeezes her and kisses the top of her bloody head. He does all of this in front of everyone. He continues to sob as the elevator dings and Jack and Haven arrive to see what all the commotion is about.

"Let me go!" Scarlet yells.

Penguin continues to hold her wrist tightly.

"Malach, what is the meaning of this?" Haven shouts.

The Behemoth stands up, still holding Jessica close and says, "Jessica is dead...it was a car accident...she didn't make it." He spits out the words and continues to sob uncontrollably.

"And you loved her?" Jack calmly asks as he steps forward out of the elevator.

Upon seeing Jack, Scarlet stands silent. It has been years since she has seen her brother.

"I guess," The Behemoth says.

"A pity then," Jack says. "Now, what's the deal with you in the Penguin suit and this woman?"

Penguin looks puzzled, as does Scarlet. Jack already knows both of them, so Penguin looks at Haven and shrugs his shoulders.

"Jack?" Scarlet utters.

Haven interrupts and says, "Lord *Ulupelu*, forgive me for not introducing you to my servants. The large man is Malach and this is, well, Penguin. The woman is your vessel Jack's sister Scarlet."

Everyone in the lobby looks dumbfounded, but knows better than to ask any questions — especially with The Behemoth in such a foul mood.

"I see. Well, that explains the feelings I am getting from Jack about her. Feelings of disdain and discontent, really. Penguin, if I may call you that, what do you have to tell us about all of this?" Lord *Ulupelu* asks.

"Roy, Nick, and the others didn't make it. Kabe and some other woman have the child, but I managed to take this one with me during my escape. I thought she would be useful."

"And this one, called Scarlet, how is she related to the others?" Lord *Ulupelu* asks as he grabs Scarlet by the face and looks her over carefully.

"She is Kabe's wife and the mother of the child," Penguin replies.

"And the child is *Kaikuci'ima*?" Lord *Ulupelu* asks. "Are you sure? Does he bear the mark?"

"Yes, my Lord," Haven says.

"Well then, they'll definitely come looking for you, now won't they?...Scarlet. But they won't dare enter this hotel — it is far too guarded. Is there any other place, maybe more secluded, that we can lure them to? *Kaikuci'ima* is too smart to attack here, we will have to set a trap for them...we'll have to lure Lord Jaguar to his own demise," Lord *Ulupelu* says.

"I know a place," Haven says. "There's an old rest stop out on highway 22 that I used to use for ritual purposes. It has a basement with one exit. We can attack them there."

"Perfect...and Jack sure doesn't like you," Lord *Ulupelu* says pointing at Scarlet. "I can feel him you know, in my head, he's still in here, in this body with me. His thoughts are my thoughts, and he sure has some nasty thoughts about you."

23

Kabe Abraham pulls the truck up slowly as he approaches Wautoma city limits. He sees that the road into town is blocked off by two police cars and that there are two officers in brown uniforms standing nearby.

"Let me take care of this," Judas says as she reaches for Kabe's shotgun.

"Are you sure?" Kabe asks.

"Yeah, just act normal. I got this. Just get him to come to my side of the truck," Judas says, pointing at one of the officers.

"Alright," Kabe says with a sigh. He feels for the machete under the seat and readies it, just in case.

The two officers motion for Kabe to slow down and to stop the vehicle. Kabe hits the brake and eases the truck to a halt. One officer walks up to the driver's side and taps on the glass. The other continues to stand in front of the truck.

"The window is broke, you'll have to go to the other side," Kabe says while pretending to finger the button. Kabe hits the button for the passenger side and rolls it down. The officer walks over and peeks his head into the window.

BLAM! Judas fires the shotgun and blows the officer's head apart. Brain, bone, and blood splatter everywhere. Pieces of the officer's skull fly into Devin's pigtails before he can duck for cover. Judas quickly opens the door, slamming it into the officer's lifeless body and fires the shotgun at the second officer as he reaches for his weapon. She hits him right in the stomach. He isn't wearing a vest. The second officer drops to his knees and tries to hold his guts in, but they burst open and spill out all over the snow staining it pinkish red. He cries out just before Judas walks over and fires the shotgun again, this time at point blank range, exploding his head to bits. The impact ricochets and sends brain matter and blood into the air, like a watermelon just burst. Judas walks back toward the truck, pulls open the door and sits down slightly out of breath. She looks at Kabe, smiles, and says, "What are you waiting for? Let's go."

Kabe laughs and says, "Damn girl, you have a mean streak, don't you?"

Judas slams the door and says, "You bet. And I'm just getting started."

"Remind me never to piss you off," Kabe says.

"Yeah me too," Devin says.

"To the Pfitzer," Judas says as she loads more rounds into the shotgun.

"You got it," Kabe says. "How many shells are left?"

"Enough."

***

"We're going to need to do something about this snow," Lord *Ulupelu* says.

"What do you mean?" Haven asks.

"You'll see."

Lord *Ulupelu* raises his arms in the air, his eyes burn yellow, then orange. He says *something* in Patamuna — *something* that begins to immediately affect the climate. *Aleluya*. The guards outside the hotel watch as the clouds disappear and the sun rises high into the sky. The snow begins to melt and thick jungle vines push forth from the ground. The wind gushes and howls. Swarms of mosquitos fly. Peccaries run. Snakes slither. The heat becomes unbearable and the moisture in the air rises.

"That's better," Lord *Ulupelu* says as he drops his arms to his sides and his eyes roll back brown. He looks at Haven and says, "You know, Jack keeps talking about his love for you, but I don't get it. You're an abomination."

"What?" Haven says, surprised by Lord *Ulupelu's* insult.

"What did you think, that just because you summoned me that I agree with what you are doing? I am a *totopu*, like Lord Jaguar...you fulfilled the prophecy by using Caribbean necromancy. What you did was wrong and you must be punished."

"How dare you! You serve me! I control you! You don't get to question me," Haven says.

"I do not serve abominations. And when I'm finished with Lord Jaguar, your power over me ends. I am the great Dragon! I will burn this world to ash for what you've done!"

Lord *Ulupelu* grabs Haven by the throat and picks her off the ground and says, "After I destroy *Kaikuci'ima*, I will rip your soul apart."

***

"There it is, just ahead, you better slow down," Judas says.

"Are you guys seeing what I'm seeing?" Devin asks. "Look! The snow is melting and I swear I just saw a macaw.

"What the hell?" Kabe asks.

"Tum tum," Zion says as he points to his stomach. "Tum, tum!" he cries.

"Ok son, just wait, I'll get you some food in a little bit," Kabe says.

"Tum tum tum tum tum tum!" Zion exclaims over and over as he starts to kick and thrash about inside the truck.

"Ok, ok!" Kabe shouts slamming on the break.

"What's wrong with this kid? Is he mental?" Devin asks.

Zion's eyes start to glow deep red. He opens his mouth and roars so loud that everyone has to cover their ears.

Judas opens the door and jumps out. Zion hits Devin in the face and crawls out of the truck. He runs toward the Pfitzer hotel — toward the main entrance.

"Zion no!" Kabe shouts. Kabe jumps out of the truck and chases after him. The two guards on top of the steps rush forward to grab Zion as he approaches.

Devin looks up, just in time to see Zion devour both guards. His agility is astounding. He quickly hops up and drives his teeth into their necks ripping out their jugulars. He opens his mouth and waves his hand as all of their bodily fluids fly into the air and rush into his maw. He drains them both dry in seconds.

"Tum! Tum!" Zion roars as he falls to the ground and shakes. Kabe tries to get to him but a swarm of mosquitos and kabura flies attack.

"Fuck!" Kabe yells as he swats at them.

The mosquitos and flies bite Kabe all over and then fly toward Judas, who quickly runs back to the truck and slams the door shut. "Close the fucking door!" Judas hollers at Devin.

"But what about Kabe?" Devin asks.

"Shut the fucking door now!" Judas yells.

***

Upon hearing the chaos outside, Lord *Ulupelu* drops Haven to the floor. "What are you waiting for? Get them!" he shouts at The Behemoth. "Penguin, take Scarlet and meet me in the back. Haven is going to take me to this rest stop of hers. That's where we'll end this."

Haven coughs and holds her throat. She now realizes what a mess she has gotten herself into. She thinks about uncle Peter, about how he was right all along, and that she has to get Jack's heart. "Give me...a minute. I have to get some stuff from upstairs. I'll just be a moment," Haven says.

"Make it quick," Lord *Ulupelu* says.

"Yes...my Lord."

The Behemoth gently lays the body of Jessica Mills down on a loveseat in the foyer, kisses the top of her head and says, "Payback will be ours, my love." He cracks his knuckles and turns to walk out the revolving door.

***

"Fuck!" Kabe screams as the mosquitos continue to swarm him and bot fly larvae begin to grow under his skin—although at an accelerated rate. They quickly start to wiggle under his flesh— to incubate.

Mosquitos in Amazonia are bot fly carriers.

"Oh shit," Devin says.

"What?" Judas asks.

"It's him, we gotta get out of here," Devin says, pointing at the figure of an enormous man who just walked through the revolving door and is standing atop the steps by Zion. "He'll kill us all!" Devin exclaims as he points toward The Behemoth.

Zion is on the ground shaking, having some kind of seizure, so The Behemoth ignores him. Tunnel vision. The Behemoth looks out toward the truck and spots Devin sitting inside.

"Oh shit. He's looking this way," Devin says, quickly ducking down in his seat.

"Think he sees us?" Judas asks.

The Behemoth raises his arms and huge tentacles burst forth with enormous spikes oozing a brown viscous fluid. He looks directly at the truck and roars.

"Yep, he sees us," Devin says, locking the door.

Kabe is on the ground, the mosquitos have passed, but the bot flies are bursting out of his flesh. They are wiggling and buzzing — spawning. Kabe shrieks in disgust. There are large flies crawling out of his face. He stands up just, in time to see The Behemoth towering in front of him. "Holy shit," Kabe says noticing the sheer size of the monster. Kabe steps back and thinks about retreating to the truck — for his shotgun.

Before Kabe can make a move, The Behemoth slams him with one of his giant tentacles, it penetrates right through his flesh and sends him to the ground. The Behemoth ensnares Kabe with both tentacles and starts to squeeze with all his might. Kabe hears his ribs crack and pop.

"Kabe!" Judas shouts as she gets behind the wheel of the truck and starts it up.

"What are you doing?" Devin asks.

"Helping an old friend."

The Behemoth continues to crush Kabe with his tentacles. Large spikes sink into Kabe's body and penetrate his muscles. He feels weak and delirious.

Judas slams on the gas pedal and smokes the tires of Nick's brown Chevy. She aims the truck right at Kabe and The Behemoth. Just as Kabe loses consciousness she guns the truck and slams into The Behemoth, driving him straight into the concrete steps. The force of the impact smashes The Behemoth's entire upper body flat and severs his head from his body. His tentacles let go of Kabe and wrap around the truck tires, popping them. Judas grabs the shotgun, but Devin stops her. "No, he's mine," Devin says. "I'm finishing this."

"Ok, he's yours then," Judas says. "I'll check on Kabe."

Devin takes the shotgun and gets out of the truck. The Behemoth's body is still pinned under the truck, his tentacles are whipping and thrashing underneath.

Judas quickly rushes over to Kabe who is bleeding out and lying motionless on the ground. She kneels down beside him and takes stock of his injuries — Kabe is also bleeding internally. In moments, he will choke to death on his own blood. Kabe coughs. He has many broken bones. The Behemoth snapped his ribs and punctured his lungs. It's only a matter of time now.

"Judas…save…Scarlet," Kabe utters.

"I will," Judas says. "I promise."

Blood pours forth from Kabe's mouth and he chokes to death in seconds.

Devin bends down to get a closer look at The Behemoth who is pinned under the truck and doesn't notice that one of The Behemoth's tentacles managed to get free. It quickly snatches Devin by the ankle and yanks him to the ground. It starts to pull hard and drag him under the truck.

"Help!" Devin cries out.

Kabe dies just as Judas hears Devin's desperate plea for help. She rushes to his aid.

Somehow, The Behemoth's other tentacle manages to get free and latches onto Devin's other leg and then around his stomach. It cinches tight, thrusting large oozing spikes into his guts.

Judas jumps to the ground and grabs both of Devin's arms. She puts both of her feet onto the side of the truck and tries to pull him loose.

"Come on! Come on!" she yells.

"Judas, you can't save me and shoot him at the same time...you have to let go," Devin says as The Behemoth pulls him farther under the truck. The tentacles wrap him up even tighter, like an anaconda. The spikes sink deeper into his nerves. Devin can't feel his legs. The Behemoth's tentacles cut off his circulation and then begin to snap through bones. The spikes tear and cut Devin's skin. They flay him open and blood begins to pool.

"No! I got this," Judas says. "It will be ok, I'm not letting you go."

Devin looks up at Judas and sees that she is struggling to hold on. He looks Judas in the eyes and says, "Then I will."

"Devin, fuck—!" Judas yells as Devin lets her hands go and is dragged completely under the truck. The Behemoth's tentacles rip him to shreds and crush him to death. A large wave of blood spews forth from under the truck and drains out under Judas' ass.

She grabs the shotgun just as one of The Behemoth's tentacles grab her by the ankle. She shoots it and sends brown and black goo flying. She quickly spins around onto her stomach, now covered in the blood and guts of Devin Sanders, and shoves the shotgun barrel in-between The Behemoth's legs. She pulls the trigger. An eruption of black goo soaks her in the face, The Behemoth's tentacles drop and go lifeless — there is nothing but silence.

24

Haven takes the elevator upstairs and rushes to room 321, where she is keeping Jack's beating heart in a silver box. She puts the heart and a black obsidian knife into a black backpack and then runs back downstairs to meet Penguin, Scarlet, and Lord *Ulupelu* — who, thanks to Haven, is currently possessing Jack's body — in the lobby.

"About time," Lord *Ulupelu* says as Haven appears in the foyer wearing the black backpack.

"I needed some girl stuff, you wouldn't understand."

"I'm sure I wouldn't," Lord *Ulupelu* says as they all make their way down a long corridor that leads to the back of the hotel.

Penguin throws Scarlet into the trunk of Roy's car and opens the door for Lord *Ulupelu* and Haven to get in. Lord *Ulupelu* gets in the passenger side and says to Haven, "You're driving."

Penguin looks at Haven and says, "I'll slow them down."

Haven nods and shuts the car door. She starts the car and drives off toward the rest stop on highway 22.

***

Judas gets up and wipes the black mess from her face. She walks around the car and sees a young boy standing on top of the steps—it is Zion—but he is significantly older. He is now about four feet tall, has medium blonde hair, is naked, and drenched in scraps of skin and blood.

"Zion?" Judas asks.

"That's what you call me, isn't it?" Zion asks.

"Yeah," Judas says. "How did you—?"

Just as Judas attempts to finish her sentence, she sees a black car pull out with Haven driving and Jack in the passenger seat. Her mouth drops. Jack looks at her and she swallows hard.

"Jack?" Judas says as she watches the car head south toward highway 22.

"Come on Zion, we've got to go...now."

Zion takes about two steps before noticing the man in the penguin suit standing in front of the door. Judas looks up and sees Penguin staring her down.

"Motherfucker," Judas says as she picks up the shotgun.

"No, I'll deal with him," Zion says, motioning for Judas to stop.

Penguin looks over at Zion and starts to walk toward him. Suddenly Penguin's feet stop moving. He is stuck. Immobile.

"Bear witness," Zion says as he raises one arm and gestures for Penguin to come toward him. Penguin's body is quickly raised off the ground about six feet in the air, his feet dangle. Penguin struggles to move, he has no control over his body. Zion snaps his fingers and Penguin's body under the suit bursts, it liquifies within seconds. First, a slimy pool of blood and mucous pours out of his suit and splashes to the ground. Then his suit follows, his penguin head bounces off the concrete. Penguin is exsanguinated. Then, Zion opens his mouth wide and makes a sucking sound. The gooey puddle that was Penguin streams toward Zion and up into his mouth. Zion sucks down every last drop and then wipes his mouth clean. He turns to Judas and says, "Now we can go, if you'd like."

Judas, awestruck, says, "Ok," in a quiet high-pitched voice. "Which way do we go?"

"South," Zion says. "We drive south."

"Do you want some clothes?" Judas asks.

"I'll borrow his. What was his name again?" Zion asks pointing at the mess under the truck.

"Devin. His name is, I mean was, Devin."

Devin's soiled clothes are no perfect fit, but they will have to do.

Once Zion is dressed, they hop into the brown Chevy and turn the engine over. It takes a few minutes, but eventually the truck starts, Judas backs it up, and they take the only road south out of Wautoma — toward highway 22.

25

Haven pulls the car to a stop, just

outside of the men's bathroom at the rest stop. The garbage can outside is putrid and reeks horribly of mold, shit, and rot. The bathrooms smell like a dumpster. No one has cleaned them since Joe Schneider, Haven's dead brother, the rest stop maintenance man, went missing many moons ago.

Lord *Ulupelu* gets out of the car and says, "Take her downstairs, I'll wait here for them to arrive. Jack seems to have a lot of history with that woman from the hotel. He calls her Judas. He seems to have some feelings for her, how cute, and how equally convenient."

"Feelings? What kinds of feelings?" Haven asks, clearly upset by this news.

Lord *Ulupelu* quickly catches on to Haven's jealousy and decides to exploit it. "Well, it seems that he cares deeply for her. He is quite concerned about her safety. One might even say he loves her."

"Impossible!" Haven shouts in disgust. "He only loves me!"

"Well, you'll have your chance to do something about that, now won't you?"

"You're damn right I will. I'll fucking eat that bitch!" Haven says, angrily storming off with Scarlet toward the basement of the rest stop.

Lord *Ulupelu* laughs and steps into the men's restroom to wait for Judas and Zion to arrive.

***

It isn't long before Zion and Judas see the black car Haven was driving parked at the rest stop.

"Over there, that's them," Zion says, pointing at the car.

Judas slows the truck down and pulls into the gravel driveway. She parks it just outside of the men's lavatory. Judas leans over and grabs the shotgun. She says, "Under normal circumstances, I'd say something like stay here or stay behind me, but by all means, I'll stay behind you."

Zion and Judas get out of the car and just as the doors shut, the men's restroom door opens and Jack walks out. Judas stops dead in her tracks. She looks like she has just seen a ghost.

"Jack? Is it really you?"

Lord *Ulupelu*, in his cleverness, decides to let Jack have control over his own body again and hides in the back of Jack's consciousness — just for this moment.

"It is."

As soon as the words leave Jack's mouth, Judas dives in to embrace him. She wraps her arms around him and holds him tight. She hasn't seen him in what feels like ages.

"Jack, I was so worried about you. I missed you so much."

"I missed you too," Jack says.

***

Meanwhile, in the basement of the rest stop, Haven pushes Scarlet against the altar and orders her to sit down. She tells Scarlet that her beloved Kabe is dead and that there really is no point in keeping her alive anymore. Tears well up in Scarlet's eyes. She bites her lip, smirks, and says, "My son is going to destroy you."

Haven pulls the obsidian knife out of her back pack, looks Scarlet in the eyes, cocks her neck a bit, and says, "I don't think so honey," before slicing her throat. Scarlet grabs her own throat with both hands and tries to hold the blood in. Haven tells Scarlet to rest now and that her son is in good hands. The last sound Scarlet hears before falling to the ground dead is that of Haven snickering.

Haven pulls out Jack's beating heart from the box and sets it on the altar. She repeats *something* in Patamuna and then blows on it.

***

"Jack, where have you been?" Judas asks.

Lord *Ulupelu* quickly takes back control of Jack's consciousness, but accidentally leaves an opening in Jack's mind for him to resurface on his own accord.

Zion gives Jack a strange look, like he knows *something* isn't quite right.

"Haven abducted me, but I'm free now, I knocked her out and tied her up down in the basement. Scarlet is there too, I'm so glad you came."

"I'm just glad you are ok, I've been so worried about you...I love you dearly," Judas says as she kisses Jack passionately. Jack kisses her back and says, "Follow me, I'll show you."

Judas gives Jack one more tight squeeze and says, "Ok, lead the way hun. I'm going to kick her ass for taking you from me." Judas looks at Zion and motions for him to follow, but he hesitates. "Come on Zion, it's ok."

Jack, Judas, and Zion all make their way down the old dusty wooden staircase into the basement of the highway 22 rest stop. They turn left and head toward an open door at the end of the corridor. The room is illuminated by candlelight.

"This way," Lord *Ulupelu* says.

"I don't like this," Zion says.

"Almost there, you'll see," Lord *Ulupelu* says.

Lord *Ulupelu* opens the chamber door and walks in. He expects to see Haven, but no one is there. He looks down and notices Scarlet face-first on the floor. His eyes go wide and he grits his teeth in rage.

"Treachery!" Lord *Ulupelu* yells.

"Indeed," Haven says as she steps out from behind the door and thrusts the obsidian knife into the back of Judas' neck.

"No!" Zion shouts.

Haven pulls the blade from Judas' nape and blood spurts forth, she hit a main artery.

Zion raises his arms and picks everyone in the room up off their feet and thrusts them abruptly to the ground. He then rushes over to Scarlet's lifeless body. Lord *Ulupelu* hits his head on the concrete, which gives Jack a window of opportunity to take control of his own body again.

Jack quickly sits up and moves over to aid Judas by applying pressure to the gaping wound in her neck, but she is losing too much blood too fast.

"I'm so sorry," Jack says.

"Jack Warren, you ruined my life...but I love you anyway," Judas says.

"Just hold on," Jack says as Judas bleeds out and dies in his arms on the cold concrete floor.

"Are you fucking kidding me? You come to her aid? You dog," Haven says.

Zion turns his attention toward Haven and thrusts his arms out, knocking everyone back off their feet again. He glares at Haven and raises his right arm in the air, picking her off the ground. Haven looks at Jack and points at the altar with his heart on it. She tells Jack that he must kill both Zion and himself. She tells him that if either survive, the world will perish.

Then, before anyone can make a move, Zion snaps his fingers and Haven explodes into a pile of blood and guts.

"Haven, no!" Jack screams maniacally.

Jack tackles Zion as hard as he can and knocks the boy out cold.

Jack gets to his feet and stumbles. He feels Lord *Ulupelu* trying to take over his mind again. He fights him with every thought and breath. Jack grabs his heart and the obsidian blade from the altar and walks over to Zion, who is still unconscious on the ground.

Jack sits down, flips the boy on his back and places his heart over top of Zion's. He thinks about Haven, about Judas, Roy, Darla, Jessica, and Joe Schneider. He thinks about the years he spent drowning in alcohol and the people he hurt along the way.

He thinks about Bill Kimball and the Stinger has-beens.

He thinks about the full fly traps in Judas' trailer, Royal Acres, and the box of ammo he left on the Noguchi coffee table.

He looks down at the faded black letters tattooed into his fingers spelling out the four-letter word **HATE** and lifts the obsidian knife into the air. "It's not a bullet, but it will do," he says as he thrusts the blade into both hearts simultaneously.

Jack falls over, his sight goes black, his breathing slows, and there is nothing but silence.

It seems Jack's mistress, suicide, won't have to wait another day.

She was a patient courtesan, unlike Judas, who would lick her lips and tell him how wet she was.